M

A

N

M

SAY UNCLE

SAY UNCLE

ERIC SHAW QUINN

A DUTTON BOOK

DUTTON
Published by the Penguin Group
Penguin Books USA Inc., 375 Hudson Street,
New York, New York 10014, U.S.A.
Penguin Books Ltd, 27 Wrights Lane,
London W8 5TZ, England
Penguin Books Australia Ltd, Ringwood,
Victoria, Australia
Penguin Books Canada Ltd, 10 Alcorn Avenue,
Toronto, Ontario, Canada M4V 3B2
Penguin Books (N.Z.) Ltd, 182–190 Wairau Road,
Auckland 10, New Zealand

Penguin Books Ltd, Registered Offices:
Harmondsworth, Middlesex, England

First published by Dutton, an imprint of Dutton Signet,
a division of Penguin Books USA Inc.
Distributed in Canada by McClelland & Stewart Inc.

First Printing, August, 1994
10 9 8 7 6 5 4 3 2 1

REGISTERED TRADEMARK—MARCA REGISTRADA

LIBRARY OF CONGRESS CATALOGING IN PUBLICATION DATA
Quinn, Eric Shaw.
    Say uncle / Eric Shaw Quinn.
        p.   cm.
    ISBN 0-525-93780-3
    1. Gay men—South Carolina—Columbia—Fiction.   2. Custody of
children—South Carolina—Columbia—Fiction.   3. Uncles—South
Carolina—Columbia—Fiction.   4. Columbia (S.C.)—Fiction.
I. Title.
PS3567.U343S28   1994
813'.54—dc20   94–551
                                                                       CIP

Printed in the United States of America
Set in Palatino
Designed by Leonard Telesca

PUBLISHER'S NOTE
This is a work of fiction. Names, characters, places, and incidents either are the products of the author's imagination or are used fictitiously, and any resemblance to actual persons, living or dead, events, or locales is entirely coincidental.

For Genie who gave me my sense of language,
for Ron who gave me my sense of humor,
for Ann who gave me my sense of style
and for Cynthia who gave me my sense of self.

To David for seeing and Peter for believing.

And to the friends who stood by me
and those who didn't.

BOOK
I

"Go on. Say it."

"Michael. Leave him alone."

"Take a hike, Bob. I'm not giving in till he says it."

"Oh, Michael. For Christ sake. He probably won't say it for six months."

"Leave him alone, Kathryn, he's obsessed."

"Say uncle, you little creep."

"Now you made him cry. Let go of him."

"I don't think it was me."

"Of course it was you."

"Try that diaper, sister. That look of concentration was a clever ruse."

"Yuck. I'm gonna change him and put him down for a long winter's nap. Say good night to Uncle Michael and Daddy."

"But he can't say uncle?"

"Shut up, Michael."

"Good night, Scott."

"Good night, son."

Kathryn hefted the baby onto one hip and waddled out of the room.

"Another drink?" Bob asked, rising to refill his own.

"No, thanks, I'm walking," Michael said, reaching for a shopping bag stuffed with bright packages. "I'll certainly miss you three this Christmas."

"Well, my parents haven't seen the baby yet," Bob said, spilling a little scotch on the bar.

"I know, I know. Fair is fair. Look, I brought your Christmas—Kathryn," Michael shouted.

"Shhh," she hissed, rounding the corner from the hall. "You'll get the baby all stirred up. You can tell you don't have any children."

"Is it my hourglass figure?" Michael giggled.

"Fag."

"Bitch."

"If you two are through stating the obvious." Bob laughed. "What did I get for Christmas, Mic?"

"Wait. Let me get yours," Kathryn said, digging under the tree.

"This hardly seems fair," Michael said, handing Bob a package. "You all are proliferating, and there's still only one of me."

"What happened to what's his name?" Kathryn asked, handing Michael his package.

"The usual," Michael said, reaching for Kathryn's package. "Two dates, and I never heard from him again. I think it's the shoes."

"You could always adopt," Bob said as he opened his present.

"I think that's illegal," Michael said. "Oh, champagne flutes."

"No," Bob said. "You could adopt children."

"Children? There's only one of me, though I do have eight champagne flutes. Thank you, sister."

"A child," Bob said. "You could adopt one child."

"I don't think Columbia, South Carolina, is ready for that," Michael said. "Can't you just see me on 'PM Magazine'?" Then Michael went on as the announcer: "He's a busy advertising executive, a father, and a homosexual. He's Fag Father, and he's here tonight on 'PM Magazine.' Get real, Bob."

"Seriously . . ." Bob started again.

"Open your present," Michael cut in. "What the hell would I do with a kid?"

"You could watch it grow up, same as everybody else does," Bob said, tearing off the paper. "Hey. All right. A radio."

"Ingrate," Michael said. "You can take this radio in the shower. I bought one for myself and liked it so well I got you one, too."

"I've been trying to get you to take a radio in the shower for years, big brother." Kathryn grinned.

"Shut up and open your Christmas," Michael said with mocking surliness.

"Seriously, Michael," Bob started again. "There's a lot of joy in seeing the little guys every day. More than I had thought."

"Look, I only live a few blocks from here," Michael said. "I'll buy a high-powered telescope and watch yours grow up."

"Oh, Michael," Kathryn squealed. "It's beautiful."

"You can't take it in the shower, I'm afraid." Michael smiled.

"Where did you get him?" Kathryn asked, seating the cherub on the mantel.

"Little shop in New York," Michael said. "Sells old building fragments. More to the left."

"He's beautiful," she said, stepping back to check her work.

"That's it," Michael said, gathering wrapping paper and stuffing it into the shopping bag. "An angel to watch over you."

"Do you regret not having any for yourself?" Bob asked, sipping at his scotch.

"No," Michael said. "Actually I bought one of those for myself, too. I can't wait to take it out of the closet, now you've got yours."

"I mean children," Bob said. "Do you ever regret—"

"I know perfectly good and well what you mean," Michael snapped. "Will you stop asking me about goddamned children?"

There was a long silence.

Kathryn got up and went to the bar to fix a drink.

Michael stared into the fire and tossed in bits of the paper he had been collecting.

"Yes, I regret it a lot," he said, not looking away from the fire. "All the time."

"I'm sorry," Bob said after a while.

"Oh, well," Michael said, dumping the last of the paper into the fire. "I've got my plants and my goldfish and the dog. And my career," he concluded, à la Katharine Hepburn, pulling the shopping bag onto his head as he turned back to them.

"Thank you for the angel," Kathryn said, crossing to hug him.

"And my radio," Bob said, rising and hugging them both in one huge embrace.

"I can always share yours, a little," Michael said in the crush. "If you don't mind."

"We'll buy you a telescope for your birthday." Bob grinned.

The laughter broke up the group hug.

"I think I'll have that drink after all," Michael said.

"Coming up," Bob said, obliging. "Where's the rest of Clan Reily?"

"Well, Ma and Pa Reily have decided to be mature about your not being home for Christmas this year," Michael said, sitting beside Kathryn on the hearth. "They're leaving the country."

"Mother, you mean," Kathryn said. "I can just hear her.

'Well'—huge sigh—'I've decided to stop worrying about my family at all'—huger sigh. 'Since my family never thinks about me' —hugest sigh."

"Kathryn," Bob chided her, handing Michael his drink.

"Thank you," Michael said, sipping.

"And Allen?" Kathryn asked.

"I think he's cornering the gold, frankincense and myrrh markets." Michael giggled. "In honor of the holiday."

"Michael." Kathryn was chiding now.

"I'm glad I'm not a member of your family," Bob said, shaking his head.

"But you are, now . . . your choice," Michael said ominously.

"Michael, seriously, you don't even know what our very own baby brother is doing for the holidays?" Kathryn accused.

"Well, neither do you," Michael shot back.

"You're much nosier than I am," Kathryn said.

"Bitch."

"Fag."

"Well, actually Allen and I are having Christmas brunch at The Alcove," Michael said. "We're swapping gifts, and I get to meet his new girlfriend."

"The one that Mother hates?" Kathryn asked.

"Does she?" Michael said, as much as asked.

"Mmm." Kathryn nodded. "What's her name? Candy, Buffy, Sniffy . . ."

"Flopsy, Mopsy . . ." Michael went on for her, laughing with her.

"Cottontail," Bob added, getting in on the joke.

"What?" Kathryn asked, sobering.

"Cottontail," Bob repeated. "You know."

"What kind of stupid name is Cottontail?" Michael went on.

"Honestly, Bob, straighten up," Kathryn said. "No offense, Michael," she added.

"Skip it," Bob said.

They laughed.

"Why does Mother hate this one?" Michael asked. "I knew she hated Bob."

"Me?"

"Sure. You're stealing her baby at Christmas," Michael said.

"She's 'not good enough for Allen,' I think," Kathryn said.

"That was the last one," Michael said, finishing his drink and rising.

"Let me get you another," Bob said, taking his glass.

"No, I've got to run," Michael said, putting the champagne glasses in the shopping bag.

"Maybe this one is she 'doesn't like the family,' " Kathryn suggested.

"No. That was Bob," Michael said, teasing them. "Where's my scarf?"

"I'll get it," Kathryn said, getting up. "Anyway, Mother hates her."

"Of course she does," Michael said, putting on his coat. "The comic value is in why."

"Here's your scarf," Kathryn said, strangling him with it.

"You two are never serious," Bob growled.

"Okay," Michael said, putting on his gloves. "I seriously want you two to be careful driving. The nuts are out for the holidays, and we might get a white Christmas this year."

He rose and headed for the front hall. "I don't know what I'd do if anything happened to you all. I've got a lot of money tied up in those Christmas presents."

"Fag."

"Bitch."

"Merry Christmas, Michael," Bob said, holding the door.

"Very Merry," Michael said, dancing down the front walk.

They watched through the storm door until he was out of sight. Kathryn stood with arms folded, looking out into the darkness. Christmas lights twinkled up and down the darkened street like fireflies out of season.

Bob put his arm around her. "We made a good choice," he said at last.

"You are so morbid," Kathryn said, pulling away.

Bob closed the door.

The cold was blurring Michael's vision as he reached his apartment. The phone on the screened porch of his second-floor apartment started ringing as he came up the walk.

"I'm coming, I'm coming," he muttered, fumbling with the

keys at the door. "Keep ringing," he yelled, wishing he had remembered to turn on the machine. He ran up the stairs and set the shopping bag on the top step as he wrestled with the lock on the French door.

"Bonsai," he cried as the door flew open. The tails of his long camel coat tipped the shopping bag and sent the champagne flutes shattering down the stairs.

"Happy New Year," he growled, running to the phone in the kitchen. "Hello?"

"Hello, darling."

"Hello, Mother."

"Were you asleep?"

"No, I just got in."

"Oh?"

"Mmm," he said, taking off his gloves and cradling the receiver on his shoulder.

"Where have you been?"

"At Kathryn's."

"Oh." Huge sigh. "How is she?"

"Call her and find out."

"I'm not calling her."

Dewars, Michael's balding, lethargic Scottie, wandered into the kitchen.

"You called me."

"You're not leaving town for Christmas."

"You are. In a minute, Dewars."

"What?"

"Talking to the dog."

"What is she up to?"

"She wants to go out, I suppose."

"Kathryn, I mean."

"Oh. We swapped gifts. You should see what she got you," he lied.

"What is it?"

"Stop by and find out."

"Oh, well." Moderate sigh. "I won't keep you. I just called to say your father and I will be by at eight."

Dewars sat down with her back to Michael and looked at him over her shoulder.

"Why?"

"So you can drive us to the airport. Our flight leaves at nine, and we want to get there in plenty of time."

"Mmm."

"So we thought we'd come by at eight."

"You won't."

"What?"

"Talking to the dog."

Dewars snorted and left the room.

"You be ready when we get there. We don't want to be late."

"Why don't you just drive out and put the car in long-term parking at the airport?"

"We could do that." Huge sigh. "We just thought you'd like to have your father's car for the holidays."

"I have a car."

"What?"

"Talking to the dog."

"Well, if you don't want the car . . ." Huger sigh.

"I'd love to. Thank you, Mother. I'll be ready."

"And your father wants you to have the oil changed and the tires rotated."

"Of course."

"What?"

"I'd be glad to."

"Okay. Well, we'll see you in the morning."

"Okay, Mom."

"Are you doing all right?"

"Sure."

"I hope you won't be lonely."

"What?"

"Well, Kathryn and Bob and the baby are going away. And your father and I are going on this cruise."

"I'll be fine."

"I just worry."

"Don't."

"Well, I do. No one should be alone on Christmas Eve."

"Mother, I give a huge party on Christmas Eve. Every year."

"Sometimes crowds are the loneliest places."

"Thanks, Mom."

"What?"

"Thanks for worrying about me. But it isn't necessary."

"Well, your father and I do worry."

"Listen, I'll see you tomorrow morning."

"I mean we have each other, and Kathryn has Bob and Scott now. And Allen has Mindy—even if she is older than he is."

"Oh, that's it."

"What?"

"Her name's Mindy. I couldn't remember. Look, I've got to take the dog out."

"Don't be lonely."

"I won't."

"See you in the morning."

"Bye."

"Now I'm lonely," he said to the silence.

He put his gloves back on and got the leash out of the pantry.

"Dewars," he called, walking in the direction the dog had gone. "Oh, Dewars," he moaned. "On the dhurrie? Jesus."

"Will you marry me?"

"Oh, Allen. Get up off your knee." Mindy laughed. "Of course I'll marry you."

"Great," he said, getting up and brushing his knee. "Then I won't have to take this back. After-Christmas returns are hell."

"Oh, my God," Mindy gasped as she opened the velvet box he had fished out of his pocket. "It's huge."

"I know." He grinned as he sat beside her. "That's why I waited till afterward. I had to be sure it was me you wanted."

"Asshole," she said, hugging him. "I love you."

"I love you, too," he whispered into her ear. "Merry Christmas."

"The merriest."

"Mmm," he muttered, leaning her back against the arm of the sofa.

"Allen?" she said.

"Yes, love," he said, kissing her earlobe.

"Allen," she said more forcefully, "what will your mother say?"

He drew back a little and looked into her face. "You're so romantic," he said, playing with a bit of her hair. "That's what I love about you."

He lowered his head and growled into the nape of her neck.

She shivered involuntarily. "Allen, stop it." She giggled, pushing him back. "I'm—stop it—I'm serious. Your mother doesn't like me very much. What's she going to say?"

"I don't know," he said, leaning on one elbow. "But I bet it'll be awful."

"She doesn't know then," she said, sitting up some.

"No," he said. "I thought I'd check with you first."

"Christ, I'm not looking forward to this," she said, wrestling herself free.

"I hope you're not talking about marrying me," he said, trying to keep it light.

"I'm talking about telling your mother," she said, rising and folding her arms over her breasts, as if to ward off a chill.

"Stop worrying about it," he said, sitting up and catching her elbow.

"I do worry," she said, pulling away. "She thinks I'm too old for you."

"That's ridiculous," he said, leaning back on the sofa. "You are only three years older than I am."

"She does," she said, beginning to pace. "The other night, when we went out there for dinner, your father and I started talking about Watergate and your mother said that I should change the subject because you weren't old enough to remember Watergate," she concluded, waving her finger in his face.

"Sweetheart," he said, wrapping a hand around the accusing finger, "you're overreacting. Mother just hates serious discussions at dinner."

"Don't sweetheart me," she said, snatching her hand out of his and turning her back. "She doesn't like me."

"Mindy," he said, rising and putting his arm around her shoulder, "stop worrying about my mother."

He kissed her neck. "I love you."

He kissed her earlobe. "And that's all that matters."

She sank with him back onto the sofa.

They held a kiss for some time.

As they broke the kiss and embraced, he said into her ear, "Besides, I have a plan."

"You see," she shrieked, pulling away and climbing to sit on the arm of the sofa with her feet on the seat cushion, "she doesn't like me."

"What are you talking about?" he said, blinking.

"Why else would you have 'a plan'?"

"Okay, look," Allen said, taking a new tack. "Mother doesn't think anyone is good enough for any of us."

"I knew it," she said, almost falling off the arm of the sofa.

"Hear me out," he said, pressing on. "Now Mother is still opposed to Bob and Kathryn's marriage, and the wedding was three years ago."

"Why on earth?" Mindy asked. "They're perfect for each other."

"And they have a beautiful baby," he added.

"Then why?" she asked again.

"Now let me think," Allen said. "Michael is always better at these."

"At what?" She was getting more confused.

"At the whys," he said. "For instance, once Mother didn't like a girl I was dating because her eyes were too close together. That's Michael's favorite."

"That's ridiculous," she said, sliding down the arm of the sofa.

"She said with my big ears and her eyes we'd have hideous grandchildren," he went on.

She was laughing.

"The girl was later a runner-up in the Miss America Pageant." He started to laugh.

"You're kidding," she said, recovering a bit.

"Swear to God," he said, raising his hand. "Ask Michael."

"Come on, think," she pleaded. "Why didn't she want Kathryn to marry Bob?"

"She said he'd never amount to anything," he said solemnly.

"But he's a very successful lawyer," she said incredulously.

"He was at the time," Allen said, nodding.

"Well, how could she possibly say that?" she asked in amazement.

"That's what Michael asked her," he said, enjoying the story. "And she said, 'There's a lot more to success than a great job and a lot of money.' "

They were both laughing.

"So you see," Allen said, hugging her, "Mother just doesn't want us to grow up and away from her and she'll grab at anything."

"All right, all right, I give up," she said, gasping. "What's the plan?"

"Michael," he said with an air of finality.

"Michael?" she echoed.

"Yes," he said. "You see, Mother and Dad are on a cruise and won't be back until after New Year's."

"And," she said.

"Well, don't you see," he said as if it were a fait accompli, "we're having brunch with Michael on Christmas Day."

"So we tell him," she said, trying to move the story along.

"Absolutely not," he said vehemently. "Anyway, we probably won't have to. With that rock on your hand either he'll know immediately or he'll accuse you of being a married woman."

"Will you get on with it?" she snapped.

"Well, you don't have to bite my head off," he said peevishly.

"Sorry," she said, taking a breath. "Okay, so Michael discovers we are engaged."

"Now that's an important point," Allen said seriously.

"What is?" she demanded, frustration mounting.

"Why are you so testy?" he chided.

"I'm sorry," she said, trying to control her voice. "But you seem to see a point that I'm missing."

"The point is," he went on, "if Michael discovers it, he'll be a part of the conspiracy—"

"Conspiracy?"

"If we tell him, he'll have to think about it and decide how he feels," he concluded, folding his hands in his lap.

"So?" she demanded.

"So?" he echoed. "Don't you see?"

"No, I don't."

"Michael knows Mother better than anyone. They're pals," he

explained. "Michael always says he's the daughter she never had."

Mindy snickered a little. "What about Kathryn?" she asked.

"Hinge-heels Reily?" Allen asked. "Kathryn was always too independent and modern for Mother. Michael's a nice old-fashioned girl. Cooks, cleans, manages a beautiful house and may still be a virgin."

"That's ridiculous," she said with a wave of her hand. "I always thought those people screwed like rabbits."

"What do you mean, those people?" he said with an edge to his voice. "This is my brother we're talking about."

"Don't let's fight about it," she said. "Tell me the rest of the plan."

"Well," he sputtered, "that's really all I know."

"What?"

"Don't you see?"

She shook her head.

"Michael knows Mother. He probably knows what she thinks of you," he explained, shrugging. "And he'll be a part of the conspiracy."

"I wish you wouldn't keep calling it a conspiracy," she said, knitting her brow.

"Well, I don't mean anything bad by it," Allen said. "It's just that, with Mother and all . . . I don't know. Anyway, Michael will be able to set her up. So all we have to do is buy her a great Christmas gift."

"A gift?" she said, still uncertain.

"And that's the beauty of the plan," he said.

"What is?" she asked.

"Mother won't be back until after Christmas, so we can get her gift on sale."

She laughed and fell into his arms. "How Machiavellian," she said. "All this scheming. What a family I'm marrying into."

"It's not too late to change your mind," he said playfully.

"What?" she said. "And give up this ring?"

"For crissake, Ann, we'll be at Michael's on time," his father called from deep inside his walk-in closet.

"Look, Ashton," she said through gritted teeth from the depths of her closet, "it takes half an hour to get to Michael's from here. If we leave now, we'll still be five minutes late."

"So? What's five minutes?" he shot back.

"You're not ready now," she screamed from inside her closet.

"Are you?" he demanded.

"Yes, I am," she said, hopping out, pulling on one shoe.

"Good," he yelled back. "Then call Michael in your spare time and tell him we're going to be a few minutes late."

"And call the airport and see if the plane's on time," she muttered as she dialed.

"And call the airport and see if the plane's on time," he shouted.

"Now check the weather," she said as she listened to the phone ring.

"I'll check the weather," he shouted, emerging from his closet.

"Don't turn on that radio," she said as he turned on the radio and began tuning through the static.

"Hello, Mother," Michael said as he answered the phone.

"Yes," she said. "It is."

"Listen," he said, "I'll call the airport. Tell Daddy he can listen to the radio in the car."

"Okay." She smiled. "I love you."

"I love you, too," Michael said. "Good-bye."

She was still smiling as she hung up the receiver. Ashton stood in his socks and underwear, cursing at the uncooperative radio. He was one of the most idiosyncratic people she had ever met—the most. He was the quintessential absentminded professor and irascible college dean. She hadn't seen the first five minutes of a movie since she started dating him thirty-three years before. She also hadn't stopped loving him—for more than five minutes—in all that time.

She sneaked up and hugged him from behind. "Get dressed, Ash," she said. "Michael's calling the airport, and we can listen to the radio in the car."

"Confounded piece of junk," he said, switching off the radio. "We need one of those with a weather band on it."

"We'll look into it after you get dressed," she said, smiling as she thought of the weather-band radio waiting for him under the tree.

"Kathryn, for crissake," Bob shouted up the stairs, "will you hurry up?"

"Okay," she screamed back. "You come get the baby ready, and I'll stand down there and scream."

"The baby would already be in the car if it were up to me," he muttered as he went for another cup of coffee.

"I heard that," she screamed.

He doubted it.

"I love you," he muttered, testing her and grinning at his own deviousness.

"Then bring me a cup of coffee and stop nagging me," she screamed.

He laughed as he went to the back of the house to the kitchen.

She had never been on time for anything. Their wedding had started late. They'd gone late to the theatre for their first date. Even the baby had been late.

He, on the other hand, had graduated early from high school, college, law school and been the youngest full partner in his law firm.

In a lot of ways, he thought as he poured the coffee, it had been her irresponsibility that had appealed to him. It seemed to balance his compulsions. It kept him mindful of what was important.

It wasn't leaving on time that counted. It was a comfortable baby.

He stood silent in the doorway of the nursery and watched. He was in love. He was content. She was right.

"Are you going to bring me the coffee?" she said without looking up.

"I love you," he said.

"I had heard that," she said, slinging a bag over her shoulder and crossing to get the coffee.

"You have the ears of a bat," he said, handing it to her.

"I know," she said. "That's why I wear my hair long. Get those two big bags, and I'll get the baby," she said, sipping gently at the hot coffee. "Are the presents in the car?"

"Yes, love," he said, nuzzling her.

"I thought you were in a hurry." She giggled.

Michael was sitting on the front steps smoking a cigarette when his parents got there at twenty to nine. They blew the horn anyway.

He went to his father's door and tapped on the window. The electric motor whirred as the glass went down.

"I'll drive," Michael said.

"I don't mind driving," Ashton said.

"Dad," Michael said, "we have this argument every time you go to the airport. Let me drive."

"Oh," Ashton said, not moving. "Well, if you want to."

"I do," Michael said. "Get in the backseat."

"Hello, darling," his mother called across to him.

"Good morning, Mother," Michael said.

"Why don't I just drive?" Ashton said.

"Because we don't have time. Now get in the backseat," Michael demanded.

"Oh, Ashton," Ann said, "let him drive."

"You two are always against me," Ashton shouted. "I don't see why—"

"Because," Michael cut in. "You drive too slowly. You don't deal well with in-town traffic. And most of all, because I can drop you and your luggage with the skycaps at the door and park the car while you check in. Now hurry up. You're late, and I'm freezing."

"Well, I'll be damned," Ashton said as he always did at this point. Then, as he always did, he rolled up the window, turned off the engine, put the keys in his pocket, unbuckled his seat belt, opened the door and got out of the car.

Ann sighed, of course.

"May I have the keys?" Michael asked without looking to see if they were in the ignition.

"What?" Ashton asked. "Oh, the keys. Certainly," he said, fumbling through his pocket and then almost handing them over. "It's this one," he indicated.

"I know, Dad," Michael said, not looking.

"I was just trying to be helpful," Ash said, patting his coat pockets as if he had misplaced something.

"I know, Dad," Michael said, getting into the car. "Just get in."

It was quarter till nine. It was twenty minutes to the airport. The flight was at nine. It was a ritual.

He started the car. The chimes sounded.

"Put on your seat belt," Ashton said, closing the back door.

"I don't wear a seat belt," Michael said.

"Neither does Kathryn." Ann sighed. "I wish you kids would. Allen wears his seat belt."

"Allen," Michael said, squealing away from the curb and making a questionable left on yellow. "Allen wears a safety chain on his zipper."

"You know, Allen . . ." Ashton began sagely.

"I'm Michael," Michael said.

"I mean, Michael," he went on. "In New York they have a law requiring you to wear seat belts."

"Mmm," Michael said, weaving around a VW and running another "pink" light.

"If you plan on pursuing this acting thing," Ashton continued, "you'll have to go up there. So you might as well get in the habit."

Michael tried not to laugh.

"That truck is turning," Ann said calmly as she jammed her brake foot against the floor.

"How is your little company coming?" Ashton asked.

That acting thing had been Michael's college major. His "little company" was he and a group of his college friends. They performed for local events and made enough to cover gas, if they were lucky.

"We're doing fine, Dad," Michael said. "We really need a permanent place to work, though. We could build a reputation and a repertoire."

"You ought to buy a place," Ashton suggested absurdly.

"I can't even get a Visa card, Dad," Michael said, trying to point out the absurdity.

"Well," Ashton said, "if you'd listen to me and save some money like Allen does."

Michael's knuckles went white as he clutched the steering wheel.

"And you ought to go down to the credit bureau and check your record." Ashton needled an old wound. "I just bet you it's that brush you had with those furniture rental people."

"Michael, slow down, this is your turn," Ann said, absolutely rigid with fear.

"I know, Mother," Michael said, taking the turn at full speed.

"If you get something on your credit record"—Ashton made a hissing sound—"that's it."

"Michael, slow down, there's a curve in the road."

"I see it, Mother."

"I wish that boss of yours would give you a raise. Have you asked him recently?"

"No, Dad."

"Michael, the pedestrians."

"I see them."

"You know you ought to look around for another job."

"I really don't want to talk about it right now."

"Michael, you're following too closely."

"Yes, Mother."

"Well, I was just trying to be helpful." Ashton harrumphed. "If you're going to take that attitude . . ."

"Michael, if you know you're following too closely, then slow down."

"Mother, we're late. Listen, Dad, when we get there, I'll pop the trunk. You get the in-flight stuff; Mother, you go on in and check in. I'll get a skycap and send the luggage in to you. You go on to the gate. I'll park and catch up."

"Michael, you need to be in the other lane," Ann said.

"Are you listening to me?" Michael demanded.

"I don't know why we should listen to you." Ashton sulked. "You never want to listen to a thing I say."

"Because I'm not catching a goddamned plane to Miami in three minutes, that's why," Michael screamed as he changed lanes and turned, without slowing down, into the airport drive.

The abrupt move, the squealing, the horns and the shouting stunned everyone into silence.

Michael screeched to a halt in front of the terminal and everyone followed orders in silence.

After his parents had gone in, he slipped the skycap some

money, which, added to the fifty cents his father would fork over, would make a nice tip. Then he parked the car, ran into the terminal, caught up with his parents and rushed them on to check in. By the time he got their stuff through the metal detectors they were ready to board and the plane was revving.

"Thank you, Michael," Ann said, hugging him.

"Sure, Mom."

"Don't forget to get the car—"

"I won't," Michael said, hugging his father. "You all have a good trip, and don't worry about anything."

"Don't be lonely," Ann called back just before they vanished.

"I won't." He smiled as he lied.

And they were gone.

As he drove back into town, he sang with the radio, thought about Kevin and tried not to be lonely.

"Is he all strapped in?" Bob asked over his shoulder.

"Hatches battened," Kathryn said, vaulting into the backseat with Scott. "We've got to stop by Michael's."

"Kathryn . . ." he began.

"He left one of his champagne glasses last night."

"We can give it to him—"

"After Christmas?"

"Okay," he relented. "We'll stop by Michael's, but we're not going in."

"Oh, he won't be there," she said matter-of-factly.

"Why not?" he asked.

"He's probably still at the airport or just leaving."

"Well, why stop by?"

"To leave his champagne glass and this bottle of Dom Pérignon."

"You sneaky devil. Just when I think I've got you pegged for the scatterbrain you are."

"Watch it, bub," she said, annoying the baby by waving things in his face. "We love you." She cooed at Scott. "Don't we, hunh? Don't we love Daddy?"

Scott cooed back.

"Yes," she went on in demented baby parlance. "And as soon

as Scotty falls asleep, Mommy's going to climb up front with Daddy and fool around."

"Slut," Bob said.

"You love it," she growled into his ear.

"Here we are," he said, turning into Michael's driveway.

She jumped from the car, ran up the front steps, left the presents between the screen and the front door and dived back into the car.

"Jesus H. Christ," she said, slamming the door, "it's getting colder by the minute out there."

"Yeah," he said, backing the car onto the street. "The radio said we might get snow for Christmas, yet."

"Oh, wouldn't that be wonderful," she said. "My first white Christmas."

As usual, the radio was a real pick-me-up, and Michael concluded his drive from the airport with James Taylor's *Don't Let Me Be Lonely Tonight.*

James Taylor—any James Taylor—was bad enough as he and Kevin shared every word of every song in common.

As Michael walked from his father's car to the door of his apartment, he thought of visits from Kevin when they had sat and sung along whole sides from the *JT* and *Flag* albums. He smiled remembering the time the two of them had gone to the movies and sung along with *Fire and Rain* on the Muzak while they waited for the feature. The thin matinee audience had applauded them.

He opened the screen door and almost kicked the champagne over. He opened the note that Kathryn had leaned against the bottle. It said, "Call him. You know he won't call. I love you— Sister. P.S. He's home for Christmas and he loves Dom."

He smiled as he gathered up his surprises and unlocked the door.

Dewars lifted her head from its indentation in the rug, near the fireplace. Michael came through the French doors, and she watched him cross the hall into the kitchen before returning to her nap.

He put the Dom in the refrigerator, rinsed the two surviving champagne flutes and put them in the freezer.

He went through the swinging door into the dining room, found his address book in the drawer of the sideboard, pretended to look up the number he knew by heart and went to the phone.

He dialed.

"Hel-*low*," Mrs. Perdue answered in her strange way. Kevin's family had run a pizza parlor and his mother had developed her strange telephone manners taking phone-in orders.

"Mrs. Perdue," he said. "It's Michael Reily. How's Christmas treating you?"

"Michael," she said, softening; he was such a nice boy. "Merry Christmas."

"Is your wayward son home for the holiday?"

"That's what I hear," she snorted. "But you couldn't tell it by me. They were in here and out so fast we couldn't make a positive I.D."

"They." She said "they." Tears stood waiting in his eyes. Calm down, he told himself.

"Well, if the authorities locate him," he said, "tell him I called to say Merry Christmas and that I'd love to hear from him."

"I'll send up a smoke signal." She laughed at her own joke.

"And Merry Christmas to you, Mrs. Perdue," he concluded.

"Thanks, Michael. Good-bye."

He sat by the phone on the porch where he had placed the call. The cold wind idly flipped the pages in his phone book. He lit a cigarette and tried unsuccessfully not to cry. He stared without focusing. After a while he realized he was cold and put out his cigarette.

"Christmas is a bitch," he said, rising to go inside.

Dewars looked up as he came back into the living room. He replaced the phone book and fumbled with the dial on the stereo until he found a station playing Christmas tunes.

Dewars snorted, rose and left the room.

"Dewars," he admonished. "These are Jesus' greatest hits."

He laughed as he went into the kitchen to begin preparing food and drink for the party.

Michael's Christmas Eve parties were a tradition for a large number of people from all over the country. Friends from high school, college, work and just friends, returning home for the holiday, were welcome. And a goodly number came.

A sizable amount of merchandise exchanged hands, an even larger amount of alcohol was consumed and Michael wasn't alone on Christmas Eve until he was too drunk to know the difference.

They started calling in around one o'clock.

"What time?"

"Same apartment?"

"Merry Christmas."

"I can't make it this year, but—"

Michael's mother had started the tradition his junior year in high school. It was the first time since grade school Michael had had any friends and Ann had been determined to encourage his friendships. He had taken the tradition with him when, at nineteen, he left home.

At six o'clock he took the phone off the hook and went to communion, downed the blood and body and rushed home to put the food out, fill the ice bucket and turn on the Christmas lights.

"Perfect," he said, looking at the Christmas fantasy he had created from mirrors, poinsettias, hundreds of white lights, red bows and candles. He lit the fire and fixed himself a drink.

The public radio station was obligingly playing every orchestra's rendition of every Christmas tune ever written and recorded.

The buzzer sounded.

It was John from Houston and then Richard from Charlotte and then Susan from Atlanta and then Laura from work. They came from everywhere, bearing gifts. They came two by two. No one came alone. All the couples smarted a bit, but Michael had another drink, got out another tray of canapés, cracked another bucket of ice and had another argument about the role of the arts in industrial society and forgot again and again.

"They." She had said "they."

The buzzer sounded.

"Excuse me," he said to Arthur, the business manager from the local Philharmonic, with whom he was discussing fund-raising.

"Meeeerrryyyyy Christmas," he shrieked, thundering down the stairs to the front door.

He flung the door open.

"Kevin," he screamed. Then he saw her standing there, hanging back a bit.

Kevin's hug was very official, not at all the one Michael had wanted, needed for Christmas.

"They." She had said "they."

"And you are?" he said to the sturdy little blond woman.

"Shanah," she said, clearing her throat. "Shanah Kline."

"Merry Christmas, Shanah," he said, taking and kissing her hand.

"Welcome to my house," he went on, leading her in and up the stairs. "Now there's only one house rule. You must meet everyone and have a wonderful time. If you're not having fun, I want you to tell me."

She was laughing already.

Kevin smiled as he closed the door and followed. Michael was the kindest and best host he knew.

Michael gave her the tour of the food and the bar, fixed her a drink and admonished, "Now, I can't fix my drinks and everybody else's, so you're on your own now."

The buzzer.

"Oops." He grinned. "More orphans nibbling at the gingerbread. Kevin, you're in charge. Ya'll have a good time now or I'll kill you."

And he was gone.

"Meeeeerrrrryyyyyy Christmas," he screamed again, hurtling down the stairs and flinging open the door. "Oh, my God!"

"And I heard him exclaim, 'ere he roared out of sight," Kevin said.

They laughed.

"So he's the one," she said. "I don't know what the big deal is."

"No big deal," Kevin said. "I just want it to be special. Gift time is at midnight. I'll wait till then."

"Only twenty minutes," she said, looking at her wristwatch.

"Great," he said. "Come on and meet everyone."

Guests continued to arrive, and the foothills of gifts under the tree grew into the Andes.

The music was switched from classical radio to rock and roll records, and midnight crept nearer.

Michael slipped on the elf hat that he had worn in a Christmas benefit in the eighth grade and every year at Christmas since. "Santa just called," he shouted, "and he's real sorry he can't be with us this year. But he said that as dowager empress and the supervising good fairy in this region, I was to do the honors. So, presents in the living room in five minutes. Fix a drink and pee. It looks like a marathon this year."

He marveled at the pile of gifts. There had been some pretty meager years in college. Lots of cards, lots of Black Label beer and very little money.

"Michael," Kevin said, startling Michael out of his reverie.

"Kevin, hey," he said, putting his arm over Kevin's shoulder.

Kevin drew back.

Michael looked at Shanah, smiled, and said, "You can sure tell everyone's working this year. Look at this glut." He pointed to the packages.

"About the presents, Michael," Kevin said. "I wanted to explain why we didn't bring one."

"We." He said "we."

"Oh, for heaven's sake," Michael said, reeling. "You're here. Both of you. That's gift enough."

"Michael," Kevin said, "I want to explain."

"No. I won't hear of it. I'm afraid there's nothing under the tree for you, Shanah. As usual, Kevin-the-Vague didn't tell a soul you were coming. But the poinsettias are—"

"We didn't get you a gift because we bought this," Kevin cut in, lifting Shanah's hand up so Michael could see the small but tasteful diamond solitaire she had slipped on. "We're getting married."

"And we want you to come to the wedding," Shanah said.

"Help us plan it." Kevin took it up. "You're so good at that sort of thing."

"Oh, my," he said. "What a wonderful Christmas present. Congratulations." He hid his tears in Shanah's shoulder as he hugged her. "Congratulations to you both."

The clock began to strike midnight. A cheer went up, and the guests poured into the living room.

"Merry Christmas, Michael," Kevin said as the sea of people washed into the room and set he and Shanah adrift.

"Presents."

"Michael, mine first."

"Michael, Michael, Michael," they began chanting.

"Okay, okay, okay," Michael shouted, waving the room to semi-quiet. "I've saved the best for first. I don't know how many of you have met Shanah. That's her over there. She and Kevin are going to be married."

The cheer went up and Kevin and Shanah were mobbed.

Michael ran for the bathroom. He splashed cold water on his face and took a few deep breaths.

"Michael, Michael, Michael." The chanting beat at the bathroom door. He wanted to stay in the bathroom until they all left.

He opened the door.

A cheer went up.

"I didn't get to pee at the five-minute warning," Michael explained to everyone. "I was getting the joyous news. Someone fix me another vodka tonic and we'll get Christmas on the road.

"Let's see, here's one for Richard," he said. "Now don't open it until they're all passed out."

Michael was burning the Christmas paper. Presents from the bizarre to the sincere littered the room in great heaps.

"We're leaving now, Michael," Kevin said. "Merry Christmas."

"Indeed it is," Michael said, drunk and a little sardonic. "I am sorry we didn't have one for you, Shanah. Oh well, fifty percent of Kevin's will be yours soon enough."

"Thank you, Michael," she said. "I had a really good time."

"Oh, me too," Michael said with the same tone in his voice.

"Michael . . ." Kevin began, then shrugged it off. "I'll talk to you later."

"Much," Michael said, rising. He shook Kevin's hand. Their eyes met.

"Merry Christmas," Michael said.

"Good-bye," Shanah said. And they left.

He didn't walk them to the door, but he watched them walk toward their car from the front porch.

The crowd was thinning out.

He remembered the champagne.

"Kevin. Shanah. Wait," he called down.

He dashed inside, got the Dom Pérignon and the two glasses out of the refrigerator. Down the stairs and out into the night. "Here, Shanah," he said, thrusting the gift toward her. "I do have something for you after all."

"Oh, Michael," she said, "Dom Pérignon."

"And two chilled glasses," Michael said, looking at Kevin. "It's Kevin's very favorite."

"Michael, I couldn't," she said.

"Please. Take it," Michael said, still looking at Kevin.

"Thank you, Michael," she said, kissing his cheek.

"No one ever leaves my Christmas party empty-handed," he said, still staring.

Kevin looked away.

"Merry Christmas," Michael said, then turned and walked back up the steps.

"Michael," someone shouted. "Telephone."

He walked up to the apartment and then out to the porch where it was cold and quiet and he could hear the caller.

He watched Kevin's car drive away. The first few flakes of snow were starting to blow in. It would be his first white Christmas.

"Hello," he said, answering the phone.

"Hello, Michael?" the caller said.

He could barely hear. Whoever had answered the phone had left the extension off the hook, and the party and Bruce Springsteen's "Santa Claus Is Coming to Town" intruded on the conversation.

"Hello?" Michael said again.

"Michael," the other party screamed. "It's Robert Miller."

"Senator Miller," Michael shouted back. "Merry Christmas. Are Bob and Kathryn and the baby there yet?"

"Michael, what's going on there?" Robert yelled.

"It's a party."

"A what?"

"A party."

"Oh. Is it snowing there?"

"Just started."

"We're having a blizzard up here."

"Great. Kathryn's never had a white Christmas. Are they there yet?"

"Michael . . . uh . . . I'm not sure . . . Kathryn's dead," the senator said quietly.

"What?"

"Kathryn's dead," he shouted. "She and Bob were killed in a car crash. Hello? Michael?"

"I'm still here."

"I tried to reach your parents. And Allen isn't home."

"The baby," Michael said.

"What?"

"The baby?" he screamed.

Someone hung up the extension, but Michael kept screaming. "The baby, Goddamnit. The baby. Is Scott all right?"

"He's fine. It's a wonder, though. Thank God for that child seat law. The car was smashed like a cockroach. Michael? Hello? Are you there?"

Michael had dropped the receiver. He threw open the door into the living room, where the party was still going on.

"Get out," he screamed at the remaining guests. "Get out."

He started pushing people toward the door.

"Take your fucking Christmas gifts and get out."

He ran to the stereo. "Shut up," Michael screamed, snatching the side arm violently across the record grooves, and hurled the record against the wall.

"Get out, all of you get out. Leave me alone."

"Michael, what's the matter?"

He slid down the wall in the dining room into a heap on the floor and flailed wildly at anyone who tried to touch him.

"Get *out*. Get *ouuuuuuuuu* . . ." He trailed off into hysteria.

The room was suddenly quiet except for Michael's wails.

Richard, an old friend of Michael's down from Charlotte, had answered the phone in the first place and went out to the phone on the porch to find out what was going on.

He came back into the room. "Kathryn is dead," he said flatly.

"Noooo," Michael wailed. "This is her first white Christmas."

Several members of the party tried to comfort him and he continued to fight them off.

"Kevin," he screamed. "Keviiiiin."

The snow was falling steadily outside.

"Where do you suppose he is?" Mindy growled, playing with her roll.

"Michael is always fashionably late," Allen said.

"Forty-five minutes is not fashionable," Mindy persisted. "Call him."

"He had his Christmas party last night," Allen explained. "Some of my earliest childhood memories of Christmas are of Michael coming at noon for Christmas with his dark glasses on and so hung over that he never took them off."

"You have a weird family, Allen."

"You think we're weird," he snorted. "You should see our Christmas pictures."

She laughed.

"Christmas at our house was always red and green," he continued. "The red of the Bloody Marys and the green faces of Michael and Kathryn."

"Kathryn?" she asked.

"Yeah," he said. "They lived together for about five years. That's why they're so close now. They're like a different family to me. Like an aunt and uncle."

"Aunts, you mean," Mindy said, turning a little ugly.

The champagne and no breakfast, Allen thought.

"Why don't we go ahead and order?" he suggested.

"Well, finally," she said. "I'm half crocked now."

"Waiter," he called, looking up. "Oh, there's Michael, dark glasses and all."

The waiter Allen had called ignored him and made for Michael. He helped Michael to his chair and said, "I'm sorry, Michael. I just—"

"That's enough, Chuck," Michael cut him off tersely. "Bring me a Bloody Mary."

The waiter left without asking if Allen or Mindy wanted anything.

"Asshole," Mindy said, startling the lady seated at the table next to them. "He might have asked if we wanted something."

"Michael," Allen said, ignoring her and glossing over the remark with bluster, "what a nice place. I want to join. You'll have to sponsor me as my Christmas present."

"Oh, God," Michael said, putting his head in his hands. "I forgot your Christmas presents." He began to cry.

Several other tables of people began to eye them with some suspicion.

"Hey, Michael," Allen said, a little stunned, "it's okay. You can give us our presents later."

Michael laughed a little hysterically.

Allen was fairly nonplussed. He smiled; then he started to laugh, too.

Mindy joined them. They all laughed for a bit.

People were staring openly.

"What's so funny, Michael?" Allen coughed.

"Nothing," Michael said, sobering a little. "Nothing at all."

This made Allen even more uncomfortable.

"Where were you all night and this morning?" Michael asked suddenly.

"I was . . . well, I—" Allen blushed and stammered. "I don't think you've ever met Mindy."

"How do you do," Michael said, looking over.

Mindy was leaning on the heel of her left hand and the enormous rock on her finger glistened where her front teeth should have been.

"Oh, my God," Michael said a little too loudly, "it's contagious."

The conversation had stopped at the closer tables and the occupants were listening intently.

"What is?" Allen said, looking around, more nervous than ever.

"You spent the night at your fiancée's." Michael grinned, triumphant in the discovery.

"Contagious?" Mindy asked.

"Kevin, an old friend of mine, announced his engagement at my party, last night—or rather I did."

"To a woman?" Mindy asked pointedly.

Michael started and aimed the unflinching glare of his sunglasses in her direction.

Allen tugged at his collar and looked as if he might melt and run all over the expensive Oriental rug.

"Yes, dear," Michael said condescendingly. "Men don't get engaged to other men."

"Oh," Mindy said, downing her mimosa. "What do they do?"

"Keep it up, honey, and I'll tell you," Michael said, getting a little ugly himself.

The adjacent tables were enjoying themselves immensely.

Chuck arrived with the Bloody Mary and took drink orders all round. Mindy and Allen ordered breakfast. Michael declined food. By the time the order was straight, hostilities had quieted somewhat, in spite of the fact that Mindy had insisted on referring to the waiter as "Michael's little friend."

The other patrons had begun to lose interest and went on with their meals.

"Allen," Michael began earnestly, "we need to talk—privately."

"About the engagement?" Mindy demanded.

Michael stared at her a moment as if he didn't know the word. "Oh," he said at last. "No, not that."

He made it sound a little distasteful, and Mindy's hackles went up again.

"Well"—she snorted—"I know you think it's contagious, but don't worry. You won't catch anything at all."

Michael burst into tears again.

"Mindy, for Christ sake," Allen chided her, wishing he were anywhere else.

The occupants of neighboring tables were watching again.

"Michael, my God," Allen said, when he showed no signs of stopping, "what is the matter with you?"

To the morbid delight of their rapt audience Michael leaped to his feet, toppling his chair, and screamed, "Kathryn's dead."

And then he ran out of the restaurant.

At Michael's apartment, a block or two away, Allen succeeded in calming his brother down after an hour of trying.

"Have you told Mom and Dad?" he asked.

"They're on a ship," Michael said. "I wired their next port of call and asked them to call me immediately."

"What about the funeral?" Allen went on relentlessly, always business first.

"I, well, they're in North Carolina," Michael stammered. "What with the snow I can't see driving up now."

He started to cry again.

"Oh, Michael," Allen said. "Don't start that again."

"We've never had a white Christmas before," he snuffled. "This wasn't what I had in mind."

"Well, we've got to do something," Allen said, pacing a bit. "I'll call Duncan's Funeral Home and see what they recommend."

"It's Christmas Day," Michael wailed. "They won't be open."

"People still die on Christmas," Allen said, dialing.

"Some romantic Christmas this turned out to be," Mindy growled, coming into the room from the kitchen. "I got engaged, it snowed, and Kathryn—"

Michael's glare brought her up short.

"Here's your tea," she said, thrusting the cup and saucer noisily into his face.

"I don't want any tea," Michael said, rising and heading for the bar. "Why is it that at every moment of crisis in my life some asshole is always trying to sell me a cup of tea?"

"I was just trying to help," she said, slamming the cup onto the coffee table.

"I hate tea," Michael said, counting ice cubes into a glass. "I never drink tea."

"It's supposed to calm you down," Mindy said, trying to catch the light in her new ring.

"It's loaded with caffeine," Michael said, dabbing Tabasco into his Bloody Mary.

"I got their answering service," Allen said, hanging up.

"Whose?" Mindy asked, looking up.

"Duncan's Funeral Home," Allen said.

"This room looks like the aftermath at Hiroshima," Mindy said to no one in particular.

"And you are there," Michael toasted, then gulped.

"They're going to call back here," Allen said, sitting down at last.

"Who?" Michael asked.

"Duncan's Funeral Home," Allen said a little testily this time.

"Did the presents explode?" Mindy needled Michael.

"Some of them," Michael said with a vicious little laugh.

"Maybe someone at Bob's firm," Allen said.

"What about them?" Mindy asked.

"Being a lawyer and all," Allen explained. "There must be an executor or something."

"Oh, God," Michael said, and then turned up the glass.

"It won't help anything if you get drunk," Mindy sniped at him.

"I fail to see, dear lady, how things could possibly be any worse," Michael said, returning to the bar.

Dewars wandered into the room and threw herself to the floor in front of the fireplace.

"Who could I call?" Allen said, thinking out loud.

"Who have you missed?" Michael said, giggling.

"I mean at Bob's firm," Allen said.

"Why not just call the wire services?" Michael suggested, still giggling maniacally.

"I don't see why you have to be so unpleasant," Mindy snorted.

"I am sorry, honey lamb," Michael said, bowing low. "Where are my manners?"

"Michael, don't," Allen sighed.

"The house is a mess, and the tea cakes are stale," Michael went on. "What can I have been thinking of?"

"Michael, stop it," Allen said more vehemently.

"Here little Mindy Sunshine has come for her first visit to the home of noted hostess Michael Maxwell and all I can think of is my dead sister. Would you like some *tea*?"

He was crying again.

"Great going, Min," Allen muttered.

"Shut up," Mindy snapped.

They sat in silence, as Michael sobbed.

Dewars lifted her head, sighed and returned to her nap amid

the bright bits of shattered Christmas on the floor around her.

The phone rang.

No one moved.

"It's ringing," Ann said.

"What the hell do you suppose he wants," Ash said. "This is going to cost a fortune."

"Probably to wish us a happy Christmas," Ann said, waving him away and then covering her free ear.

"Hello?" she said into the phone. "Allen? What are you doing there? . . . What? . . . Merry Christmas to you, too, dear. . . . What's all that racket? . . . Well, put him on. . . . Well, why not? Has he been drinking? . . . Who is? . . . How is Mandy? . . . What? . . . Oh, Mimzee, of course—how is she?"

"Ann, this is costing a fortune," Ash growled.

"Shhh. What is it, Allen? . . . What could be so bad? Just tell me."

"Ask Michael if he took the car in," Ash insisted.

"Ashton, shut up. Allen, sometimes the best way is just to say it right out. I'm a tough old lady, I can take it. . . . Well, then put him on and let him tell me. . . . Then you'll just have to tell me yourself if Michael can't. . . . A white Christmas? Wouldn't you know I'd miss it."

"He wrecked the car," Ash said to himself. "Ask him if Michael wrecked my car."

"Ashton, go and count the towels. Listen, baby, Annie's getting annoyed, and your father is driving me crazy. Now just tell me."

There was a long silence.

"What is it? What's he saying?" Ash demanded.

"Yes. I'm still here," Ann said, and then pressed her lips together hard.

"I'm all right," she said at last. "The baby? . . . I see. Well, take care of your brother. We'll be back as soon as we can. Call Mr. Stockbridge at Bob's firm. . . . Well, he's the senior partner. I'm sure Bob has taken care of it. . . . No, Kathryn was complaining about it to me the other day—" Her voice broke. "No," she said, recovering. "We'll be right home, baby. Good-bye." She hung up the phone.

She sat staring at the lurid hotel wallpaper for a time.

Ash stared at her. She looked as she had never looked in their thirty-odd years together.

"Ann?" he said at last.

"We're leaving," she said simply.

"Why, what's happened?" he asked, sitting beside her and putting his arm around her.

"They're having a white Christmas," she said to the wallpaper pattern swimming in front of her unblinking eyes. "And we're missing it."

Robert Miller sat staring out the den window at the snow.

His wife, Sylvia, came in with coffee in huge white steaming mugs. She pushed one of the cups into his hand. She sat and stared, red-eyed, trying to see what he was looking at.

Scott's cry's rang out.

"I'll go," she said, putting down her cup and rising.

"I wonder if that's wise," Robert said flatly.

"What?" she asked.

"Shouldn't we have left the baby at the hospital?" he said, still expressionless.

"The baby is fine. The doctor said so. I just couldn't leave him . . . there."

She held her tears back and darted out of the room.

Robert sipped at his coffee. They had not been to bed. They had been awaiting the arrival when the news came. The accident had been only a few miles away, and the local authorities had recognized the name from the registration. It was a largish city, but Robert Miller III was notable there because of his famous father.

The former U.S. senator sat staring at the lifeless Christmas tree surrounded by unopened gifts. The lights still glinted, awaiting the return of the prodigal.

Bob had been their only child and, while public life had kept Robert away most of the time, his namesake had been a source of constant pride. Always first. Always best. Not like so many of the children of his peers in the Senate.

"God damn her," he shouted.

"Shhh," Sylvia hissed, coming back into the room. "I've just gotten him settled down."

"It's all her fault," he ranted on.

"Robert," she said, shocked.

"It's true," he said, staring straight at her for the first time since the news came.

"Robert, don't say that."

"For them to find him like that."

"I won't listen to this," she said, beginning to cry.

"That stupid white trash—"

"Stop it."

"That whole goddamn crazy family. We should never have allowed this."

"We couldn't have stopped it."

"I stopped the story right enough. I can just see the headlines, SENATOR'S SON FOUND DEAD WITH HIS PANTS DOWN."

"Damn you, Robert Miller," she said, crying in earnest.

"And her with her—" He broke off. "Well, she got what she deserved anyway."

Cries of anguish racked Sylvia's body.

"I'd have cut off both her arms if I could have prevented this."

Sylvia screamed and ran from the room.

Robert stood for a moment, listening to his wife's sobs recede into the vastness of their house.

"Damn you," he screamed, kicking a gaily wrapped package against the wall. It made a shattering sound as it hit, its contents destroyed, the beautiful package undisturbed.

"Damn you, Kathryn Reily. God damn your soul."

"Senator. Mrs. Miller," Allen said, rising to greet them as they approached the appointed room at Duncan's Funeral Home.

"Allen," Robert said, brushing past.

"Hello, Allen," Sylvia said, taking his hand and then embracing him.

Allen and Michael were taking their turn receiving, although for the most part it was Allen. Michael sat, unshaved, hiding behind dark glasses and drinking still, in the anteroom where they were to greet guests before the services. For his part he was oblivious of the steady stream of arrivals.

"Michael, darling, I'm so sorry," Sylvia said, sitting on the sofa beside him and trying to embrace him.

Michael did not respond.

"Come, dear," she said softly. "Come in and sit with me."

"What an event," Michael said, unmoving. "Everybody who's anybody is here. Kathryn would have liked that."

"I'm sure she would have," Sylvia said to comfort him.

"I hate it," Michael said, shrugging her off and taking another sip of the drink he had badly disguised in a coffee mug.

It was true. The room was filling fast with distinguished mourners from all over the country. Of course, the senator's reputation had brought a slew of dignitaries from governors to foreign diplomats.

Dean Reily, Allen, Kathryn, Robert, and Michael, however, were not without reputation.

The odd mix of politicians, advertising personae, theatrical luminaries, stockbrokers, educators, lawyers, business people, and Kathryn and Michael's more decadent associates had made for an event worthy of media attention. However, the reporters, TV cameras and the curious were held at bay by a fair number of police and security personnel.

Michael had been the catalyst that brought the strange funeral party together. His advertising agency had handled the senator's campaigns for years and it had been at a fund-raiser for the senator that Michael had put together that Kathryn and Bob first met.

"We all hate it, sweetie," Sylvia said, still trying. "This is part of the price for public life."

"What?" Michael said loudly enough to attract attention in the obsequious quiet. "Public death?"

Allen began frantically to shake hands and to try to move the long line of mourners inside.

"Michael," Sylvia said a bit sharply. Then, changing tones: "Where are Ann and Ash?"

"They're home primping for the seven o'clock news," he said bitterly. "They should have gotten Duncan's to do it. The happy couple never looked better."

He began to cry. Loudly.

Sylvia turned her pleading, tear-brimmed eyes to Allen, who shrugged and went on greeting the bereaved.

"Come on, Michael," she said, fighting for control. "Let's go on inside."

"No," Michael shouted, leaping to his feet.

"Michael," Sylvia gasped, a little stunned by the outburst.

"I won't go in there."

The line had stopped dead. They stood staring as Allen pushed through their ranks to get to Michael.

"I'm not attending this morbid premiere," he continued, stumbling toward the door.

"Michael, please," Allen said, reaching him at last and grabbing his arm.

The ensuing struggle overturned a spray of flowers and stunned onlookers into silence and inaction.

Michael broke free and ran toward the door. As he ran into the frozen shock of the world outside, flashbulbs popped and TV lights went on. The blinding onslaught brought him up short.

"Michael. Come here." A voice broke the silence of the moment frozen forever on yards of film and videotape.

Michael obeyed. "Where have you been?" He wept as he fell into Kevin's arms.

"I'm here now," Kevin said.

Kevin waited in the idling limousine in the darkling twilight.

The grave maintenance crew waited, leaning on shovels, holding their hands under their arms and pacing to keep warm.

The graves stood like red wounds in the snow.

Michael sat, alone on a folding chair under the funeral home canopy.

As the last light of the day faded away, he rose and crossed to lean on Kathryn's coffin. "Alone at last," Michael said. "I love you. I always thought I'd be first. I'm not sure I can do this alone." He cried softly; tears dropped onto the shiny polished surface of the mahogany coffin.

The automatic lights in the cemetery came on as they would

eternally. Snow began to sprinkle itself over the scene, frozen like some bizarre paperweight.

Kevin got out of the car and walked to Michael. He stood behind him for a moment, not speaking. "Michael," he said at last.

"Happy New Year, little sister," Michael said. "See you around."

~ ~ ~

Michael had reluctantly decided to attend the reading of the will. Actually, his mother had shamed him into coming. He had spent all of New Year's Day in bed refusing to answer the door or the phone.

Ann had borrowed Kevin's keys and let herself into Michael's. "Thank goodness you're all right," she said, bursting into his bedroom.

"How did you get in here?" he asked, staring at the wall.

"Kevin had a key from the time he house-sat for you," she said, picking up dirty clothes off the floor. "This place looks a mess."

"Sorry," Michael said.

"Michael," she said, sitting on the edge of the bed, "you can't stay in bed for the rest of your life. Or drunk either. We're all sorry Kathryn's gone. She was my daughter," she said, choking a little, "and I get emotional just thinking about it. But I've got two sons and a husband and a grandson to think about."

"And a daughter-in-law," he added, rolling over and reaching for his cigarettes.

"I don't want to think about that," she said. "I've had enough tragedy in my life recently."

They laughed.

She kicked off her shoes, and they both sat up in bed and smoked in silence.

"She is a delight, isn't she?" Michael snorted.

"Who, Mimzee?" Ann asked.

"Mmm." Michael nodded. "Mandy, I think."

"Whatever," Ann said. "What will we do with her?"

"We could pay her off." Michael grinned. "How much have you got?"

"Not as much as Allen," she said, blowing smoke at the ceiling.

"And God knows she knows it," Michael said. "She is definitely after his money."

"You know they're reading the will tomorrow," Ann said offhandedly.

Michael turned over again and stared at the wall.

"You know you're mentioned," Ann continued in the same tone.

"I'm not going," Michael said.

"Michael," she chided, "of course, you'll go."

"I'm not."

"Of all the childish nonsense," she said, her voice getting sharp. "You know, this didn't happen just to you. It happened to all of us. And you have done nothing but make this harder for everyone with your amateur theatrics. And now you refuse to go and hear the last words of your dead sister and her husband. Well, that is the end."

She was crying. "I'm so ashamed of you I could just die. If this is how you're going to act at my funeral, then don't come."

He tried to hug her, but she pulled away. "You just stay in bed and feel sorry for yourself. I need a little comforting, not a lot of childish, emotional wallowing. You selfish, spoiled beast."

The door slammed, and she was gone.

And he was dressed, shaved, showered, sober and dry-eyed at the lawyer's office the next day.

The reading was to be in the boardroom at the law offices where Bob had been a partner. The huge, forbidding oak and leather chamber, surrounded with oil paintings of oak and leather gentlemen in heavy gold frames, was made more forbidding by its occupants.

Everyone was furious by the time Michael arrived.

Bob's father hadn't spoken to anyone since his arrival. Sylvia was furious because he hadn't.

Allen had insisted on bringing Mindy, which made Ann furious, which made Mindy furious, which made Allen furious.

Ashton was furious because everyone else was.

"Hello," Michael said as he came in and took a seat.

Everyone was furious at Michael. His behavior at the funeral home had been splashed all over the news and the papers. No one spoke.

"Did they already read the will?" he asked.

No one spoke.

"Did you see my picture in the paper?" He grinned.

Everyone glared.

"I don't suppose everyone wants to come over for coffee and sandwiches afterward," he said into their angry stares.

"I'm sorry I'm late," Bill Stockbridge, Bob's senior partner and mentor, blustered, coming into the room. He had not read a will or been executor of anyone's estate for years. But Bob had been special, his protégé of sorts, and he had consented, not really thinking he'd ever live to see the day.

"Let me start by saying how sorry I am. We all feel the loss here and know it must be worse for you. I have to say I never really thought I'd have to do this. Let's begin, shall we?"

He put on his reading glasses and unfolded the document. He looked down and opened his mouth to begin to read and then closed it again. He looked over his glasses at all the bloodshot eyes looking at him. He sighed. He set the will on the table before him. He took off his glasses and set them on the will. He squirmed a bit as he fished pipe and tobacco out of his pocket.

Everyone stared in uncomfortable silence. Stockbridge's odd behavior made them all wary of the contents of a will that they all had believed would be routine.

"Well, it's like this," Bill began at last as he sucked his pipe to life. "When Bob and I sat down to write this thing . . . Well, hell I never expected to live long enough to read it . . . let alone that anyone would ever have to. That is, you see, well . . . this will was written after Scotty was born. And well . . . I never thought both he and Kathryn . . . Well, don't you see?"

"No. We don't see," Michael said at last. "What does it say?"

"Well, basically, they left everything to one another in the event of one or the other dying."

"Yeah," Allen said. "Go on."

"And in the event they both died why, you're all mentioned for this and that but most everything goes to Scotty."

"Naturally," Robert harrumphed.

"And there are provisions for distribution in the event Scotty predeceased them. And in the event that any of you-all predeceased them."

"Thorough." Michael smiled and lit a cigarette.

"So what's the problem?" Allen asked.

"Well," Bill went on, "Scotty is a minor."

"Don't tell me that that isn't covered," Michael said in aston-ishment. "He covered everything else."

"Oh, it's covered," Bill said, staring at Michael.

"Well, what's the story?" Allen said.

"Well," Bill stammered, "the codicil covering executorship and guardianship names . . ." He trailed off.

"Well?" Ann said, no longer able to stand it.

Both she and Sylvia figured one or both of them would handle it.

"It names Michael," Bill blurted out.

"Me?"

"Michael?"

"Him."

"The fag?"

"Watch it, Muffy," Michael snapped.

"Mindy."

"Who cares?" Ann cut in. "No one even invited you."

Mindy started to speak, thought better of it and sulked instead.

Everyone sat in stunned silence. No one knew quite what to say. They stared at one another for several minutes. At last Mi-chael broke the silence. "I guess this means we are definitely on for coffee and sandwiches at my place."

It was a somber and silent crowd that gathered at Michael's.

Ann, Ashton, and Michael had been first to arrive. They made coffee and set up chairs enough in the living room in stony silence.

Allen and Mindy had gone by the delicatessen to pick up sand-wiches Michael had ordered.

Robert and Sylvia stayed behind to talk with the lawyer.

Michael, in his sheer terror, switched into good-host automatic pilot and fluttered and fussed, making sure everyone was comfy and well provided for. Several members of the party preferred something stronger than coffee, as did Michael. But considering the dressing down Ann had given him the day before, he thought better of it and stuck to coffee.

Everyone picked up Michael's tone and chatted around the topic at hand. Careers, retirement, money, old times, new invest-ments, everything but custody was discussed.

Michael stared at his sandwich and wondered what to do next. As he caught the furtive glances from around the room, he realized everyone was waiting for him to speak. Everyone, with the possible exception of Mindy, was afraid to offend him.

Michael cleared his throat. As if to prove his theory, the room fell into immediate silence.

Ready or not, he thought.

"Well," he said nervously, "I suppose you're wondering why I've asked you all here."

He laughed a little.

Everyone laughed a little.

"I'm not really sure how I feel right now, other than nervous," he said.

Another little laugh.

"Well," he pressed on, feeling as if he might throw up. "Let me start by saying no one in that room was more surprised than me."

Everyone made oh, so understanding noises. Everyone except Ann, whose hard stare Michael avoided.

"I feel like I'm holding a press conference," he went on.

He smiled.

Everyone smiled.

Except Ann.

"At this point I'm not really even sure what's expected of me. I mean legally, what being a guardian or an executor even means. But, um, I wasn't ever expecting children as a part of my life, I'm sure you all know."

Mindy snorted. Allen elbowed her into silence. They exchanged a look.

"And, um, I loved Kathryn and Bob . . ." He fought for control. "But I'm not sure they made the best decision."

Now the room erupted. This was what everyone wanted to hear and now they all had something to say.

Except Ann.

"Of course you didn't."

"We understand."

"What would you do with a baby?"

"Too much responsibility for one person."

On and on it gushed.

Michael was a little overwhelmed.

"I think I can help clear this up a bit," Robert began in his senator voice.

Everyone fell silent.

"I stayed behind and spoke with Bill Stockbridge, and he thinks"—Robert paused, shifted to his folksy campaign straight-talk tone—"Well, the long and the short of it is the decision is yours, boy. Michael, if you don't want to take on raising this child, why, you just say the word and we can work this thing out quietly and to your satisfaction."

Another uproar of consoling, understanding and generosity from everyone.

Except Ann.

"Well," Ann said in a tone that brought the din up short, "this is too important an issue to be decided in the next five minutes. Michael, you sleep on it and see how you feel. The rest of you go home. When Michael is ready, I think he should talk with the lawyer and they can tell us what's what then."

There was a lot of "here, here," "sleep on it," and "it's totally up to you" as everyone gathered up to leave.

No one noticed Ann as she hugged Michael and whispered into his ear, "Take the phone off the hook and don't answer the door. I'll be back later."

Michael was staring at the lunch things in the twilight. He had sat smoking and finishing the coffee for several hours after the mob had left.

It had been an overwhelming afternoon.

The "Congratulations, you're a father" revelation of the will had been stunning. The family reunion had been draining. But the greatest shock of the day had been Ann. Her total lack of support or open hostility or anything else had been unsettling, but her little diversion at the end had been the most off-putting of all.

Ann was a hardworking, self-sacrificing, no-nonsense lady. She did not believe in ghosts, the Loch Ness monster or hyperbole. Never had. And had not permitted her children to indulge in such beliefs.

Her God was a rational being who commanded the universe

to behave in an orderly and explainable way. She could not even abide science fiction movies.

And yet this cracker-barrel Socrates was advocating the most cloak-and-dagger behavior.

What was more surprising was her insight into the situation. Since their departure the senator and Mrs. Miller had been to the door twice and he had sighted Allen and Mindy circling the block.

So he sat alone in the dark, afraid to go near a window.

"This is ridiculous," he said aloud.

Dewars snorted.

"It certainly is," Ann said, suddenly coming in from the kitchen.

Michael shouted and overturned a chair in his fright.

"Shh," she hissed. "I think Bob's mother and father are out there."

"Mother, what is all this about?" he demanded, rubbing the ankle he had barked on the chair.

"I'd say it's about time you grew up," Ann said, switching on the lights.

"What are you talking about?"

"Wait a minute," she said, going out onto the balcony and turning on a lamp.

"Michael," she shouted.

"What?" Michael said, frustration creeping into his voice.

"Would you bring me a cup of coffee?" she shouted.

"Sure," he said, storming into the kitchen.

"Here, I'll help you," she shouted, coming back inside.

"I can pour coffee by myself," Michael snarled as she came into the kitchen.

"I don't want any coffee," she said matter-of-factly.

"Then why—" he began.

"I wanted Robert Miller to know I was here," she said, climbing onto a barstool in the kitchen.

"How did you get in here?" he asked. "And what are you up to?"

"I came in the back way with Kevin's keys," she said. "I parked one street over."

"You climbed over the fence in my backyard?" he said, taking the other barstool.

"And I'm here to talk to you before the deal makers get here."

"I think your panty hose are on too tight," he said, taking a sip of her black coffee and making a face.

"Here," she said, handing him the creamer. "I want to talk to you about Scott and the future."

"Oh, God," he said, spooning creamer into the cup. "You want the baby. That's what this is all about."

"No, Goddamnit," she snapped. "That is not what this is about."

Ann could be a docile and easygoing person and had allowed her husband, her children and even the family pets to push her around. But, when she said "Goddamnit," it was time to shut up, listen and say "yes, ma'am" when she was finished.

Michael did.

"This is about you," she said. "It's time you grew up. I love you, Michael. Everyone loves you. And a big part of why everyone does love you is that you have remained the child we all were, once. You run and play. We scrimp and save. You wear silly clothes. We choke in gray wool. You laugh and chatter. We attend real estate investment seminars. You are always broke. We loan you money. You say terrible things to us. We laugh. We love you. We envy you. We live through you. You are our connection with our youth."

There were tears in her eyes.

"But the time has come for you to grow up. To accept the responsibilities of growing older. There is joy there, too. A different joy. A quiet joy. But there is joy. And there's pain. It's accepting the pain and the joy that makes you a grown-up."

"Is this a scene from *Peter Pan* or are we headed somewhere?" Michael asked, trying to lighten the mood as much as to find out what Ann was up to.

"Shut up, Michael," Ann snapped. "I've stood by as long as I'm going to. I'm not fooled. This decathlon of superficiality you have chosen to call your life is just a mad dash from reality. And that reality is that you're alone."

"So what do you want me to do?" Michael snorted. "Find a nice boy and settle down?"

"You already have," she said, rising to get herself a coffee mug.

"What?"

"I'm talking about Scott," she said, pouring. "How long has this coffee been here?"

"An hour or so."

"Mmm." She sipped.

"What about Scott?"

"Scott is your chance not to spend your life alone."

"Mother . . ."

"Hear me out. I have found fulfillment with your father that is one of the most wonderful parts of my life. But the most wonderful part, the most fulfilling thing that has ever happened to me is having children. Watching you grow up to become who you are, sharing your life, the good and bad, right from the start. It has made my life . . ." She paused, searching for the word, shrugging and shaking her head. "It's made my life."

"So you think I should keep Scott?" he asked, incredulous.

She smiled and nodded.

"Are you crazy?" He snorted.

"Maybe," she said, still smiling.

"In the first place, I don't know anything about children—babies—I wouldn't know what to do," he said, pacing the kitchen.

"Neither did I when you were born."

"You had nine months' notice."

"And now I have nearly thirty years' experience and a telephone." She smiled still.

"I have a career and a busy life. What would I do with a baby?"

"Share your life," she said, pouring more coffee for them both.

"Well," he began again with a harder edge in his voice, "beyond the metaphysical consideration of spiritual rewards, how do you suppose the rest of the concerned parties would react?"

"They'll hate it," she said, handing him his cup.

He sipped and thought. "They'll drag me to court," he said at last.

"Most certainly," Ann said.

"And everyone gets hurt and I lose," he said. "So what's the point?"

"Why are you so sure you'll lose?"

"Given the choice of a college dean and his wife, a senator and his wife, an up-and-coming young businessman and his slightly older wife-to-be and a crazy faggot who writes TV commercials

and throws cocktail parties for a living, who would you pick?"
he demanded.

"It doesn't make any difference who I would pick. Or a judge,"
she said. "It's who Kathryn and Bob would pick. And they picked
you."

"Wills can be broken," Michael said, slamming his mug down.
"Especially when the facts of my sexual proclivities are brought
from under their rock into the harsh light of judicial impartiality
and what's best for the child."

"Balderdash," she said with a little laugh. "You're just an old
maid, Michael."

"Mother," he said, astonished.

"Well, it's true, isn't it?" she said, still amused. "Kathryn's sexual activities were more suspect than yours. You're the only one
who adopted your mother's outdated values and morals. You're
just an old-fashioned girl."

Michael's mouth hung open.

"Don't think I haven't heard you and your sister whispering
and giggling all these years."

"Well," Michael said, finally regaining the power of speech.
"Road-whore or not, I am gay."

"Bill Stockbridge says—" she began.

"You have been busy," he cut in.

"He says the will makes mention that they were aware of that
fact and still felt you best qualified to raise their child as they
would have," she concluded. "In addition, Bill Stockbridge himself is already retained, as a stipulation of the will, to represent
you and advise you in administering the estate until Scott is
twenty-one."

"How do you—"

"Here's a copy," she said, pulling the cumbersome document
from her purse.

"Look, Mother," he said at last, "I appreciate what you're trying to do and what Bob and Kathryn tried to do, but I don't think
this is what they intended."

"Of course it is."

"They did not plan for me to raise their child from the cradle,"
he was shouting.

"Of course not," she said soothingly. "But they did want you to raise their child if they couldn't."

"Well, I'm not going to," Michael said, teeth clenched. "Even if I wanted to, they'd take him away from me. At least this way I can avoid the pain . . ."

The words died in his throat. He stared into her eyes and she into his.

Dewars' nails clicked onto the linoleum and she cocked her head and gave Michael that "this-is-your-last-chance-buster" look.

"Well," Ann said with an air of resignation, "you avoid the pain, baby. Make your best deal. I'm sure Allen and Mindy will make lovely parents."

She finished her coffee, snapped her pocketbook shut and kissed Michael on the cheek.

"I tried," she said. "They'll be here in a minute. You better take the dog out. Good night, dear."

"It's for the best, Mother," he called after her as she marched down the front stairs. He knew she was crying. He heard the front door close. He got Dewars' leash out of the pantry and they went down the back stairs together. He sat in the darkness on the cold cement steps as Dewars negotiated the last patches of snow. The cigarette tasted good and he tried to think only of smoking as he leaned against the iron railing.

"Michael?"

The voice startled him back to reality.

"Doesn't anyone just come to the door anymore?" he muttered as he rose and stomped out his cigarette on the step.

"Dewars," he called, "come on, hurry up, we have more company."

"Michael?"

"I'm coming, Robert," he called back. "We're out here."

"Take your time," Robert called back. "We'll wait."

Dewars took her time and at length they returned to the house.

"Robert, Sylvia," he said in greeting as they came back in. "Coffee?"

"No, thanks," Robert said, smiling affably as Michael and Dewars came into the living room.

"Sylvia?" he asked.

"No, thanks, Michael."

There was an embarrassed silence.

Dewars crossed to her spot at the fireplace, surveyed the others in the room, snorted in disgust and threw herself to the floor.

"What a wonderful little dog," Robert said. "How long have you had her?"

"What's the deal, Senator?" Michael said, flopping onto a sofa.

"What?" Robert said, a little shocked.

"Let's don't beat around the bush, mmm?" Michael said, lighting a cigarette. "What compromise package have you come to offer? Let's get right to the negotiations. We'll worry about PR later."

The "oak and leather room" at Bob's law office was more terrifying than Michael had remembered. Maybe because it was empty now. Or maybe because it was soon to be full again.

In any case, Michael sat chain-smoking, waiting for everyone to arrive so all the final papers could be signed and witnessed.

"The deal" had turned out to be pretty lucrative. Michael was to take ownership of Bob and Kathryn's expensive condominium at the beach and he would receive fifty thousand dollars in cash, stocks and negotiable bonds. The remainder of Bob and Kathryn's holdings—stocks, securities, real estate, their house, some office buildings and a share in a shopping mall—would be set up in trust and administered by a board of directors, of which Michael would be chairman, a salaried position.

"Scotty, Inc.," Michael called it.

All in all he had been fairly shocked at the size of the estate. Bob had been more successful than he had thought. Though much had been inherited from his prominent family, Bob had parlayed what he had gotten into substantial holdings.

Michael was greatly relieved that he was not going to have to keep up with it all. His primary role would be to sign papers until Scott was old enough.

Scott was to go to live with the Millers during the year and spend summers with Ann and Ashton. Custody passed to the Reilys first and then to Allen and Mindy, in the event that all grandparents died before the child reached twenty-one years of age. In the event that absolutely everyone died, Michael took custody.

"How do you feel?" Bill Stockbridge said, scaring the bejesus out of Michael as he came into the room.

"Like Judas Iscariot," Michael said, stubbing out his cigarette.

"That's not fair," Bill said, arranging papers on the table.

"You're right," Michael said, lighting another. "I'm a much better negotiator."

Bill snorted and went on shuffling.

"Right in here," Bill's secretary said, ushering in the Millers and Ann and Ash.

Ann was carrying the baby.

Michael was a little startled. He hadn't seen Scott since Christmas Eve with Kathryn and Bob, and hadn't expected to see him there.

"Here, Michael," Ann said, thrusting the baby into his hands. "You hold him."

"Mother, I—"

"He's no threat to you now," Ann said a little icily. "Go on."

"Thanks, Mom," Michael said, giving up.

"Everything ready?" Robert asked Bill absurdly.

"Just the formality of signing," Bill said. "Then off to probate, though with all concerned parties signing, that shouldn't be a problem."

Allen and Mindy arrived.

Sylvia, Ann and Ash sat talking. Robert and Bill blathered on about legal matters that didn't bear discussion again.

Michael sat with Scott. "Say uncle, Scott, say uncle."

"I see we're all here," Bill said, quieting the crowd.

"Say uncle." Michael's voice rang out in the silence.

Everyone stared. Michael blushed. They smiled.

"Sorry," Michael said sheepishly.

"Well, yes," Bill began. "Now I know everyone is familiar with the terms set out by this agreement. But, just for the sake of clarity and to avoid later misunderstanding, I'd like to review everything verbally and then we'll all sign. Okay?"

Everyone nodded and made agreeable noises.

The baby grabbed Michael's right index finger and began to tug and laugh.

Bill began rumbling through the document.

Michael tried to pay attention, but the baby kicked and

screamed with delight. "Shhh," Michael hissed, leaning in close to the baby's face.

Scotty let go of the finger and grabbed Michael's hair.

"Ow, stop, let go," Michael said under his breath.

Scotty squealed with laughter.

Michael giggled.

Bill looked over his glasses and then returned to reading.

Michael managed to pry the baby's grip loose from his hair.

The others began signing.

"Uuuuuu-Caaaaa," Scott screamed.

"He said it," Michael shouted.

"Michael, we're ready for you," Bill said, patiently holding out the pen.

"He said uncle," Michael said in delight.

"Oh, I doubt it," Mindy said, crossing over. "Here, let me hold him while you sign."

"Sign?" Michael said uncomprehendingly.

"The papers," Bill said, pushing the pen at him as if it might help explain.

"Oh," Michael said, realizing. "Of . . . course."

"Here. Give him to me," Mindy said more forcefully.

"I—okay," he said, handing the baby over. "Didn't you hear him say uncle?"

"Just gurgling," Mindy said, taking him. "He doesn't know what it means."

Scott threw out his arms and began to scream, "Uuuuuu-Caaaaa."

"The hell he doesn't," Michael said, taking the baby back. "He knows me."

"Michael," Robert said, "if you could just sign now, we can get on with this."

Michael looked up into all the staring faces.

Scott gnawed on his chin.

He looked into Scott's face, then up again. Bill was bringing pen and paper to him.

"It would really be a lot easier if you just gave him to me," Mindy said, getting a little testy.

Michael took the pen with his free hand. "It certainly would be, wouldn't it, Mindy?" he said.

He looked into Ann's face. She smiled under knowingly arched brows.

"No," he said matter-of-factly.

"What?" Bill said, still shoving the papers at him.

"No," he said again. "I . . . can't. I just can't."

"Michael," Robert said, trying to remain calm, "we discussed this. If there's something else you want—"

"No."

"Then just sign the paper, Michael," Sylvia said soothingly, walking slowly toward him as if he were holding a gun on them all.

"Yes," Michael said.

"That's better," Bill said. "Then just sign right—"

"No. I mean, yes, there is something else I want," Michael said. "First I want not to make this decision. But I can't have that. Second, I want to avoid a fight, and I'll bet I can't have that either. And I want to—I have to keep the baby."

"What?"

"Michael, we agreed."

"Give me the baby now."

"Michael, I love you."

"Let's get out of here, Mom."

"I already put the baby seat in your car." Ann grinned.

"You're a fiend, Mother."

"Uuuuuu-Caaaaa," Scott screamed.

"Good-bye, everyone," Michael said to the angry mob, his family.

"I'll see you in court," Robert shouted over the uproar.

Michael woke up with a start. Someone is screaming, he thought in a panic.

"Scott is screaming," he said out loud. He squinted as he tried to focus on the glowing red numbers on the alarm clock. "Scotty is screaming at two-oh-seven," he said. He flung back the covers, put on his robe and slippers and shuffled across the hall to Scott's room.

The thought of staying at Kathryn's was too much, so Ash and Michael had moved some essential items over to Michael's and set them up in his office. Michael had chosen the room as his office because it was smaller, sunnier, away from the street and therefore quieter. It made a pretty nice nursery.

Michael opened the door and shuffled over to the crib. He leaned over, looked into Scott's face and said, "What? What is it? Stop screaming. It's two in the morning. Stop screaming."

Scott went right on screaming.

Michael leaned closer to Scott and screamed.

Scott paused, looked at Michael and then began screaming again.

Michael screamed again.

Scott stopped, looked and screamed. Then he stopped again and looked.

Michael screamed.

Scott screamed a little and laughed.

Michael laughed and picked him up.

"Now. What's wrong. Hunh. Oh, that. Say diaper," Michael said, laying the baby on the top of the Bathinette the Millers had given Kathryn.

"Uuuuuu-Caaaaa," Scott said.

"That's me," Michael said. "Now say Di-Per," he went on, holding up the example. "Di-Per. It'll help out a lot if you learn to tell me what you want. This screaming is out.

"And I don't know who got you started on this sleeping schedule," he said, powdering. "But it has got to go. If I went to bed at seven in the evening, I'd be up at two in the morning, too. You're going to start staying up.

"Di-Per," he said again, waving a cleaner example this time. "Di-Per.

"Say it, Scott." He was fastening the tapes. "Say Di-Per."

Scotty laughed and kicked.

"Now you're supposed to get a bottle," Michael said, hefting Scott onto his hip. "How you can drink milk at this hour is beyond me."

Michael switched on the kitchen light, took a bottle out of the fridge and put it in the microwave. He programmed the machine, yawned and hit the start button. The machine sprang to life.

"Durrr," Scott said, thrusting a hand at the machine.

Dewars came clicking into the kitchen.

She cocked her head and eyed them suspiciously.

"That's the microwave, not Durr," Michael said, but Scott was no longer paying any attention.

"Bow, bow, bow, bow, bow," Scott shrieked, bouncing.

"That's Dewars," Michael said, squatting so Scott could get a better look.

"Da-pa," Scotty shrieked.

"No, Dewars," Michael sat, patting the dog. Dewars winced and clicked off to the water bowl.

"Di-per," Michael said, patting Scott's diaper.

"Da-pa," Scott said, patting his diaper.

"Excellent," Michael said, hugging him.

The microwave beeped.

"Eeeee," Scott screamed with delight.

"A bottle and off to bed for you," Michael said, testing a squirt on his wrist. "An excellent year," he said, handing it over.

It was three when he went back to bed.

It was seven when the radio alarm went off.

"Oh, my God," Michael said to the ceiling.

"You look like ten pounds of shit in a five-pound sack."

"Thanks, Al," Michael said to Alice Leigh, the office manager at Gilliam and Company, the ad agency where he worked.

"Anytime, Mic," she said, wrestling with the coffee machine.

"Don't call me Mic."

"Don't call me Al."

"Coffee ready?"

"Does it look ready?"

"No."

"Well, it is. Have a cup," she said sarcastically.

"Ah, kind words from a sympathetic coworker in a time of trouble."

"Surely, you don't want me to act—"

"No, I don't. And don't call me Shirley."

They laughed.

"There's cheese Danish."

"Blech."

"You doin' okay?"

"Fine."

"How did the settlement go yesterday."

"Not so well."

"Oh."

"I'm a mother."

"Oh, Michael. You didn't?"

"I did. Where's the newspaper?"

"Must still be outside."

Out in the parking lot Crawford, one of the writers from the agency, pulled up.

"Michael," he shouted, "how are you?"

"Fine," Michael said, stuffing his arm into a juniper bush and fishing out two newspapers—neither current.

"You look really good," Crawford said, getting close enough to pat Michael on the shoulder.

"Thanks, Crawf, so do you," Michael said, smiling to himself.

"Today's?" Crawford said, indicating the papers.

"Both of 'em," Michael said, thrusting them into Crawford's hands.

Crawford laughed his insincere laugh.

Crawford disliked and was jealous of Michael. Michael disliked and was jealous of Crawford. It was an interesting arrangement.

"There it is," Michael said, crawling under the steps to fish out yet another paper.

"I'm going on in. See you around," Crawford said.

"We'll do lunch." Michael smirked.

Crawford laughed insincerely.

Michael followed him in. "Coffee ready?" he asked Alice.

"No," she said, taking a sip of hers and taking the paper from him. "Your mother's on the phone."

"That was fast," he said, getting coffee.

"What?" Alice asked, taking out sections of the paper.

"She's keeping the baby. I figured it would be longer before she called."

"Mmm. You got the kid already?"

"Umm-hmm. Give me that back," he said, snatching at the paper.

"I had it," she said, snatching back. "Talk to your mother."

He sat at the receptionist's desk to take the call. He and Alice and Crawford were the first ones there. As usual. Frankie Gilliam would probably be next if he was in town and didn't have a breakfast meeting. The rest of the staff trickled in between nine and ten.

"Hello, Mother," he said as he punched the flashing button.

"Hello, Michael," she said. "Where are the diapers?"

"They're in the closet in the office. Scott's room," he said. "Listen, if he needs to be changed, make him say diaper first."

"What?" Ann said.

"I'm trying to get him to say what he wants instead of screaming," Michael explained.

"That's ridiculous," Ann said. "He can't say—"

"Yes, he can. He said it last night and this morning," Michael argued, slurping his coffee.

"How am I supposed to get him to stop screaming long enough to say anything?" she asked in exasperation.

"Scream back," he said reasonably.

"What?" she said, a little shocked.

"Scream back at him until he starts laughing," Michael explained.

"Michael, that is the most ridiculous thing I've ever heard."

"Be that as it may, I want to start encouraging him to verbalize as soon as possible and I don't want to reinforce his screaming."

"Who are you, Dr. Spock? You said not a week ago you didn't know anything about babies. Now one night, and you're an expert."

"And don't baby-talk around him either."

Ann laughed. "All right, I'll do my best," she said. "But you're going to have a hell of a time getting a nanny, I can see."

"We start interviewing tomorrow afternoon."

"We?" Ann asked.

"Yeah," Michael said. "I thought Bill Stockbridge should be there. For propriety's sake. If, I mean, when, Robert Miller drags me into court, I want everything to be on the square. I'm asking for a degree in early childhood development or two years' experience with children."

"Expensive," Ann said, lighting a cigarette.

"I guess," he said, gesturing with a half-eaten biscuit. "But I'm going to have to be prepared to compete with the old 'offering the kid advantages' routine, I don't want to look slouchy.

"Alright, Mom. Is that it? I gotta go."

"See you at lunch," she said.

"Okay, bye," Michael said, hanging up. "Give me the newspaper, Alice. I don't want to have to hurt you."

". . . And I really think this job will give me the opportunity to put a lot of things that have just been theory up until now into practice."

"Well, that's all I have," Michael said brightly to the last in a string of applicants. "Thank you, Anna."

"What? Oh, yes, thank you," Bill Stockbridge said as if waking suddenly from a nap.

"Cindy has your number?" Michael asked.

"Yes, sir," she said.

"Well, we'll be making a decision in the next couple of days," Michael said, rising. "We'll let you know."

"Thank you both," she said, following Michael's lead and rising. "And may I just say what a brave thing I think you're doing."

"Thank you, Anna," Michael said, a little put off but not showing it much.

There was an uncomfortable pause when Bill was supposed to rise but didn't.

"Well," Anna said at last, slapping her arms limply on her sides in a huge shrug, "I hope I'll be seeing you."

Michael saw her to the door, then returned to the living room, where they had been conducting the interviews.

Neither man spoke. Michael lit a cigarette and went for more coffee. "Coffee?" he called from the kitchen.

"No, thanks," Bill called back.

When Michael returned, Bill was tamping tobacco into his pipe. "The grandmotherly one we saw around lunchtime was nice," Bill said at last. "Lots of experience."

"I would rather have had lunch," Michael said flatly. "Besides, her children sounded ghastly, and her husband left her. Not very promising."

"Well, these things take time," Bill said perfunctorily.

"Too much time," Michael said. "I'm starving. Let's go get lunch."

"Mmmkay," Bill said, rising. "Good Lord, it's nearly four o'clock."

"Yeah, and Mom'll be back with the kid in a couple of hours," Michael said, finding a coat. "Let's get going."

"You know, Michael," Bill said, "have you considered that maybe it would be better if you went ahead—"

"Yes. I have," Michael said, buttoning. "It's like mercy killing."

"It is?" Bill said, blinking in amazement.

"Yeah," Michael said. "To me it's not so much the question of whether or not the person is suffering, but for whose benefit they're being cut loose. It's certainly more convenient for the family to be shed of the burden. But they always say, 'So-and-so's better off.' Still in all, it's their misery they're thinking of. It's all I. 'I couldn't stand to see him suffering.'"

"You should have been a lawyer, Michael," Bill said, a little amused, as they started down the stairs to the door.

"I couldn't stand all the schooling," Michael said. "Let's go to the Urb. I feel like a tabouli salad."

"Sure," Bill said with very little conviction.

The Urb was the Urban Greenery, a vegetarian restaurant and one of the last vestiges of the sixties counterculture left in Columbia. The owner, a hippie-cum-businessman and a friend of Michael's, had started with the operation when it was a commune of sorts. But as communes fell out of fashion in favor of salaries,

Randy Green had gotten a loan through the Small Business Administration, moved the operation to an up-and-coming district in the city and, with a little marketing assistance from Michael, made the Urb a chic and successful health food restaurant.

Michael was a frequent visitor because of his friendship and because it was only a block from his house.

By the time Bill and Michael arrived, the lunch rush was over and the help was setting up for dinner. The restaurant had that informal "come sit in the kitchen" quality that empty restaurants take on. And as Michael was more family than client, no one paid much attention when they arrived.

Randy's daughter, who had been sitting at the juice bar coloring, was the first to spot them. "Uncle Michael," she shouted across the vacant room.

"Nicky," he shouted back as she ran to embrace him. "Here," he whispered into her ear as he slipped her a chocolate mint that her holistic father strictly forbade. "Don't let Randy catch you. And don't implicate me if he does."

"Michael," Randy said, emerging from the kitchen, wiping his hands, "what have you been up to? Strike that," he said, blushing. "Sorry about your sister."

"Thanks, Randy," Michael said, smiling. "This is my lawyer, Bill Stockbridge. Bill, this is Randy Green."

"Nice to meet you," Bill said, extending his hand a little tentatively.

Despite the success of the business, Randy remained in an arrested state of development. His hippie locks remained unshorn and were tucked under a red bandanna tied to his head for kitchen work.

Because of the beginnings of the business and Randy's continued commitment to an era long gone, the staff and even the restaurant itself had a quality of being refugees from time.

How Randy made contact with the offbeat staff members was a source of continuing amazement to Michael, but Randy's staff was always composed of fellow adherents to the doctrines and styles of days gone by.

"Nice to meet you, too," Randy said, shaking Bill's hand firmly. "You here for lunch?"

"If we could," Michael said. "I have got to have a tabouli salad."

"No problem," Randy said, taking up a couple of menus from the counter.

At that moment a similarly clad gentleman emerged from the kitchen, carrying an enormous plastic container. "Gray," Randy said, addressing him, "you've got your first table of the evening. Michael, this is Graham Rambeaux—Gray."

"How do you do?" Michael said, inclining his head a bit.

"Well, and you?" Gray nodded back.

"French?" Michael asked, judging the tangible accent.

"Canadian." Gray smiled.

"Gray's been with us since before Christmas," Randy said, coming around the counter. "If we ever saw you around here, you'd know. He works during the day with Anise and waits tables for me at night."

Anise was Randy's wife, sort of. Formerly in charge of child care at the commune, she had returned to school and now operated a Montessori school.

"Well, you didn't come to my Christmas party," Michael said.

"I never come to your Christmas party," Randy said. "Where do you want to sit?"

"By a window near the garden," Michael said. "Well, you shouldn't complain about my not visiting if you won't visit me."

"Your parties are a little bourgeois for me," Randy said, seating them. "Here you go."

"Bob Dylan is a little bourgeois for you." Michael grinned.

"Gray will be right with you," Randy said, smacking him with a menu.

"I've never been here before," Bill said confidentially when they were alone.

"Oh," Michael said, feigning surprise. "Well, don't order anything with carob in it. It tastes like Ayds diet candy. Other than that, everything's pretty good."

"Nicky," Randy shouted, "what is that all over your mouth?"

"Nothing," she said, eyes as big and shiny as wading pools.

"It is not nothing," he went on. "It's chocolate. Where did you get it?"

"Uncle Michael," she said without a moment's remorse.

"Michael," Randy shouted.

"She must have picked my pocket," Michael said from behind his menu. "Probably learned it from one of your scalawag friends. May we smoke?"

"God, you're a bad influence," Randy yelled. "Yes, go ahead. Crack the window and quit if anyone comes in."

Eventually Gray took the orders and Bill and Michael got lunch.

Afterward, as it was still too early for dinner trade and the side work was done, Randy joined them. Gray, a little bored but not bold enough to pull up a chair, hovered around the table enjoying the conversation, if not joining in.

Michael began describing the interviews with the child care candidates, rising to imitate mannerisms and walks. Everyone had a pretty good laugh.

"Well," Bill said at last, "I've really got to be going. I hope you won't take offense, Randy, but I've had a better time than I expected. Thank you."

"None taken," Randy said. "You turned out to be less of a bore than I thought."

Everyone laughed.

Gray brought the check, which Michael and Bill fought over. Randy won by tearing it up and refusing to accept payment. "Late Christmas," Randy said, waving off the cash. "Listen, Michael," he went on as they walked toward the front, "you ought to consider leaving Scott with Anise."

"Thanks, Randy," Michael said, patting his shoulder. "But I've got to compete with Senator and Mrs. Miller and I don't think day school beats a full house."

"Just a thought," Randy said, holding the door. "Take it easy."

"See you, Randy," Michael said, slipping him a chocolate mint. "Don't let Nicky see that."

"I won't. Thanks."

"Nice place," Bill said as they started up the street.

"Yeah," Michael said, pausing to light up. "I'd go more often if they'd let you smoke."

"Mr. Reily."

Michael turned. It was Gray.

"Yes?" Michael said, wondering what he might have left on the table other than a tip.

"May I speak with you a moment?" he asked.

"Well, I suppose," Michael said haltingly.

"Michael," Bill said, "I really do have to run. I'll talk to you tomorrow."

"Right, Bill," Michael said. "I'll call Cindy and let you know when round two is. I'm going to try for Saturday, if that's okay."

"That'll be great." Bill waved. "See you."

"Mr. Reily."

"Michael."

"Michael," Gray began again. "I understand you are looking for someone to care for your child, no?"

"Yes," Michael said, "I am. Do you have a girlfriend you'd like me to consider?"

"No," Gray said. "I would like for you to consider me."

"You?"

"Yes," he went on. "I have much experience with children. I have Montessori training and a degree in art history. I can cook very well; I cook here sometimes. And I speak French."

"French," Michael said, puzzled.

"Yes. I could teach the child French as well as English. And much about art. I was a very good student at university."

"Well, I, uh . . . would be delighted to er . . . consider you," Michael stammered. "But what about your jobs with Anise and Randy?"

"Alas, they are part-time and do not pay well," Gray said with a shrug.

"Well, the position is full-time," Michael said. "But it's live-in."

"That would solve much," Gray said. "For I am staying with Randy and Anise for over a month now and cannot afford to move out."

"Well," Michael said, unable to think of anything else.

"Please consider my offer," Gray said urgently. "I must get back to work now. If you wish to talk more to me, you may call here, at the school or Randy's."

"I'll do that," Michael said, smiling affably.

"Thank you, Mr.—" Gray began and then stopped. "Michael. I am the best choice, I assure you."

Randy looked at the clock. It said four-fifteen.

"Who the hell can be calling at— Hello?" he said angrily into the phone.

"Randy? Michael," Michael said.

"What in the hell do you want?" Randy demanded.

"Do you hear that?"

"What?"

"Listen."

"Di-Pa. Di-pa. UuuuuuCaaaaa."

"What do you suppose that is?" Michael demanded, returning the receiver to his ear.

"The war cry of a band of irate Pygmies?"

"Is Gray there?"

"Yes, but Christ, he's asleep. It's four o'clock in the morning."

"Four-seventeen." Michael corrected him. "Get him up. He's going to have to get used to it."

Michael had hired Gray over the objections of Bill Stockbridge and his mother. Ashton had been his strongest supporter in the decision. Oblivious of public opinion and an educator, Ash thought that Montessori experience was an excellent qualification. "You hire the best qualified, not the most popular," he said.

Still, even Michael had had some reservations when Gray's luggage consisted solely of a guitar, three pairs of very old blue jeans, a half dozen T-shirts with various slogans emblazoned on them and the remains of a pair of tennis shoes. No socks. No toilet articles. No underwear.

After some very brief soul-searching Michael had broached the subject. "Look," he said after a few perfunctories following dinner one night, "I know and you know that outward appearance is irrelevant."

"Yes, I would say so," Gray said earnestly as he sat on the living room rug playing with Scott.

"But these are hard times for liberals." Michael began again.

"Particularly for me. Scott's grandfather is suing to take Scott away from me."

"Oh?" Gray said, looking up at Michael. "Not Ash."

"No. Not Ash," Michael said, looking away. "Scott's paternal grandfather."

"I did not know," Gray said, watching as Michael paced around the room.

"Well, it's not my favorite topic," Michael said. "The thing is —is that . . . well, if it were up to me, but it isn't—"

"You don't want to hire me?" Gray asked, oblivious of Scott's swinging on his beard.

"No, no, no. It's not that at all," Michael said, sitting at last. "It's that, well, we really have to keep up appearances."

"Yes," Gray said.

"Yes. Well." Michael was on his feet again. "You're . . . very well qualified to care for the baby—"

"But I look like a Bolshevik?"

Michael laughed. "Well, a little Leninist," he said.

"Michael," Gray said, smiling. "I would wear expensive Italian suits if I could afford them. I look like the Bolsheviks because they were poor men and so am I. I am not offended, and I will try to improve my appearance. This is the best job I've ever had. I will spend my money on better clothes."

"We can help a little bit," Michael said, greatly relieved.

And that was that.

To the various delight and dismay of Michael's clothiers, hair-dresser and Gray, Michael undertook an immediate Pygmalion transformation. After a fight Gray was allowed to keep his mustache, though he lost his beard and most of his hair. Tennis shoes gave way to Top-Siders, blue jeans to khakis and "No Nukes" T-shirts to Ralph Lauren button-downs.

"Scotty, Inc." had its first employee and, as Ashton pointed out, Gray looked more conservative than Michael.

All in all, Gray was more pleased than he had expected with the overnight metamorphosis. Though he had bucked at the new look originally, the new respect that came with it was a pleasant surprise. On previous trips to the farmers' market with Randy for vegetables, good deals were hard to come by and contempt was thinly veiled. Now his weekly arrival in Kathryn's Volvo station wagon was like the appearance of visiting royalty.

His knowledge of the market and new guise brought respect and good deals. Instead of insults to his back it became, "Nossir, those aren't for you. I set these here aside to show you."

What's more, Kathryn's charge accounts brought admission to the finest shops.

If Gray was enjoying the privileges of running a household on the grander scale afforded by the estate, Michael was enjoying living there. His once-humble, if fashionable, apartment, had been transformed into a bastion of quiet comfort. The plants flourished, the food was excellent and the house was spotless. But more than that, the house was full.

"Good morning, Al," Michael said, shoving into the tiny office kitchen.

"Good morning, Mic," Alice said, shoving back.

"Don't call me Mic."

"Don't call me Al. What's in the tin?" she asked, snatching the newspaper.

"Some bran muffins Gray baked," Michael said, prying off the lid. "Posta be good for ya."

"Hey, Mikey," she said, tasting one. "I like it. No wonder you look so good lately."

"Yes, motherhood agrees with me," Michael said, pouring himself a cup of coffee.

"Seriously," she said. "You've been downright pleasant lately."

"Don't let it get around," he said, pouring her a cup.

"These are really good," she said, taking a second muffin.

"Tell me about it," he said as they went out to sit in the reception area. "The man is a gem. I keep going outside and checking the house numbers to make sure I'm in the right apartment. Give me some of the newspaper, will ya?"

"Is it just vegetarian?" she asked as she tore off the upper left corner of the front page of the paper with the weather report on it and handed it to him.

"No," he said, snatching the rest of the paper off her lap. "We had a discussion about that. He said he felt that he couldn't prepare flesh and I said I respected his feelings and would give him

a very good reference. He's particularly good with veal. Here."
He handed her all but the front section and sales papers.

"Thanks," she said, laughing at the story. "Marriage agrees
with you."

"Bite your tongue," he said, playfully slapping her hand.
"There are spies everywhere. Besides, you can't fire a wife."

"How is that going?" she asked.

"How is what going?"

"The lawsuit."

"Oh, that. Who knows? They haven't even scheduled a hearing.
No word anyway."

"That's odd."

"I guess."

At that point Crawford stormed into the office.

"Good morning," Michael said. "There are some muffins. Have
one if you—"

"Good morning, Alice," Crawford said, crashing around in the
kitchen. He emerged with a cup of coffee and strode past them.

"What's the matter with him?" Alice asked.

"You noticed that, too?" Michael said. "I suppose I've done
something. Probably a good job again."

"No!"

"Yes!" he said. "It really seems to make him angry."

"He's such an asshole," Alice said, rifling through the paper.
"So are you. You gave me all the lousy sections."

"You got *Jumble.*"

"Good morning," Frankie Gilliam, the ad agency's owner, said,
bursting through the door.

"Morning, Fran," they said in chorus from behind their
newspapers.

"Don't let me disturb you," he said.

"Don't worry about it."

"No problem."

"I love the respect and adulation of being boss the best," he
said, heading for the kitchen. "Is there coffee?"

"No, we're all out," Alice said from behind the paper.

"That's a shame," he called back, pouring a cup. "What are
these?"

"Bran muffins," Michael said. "Don't have one. It might improve your health and your early demise will increase my opportunity for advancement."

"I won't," he said, stuffing most of one into his mouth. "They're terrible," he gargled, taking another. "And, just for that smart remark, I'm not going with your creative on the insurance pitch after all," he said, standing in front of them, grinning.

"Oh, Frankie, that's wonderful," Michael said, tossing the paper aside.

"If you hug me, I really will change my mind," Frankie said.

"So that's what was wrong with Crawford," Alice said, lowering the paper.

"It's not perfect," Frankie said seriously. "We've got a lot of work to do and the presentation is the first of next week, but you're it."

"I'm ready," Michael said, rising. "What's first?"

"I've marked up the copy and Ellen's pencils," he said over his shoulder as he headed down the hall. "I'll give it to you in a minute, and we need to meet as soon as Ellen gets here."

"Have a good day, Al," Michael said, gathering up his coffee and belongings.

"You, too, Mikey," Alice said, returning to the paper.

"This is a more important point than your copy makes it," Frankie said as he, Michael, and Ellen huddled around the table in his office. "The research makes name identification a real positive."

"But the client feels like locally they aren't as positively received as the research indicates," Michael said.

"The survey is from Delaware, not here," Ellen said, leaning back.

"True enough," Frankie said, chewing up a pencil. "So how do we deal with that?"

"We're recommending research as part of the start-up," Michael said. "We give 'em what they want on the creative now and then we test it against more specific creative later."

"Okay, I can go for that," Frankie said, leaning on the table. "Where does that leave Ellen on the mock-ups for the print work and story boards?"

"It's the same thing," Ellen said.

"Excuse me." Alice's voice rang out from the intercom. "Michael, you have a call."

"Could you take—" Michael began.

"It's Gray," she cut in.

"Okay, I'll take it, thanks. Hello?"

"Michael?"

"Who were you expecting? Is Scott okay?"

"He's fine. Listen, I think I'm going to have Cornish hens instead of swordfish steaks. Your mother says Allen is not too fond of seafood."

"That's fine. Is there anything else?"

"No, that's it. I just wanted to be sure. I'm getting ready to go to the market. Do you want anything?"

"Yes. Anything will be fine for me."

"Okay." Gray laughed. "I'll see you at lunch."

"No. I won't be home for lunch. I have too much to do here."

"Oh. You will eat, though."

"Probably. El and Fran and I have a lot to do, though, so I've got to go. Oh, while we're at it, I'm probably going to have to work over the weekend," he said, looking at Frankie, who nodded vigorously. "And I'll be out of town the first of next week. So if you could . . ."

"No large deal," Gray said.

"Thanks, Gray. I'll see you tonight."

He hung up.

"What was all that about?" Ellen said as he returned to the table.

"Oh, my brother and his fiancée are coming to dinner, and Gray is coming unglued. You'd think it was the king of France."

"Oh," Frankie said. "Then a dinner meeting is out?"

"I'm sorry, Fran," Michael said. "We'll all be fresher at breakfast anyway."

"It's me," Michael shouted up the stairs as he returned home.

"Uuuuuu-Caaaaa," Scott screamed.

"Hello, darling," Michael shouted back.

"Hello, Michael," Gray called, coming to the top of the stairs. "Did you get the wine?"

"Yes, but I still don't know what was wrong with what we've

got," he said, handing it over as he got to the top of the stairs. "Allen doesn't know fine wine from fine-tuned. And Mindy strikes me as the sort who would serve classic Coke at formal dinner parties."

"Michael," Gray said with disapproval, "this is your brother and the woman he is to marry. You want things to be gracious in your home."

"You're a sloppy sentimentalist," Michael said, rushing past him. "Where's my— There he is."

"Uuuuuu-Caaaaa," Scott screamed from the playpen Gray had set up in the small hallway adjacent to the kitchen at the top of the back stairs. Michael had moved his office into the space from what had become Gray and Scott's room.

"Scott," Michael screamed back, reaching down to pick up the baby, "I see you're taking over my new office."

"Besides," Gray said, crossing to stir one of the pots on the stove, "you want your brother to give a good report on Scott's home."

"What?" Michael said, not remembering the previous conversation. "Oh. Don't be ridiculous. Allen is on our side."

Michael snitched a carrot off the butcher-block table Gray had built. Gray slapped his hand.

"Did you eat lunch?" Gray asked.

"Yes, yes, I ate lunch," Michael said, surveying the dining room. "Gray, there are only three places set at the table."

"Someone else is coming?" Gray asked, coming into the dining room, drying his hands on a dish towel he had tucked partially into his pocket.

"God, I hope not," Michael said.

"Scott is too young to sit at the table," Gray said. "I will not—"

"Not Scott, you, you mukluk."

"Me?"

"Well, you needn't look so shocked," Michael said. "Of course you."

"No," Gray said. "It would not seem proper. I will serve dinner."

"Oh, for rice cake," Michael said. "For a Bolshevik you're pretty class-conscious. We are a family. I'm not going to have you eating out in the kitchen like a scullery maid. And that's the end of it.

"You know," he said, intentionally changing the subject and crossing out onto the screened porch, "I think it's warm enough to have drinks out here."

"You are the kindest, best man I know," Gray said, throwing his arms around Scott and Michael and kissing both Michael's cheeks.

"Stop that. You're going to knock me down, you French ninny," Michael said, wobbling.

"I'm sorry," Gray said, rushing off. "I'll move the hors d'oeuvres out here."

"These are excellent," Mindy said, munching one of the canapés. "What are they?"

"Who knows?" Michael said, sipping his martini. "You'll have to ask Gray."

"He's certainly a wonder," Allen said, taking a seat. "Even Mother likes him. And your place. I don't know, it looks finished."

"Finished?" Michael echoed.

"Yeah. Before it was like, well, it was always nice," Allen went on, "but it looked like no one lived here."

"Well, no one did really," Michael said. "I slept here and watered the plants, but I was out a lot. Most of the time. It's Scott's doing."

"Scott?" Mindy said, wolfing down some more canapés.

"Yeah. Well, Gray wouldn't be here if it weren't for Scott. And he's made the difference."

"Where did you find him?" Mindy asked in that annoying tone that usually precedes "Good help is sooo hard to find."

"In the window at Presbyterian Hospital, as I recall," Michael said obliquely.

"What?" Mindy said more than asked.

"He means Scotty." Allen smiled. "Scott was born at Presbyterian."

"Oh," she said, not acknowledging the joke. "I meant Gray."

"On the street," Michael said casually.

Mindy choked a little on her seventh canapé.

Allen looked a little startled.

"Oh, come on," Michael said. "Joke? Gray waited table for Bill Stockbridge and me at the Urb. He overheard us talking with Randy—Green. You remember him, Allen?"

"Of course," Allen said, not remembering and getting more rather than less alarmed as the story progressed.

"Anyway," Michael said, beginning to hate the conversation, "he approached me on the street as we left and I hired him at four o'clock the following morning."

"Four o'clock in the morning?" Mindy asked a little over-anxiously.

"I thought he was a Montessori teacher," Allen said, trying to head off the line of questioning.

"He was," Michael said, lighting a cigarette. "Part-time. And part-time he was a waiter. In a way he's still both."

"Here are the drinks," Gray said as he strolled onto the porch with the tray.

Dewars bounded behind him.

"I don't think I've ever seen that dog move that fast," Allen observed as he took his scotch. "Thank you, Gray."

"Gray has improved everyone's diet." Michael smirked. "And Dew Dew spends more time outside now with Gray and the baby."

"Dew Dew?" Allen laughed.

"That's what Scott calls her," Michael said.

"Here, Michael," Gray said, handing him another martini. "I brought you a fresh one. I'm sorry I was so long, but I am trying to convince Scott that it is bedtime already. Michael keeps him up so late usually."

Gray sat on the arm of Michael's chair.

"Oh. Sit here," Allen said, taking his feet out of the only remaining chair.

"Be comfortable," Gray said, waving his hands. "I'm fine here. Besides, dinner will be ready soon, so I'll have to go to the kitchen in a moment."

Allen tried to avoid Mindy's look. He put his feet back up and stared off the porch into the rich, warm sunset that was then at about eye level from their second-floor perch.

They sat in silence in the dull glow, enjoying the moment. Each in his own way.

"Music," Michael said suddenly.

"What?" Allen said, blinking in surprise.

"We need music," Michael said, rising. "To fill the pauses."

"I'll check dinner," Gray said, rising as well. "Not too loud, eh, Michael? The baby?"

"You got it, Grandma," Michael said, leaving.

"Seriously . . ." Gray began as he followed.

"Where is it?" Mindy asked as soon as they were alone.

"I really don't think we should," Allen said, looking troubled.

"Well, we've gotten this far," Mindy shot back. "I'm going through with it."

"I don't know, Mindy . . ." he began.

"Where is it?" She pronounced each word.

"It's usually on the sideboard thing in the dining room," he said with no conviction.

"Fine," she said.

"It's *The Big Chill*," Michael announced as he returned to the porch. "I hope you're not sick of it."

"No," Allen said blankly. "That's fine."

"Well, you both look like you just bought a time share," Michael said, laughing.

"Michael," Gray said sharply as he returned to the porch, "that is too loud."

"It is not," Michael said, dancing around the porch.

"I've got to go to the powder room," Mindy said, rising.

"Mindy, don't—" Allen said, and then stopped short.

"What?" Michael said, bursting into peals of laughter. "God, you two are close."

"I'll be right back, Allen," she said, playing on the moment. "Excuse me."

"Michael," Gray began again, "I'm going to turn it down. You'll wake the baby."

"It's my turn to wake him up," Michael said, spinning wildly.

"Michael," Gray said, stamping his foot.

"All right," he said, calming himself as the song died in the background. He reached and took Gray's hand understandingly. "You're right. But one thing," he said gravely. "First let's dance," he screamed, spinning Gray under one arm and into the next tune.

———

"Good night, Michael," Mindy called one last time as she climbed into the car. "Everything was lovely. Thanks so much."

"Good night, Mindy. Night, Allen." Michael waved from the porch.

Allen got in at the driver's side and they slammed their doors.

Michael went inside and the porch light went off as Allen pulled his car away from the curb.

"They're obviously sleeping together," Mindy said triumphantly.

"What?" Allen said with a little too much shock. "Don't be ridiculous."

"Oh, Allen. Come on." Mindy chided him. "They're pretty cozy to be just employer and employee. Gray sat at the dinner table."

"That's your proof?" Allen snorted.

"Not all of it. No," she said. "There were plenty of other suspicious moments."

"Jesus, Mindy," Allen sighed. "I don't know how much more of this I can stand."

"Sweetheart, it's for the baby," she pleaded, whining a bit.

"Well, no one ever mentions the baby unless it's time to justify some more inexcusable behavior."

There was a longish pause.

"Anyway," Allen said at last, staring straight ahead, "I don't think a little household democracy means Michael is shacking up with the help."

"Think what you want," Mindy said tartly. "I know what I saw. And," she said, pulling Michael's address book triumphantly out of her purse, "this will provide us with all the proof we need. Michael's little black book. It's really black."

"Proof of what?" Allen said, turning the car violently. "What are we proving?"

"I'm sick of this conversation," she said, drumming her fingers on the cover of the book. "We're proving that Michael is an unfit parent. You know that. I know that. All God's children know that."

"Why?" Allen growled. "Because he sleeps with boys?"

"You make it sound like it's no big deal," Mindy said, shocked.

"Well, I just wonder how big a deal it is," Allen said evenly. "That house seemed like a pretty stable environment to me."

"I'm sure Bluebeard gave lovely dinner parties," she huffed.

"Bluebeard?" Allen asked incredulously.

"Well," she began, petulantly flipping into the address book, "we'll just see what Albert Asbul has to tell us about your brother."

"Yes," Allen said nastily. "His testimony should be electrifying. He's our insurance agent."

"He's just a name I picked at random," she said, snapping the book shut.

"Yes, I know," Allen said. "And he's a good example of who you'll find in there. Friends, relatives and business associates. Just like anyone's address book."

"I just don't understand how you can say that," she said at last.

They rode in silence. Allen pulled into the parking garage at his condo and drove the car to his reserved space.

"What would you do if one of our children turned out to be, you know, like Michael?" she asked seriously as they walked to the elevators.

"I don't know," he said at last as the elevator arrived.

They climbed in. Allen pushed the button for their floor.

"Ruining his life wouldn't be at the top of my list," he said as the doors closed.

～ ～ ～

Michael was up early the morning after the dinner party. He and Frankie were on for breakfast to go over some of the details of the proposal that needed ironing out.

Michael enjoyed making the pitches as much or more than actually doing the blood-and-guts work of production and the prospect of making the pitch had his spirits up. He was singing with the radio and dancing around his bedroom as he got ready for his early meeting.

He glanced out the window as if to confirm the radio announcer's prediction for a warmer, sunny day. The leaves in the tops of the trees were beginning to show and the world had a fresh green cast to it.

He looked again. There was a van from one of the local TV stations parked out front. Several people were milling around and one of the local on-the-air personalities was speaking sincerely to a video camera perched on the shoulder of an associate.

Michael knit his brow as he stood tying his tie.

The neighborhood was a popular one. Very urban-residential and adjacent to an up-and-coming shopping and entertainment district. It was the site of frequent parades, street parties and jogging marathons. What puzzled Michael was that he generally knew about these events months in advance, through his connections.

Have to tell Momma my house is gonna be on the news, he thought.

"And at the top of the news," the radio announcer said as Michael punched a pin through the lapel of his jacket, "former U.S. Senator Robert Miller is suing local advertising writer and former campaign aide Michael Reily for custody of his grandson. The suit, which revolves around Reily's alleged homosexuality, charges that he—Reily—is unfit to act as guardian for the child, son of Reily's sister and Senator Miller's son, who were killed tragically on Christmas Eve in a car accident. Neither Reily nor

Senator Miller has been reached for comment, but Hamp Taylor, WAXX reporter, is standing by live at the home of Reily—"

Michael stared at the radio.

"Michael," Gray called. "Michael?" He burst into the room. "Michael," he said again. "There are reporters in the backyard."

"What?" Michael said, still dazed.

"I went out to walk Dewars, and we never made it down the steps. They thought I was you. They started asking me for my first reaction to the charges. Michael? What charges? What's going on?"

Michael stared at him.

The phone started to ring.

"Are you all right, Michael?"

"Hello," Michael said expressionlessly into the bedside extension.

"What in the pluperfect hell do you think you're doing?" Robert Miller screamed into the phone.

"What?" Michael asked, still stunned.

"The goddamned news media is blocking the gates here," Robert shouted. "Someone said the national people just got here."

"They're here, too," Michael said, looking out the window.

The doorbell rang.

"What kind of stunt are you trying to pull?" Robert demanded. "If you think—"

"Wa-hai-hait a minute," Michael said, snapping out of it. "What do you mean, what am I trying to pull? I didn't invite these people to this surprise party," he yelled. "Shit, I don't even have gates. They're trying to beat down the door. Gray, do not answer it."

"Well, I sure as hell didn't do this," Robert snapped.

"You filed the damned suit," Michael said angrily.

"Yes, but I didn't plan on anything like this," Robert shot back defensively.

"What were you expecting? High tea?"

"You're the publicity person."

"You're the public figure."

"This is just the sort of thing you'd pull."

"Why on earth would I do this?"

"To embarrass me."

"Well, it's brought a pretty strong blush to my cheek, too."

"I want you to call it off." Robert was screaming again.

"Me?" Michael almost laughed. "Drop the suit, and it'll die a natural death."

"I knew it. That's why you did this. You can damn well give up the kid if you want this to go away."

"It seems to me you've got a stronger hand to have led this trump. I'm the one being call a Communist buttfucker on the morning news. And it's not going to work."

Michael slammed down the phone.

It started to ring again. The doorbell continued.

"Uuuuuu-Caaaaa," Scott screamed.

"Oh, Kathryn." Michael sighed, staring at the phone. "Why did you do this to me?"

The door of the fashionable duplex opened slowly. Members of the press rushed across the yard, jockeying for position around the small porch.

The neighbor from downstairs, who had been set upon as she came out for her morning paper, peered through the window in her door.

A lone figure emerged through the front door wearing a brown paper bag on his head.

Cameras reeled and clicked in the silence. An uncomfortable hush fell over the small crowd of reporters, photographers and cameramen.

Slowly the bizarre figure edged toward the front step. The press actually backed up.

"Surprise," Michael said, snatching the bag off his head. "It's me."

There was some nervous laughter.

"Oh, come on," Michael said. "I think that was pretty original for thirty minutes' notice. If you'd phoned ahead, I could have popped out of a cake."

More earnest laughter then, and the questions began.

"Wait, wait, wait," Michael said, waving them off. "I'm not answering a bunch of questions, because frankly, I'm not real sure what's going on. I have never been served with any papers. I do have guardianship of my nephew. And I did work as a consultant on Senator Miller's campaigns. Anything further, you'll have to ask Senator Miller.

"That's it. I've got to go now. I'm late," Michael concluded, pushing into the crowd. Then, just as he got through, he turned. "Oh, one more thing. Please don't upset the baby. I know you're only doing your jobs, but he is only a baby. Thanks."

With that he dived into his car and roared away.

He lit a cigarette and switched on the radio, out of habit. "And that was Hamp Taylor, live from the home of alleged homosexual—" He turned the radio off and rode in silence.

He drew up to the hotel where he was scheduled to meet Frankie for breakfast. More members of the media waited on the curb out front. As he slowed to turn into the parking lot, Chaz Montreau, the general manager and a friend and client of Michael's, stepped from the curb and signaled Michael to stop.

Chaz jumped into the car. "Get out of here," he ordered.

Michael obeyed.

"They nabbed Frankie on his way in this morning," Chaz said. "He's at my house, waiting for you. What the hell is going on? Got another cigarette?"

"Here," Michael said, pulling the pack from his pocket. "And I don't know what's going on. I sure as hell don't know how they knew to look for me there. My house looks like some bizarre block party. Where do you live?"

"In The Grove," Chaz said, lighting the cigarette and putting the pack back in Michael's coat pocket. "Frankie hit the ceiling. You know how he hates speaking in public."

"Great," Michael said, hitting the steering wheel with his open hand. "Just great. Why is this happening to me? Miller must be out of his mind."

"You think Miller did this?" Chaz asked. "Go left at the light."

"I don't know what to think," Michael said, squealing around the corner. "I only know that if I had pulled this, I'd be better prepared. And Miller's the only other camp involved. So . . ." He shrugged in conclusion.

"That's clever," Chaz said, imitating the shrug. "So . . . I'd come up with a better answer than that. Frankie's pretty steamed getting caught off guard like that. It's the next right."

"I would, Chaz, if I had a better answer," Michael said, turning the car under the canopy of old trees and old money that was The Grove.

"Well, how would Miller know about your meeting with Frankie?" Chaz said.

"I don't know," Michael said emphatically. "But I sure as hell wouldn't set the trap and then jump in it."

"It's the gray one there on the left," Chaz said, smashing the cigarette out.

The two men got out of the car and walked in silence to the door.

Chaz opened the door. "He's in here," he said, leading the way.

"Nice place," Michael said as they walked down the hall of the stately old place Chaz had bought and restored after his divorce.

"Thanks," he said. "In here."

Chaz opened a pair of old sliding wooden doors. Frankie sat at the breakfast room table, sipping coffee and eating some bagels he had brought from the hotel. He looked up from the paper as Michael entered.

"Hi, Fran," Michael said.

Frankie stared.

"I guess you don't want to talk creative on the insurance company pitch," Michael said, laughing nervously.

"See you," Chaz said, pulling the doors shut.

"Coward," Michael muttered as he crossed to get himself some coffee. "Well," he said, stirring his cup, "are you just going to sit there like Buddha or do you speak?"

"What do you want me to say?" Frankie said in studied calm.

"You might ask me how I'm doing," Michael said a little hotly. "No one's asked me that yet."

"Michael," Frankie said, handing him the paper, "what the hell is going on?"

"That I have been asked?" Michael said, looking at the article with his picture on the front page.

"Well?" Frankie demanded, throwing the paper down as Michael made no move to take it.

"Well what?" Michael said, taking a sip of his coffee. "Do you think I'd look this stupid if I knew?"

"The paper bag was pretty funny," Frankie snorted.

"Already?"

"Eight twenty-five report."

"God, what'll I do for the evening news?" Michael smiled. "Any word from my worthy opponent?"

"None," Frankie said quietly. "You can't come with me to pitch the insurance people."

There was a long silence.

Michael wasn't really shocked. He had realized it earlier on some level, but this was the first time it really became clear. The first time it had been said out loud.

"No, I guess I can't," Michael said at last.

"And you couldn't be on that shoot. And you can't go to a dinner meeting. There are a lot of can'ts lately," Frankie said without looking away.

"Who?" Michael said, staring into his cup.

"Crawford," Frankie said, still staring.

"God," Michael sighed.

"I don't know why you two don't get along better."

"He'll do a fine job," Michael said tonelessly.

"Michael?"

"What?"

"Maybe . . ." Frankie sighed wearily and looked away. "Maybe it would be better for the time being if you . . . took some time. Just until this thing is settled."

Michael sat staring into his reflection in the glass table for a long time. He tapped his pen on the frame. He lit a cigarette. He drank some coffee.

"And then what, Frankie?" Michael asked, breaking so long a silence that Frankie jumped. "And then what?" Michael asked again. "Then come back to work and we'll all pretend nothing's happened?"

"Michael, don't get dramatic," Frankie said, fidgeting with a bagel.

"I'm trying not to be," Michael said solemnly. "I don't want to pretend that at the end of this script everyone lives happily ever after. Especially when we know that's not the ending. Not to this play," he went on, stubbing out a cigarette. "We both know if I leave, I'm not coming back. Win, lose or draw I will always be 'alleged homosexual' Michael Reily. I wouldn't even hire me to do PR."

"Maybe," Frankie said, making patterns in the cream cheese with his fork.

"Maybe hell, Frankie," Michael snapped.

They sat for a long time in the web of shadows the mullions on the breakfast room windows cast over them in the strong, unfiltered late-winter sun.

"Good-bye, Frankie," Michael said, rising to leave. "Good luck with the insurance folks."

"Thanks, Michael," Frankie said. "Good luck."

"Heeeeey, I'm not in right this minute or I very possibly don't feel like answering the phone. Anyway, you know the routine. First obnoxious tone, then time, date, phone number, height, weight, color of hair and eyes, marital status, astrological sign, blood type, childhood illnesses, any history of mental illness in your family—the usual. See-you-later-bye. Beeeep."

"Michael? Allen. If you can hear me, pick up. Michael. Oh, Michael. Listen, it's Allen. I really need to talk to you—"

"Allen?"

"Gray? Where is Michael? Is he okay?"

"Oh, he's fine, I guess. He left awhile ago. He had a breakfast meeting."

"Where?"

"At The Inn with Frankie. Don't tell, though. I'm not supposed to."

"I won't."

"Anyway, he's supposed to be back at three."

"Look, if he hasn't seen me by then, have him call me, would you? The whole family is worried."

"Oh. I guess they are. Well, everything's fine. Well, not fine but okay. I'll call Ann and tell her."

"That's good. I'll try to track Michael down. See you soon, Gray."

"Good-bye."

Gray began dialing immediately after hanging up and got through right away.

"Hello?"

"Hello, Ashton?"

"Hello, Gray," Ashton said jovially. "And thank you for calling campaign headquarters. We don't know anything either, but that hasn't stopped everyone from calling. Ann's lying down. She fielded the first-wave assault. This is about the four hundredth telephone call."

"Are there reporters out there?"

"Not many anymore," Ash said. "Of course, they could be hiding. They got the paperboy and two of the neighbors in surprise attacks. Gray, what's going on?"

"Everything is fine here."

"Where's Michael?"

"At breakfast or the office by now."

"After all this?"

"Well, he said we should go about business as usual."

"Just another ordinary day."

"Did you see him on television?"

"With the paper bag?"

They laughed.

"He's a good kid," Ashton said.

"I watched from the porch," Gray said proudly. "He was very clever."

"So Michael didn't have anything to do with all this?"

"No, he was very much surprised."

"Well, then I guess Robert Miller really is a son of a bitch."

"I guess. Well, tell Ann we are fine and surprised. I only called because Allen said you would be worried."

"Thanks, Gray. I'll tell her. Bye."

He hung up the phone and went to the foot of the stairs. "Ann? Ann."

"What?" she wailed from her bed.

"That was Gray."

"Oh, God," she said, rushing to the top of the stairs. "Is the baby okay?"

"Fine," Ash said.

"Then why did he call?"

"Just to say everyone was okay."

"Well, of course they are. What foolishness. We're not having a tornado. Sounds like Allen to me."

"Allen told him we were worried."

"Why on earth?" she said, coming down the stairs. "Annoyed, yes. Worried, no. You want some coffee?"

"Just made some," he said, hugging her as she reached the foot. "Try that exhaust fan in the downstairs john."

"You fixed it," she said, crossing down the hall to the bathroom door. She reached in, flipped the switch and all the lights went out.

"Well, almost," he said in the darkness.

"Doesn't rattle anymore," she said, laughing. "Turn on the lights. I flipped the switch back."

The lights came back on as she poured the coffee. "That's it," she called.

"Are they on yet?" he called from the service porch. Then he turned them out again.

She got cream out of the refrigerator.

The lights came back on again.

"How about now?" he shouted.

"That's it," she shouted back, getting some cookies out and placing them carefully on a plate.

Half the lights went out.

"Is that it?" he screamed.

She put the cookies and the coffee on the table in the den and went out to the service porch.

The lights went on and off.

"Ash," she said, "your coffee's ready. There are cookies, too."

"I'm coming," he said, shining a flashlight on the circuit breaker in the brightly lit room and flipping switches randomly.

She closed the door and returned to the den. The television sprang to life periodically. She leafed through the paper and drank her coffee.

The phone rang.

She let it ring awhile and then rose in frustration to answer it. "Hello?"

"Hello, Ann? Sylvia."

"Hello, Sylvia."

"We've just gotten into town."

"Great," Ann snapped. "We were just leaving."

"Listen, Ann," Sylvia said apologetically, "I'm sorry about all this. But you've got to know we didn't have anything to do with it."

"I don't know anything of the sort," Ann said tensely. "I sure didn't start all this. And there wouldn't have been any news if you hadn't filed the suit."

"I know it," Sylvia said in disgust. "Robert has just been crazy since Bob died."

"I guess I can understand," Ann sighed.

"Look, Robert doesn't know I'm calling," she said. "I think we've got to get the family together and fight this out in private."

"It's a little late for that, don't you think?"

"Well, we can't let this go to court, Ann. It's bad enough as it is."

"Ask Michael," Ann said as she watched the hall light go on and off. "It's really up to him, isn't it?"

"Look. We're staying at The Inn. See if you can't get Michael over here. We'll have dinner at the restaurant about eight."

"I haven't heard from Michael, but if I do, I'll have him out here for dinner at eight. You get the senator out here and we'll talk. I don't think a restaurant is any place for this discussion."

"You're right," she said. "Okay, I've got to go. Here he comes. Bye."

She hung up the pay phone in the lobby of the hotel as Robert and the bellman came trundling toward the elevators.

"Everything all right?" she asked, putting her earring back on.

"How did the press know we were coming?" he demanded.

"I'm sure I don't know," she said.

"Well, it's a good thing we got in the side way. They're thick as thieves out front." He snorted.

"Hey!" someone called from the front doors across the lobby. "Senator Miller."

It was Mindy. And Allen.

It was also a media stampede.

Everyone sat in silence in Ash and Ann's den. A pine fire hissed and spit in the fireplace. Ann continued to rock an already sleeping Scott, the chair creaking like some annoying timepiece.

"Where the hell is Michael?" Allen asked, rising to fix himself another drink.

"I wish I knew." Gray shrugged, shifting from one cheek to the other on the hard surface of the hearth. "I feel bad about leaving the house empty."

"You did the right thing, Gray," Sylvia said soothingly. "Who knows when he'll be back? And things are a lot quieter out here, for the baby, I mean."

Robert growled and shifted around on the sofa beside her.

"He said he'd be back around three?" Mindy asked.

"And it's almost seven now," Allen answered absently. They'd been over this territory before.

"He was supposed to go to work," Gray said, his eyes not focused on anyone in particular.

"But Frankie hasn't seen him since this morning," Allen continued. "Where could he be?"

"Kathryn would know," Ash said, an odd glaze settling in his eyes.

Silence returned.

Mindy rose and turned on the TV.

"Turn that thing off," Robert snapped.

"It's time for the news," Mindy said, returning to her seat.

"Exactly," Robert said, rising to do it himself.

"Well," Mindy said confidently, "we're not the only ones looking for Michael."

Robert stared at her a moment. It made some sense. He shrugged and returned to his seat.

When the commercials were finally over, the news came on. "Good evening. In the news tonight former U.S. Senator Robert Miller plans to sue local advertising executive and former campaign aide Michael Reily for the custody of his grandson."

"Jesus," Robert said, sinking into the sofa and covering his eyes.

The family watched in states varying from mirth to horror as Michael emerged from the apartment wearing a paper bag over his head and then looking calm and jovial with the press. At the end of the clip they cut directly to the lobby of The Inn where the senator, Sylvia, Allen and Mindy had been caught earlier. They looked anything but calm and jovial.

"Senator and Mrs. Miller were in town unexpectedly today.

Seen here with Reily's brother and family friend Mandy Thornton."

Mindy snorted.

"When asked to comment on the allegations, the senator had this to say."

There was a moment of silent footage where the senator appeared to be yelling at Mindy, and then the sound came up. "What?" Senator Miller said, looking at the camera like a deer in the headlights. "Oh. Well. I . . . well, yes. I am trying to get custody of my grandson. But, um, no formal charges have been filed yet."

He looked pleased for a moment, and then another reporter asked, "Do you plan to file charges? And if so, on what grounds?"

The senator's smile slipped, and he began pounding the elevator button behind him. "Well," Robert stammered on the screen, "I'm not sure. I am still hoping that this thing will work out quietly."

The press laughed.

Another reporter asked, "Is it true you're asking for custody because you allege Mr. Reily is a homosexual?"

"I—I have nothing further to say at this time," Miller said flatly, his face blanching.

With that the elevator opened and the small party climbed aboard.

"A check with sources in the family court indicates that Miller has indeed filed charges alleging Reily is unfit as a parent due to his homosexuality. Since this has been revealed, neither party has been available for comment. This is Sheryl Thomas, TV Eleven news.

"In other news the federal government today—"

"Well, great. Just great," Miller said, shutting off the set. "Now I'm a liar. Turnbul was not supposed to file those charges yet."

"Why didn't you just say no comment?" Ashton asked.

"You're never supposed to say no comment," Miller said. "Makes you look guiltier. I learned that a long time ago—from Michael."

"Well, at least they got your name right," Mindy sulked.

"Oh, shut up," Miller shouted. "This is all your fault."

"My fault?"

"Yes, if you hadn't shouted my name across the lobby—"

"Don't yell at me. I'm on your side. Remember? You'd never have gotten the book at all without—" She stopped short.

The room fell silent again.

"What book?" Ashton asked evenly.

"I'm taking the baby to bed," Ann said, rising.

"What book?" Ashton asked again once she was out of the room.

Robert and Mindy stared.

Allen finished his drink.

"No comment?" Ashton asked sardonically.

The phone rang. No one moved.

"Ashton," Ann called.

The phone continued to ring. Finally Ashton crossed out into the hall to answer it.

"Hello?"

"Mr. Reily?"

"Look. I don't feel like answering anymore—"

"It's Kevin Perdue, Mr. Reily. I just saw the report."

"Oh, I'm sorry, Kevin. I thought you were another reporter."

"No. I just called to say how sorry I was about all this. And to ask you if you know where Michael is?"

"Well, that's the sixty-four-thousand-dollar question," Ashton said.

"You haven't seen him?"

"Not all day. He left for the office this morning, and no one has seen him since. We're all here waiting for him."

"Oh. Well, it doesn't matter. I just wanted to know if I could help out. If you see him, tell him how sorry I am and that I think he'd make a great parent."

"Thank you, Kevin. Good-bye."

Ashton hung up the phone. He stared for a moment at a large family portrait on the wall there. He and Ann stood young and smiling. She held a baby, Allen. Kathryn and Michael, dressed up like little grown-ups, stood beside them.

"Ashton?" Ann said quietly as she saw the tears in his eyes. "You okay?"

"No," he said at last. Then more stridently: "No, I am not."

With that he stormed back into the den. "What book?" he demanded. "What the hell is going on here? I think it's time you all came clean. I've lost one of my children and I can't find the other one."

"You have three children," Mindy said.

"We'll just see about that," Ashton said, his voice rising. "What are you not telling me, Allen? What have you done?"

Allen sighed and stared into his glass.

"Only what you should have been doing yourself," Mindy said at last.

"What is that?" Ashton demanded.

"Looking after the interests of your grandson," Mindy said, matching his volume.

"By turning his life into a three-ring circus? How dare you come into my home and disparage my family? You social-climbing little fool," Ash shot back through teeth gritted so hard they hurt.

Tears of anger stood in Mindy's eyes. She rose slowly, unsteadily.

Allen looked on, unable to speak, unable to take control.

"I did what I did gladly," she said at last. "And I'd do it again. You're the fool. Michael is the one you should disown. This is all his fault. You should have had him locked up years ago with the rest of the deviants."

With that she ran out of the room.

"Wait," Ann said, following her. "Don't go in—"

And all the lights went out.

Kevin drove through the darkness. His headlights cut a narrow path through the ominous quiet of the exhausted neighborhood. It had once been a beautiful place, but time and the automobile had moved interest elsewhere. And, it seemed, the light.

The infrequent streetlights illuminated homes in need of paint, warehouses filled with God knows what and the occasional fearsome and fearful resident of such an area.

At length Kevin arrived at the city reservoir, the banks of which were being turned into a park in an effort to help restore life to the area. The park itself was closed at sunset. Kevin drove on to the entrance of the waterworks. He negotiated the long, bumpy drive. Bits of light and life shone through the painted windows of the plant. He parked his car and got out. He walked into the underbrush and stumbled through the woods until he came to a hole in the fencing surrounding the park.

Kevin loved this place. The continuous flow of water through the canal there seemed to drown out noise, thoughts and distraction of the world outside. He came here often to be alone, to think. He walked down the paved path, coming eventually to its end. He swung himself confidently around the fence that ended at the bank of the canal.

The path turned to dirt on the other side of the fence and the light of the park faded. He walked on.

At last he came to a large outcropping of rocks. He climbed onto the surprising flatness of the large rock at the top.

"How are you, Michael?" Kevin said to the figure sitting at the edge nearest the water.

"You're the first person to ask me that all day," Michael said without looking.

"I've always said you hung out with the wrong crowd," Kevin said, sitting beside him. "Well," Kevin said after a long pause, "you've had all day to think about it. How are you?"

"Great," Michael said. "You know, it's really funny."

"What is?"

"I feel like an innocent bystander. Like I'm standing watching some horrible accident. Only once the tragedy is over, the whole crowd turns and blames me for causing the whole thing."

"Everyone is worried about you."

"Everyone is worried about themselves, their little lives."

"That isn't fair, Michael."

Michael's laughter rang out in the silence of the winter wilderness. "Unfair? You want unfair? I'll give you unfair. My sister was killed for Christmas, I became a mother for New Year's and I lost my job for Valentine's Day. You know my life wasn't great before, but it had its moments. Now it's just totally out of control."

He was crying.

Kevin shifted uncomfortably. "I figured you'd be here," he said.

"I'm surprised you came," Michael said, lighting a cigarette with unsteady hands. "Where's Shanah?"

"At home. Asleep probably. We were on a commercial shoot in the middle of nowhere. We just got back when I heard about all this on the news."

They sat for a moment.

Kevin began to laugh.

"What is it?"

Kevin tried to speak but couldn't quite.

"What is so funny?"

Kevin rolled around on the rock, his laughter building rather than subsiding.

"Kevin," Michael pleaded, beginning to laugh. "What is it?"

They were both laughing.

"The paper," Kevin gasped. "The paper bag."

They were both laughing and rolling around. They rolled into each other. Kevin put his arms around Michael and they laughed until tears streamed down their faces.

They looked into each other's eyes and the laughter died in their throats. They stared for a moment.

"I do love you, Michael," Kevin said at last. "In my own way."

"But you're going to marry Shanah," Michael said, sitting up.

"I don't love you that way, Michael," Kevin said, staring up at the stars. "I can't."

"Yes," Michael said, rising. "That was a Christmas present I had forgotten."

"I'm sorry about that," Kevin said. "I thought the Christmas party would be a good time. That you'd be happy and it wouldn't matter—so much."

"You were wrong," Michael said, climbing down.

"I couldn't have known about Kathryn," Kevin said, following him.

"It had nothing to do with Kathryn," Michael said, fighting through the underbrush.

"What?" Kevin asked, following too closely, the branches in Michael's wake slapping him in the face.

"You left before I found out about Kathryn or don't you remember? You left me to deal with Christmas and death and all this alone."

"You have always expected too much from me," Kevin said, dashing to catch up with Michael, who was already on the path.

Michael stopped short and turned. Kevin almost ran into him in his haste in the darkness.

"All I have ever expected, ever wanted was to have a plain ordinary life. I want to have what the rest of the world wants. Someone to love and to share my life with. Something to do—a job, a purpose. And someone to share the successes and the failures with. That's it. But because, for whatever reason, I turned out different from the rest, everyone acts like it's an unreasonable request. Even though they want the same things. I didn't pick this. My God, it would have been easier not to be gay. But because of that . . . Do you know what they said on the news today? 'Alleged homosexual Michael Reily,' like 'alleged murderer.' It's not a crime. It's not even my fault. But I'm going to go to trial for it. I'm already being punished."

"I'm sorry, Michael," Kevin said after a moment. "It's just tough for me to deal with."

"Oh, is it?" Michael said sarcastically. "Well, if I can deal with the fact that you don't love me, you can deal with the fact that I do love you." And he turned and walked away.

"That's really clever," Kevin said, following.

"Send a fan letter to Harvey Fierstein; it's his line."

"It doesn't solve much."

"I don't have any solutions."

"Michael, why are we fighting?"

"Forgive me if I'm not in a good mood."

"Michael, wait."

Michael was swinging around the end of the first fence. "I'm going home to defend my little piece of reality."

"Michael. Michael, I'm sorry. Please wait. Let me drive you. You know you don't see well at night."

"Things were never clearer."

"Michael, everyone is at your parents'. That's what I came to tell you."

Michael was climbing through the hole in the fence.

"Michael," Kevin called out, "please wait for me."

"I've waited long enough," Michael called over his shoulder. "There's only one person who needs me now."

Michael broke through the edge of the brush. Kevin could hear footfall on pavement. A car door slammed in the distance. An engine started and ebbed away.

The lights in his parents' house were flashing on and off as Michael pulled into the driveway. He could hear a tremendous disturbance from inside: voices raised, doors slamming. He walked in the front door and followed the noise to the den.

As he opened the door, the lights came on again. Everyone froze.

Gray sat red-eyed on the hearth. Allen and Mindy were in each other's arms on the sofa. The Millers stood on either side of them. Ann had her back to him but turned to face Michael as the others fell silent.

"That should do it," Ashton said, coming back into the room from the kitchen door. "Michael."

"Hello, everyone," Michael said, tight-lipped. "Where's Scott?"

"He's upstairs," Ann said. "What happened to you?"

Only then did Michael realize that his clothes were torn and dirty.

"Were you in a fight?" she asked.

"Nope," Michael said. "Just at a picnic."

"Well, I'm glad you're here," Robert Miller said.

"Oh, really?" Michael smirked. "Well, I'm not staying. Gray, get the baby and go home."

Gray rose.

"Wait just a minute," Robert said.

"Now, Gray," Michael commanded.

Gray left the room. Ann rose and followed him out.

"We need to talk," Robert demanded.

"We have nothing to say," Michael cut him off. "You want a fight. You've got one. But I should warn you, you've made a serious mistake. I now have nothing left to lose except Scott. I was fired today. My reputation just sank into a sea of multimedia innuendo. And frankly, I'll fight you to the death to keep Scott now."

"I'm leaving, Michael," Gray called.

"I'll be right home," he called back.

The front door closed.

"Michael," Robert said, "let's try to calm down here. I don't want things to get ugly. I never have."

"Well, you blew it," Michael said, turning. "Good night."

"Michael, wait," Robert began, and the lights went out again.

There was a loud crash. And Michael heard his mother's laugh over the senator's curses as he reached the door.

"Good night, Michael," she called.

"Thanks, Mom."

"Don't thank me. Thank your father. He fixed the bathroom fan."

～～ ～～ ～～

"All rise."

All did.

The day had arrived.

Family court, usually a quiet wing of justice reserved for settling private disputes and youthful skirmishes with the law, had been transformed into the center attraction. The people's right to know had turned into a source of national gossip. Each new development had been watched, analyzed and reported since the explosion that started it all.

Both sides had been asked to appear separately and together on various talk and news shows. All offers had been declined by both sides.

Nothing deterred the media. They began camping on Michael's and the senator's doorsteps. Family members, friends and associates were harassed.

Michael's neighbors complained so bitterly that he had to get a court injunction to avoid eviction.

That did not, however, stop less civilized harassment. Hate mail poured in on both sides. Bricks were tossed through Michael's window, his car was vandalized and attacks of all kinds increased to the point where the police had to be on constant duty.

Eventually "Scotty, Inc." bought a high-rise, high-security condominium and Michael moved.

The press followed.

The tabloids had a field day. Splashy headlines were there for the taking. Confessions from former lovers of Michael's ran in several papers. Michael had never met any of them. Michael dealt pretty well with most of it. He found the "true confessions" amusing.

All the attention and bright lights showed their harsh glare on this first day of the suit.

The judge, one Winnifred Dukes, had been driven to injunctions and contempt charges to get the press to leave her alone.

"Be seated," Judge Dukes said to the mob. "I have something to say. Family court is a place where private matters are settled privately. Due to the unusual nature of this case, I am willing to stand for a certain amount of attention from the fourth estate. This is, however, a court of law and not a press conference. Interviews, photographs and video cameras do not belong in my courtroom and will not be tolerated.

"Further, the events of each session of this suit will be strictly private at my discretion. That is, I will decide at the end of each day whether or not there is genuine public information or pure sensationalism involved. What that means is that there is now a gag order in effect and I will lift it or not on a daily basis. My decision will be announced by the court crier within one hour of adjournment each day. Is that clear?"

There was a general disturbance.

"Order, order. The alternative is I clear the courtroom and you find out nothing."

The disturbance died down.

"The court will now entertain any opening motions," Judge Dukes said perfunctorily. "Mr. Turnbul?"

"None, Your Honor," Harvey said, almost rising.

Harvey was a good lawyer with grand political aspirations. Representing industrial leaders in labor disputes, he had come to the attention of Senator Miller. He had won and won big. And it was a big win that Robert Miller was after.

On the other hand, it was the senator's big name that Harvey was looking for. The case had the earmarks of the sort of splashy press coverage that he needed to give him name recognition before he announced for the attorney general's race.

"Mr. Stockbridge?" she asked.

"Yes, Your Honor," Bill said, rising. "We move for dismissal on the grounds that the allegations are irrelevant to the soundness of the will and therefore inappropriate for a dispute of this nature."

"Mr. Turnbul?" she queried.

"Your Honor, we feel that the moral fitness of Mr. Reily is of primary interest here, but we are also prepared to present evidence as to the diminished capacity of the testators if the court feels it necessary."

"What?" Sylvia's voice rang out.

There was a general disturbance during which Sylvia and Robert whispered animatedly over the railing that separated their seats.

"Order," Judge Dukes said, pounding her gavel. "Gentlemen, approach the bench."

They did.

"Mr. Turnbul," Judge Dukes began as she crooked the microphone away from the conversation, "would you care to elaborate?"

"Certainly, Your Honor," Turnbul said, beaming. "We realize that the moral fitness of the specified guardian is not necessarily at issue in matters of this nature. But there is a small child to be considered."

"Your Honor," Bill muttered, "in contesting a will, it is the testator's capacity and fitness that are at issue, not those named in the will."

"If Your Honor please," Turnbul cut in. "We are aware of the specific point of law and we are prepared to introduce evidence and testimony enough to cast doubt on the moral judgment of the late Mr. and Mrs. Miller. We had, however, hoped to avoid any unnecessary unpleasantness."

"Oh, come on, Harvey—" Stockbridge began.

"Mr. Stockbridge," Judge Dukes said peremptorily, "the court recognizes the validity of your opening motion. If, however, Mr. Turnbul is prepared to answer the tenor of that motion by disproving the fitness of the testator, we have no choice but to grant him that opportunity unless you wish to withdraw the motion."

Bill Stockbridge looked at Harvey's unrestrained grin, then at Judge Dukes' brooding knitted brow. "A moment with my client, Your Honor?" he asked at last.

"Granted," Dukes said, leaning back in her enormous black leather chair.

Counsel returned to their respective desks.

"What's up?" Michael asked.

"The situation is this," Bill sighed. "They're playing flinch. If we don't withdraw the motion, they're going to smear Bob and Kathryn and then you. If we do withdraw, then they'll smear only you. So, do we flinch?"

"Jesus," Michael said at last. "No, we don't. We let them smear the parents and then we use it against them later if we need to."

"Are you sure you wouldn't like to be a lawyer?" Bill said, smiling kindly.

"I never want to be in another courtroom again," Michael said.

"Your Honor," Bill said, straightening and facing the bench, "we stand."

"Very well," Judge Dukes said. "Mr. Turnbul, you may proceed."

"Yes, Your Honor," Harvey said, rising. "We call Officer Richard Blanche."

Bill looked at Michael. Michael shrugged.

Officer Blanche was sworn in.

"Please state your name and occupation."

"Officer Richard Blanche, North Carolina highway patrolman."

"Officer Blanche," Harvey began, pacing in front of the witness box, "where were you on the evening of December twenty-fourth of last year?"

"I had drawn special duty, sir. It had started snowing around noon and because of the hazardous driving conditions and the Christmas Eve traffic, a lot of us had been put on to try and cope with problems."

"I see," said Mr. Turnbul. "And did you encounter any problems that afternoon?"

"Yes, sir," Officer Blanche said. "All sorts."

"Were any of those fatal?" Harvey continued.

"Well, yes, sir," Blanche said. "One was."

"Could you tell us about it?"

"Yes, sir," he went on. "About four-thirty on I-seventy-seven on the approach to the city, I encountered an accident that had proved fatal to two of the occupants of a late-model gold BMW sedan."

"You are referring to the accident which killed Mr. and Mrs. Robert Miller of this city?"

"Yes, sir," Blanche said, shifting a bit in his chair.

"In your judgment as a professional in these matters, what appeared to have happened in this accident?"

"Objection," Bill said, rising. "The question calls for a conclusion on the part of the witness for which no foundation has been laid."

"Your Honor," Harvey said quickly, "in fatal accidents the state is willing to accept the conclusion of a qualified officer as to the probable cause of an accident when no witnesses are available."

"Overruled," Dukes said after a moment. "The witness may answer."

"Yes, Your Honor," Blanche said, nodding to the judge. "The car appeared to have run off the road and crashed into a cement embankment."

"Was there any evidence that the car had skidded, slid or in any way been forced off the road?"

"No, sir, there was not," Blanche said, his voice dropping.

"Would you tell the court what you found on further investigation?"

The officer shifted and tugged at a pants leg.

Michael put his face in his hands.

"Well, first off I found a baby alive in the car seat, in the back of the vehicle."

"How did you know the child was alive?"

"It was crying, sir."

"Did you attempt to rescue the child?"

"I did, but the doors were stuck shut, so I radioed for help."

"What else did you find in the car?"

Ashton took Ann's hand and squeezed as he fought back tears.

"Yes, sir, in the front seat were the remains of a man and woman."

"Was there anything . . . unusual about the condition of those remains?"

"Stop it!" Sylvia screamed.

"Sylvia," Senator Miller hissed, "sit down."

"I won't listen to this," she screamed.

There was an uproar as Sylvia Miller was helped from the room.

"Do you wish to continue, Mr. Turnbul?" Judge Dukes asked afterward.

"Yes, Your Honor," Harvey said, bowing his head cockily in

the judge's direction. "Officer Blanche, was there anything unusual about the remains?"

"Well, yes, sir," Blanche said, clearing his throat.

"Please describe for the court just what you found."

"Well, sir, there was a lot of blood and I couldn't actually get
into the car, but as best as I could make out, the woman Mrs.
Kathryn Miller's arm had been torn off."

There was some rumbling, but everyone wanted to hear what
was next, so it was controlled. Judge Dukes tapped a warning.

"Was there anything else?" Turnbul asked.

"Well-um, he's, the-uh, gentleman-um, Mr. Robert Miller, had-
um . . ." Officer Blanche trailed off.

"Yes, Officer Blanche, we didn't hear you."

"He had his pants down," Blanche said so strongly that there
was mike feedback.

The courtroom erupted.

"Order," Judge Dukes screamed.

"Your witness," Harvey Turnbul said, crossing away from the
stand.

"We will not participate in this," Bill Stockbridge said, rising.

"Mr. Stockbridge," Judge Dukes said, "you will confine yourself to yes or no. This court does not need editorials."

"Yes, Your Honor," Bill said, sitting down.

"And you, Mr. Turnbul," Judge Dukes said, brandishing her
gavel, "you had better have an excellent reason for introducing
this sort of lurid evidence in my court."

"Our meaning will become clear as we proceed," Harvey said
deferentially.

"It had better, Mr. Turnbul," Judge Dukes said threateningly.
"Proceed."

"Thank you, Your Honor," Turnbul said, treading lightly. "The
plaintiff calls Frank Lester."

Mr. Lester was seated and sworn.

Harvey Turnbul oozed forward, hands clasped behind his
back. "For the record, sir," he began, "state your name and occupation."

"Frank Lester, county coroner," Lester said, leaning up to the
microphone.

"Mr. Lester," Harvey said, "you have heard the testimony of

Officer Blanche as regards an automobile accident on the evening of December twenty-fourth of last year."

"I have."

"How were you involved?"

"I had occasion to examine the bodies when they were brought in."

"Please tell the court what, if anything, you found in your examination that might be termed out of the ordinary."

"Could I have some water?" Lester asked, looking to the judge.

"Bailiff," the judge said with a wave of her hand.

The water was brought.

"Better?" she asked.

Lester nodded.

"Proceed," she said.

"Mr. Lester. I ask you again—" Turnbul began.

"I remember the question," Lester cut in. "Your Honor, I have been a pathologist for the county coroner's office for seventeen years. I have examined and testified about the grisliest details of murders and accidents and deaths. All kinds. Never at a probate hearing—"

"Your honor," Turnbul said, "please instruct—"

"Hold your horses, Turnbul," she snapped. "Go on, Mr. Lester."

"Well, Your Honor," Lester went on, "the details in this case are pretty—lurid, as you call it. And well, I guess the family knows. But as justice isn't in question here, I just don't think everyone needs to know."

"Here, here," Michael muttered.

"Your Honor," Turnbul said, "the plaintiff does not wish to cause undue sensationalism in this case, but we are trying to establish the mental capacity of the testator. It is our feeling that it was diminished enough to bring about his death and hence was inadequate to make the proper judgment as regards the custody of the child. Now the plaintiff did not wish this evidence introduced, but the defense has insisted."

"Mr. Stockbridge?" Judge Dukes asked.

"Your Honor," Stockbridge said rising, "we object to this whole line of questioning as totally irrelevant to determining mental capacity. Hundreds of people do foolish things that get them killed every day. It doesn't mean they are bereft of good judgment."

"Granted, Your Honor," Turnbul said, taking the point. "But the events that brought about the deaths of the testators rattled a veteran pathologist and sent one of the plaintiffs from the room in tears."

"Gentlemen," Judge Dukes said after a pause, "this is only a hearing. And as there is not a jury, only myself to pass judgment in this matter, I will hear the evidence and determine whether it is germane to the issue of competency. I will, however, clear the courtroom."

The disturbance was enormous, but in due course the court was cleared of all but family and witnesses.

"All right, Mr. Lester," Judge Dukes said. "Suppose you tell me what is so shocking about the deaths of these two young people."

Lester took a huge gulp of water, then a deep breath. "It was pretty ugly, Your Honor," he began at last.

"Up, up, up," Judge Dukes intoned, cutting him off. "Just the facts, ma'am."

They exchanged a smile.

"Yes, Your Honor. As you know, Mrs. Miller was dismembered. This apparently was caused by the steering wheel. Her right arm was found in Mr. Miller's lap. Mr. Miller was also . . . dismembered. If you receive my meaning."

"Please be specific, Mr. Lester," Judge Dukes asked, knitting her brow.

"A portion of Mr. Miller's genitals was . . . missing."

There was a long pause.

"It was still in Mrs. Miller's right hand."

"Court is in recess for lunch, though I doubt anyone will want to eat. I will see defendant, plaintiff and counsel in my chambers in one hour," Judge Dukes sighed with an irritable tap of her gavel.

Michael sat by a window in Judge Dukes' office, smoking. Bill Stockbridge alternately paced and tried to light his pipe. Harvey Turnbul and the senator sat in the two chairs in front of Judge Dukes' ornate French writing desk.

The office was in the sleek new judicial building and all but the desk was in keeping with that style. Synthetic tweed upholstery, Formica cube furniture. Official, imposing, quiet.

Presently the judge came bustling into the room. "Don't get up," she said, crossing past them into a small dressing room at the back of the chamber.

She emerged looking less official, without her robes, but no less severe. Gray wool suit, silk blouse, a custom match for the official and imposing office.

"Well, Mr. Turnbul," she said after regarding the occupants of her office for a moment, "that was one of the most distasteful experiences of my entire judicial career. Senator Miller, I am glad I'm not a member of your family."

She reached and depressed a button on her desk. "Come in here and bring that machine," she said into the intercom, holding up a hand for quiet. "Before you speak, I simply could not see putting the rest of the party through this," she said, sitting down.

The stenographer came into the room.

"All right," the judge began. "Now for the record, Mr. Turnbul, why on earth did you feel it essential to the judgment of competency in a probate hearing to introduce that sort of testimony? I warn you if I don't like your account, I will have the entire matter stricken and entertain motions for dismissal."

"Your Honor," Turnbul said, rising, "distasteful though it might be and I assure you that the plaintiff preferred not to introduce—"

"Mr. Turnbul," said the judge, "I do hope you are not preparing to make the court responsible for the introduction of your testimony."

"No, Your Honor."

"Good, then simply explain your purpose to me."

"Yes, Your Honor," Turnbul said obsequiously enough to address Judge Dukes' rather icy glare. "It was introduced in order to prove that the primary testator—that is, the younger Mr. Miller—could be coerced into considerable lapses of judgment by his wife.

"There was no evidence of skidding or other automotive failure. There was no evidence that another vehicle was involved. The deceased was even driving an automobile designed and built by people accustomed to just such hazardous driving conditions.

"Yet in spite of the fact that it was snowing and that his entire family, including the child whose interest is in question here, was present in the car, there is every indication that he was involved in behavior that presented a clear and present danger to himself and his family and at the instigation of his wife.

"Your Honor, it is our contention that the testator, Mr. Robert Miller the Third, by his very death demonstrated extreme short-sightedness and highly questionable judgment with regard to the best interests of the child. And further, that the secondary testator, Mrs. Miller, the sister of the defendant, was capable of leading him into making grievous errors in judgment. In light of these facts we feel there are adequate grounds to question the soundness of the selection of Mr. Reily as guardian for the child."

Harvey inclined his head ever so slightly to the judge and sat down.

Judge Dukes tapped her chin with a pen. She regarded Senator Miller for a long moment, then turned abruptly to where Bill Stockbridge and Michael sat in stunned silence.

"Mr. Stockbridge," she said at last.

"Yes, Your Honor?" he said, looking up from his shoes.

"Have you anything to say?" she asked.

Bill looked at Michael, who nodded.

"Your Honor," Bill said, "it is hard for the defense to believe that destroying the memory and sullying the graves of the child's parents by pouring the details of their gruesome and tragic deaths into the mills of the press like so much grist is the act of persons in whose hearts rest the better interests of the child. We thank Your Honor for clearing the courtroom when you did."

Harvey Turnbul's knuckles went white as he clutched the arms of his chair.

"Further, we thank you for sparing the rest of the family the sickening spectacle of a father destroying the memory and reputation of his own son in support of his own personal prejudice.

"Finally we invite proof that these same heartless monsters who would subject a child to such public scandal might in any way be better suited as guardians of the interests of the child whose life and name they seem bent on destroying. Thank you, Your Honor."

His name isn't first on the door by accident, Harvey thought, regarding Stockbridge, who sat serenely lighting his pipe.

The judge sat with her chin resting on the heel of her hand, her fingers resting on her nose. She stared down her fingers at the burl of the wood on the top of her desk until it swam before her eyes.

"Gentlemen," she said into her hand, "your points are well taken. It is the feeling of this court that the plaintiff has, in however questionable a fashion, cast some doubt as to the judgment, if not the competence, of the deceased. This court will hear what testimony and evidence the plaintiff has to present as to the soundness of the decision of the late Mr. and Mrs. Miller with regard to the guardianship of their child.

"It is also the feeling of this court that one error, no matter how fatal, does not erode the capacity of a testator. Therefore, the burden of proof in this matter rests entirely with the plaintiff.

"What's more, on the basis of the behavior of the plaintiff thus far, the court will also render its judgment on the future actions of the plaintiff as to their fitness as guardian or to select a guardian for the child. We are at recess until nine tomorrow morning."

"I'm going home," Sylvia said without looking at Robert.

"What?" Robert said, crossing farther into their hotel room and closing the door.

"I'm going home," she repeated.

"Why are you sitting in the dark?" Robert asked, crossing to the lamp.

"For the same reason I'm going home. Because I can't stand to look at you."

"Oh, for Christ's sake, Syl," he muttered, fumbling with the switch. "I've had enough drama for one day."

"Your own son," she said, shaking her head.

"I didn't want to—"

"Just shut up," she snapped, looking at him for the first time, her eyes red and smeared. "If you say you did it for Scotty, I'll scream."

"Listen, Syl—"

"No, you listen." She was shouting. "I'm going home and pack my things and I'm leaving. Our son is the only reason I've stayed with you this long, and now you've destroyed that. I won't sit for the portrait mongers day after day while you destroy our grandson and someone else's son in the bargain. I don't know what you want out of this anymore, but I hope you get it," she said, turning away again.

"What do you want me to say?" he said softly. Finally.

"Nothing. Nothing else. Just get out," she said haltingly.

He stared at her back. Her blondish gray permanent looked hard and cold as it glinted in the harsh light of the single lamp. He remembered when it had been soft and truly blond, falling loosely about her shoulders.

She had looked so young and so proud when she sat on campaign platforms as he began the trek from mediocre businessman to firebrand politician. Life and belief had been so strong in them then. They had been right. And yet now they were wrong. The things they had believed so strongly in their youth had aged as badly as they had.

He had not been voted out of office; he had given it up because he was no longer sure. Politics had stopped being about what they had felt so strongly once. At the end it was about raising money, getting reelected. It was about image. It was about compromise. It was about stopping young people who felt strongly about what they believed.

His youth and his beliefs were gone. He saw it reflected in his wife's dyed blond hair. He turned and left the room.

The air in the courtroom was possessed of that strange vacuumlike quality that often precedes a violent summer storm. Details of the closed session of the day previous had, of course, been discovered through the North Carolina coroner's office and their meanings surmised by a hundred clacking tongues and typewriters. It was not a leak, but it was an unanswered question hanging, waiting for Judge Dukes' answer.

The senator looked tired and preoccupied, his wife still absent. Ann and Ash were drawn and silent as they sat behind Michael, who leaned pensively on the desk. Allen looked starched and proper, but his face was vacant of its usual attentive confidence. Even Mindy looked a little ragged as if the limelight she had sought and found here had scorched and melted her with its intensity.

"All rise."

"Be seated," Judge Dukes muttered. "Let me open today's proceedings by saying two things for those anxious little tape recorders. First: No comment. Second: There is a member of a certain North Carolina coroner's staff looking for work. Mr. Turnbul, proceed."

"Your Honor, we call Joshua Remington," Turnbul said, almost standing.

"Private investigator," Bill Stockbridge hissed into Michael's ear.

"State your name and occupation," Harvey Turnbul said, cantering back and forth in front of the witness box in an effort to contain himself.

"Josh, uh, Joshua Remington," said the stalwart dark man as if clearing his throat. "I'm in confidential inquiries."

"You are licensed to practice in this state?" Harvey said perfunctorily as he clenched and unclenched his hands behind his back, belying his apparent calm.

"Yes, sir," he answered, shifting his weight to his left hip and leaning into the microphone.

"Please tell the court how you are involved in this case," Harvey said, stepping aside as if to make way for the answer.

"Yes, sir. Myself and my operatives were hired by Senator Miller to make certain inquiries into this case."

"You yourself?" Harvey posed the words as a question.

"I was part of the continuous surveillance of Mr. Michael Reily."

"And what specifically were you looking for?"

"Well, we were assigned to observe Mr. Reily's behavior to determine whether or not he was engaged in any morally questionable behavior."

"Jesus," Michael said into the palm of the hand on which he still leaned.

"And what did you find?"

"There were several incidents which we considered questionable."

"Your Honor, we object," Bill Stockbridge said. "The witness is a private eye, not an arbiter of public morality."

"Sustained," said Judge Dukes. "The witness will confine himself to factual information and avoid drawing conclusions.

"Mr. Stockbridge, I would remind you that this is a probate hearing, not a criminal case. As there is no jury, we can trust the judgment of the court in these matters and allow some time-saving latitude in the proceedings. It may surprise the audience to learn that I have heard messier cases than this, though none noisier."

The laughter broke the clouds of tension for a moment. Michael smiled.

"The witness will proceed," Dukes said.

"Thank you, ma'am," he said, and cleared his throat again.

"On the evening of February twenty-first, Mr. Reily returned from work at five forty-five P.M. He was observed walking to the front door of the house which he at that time shared with Jacques Graham Rambeaux. This is a photograph of Mr. Rambeaux obtained by one of my operatives from the *San Francisco Chronicle*. As you can see he is participating in the 1983 Gay Pride March."

He handed the photograph to the judge.

"As the judge can see in this enlargement, Mr. Rambeaux is the one wearing the T-shirt inscribed 'I like Boys'."

"I didn't know," Michael said, anticipating Bill's question.

"In what capacity was Mr. Rambeaux present in the Reily household?"

"It's difficult to say," said Remington.

"How so?" asked Turnbul.

"Mr. Reily was first observed with the young man on the street near his home. Then, much later that night, Mr. Rambeaux arrived with a guitar case and flight bag—four forty-seven A.M. on the morning of the fifteenth," he said, referring to a small notebook.

"And how was he received at such an hour?"

"Mr. Reily met him at the door and embraced him. As you can see in this photograph. Ostensibly, Mr. Rambeaux appears to be caring for the child as well as the house and Mr. Reily. But there are certain inconsistencies."

"Such as?" Turnbul asked, barely able to repress his grin.

"Well, Mr. Reily has been observed buying the young man expensive clothes and other personal items. He has given Mr. Rambeaux the use of the late Mrs. Miller's silver Volvo station wagon and access to her charge accounts. And Mr. Rambeaux has remained in the house, even since Mr. Reily lost his job and is at home most of the time."

"And on the night in question?" Turnbul asked, beaming.

"Yes, sir. As I said, Mr. Reily walked to the door and had a brief verbal exchange."

"What was said?"

Remington again checked his notebook. "Mr. Reily called, 'It's me.' The child was heard. Then Mr. Reily called, 'Hello, darling,' and Mr. Rambeaux answered, 'Hello, Michael.' "

The storm was building and Judge Dukes banged more earnestly.

"Go on, Mr. Remington," Turnbul prompted.

"Yes, sir. Well, Mr. Reily went inside then and closed the door and we heard nothing for around five minutes and then Mr. Reily came out onto the second-floor porch. He was talking, but it was unclear what he said and he was holding the child. Mr. Rambeaux followed him out onto the porch and, as you can see in this photograph, he kissed Mr. Reily."

It was a typhoon, and it was some minutes before the storm had passed.

"All right," Judge Dukes said. "Last warning. Proceed, Mr. Turnbul."

"Thank you, Your Honor," Turnbul said, bouncing on the balls of his feet.

Michael was whispering earnestly to Bill Stockbridge.

"Now, Mr. Remington, did anything else happen that might be of interest to the court in this matter?" Turnbul crowed.

"Well, yes, sir," Remington said, shifting to the other hip. "Later that night Mr. Rambeaux was observed sitting in the same chair with Mr. Reily. As you can see in this shot. And even later on Mr. Reily was observed dancing with Mr. Rambeaux."

Michael laughed, causing an odd ripple of reaction.

"Anyway," Remington concluded, "about then they went back inside and our observation was curtailed."

"I see," Turnbul said, raising his eyebrows and deepening the lines above them. "So on the night in question Mr. Reily was heard calling Mr. Rambeaux darling and seen kissing him and dancing with him?"

"That's correct," said Remington.

"And Mr. Rambeaux is a known gay activist, whom Mr. Reily met on the street, took into his home in the middle of the night, for whom he bought expensive gifts and who is caring for the child in question?"

"Yes, sir," Remington said, nodding.

"Just the facts, Mr. Stockbridge," Turnbul said, nodding to his opponent.

Stockbridge inclined his head in response.

"Mr. Remington," Turnbul said, turning back, "was there anything else worth noting?"

"Well, sir, the following evening, that's the twenty-second, when this mess really blew—"

"Mr. Remington," the judge cautioned.

"Sorry, ma'am. The day the press got hold of the details of this suit—"

There was some laughter. Judge Dukes smiled and waved a warning finger.

"Well, that evening," Remington began again as the laughter

died. "That evening Mr. Reily was observed going to the River-banks Park. He drove into a restricted area near the waterworks, parked his car there and climbed into the park through a hole in the fence near the reservoir. The park was closed. He proceeded through a wooded area to the trail in the park and from there he climbed onto a rock outcropping on the bank of the river."

Michael put his face in his hands.

"What did Mr. Reily do then?" Turnbul asked, prodding Remington along.

"Well, nothing really," Remington said. "He sat for a while smoking what appeared to be cigarettes—"

"Your Honor," Stockbridge said with an edge in his voice.

"Mr. Remington, watch the innuendo. Stick to facts," the judge said, matching Bill's quiet warning tone.

"Sorry," Remington said.

"Go on," Turnbul said over his shoulder as he walked away from the witness toward his desk.

"Well, sir, after the sun went down, he was joined by another gentleman using the same route. We have since identified the gentleman as a Mr. Kevin Perdue; you can see him in this picture, taken at Mr. Reily's sister's funeral. He is the one with his arms around Mr. Reily. The picture appeared on the front page of the local paper among others."

"And what did Mr. Perdue do once he had also broken into the park?" Turnbul asked.

Stockbridge cut his eyes at Turnbul, who was already returning the look, smiling.

"He, um, climbed up with Mr. Reily on the rock."

"And then?"

"Well, they appeared to talk for a while, we could not get close enough to hear what was said, but after a moment they started laughing and rolling around on the rock. And then they kinda rolled into each other's arms and lay that way for a while, as you can see in this photograph."

"How long did this last?" Turnbul asked, rising above the receding tide.

"Not all that long," Remington said. "After a minute or two Mr. Reily started yelling and got up. We were able to hear some of this." He referred to the notebook. "We heard Mr. Reily say,

'But you're marrying Shanah.' Shanah is the name of Mr. Perdue's fiancée."

"Please go on," Turnbul said, half sitting on the edge of his desk.

"Well, after a minute, Mr. Reily climbed down off the rock and sort of ran out of the park. Then Mr. Perdue followed. They shouted back and forth, and we made out bits and pieces of what was said. They shouted something about Christmas and the defen—I mean Mr. Reily's sister, Kathryn, and then Mr. Reily shouted real loud and clear, 'If I can deal with the fact that you don't love me, you can deal with the fact that I do love you.'"

Michael held his hands over his face to hide the tears.

"Now," Harvey Turnbul said, almost skipping forward from his perch, "about this sudden interest from the press that had begun that morning. Were you able to determine the cause of this sudden burst of energy on the part of the media?"

"Well, sir," Joshua said, reaching for his folder, "we were able to obtain from a local reporter a copy of this press release detailing the early aspects of this suit."

"Is there anything distinctive about the release?" Harvey asked, lacing his fingers over his stomach and goose-stepping in front of the witness box. "Anything that might indicate the point of origin?"

"Well, it's on Gilliam and Company stationery."

"Crawford," Michael muttered, smearing the moisture down his face as he dragged his shielding hands to his chin.

"What?" Bill Stockbridge asked in a whisper.

"Thank you, Mr. Remington," Harvey Turnbul was saying. "Your witness, Mr. Stockbridge," he concluded smugly and strode back to his desk.

"Mr. Stockbridge?" Judge Dukes asked, swiveling like some great metronome in the huge black leather chair. Combined, her black robes and chair gave her severe owlish face a disembodied quality. "Do you have any questions of this witness?"

Bill Stockbridge looked up from the desk, where he and Michael whispered as Bill scribbled furiously on a yellow legal pad. "A moment, Your Honor," he said.

"How about five?" Dukes said absently, tapping the tips of her fingers on the great desk in front of her. "The court needs to powder its nose."

"Thank you, Your Honor," Stockbridge said.

"Mr. Remington," Bill Stockbridge said as he stalked up to the witness box, yellow notepad in hand.

Court was back in session. Hardly anyone, save the judge, had left during the brief recess. But then her seat at the proceedings was secure. Michael and Bill had moved to a small antechamber just off the courtroom. The senator had risen to stretch his legs and to speak with Mindy and Allen, who sat behind him.

The courtroom, insofar as the family was concerned, had been divided like some hostile wedding party, each sitting on their prescribed side and behaving as if alone, neither speaking to nor acknowledging the existence of the other side.

Ash and Ann sat, as they had, behind Michael. Michael had forbidden that Gray, or the baby, set foot in the courtroom. In fact, they never left the protective confines of the high rise, spending afternoon strolls in the rooftop garden. Randy Green brought fresh fruit and vegetables, and the shops Gray had visited brought whatever was needed.

Ash had not spoken to Allen or Mindy since that night at his house. After Michael had left, he had said simply, "There is nothing left to say. Get out of my house."

They had left in silence.

Ann had called Allen occasionally to ask how he was and to plead with him to make amends with his father and brother. She had spoken to Mindy only if she answered the phone. And then only to ask for Allen.

"Fuck 'em all," Mindy had said one night after Ann had called and after about five glasses of wine. "They're just sore 'cause they're gonna lose," she slurred.

"You're drunk," Allen had said quietly without looking up from the day's *Barron's*. "Go to bed."

Bill Stockbridge looked over the tops of his reading glasses at the large dark man on the witness stand. "Was Mr. Reily the only person that you and your operatives spied on?" he asked with special distaste.

"There were others under surveillance," he replied, stressing the word "surveillance" defensively.

"Who?" Bill asked so abruptly that everyone including the witness waited for the rest of the question. "Well?" Bill demanded, narrowing his eyes. "On whom else were you spying?"

"Your Honor—" Harvey Turnbul began.

"Your Honor, counsel brought in this whole line of questioning."

"Your Honor, Mr. Stockbridge is intimidating the witness."

"All right, boys," the judge said with a sharp bang of the gavel. "Mr. Turnbul, you started this. Mr. Stockbridge, it isn't necessary to rough up the witness. Proceed."

"Mr. Remington," Stockbridge asked with a mocking smile and tone, "about whom else were you making confidential inquiries?"

"A number of people."

"Their names?"

"Dr. and Mrs. Ashton Reily, Allen Reily and Mandy Thornton, Kathryn Reily Miller, Robert Miller III, you, Frankie Gilliam, Graham Rambeaux, Randy Green—"

"That's enough," Bill Stockbridge cut him off amid the shock wave rolling around him. "You ought to be able to retire off the money from this inquisition."

"I've done all right," Remington said.

"All right?" Bill said, chuckling and raising his eyebrows. "How much has the senator paid you for your testimony here today?"

"Your Honor—"

"Mr. Stockbridge."

"Sorry, Your Honor. Mr. Remington, how much has the senator paid you to gather the confidential testimony you've presented here today?"

"Around fifty to seventy-five thousand . . ." he muttered, and trailed off.

"Seventy-five thousand dollars?" Stockbridge said, and then gave a long, low whistle.

"About."

"You mean it could be more?" Stockbridge said even louder than before.

"No. No more than that."

"That's a lot of money. You must feel very indebted to the senator?"

"Your Honor—"

"I withdraw it."

"How long did it take you to earn all that money?"

"Around two months."

"Two months," Stockbridge said, nodding.

"Yes, sir," Remington said, shifting uncomfortably from one cheek to the other.

"And in all that time only these two incidents seemed suspicious."

"Well, no," Remington said evasively.

"You mean, there were other equally heinous incidents you've left out?" Bill asked, shocked. Pretty risky, Stockbridge, he thought.

"Well . . ." Remington said, looking at the wood grain of the side of Judge Dukes' desk.

"Well?" Bill asked hotly.

"Well, nothing specific," Remington said, shifting his gaze to his hands.

Bill Stockbridge rocked back on his heels and smiled. Pretty good for an old corporate lawyer, he thought.

"Do you mean to tell me that in sixty days of watching a sizable portion of the population of the state of South Carolina, the only instances of hugging and kissing and—dare I say it—dancing, that you observed were these two miserable stories?"

"Well, no," Remington said. "If we're talking about everyone."

"Well, nearly everyone, it seems to me." Stockbridge smirked. "Why? Did you think I meant only my client?"

"Well, naturally I thought—"

"That I meant my client because he's on trial here?"

"Your Honor," Turnbul said, sitting forward.

"Let me remind you that this is a hearing, Mr. Remington. We're here for all the facts."

"Your Honor," Turnbul said standing, "we object to all of this line of badgering."

"And to determine who is best suited to raise the child," Bill continued.

"Sit down," Judge Dukes said. "Control yourself, Stockbridge."

"Sorry, Your Honor," Bill said, smiling wryly.

Harvey started to say something, spluttered and then slouched in his chair.

"So, Mr. Remington," Bill said, holding his glasses and his notepad behind his back, "tell us about this rampant hugging and kissing and dancing that you and your dedicated employees observed."

"Look, most of what we observed was pretty innocent." Remington sighed, looking squarely at Bill's handkerchief.

"Kissing and hugging and dancing? Innocent?" Bill said, bushy gray eyebrows raised. "Yet Mr. Reily's flirtation with decadence seemed—guilty?"

"Suspicious."

"Describe for the court," Bill began again, tossing his notes onto the desk, "describe the criterion for suspicious."

"Well, um, out of the ordinary," Remington said at last.

"Out of the ordinary?" Bill said, tapping his chin with his index finger. "You think a single man suddenly encumbered with the care of a child hiring a housekeeper is out of the ordinary?"

"It is if the housekeeper is a gay activist."

"That's right, but you're the only one who knew that, well, you and the senator. And you thought there was something wrong with that?"

"It didn't seem in the best interest of the child, no."

"So you kept it a secret. I see." Bill nodded and paced in front of the witness. "Now let's talk about these suspicious incidents. The expensive gifts. What were they?"

"Clothes mainly."

"I see." Bill picked up one of the photos from the table in front of the judge. "Now I see here that the night Mr. Rambeaux arrived he was carrying a small flight bag and a guitar case. Did he ever bring other luggage?"

"No, sir, not that we saw."

"Now do you suppose his wardrobe is in the flight bag or the guitar case?"

"Well, I—"

"Maybe Mr. Reily was just buying Mr. Rambeaux some clothes because he didn't have many? Is that possible?"

"Well, yes."

"And this hug here in the picture. If you can bear it, please look on this shocking scene and tell me what lights are on in the house."

"The lights in the front and rear rooms in the house on the left-hand side."

"The bedrooms?"

"I'm not certain."

"Those are the bedrooms. Now doesn't that seem suspicious to you? That at nearly five o'clock in the morning the lights are on in the baby's room? Do you suppose Mr. Reily is relieved that someone has arrived to care for a child awake at nearly five in the morning?"

"Yes, I suppose that's possible."

"And it's equally possible that the hug is one of relief?"

"Well, I don't—"

"Is . . . it . . . possible?"

"Yes."

"I see. Now this kiss here. Right on the front porch. Did you discover that Mr. Rambeaux is of French ancestry?"

"Yes."

"Have you seen photographs of Charles de Gaulle kissing soldiers on both cheeks after pinning a medal on them?"

"I think maybe."

"Did you think that was suspicious?"

"Well . . . no, not really."

"But you found it suspicious when Mr. Rambeaux, who arrived without clothing much beyond the shirt on his back, who was clothed, housed, fed, paid and driving a silver Volvo turbo thanks to this man, in the custom of his culture kissed Mr. Reily on both cheeks?"

"Yes."

"He did in fact kiss him on both cheeks?"

"I . . . no . . . well." Josh Remington's mouth snapped open and shut. "I don't remember."

"You don't remember?" Bill asked, looking very shocked indeed. "This incident was so shocking that you took a photograph and described it in detail in a court of law and you don't remember?"

"I'm not sure."

"That hardly seems worth seventy-five thousand dollars," Bill said, shaking his head sadly at the senator.

Senator Miller, veteran of twenty-seven years of filibuster and firebrand senatorial politics, blushed and looked down at his shoes.

"Well," Bill said triumphantly, "let us assume that since this photograph shows Mr. Rambeaux kissing Mr. Reily on the right cheek that he did indeed kiss him on the left, as is the custom among thousands—millions—of his countrymen, and that there is nothing suspicious about it. And why don't you bring in the rest of the photographs you have taken of all the people Senator Miller has had you following? Your Honor?"

"So ordered."

"Now the shouts of endearment from the street. You testified that Mr. Reily shouted something and then the baby made a sound and then he said, 'Hello, darling.' Is that right?"

"Well, there—"

"Is . . . that . . . right?"

"Yes."

"Does that seem suspicious?"

"Well . . ."

"Your honor . . ." Harvey began.

"Let me put it this way. If a baby responded to the sound of your voice, would you then speak to someone else?"

"I guess not."

"I should hope not; someone might think it suspicious. Where were you while you observed all this suspicious behavior?"

"We were concealed in a stand of nandina along the edge of the property."

"Hiding in the bushes?"

"We were—"

"Your Honor," Harvey Turnbul sputtered, "I think this has gone just about far enough."

"Confidentially inquiring in the bushes?"

"Your Honor?"

"Mr. Stockbridge."

"Sorry, Your Honor, I was just curious."

"Now did Misters Rambeaux and Reily spend a quiet evening at home that evening?"

"No, sir. They were joined by Mr. Reily's brother and his brother's fiancée, Mandy Thornton."

"Were they present during the notorious arm sitting and dancing incidents?"

"Yes, sir," Remington answered flatly. He was a defeated man. Shoulders slack, answers quiet. He really wanted a cigarette.

"Were Gray and Michael the only dance partners that evening?"

"No, sir, Mr. Reily also danced with Miss Thornton and his brother."

"That's pretty sordid," Bill said, playing the house broadly. "How about kissing?" he went on. "Did Mr. Reily kiss anyone else that evening?"

"Yes, sir, he kissed Miss Thornton good night."

"No!" Bill said, obviously enjoying himself.

"Mr. Stockbridge," said Judge Dukes, to whom it was also obvious, "is there a point to all this?"

"Yes, Your Honor," Bill said, suddenly serious. "Our point is that if you hide in anyone's bushes long enough, you're bound to come across a few incidents that, when taken out of context, seem suspicious. It is our intent to point out the selective manner in which these incidents were chosen and the innocence inherent in these incidents."

"So noted," said the judge absently. "Now let's move along in a less theatrical fashion."

"Yes, Your Honor," Bill said. "Mr. Remington, are you aware that Mr. Reily's advertising firm had a long-standing relationship with Senator Miller?"

"Yes, sir."

"And are you aware that Mr. Reily's firm employs nearly one hundred people in five cities around the Southeast?"

"No, sir, I was not aware of that."

"You may believe me that is true," Bill said, crossing back to his desk. "So," he said, turning back and raising his voice, "hundreds of people, including Senator Miller, had access to this stationery," he said, holding up the press release. "And it would have been possible for any one of them, including Senator Miller, to send out the press release?"

"Well, I don't—"

"Was . . . it . . . possible?"

"Yes . . . it . . . was."

"No further questions."

The day in court continued pretty much along these lines. Harvey Turnbul called witnesses, and Bill Stockbridge humiliated them.

Allen had been sullen and terse with both lawyers, answering yes or no whenever possible. He had been called to substantiate previous testimony regarding the evening of the dinner party, but the line of questioning had seemed petty by then.

And Bill had substantially embarrassed both Allen and Mindy by calling their unmarried living situation into question.

The only real drama had been an outburst from Allen. "You're trying to make Michael's perverted life seem okay."

"No," Bill had answered calmly. "You're trying to make it seem perverted."

Mindy had been even less reserved, answering Harvey's questions in obviously staged cooperation. She had been hostile and baiting with Bill, snapping her answers at him and becoming vocally combative on several occasions. She had become red with rage as Bill questioned her living arrangement with Allen in the same terms that Harvey had questioned Gray's with Michael.

"Has he bought you expensive gifts?"

"I don't see—"

"Has he?"

"Well, yes."

"Are you there ostensibly as a housekeeper? I remind you that you are under oath. And that I have seen the apartment."

It had been a triumphant day for Michael.

"Kissing and hugging and dancing—oh my," Michael said, dancing around and laughing.

"It went really well," Bill Stockbridge said as they rode the elevator to Michael's.

"We didn't talk about Kevin," Michael said flatly, staring at the blinking numbers as the floors ticked past.

"We didn't have to," Bill said.

"It was just as well. So the topic just vanishes?" Michael asked as the elevator doors opened.

Bill didn't get the chance to respond. The abrupt appearance of Gray, standing with his guitar case outside the elevator door, interrupted.

"Where are you going?" Michael asked.

"I'm leaving," Gray said, pushing into the elevator.

"Leaving?" Michael said, jumping back onto the elevator.

The doors closed, leaving Bill stranded in the hall.

"What do you mean you're leaving?" Michael demanded hotly. "Where's the baby?"

"He's asleep," Gray said, pushing the elevator button for the lobby.

"Alone?" Michael asked, a little stunned. "Talk to me."

Gray said nothing.

The elevator started to descend.

Michael ran his fingers down the row of buttons.

Vera Dillingham was an elderly widow of the proper blue-haired persuasion. Her husband had died five years before of a heart attack suffered on the eleventh hole of the golf course to which they had belonged ever since GE had moved them to the state nineteen years before. She had become the ultimate golf widow.

After his death their home, built to accommodate their three children and their life together, had seemed gloomy and empty.

The memories, good and bad, haunted every corridor and room.

So, when her friend Jo Ann, also a recent widow, had spoken in glowing terms of the tax advantages and cheery merits of selling the family dinosaur and moving into a modern condominium, it had seemed a great idea.

Actually Jo Ann, who had lived across the street from Vera for seventeen years, was bored and lonely. And while there had indeed been tax advantages, condominium life had not been cheery until Vera had moved in upstairs.

It hadn't been too terrible a fib, for Vera and her old friend did have a pretty good time. They shopped together, went to the beauty parlor together, and every Tuesday night went to dinner at J.J.'s, an overdressed local steak house that catered to the Vera and Jo Ann crowd, and then to bingo at the church.

It was Tuesday evening.

Vera stood, pillbox hat and veil nailed to her blue hair, smelling of powder and perfume, and waiting for the elevator to take her down to meet Jo Ann for "a little sherry" before they went out.

She was thinking how annoying she found Jo Ann's flirting with the "help" at J.J.'s, so it wasn't until after she'd actually stepped into the elevator that she realized that one of the occupants was screaming.

"Goddamnit, Gray," said the young man, who was tugging at the guitar case held fiercely by the only other occupant, "you can't just leave me."

"Oh, dear," she said as the doors of the elevator snapped shut behind her.

Albert Hoffman was fifty-two next month, or so he'd say if you asked him. He was actually fifty-five and had been divorced since he was fifty-two, from his wife of thirty-three years.

They had run a small delicatessen together since shortly after their marriage. They had set up the shop with money Faye had inherited from the demise of her ninety-three-year-old great-aunt Rose, with whom they had lived after their marriage.

The deli had done well and Al had given Faye everything she had wanted for thirty-three years. Everything except an orgasm, which happily she had received, if belatedly, from the kosher meat man, with whom she had left three years previously.

To be truthful, Albert was somewhat ambivalent as to whether he was sorrier to lose his helpmate of thirty-three years or a steady supplier of kosher meats. Worse still, Faye and Kosher Meats had gone into competition, with money Faye had exacted as part of a buyout divorce settlement centering on the deli.

Aside from the drain on his business, life was still pretty good to Albert. He had used his half of the handsome profit they'd turned selling their house in The Grove to a local hotel owner, to buy a luxury condominium. He had "a girl" in three times a week to do the cleaning. And the deli provided a good living as well as a good diet. What's more, his life was free of Faye's screeching voice and PBS.

He brought home sandwiches, potato salad and beer and sat in front of the all-sports cable network until he fell asleep.

Tuesday night was the fights. In preparation for an evening's vicarious violence he was emptying the large plastic bucket he kept by his TV chair to catch beer bottles. The "girl" didn't come till tomorrow.

As he walked down the hall to the garbage chute, the elevator doors opened and a small older woman fell backward into the hall.

Without thinking Albert dropped the bucket, sending Bass Ale bottles echoing down the marble hallway, and caught Vera Dillingham in his arms.

She had stepped back, leaning against the elevator doors, in an effort to get away from the fight taking place in the elevator.

Albert was unaware of this impulse to escape and stood her up and back into the elevator.

"Are you all right?" Albert asked as he stepped in with her, followed by the clatter of a number of Bass Ale bottles.

The doors closed behind them.

"It's no large deal," Gray said.

"The hell it isn't," Albert said. "She could have hurt herself."

"I'm fine," Vera said, obviously not fine. There was no social dictum that she knew of for being in an elevator during someone else's fight.

In fact, the only social obligation she could think of was to face the doors, which she did.

The doors reopened and Vera found herself more or less face-to-face with the large black visage of Ella Jenkins, the belligerent maid to the thin and obliging Boyds on the twenty-second floor.

Stunned and unable to get off without pushing the rotund obstacle out of her path, Vera gestured nervously with her head toward Michael and Gray and said, "Take the next car."

Ella interpreted the entire incident, as she usually did, to be a racial slur akin to "go to the back of the bus." The clipped terror of Vera's voice seemed curt and the warning toss of Vera's head seemed haughty.

"Hunh-uh," she said, shoving into the car. "I've been on my feet all day and I s'pose I got as much right to ride as you."

"I demand some kind of explanation for this," Michael screamed suddenly into Ella's face.

Unaccustomed as she was to that sort of treatment from the obsequious Boyds, or anyone else for that matter, she considered the comment carefully for about three seconds and then screamed into Michael's face, "What did you say?"

"You stay out of this," Michael snapped.

Vera saw her chance. As Ella stepped further into the elevator, she edged to get out before the doors closed again.

Unfortunately the reason Ella had stepped forward was to get enough swinging room to strike Michael with her shopping bag. The result was that she clobbered Vera Dillingham with her purse, her coat and two bottles of Blue Nun wine she had concealed in a Macy's shopping bag under her purse and her coat.

In spite of the fact that one of the bottles was half empty—which perhaps explained why Ella was more belligerent than usual—the blow knocked Vera senseless into the arms of Albert Hoffman. Again.

She moaned as she saw the doors to the elevator close. Again. And still louder when she saw from her perch, draped over Al's shoulder, that all the buttons were lighted.

"Are you crazy?" Albert said as he propped Vera against the wall of the elevator.

"Who are you talking to?" Ella said, reeling on him.

"I'm waiting for an explanation," Michael said, yanking on the guitar case.

"I'm takinayou, you crazy lady," Albert said, pulling down on Vera's cheeks to get a look at the whites of her eyes. He wasn't

sure what he would see but he remembered that he'd seen someone do it on some show he'd watched with Faye on PBS. "What
have you got in that bag? Cannonballs? You knocked her silly."

"I don't want to talk about it," Gray began repeating.

Ella looked for a moment at Gray. Albert took that opportunity
to rush her and try to wrest the bag from her hand.

Michael began to laugh at Gray's inept "Idonwannatalkaboutit" singsong belabored through the thick French accent.

The elevator stopped again.

Vera felt herself sliding down the wall where she leaned.

The doors opened.

The struggle ensued, but as Ella was more than twice Albert's
size, she was having a pretty easy time of it. She held Albert off
with one hand and drew back the shopping bag with the other to
improve her swing at him.

"Gray," Michael said, "stop doing that, and talk to me."

The backward trajectory of the shopping bag placed it outside
the car as the doors closed on the empty hall of the twenty-first
floor. They also caught the shopping bag in mid-swing halfway
in and halfway out, causing Ella to lurch forward as she swung
and then backward as the bag was snatched away by the doors
of the elevator. As she fell back, her solid hold on the front of
Albert's shirt caused him to fall with her.

They listed dangerously in that direction until the downward
motion of the elevator brought the business end of the shopping
bag to rest on the marble floor on the twenty-first floor, where it
remained, separated from the rest of the party.

Slowly Ella began to rise off the floor of the moving elevator,
pulled by her firm grip on the handles of the stationary shopping
bag. And slowly Mr. Hoffman began to rise, pulled by her equally
firm grip on him.

Macy's shopping bags are designed with double reinforcement
around nylon handles. In this way, reasoned the executive vice-
president in charge of operations and, presumably, shopping
bags, the customer could load up with more merchandise.

However, the combined weight of Ms. Jenkins and Mr. Hoffman proved too much for the heavy-duty construction, and the
bag gave, sending Ella and Al to a crash landing on Vera Dillingham inside the elevator. Meanwhile, up on the twenty-first

floor, liberated from the torn remains of the shopping bag, the two bottles of Blue Nun wine, one already opened, went clattering to the door of 2107.

The disturbance aroused the occupant of 2107, a Mr. Johnson, who was inside minding his children while his wife was in the laundry room in the basement. He was fond of Blue Nun and assumed his wife had brought the bottles for him as a surprise.

The disturbance also startled Gray enough that he stopped saying, "Idonwantakboutit." Which pleased everyone in the elevator.

"You can't leave the baby and me," Michael said in the relatively silent opportunity.

Ella had found a Bass Ale bottle with her hand and was preparing to strike Al Hoffman with it when the doors opened.

Gray's response was covered by the earsplitting scream of Jo Ann Henson, who was horrified to see "that nice Mr. Hoffman" and the Boyds' maid sitting on her dear friend Vera Dillingham.

This was followed by the alarming bellow of Albert Hoffman, who cried out in pain as Jo Ann inadvertently drove her spike heel into the back of the hand he was using to push himself up from the floor.

"What?" Michael asked as the noise subsided and the doors closed.

"Vera, are you all right?" Jo Ann said to her inert friend, who obviously was not.

"Because I got this today," Gray repeated, pulling a blue sheet of paper from his pocket.

"A subpoena," Michael said, recognizing it at once.

"A subpoena?" Al asked, looking away from Ella long enough to give her the chance to take a cut at him with the beer bottle.

The elevator lurched to a stop and she instead struck Jo Ann in the kneecap.

"Do I meddle in your business?" Michael asked, looking at Al Hoffman for the first time. He was more than a little surprised to see Mr. Hoffman sitting astride the Boyds' maid in a public elevator.

Mert Hager had had a full and exciting life. He had been a marine in World War II and then a policeman in the sixties and seventies. Between the war and the social unrest, he had had enough excitement. He had tried retirement, but in spite of his two generous pensions, he and his wife had driven each other insane.

So the job as a shift watchman at the luxury high-rise had been an excellent solution.

It gave him a reason to be out of the house for a while every day. And sitting at the desk in the posh lobby reading and occasionally watching the TV monitors that surrounded him suited his need for quiet. He especially enjoyed the evening shift. There were only minor comings and goings to monitor and no heavy packages to deal with. He could read in peace.

He was, in fact, deep into an exciting Robert Ludlum novel. Which perhaps explains why he overreacted when the elevator doors opened and Mrs. Henson from 1902 rode out of the elevator on the back of Ella Jenkins, the Boyds' maid from 2201, followed by Mr. Hoffman of 2309, who was hurling beer bottles and profanity at them both.

Pushing the alarm button had probably been warranted, but the warning shot he'd fired into the crystal chandelier had probably been ill considered.

Who can say?

Betty Ann Johnson had just started as a senior English teacher at a local private school. She had been lucky to get a job so quickly, but the previous instructor had become pregnant and decided to leave at the last minute.

Betty Ann and her husband had just transferred from St. Louis with the paper company for which he worked. She had hated uprooting the kids, but the job was a nice promotion and if he hadn't taken it, it might have been a long time before such an opportunity came along again.

She sat in the relative quiet of the laundry room, grading papers. Her husband was upstairs with the kids.

She was actually a little sorry that her new washer and dryer were due to arrive later that week and she would be denied the peace of a laundry room hardly anyone in the luxury high-rise ever used.

The ring of the elevator bell annoyed her because she knew company would disturb her quiet.

She looked up and was startled to see a guitar case clatter across the floor. This was followed by a lanky blond man with a mustache.

Another man, shorter and darker, stepped out, quickly reached back in the elevator for a second and then ran across the room to the guitar case and kicked it out of the grasp of the blond man, who was just bending over to pick it up. The darker man then tackled the blond man and they rolled around on the floor for a time.

The elevator doors closed.

She watched as the struggle continued until both men collapsed in laughter.

"Gray," the darker man said as they stopped laughing, "lookit, a subpoena is not the end of the world. Why leave?"

The blond man became sober and said quietly, "I know what happened today in court. About me."

"Then you also know that we took the day," Michael said.

Gray began to cry. "I should have told you," he sobbed.

"It doesn't make any difference," Michael said. "That's our whole point."

"But I am in love with you," Gray wailed.

"Oh, God," Michael sighed, holding his sobbing friend. "Let's go back upstairs."

As he helped Gray to his feet, he noticed Betty Ann Johnson staring at them openmouthed from amid her partially folded laundry.

"You're not some goddamned private eye, are you?" Michael shouted at her as he poked at the elevator button.

"I'm . . . no," she said. "I teach senior English."

"Thank God," Michael said as he helped Gray onto the elevator.

"You forgot your guitar," she said to the elevator doors.

"Look, we'll just go for a few minutes and then leave," Clive Royal said to his wife, Louden.

She did not believe him. She snorted.

In their role as the chairman of the board—and spouse—of a large local bank, their social schedule was filled with a lot of obligatory appearances at stupid parties given to support the museum or the animal shelter or some other public cause. The job as chairman was largely ceremonial since the bank had been bought out by a large national chain. Clive felt his social calls more keenly now since that was really all he did.

His contract from the merger paid him an obscenely large amount of money to be the "local face" for the bank. Bank operations were handled by a much younger man sent down from the New York office.

The only thing Louden Royal felt keenly anymore were the vodka stingers she started drinking at lunch.

Which was another reason Clive enjoyed the parties. It was a break from spending the evening with Louden.

"You'll go in and ignore me all night," she snarled, lipstick showing on her teeth.

Clive was about to make one of the conciliatory, placating and meaningless remarks that had given rise to his successful career in banking when the doors to the elevator opened.

This ordinarily would not have stopped him making his remark, but this particular elevator arrived with an elderly woman, wearing a hat and white lace gloves, sprawled on its floor.

"Dear me," Clive said instead.

"Wha—oh, my," Louden said, noticing. "What should we do?" she asked listing slightly, from either the shock or the Wolfschmidt.

"Something, I expect," Clive said, blocking the close of the door with his left arm.

"Yes," Louden murmured. "Something."

All in all, it had been a more eventful evening at Saluda Hill Luxury Condominiums than had been seen in a long time. Actually nothing had ever happened there before. So the evening had taken first place pretty easily.

When the police arrived in response to the alarm, they had found a large older man in riding livery—the homeowners' association having eschewed military uniforms as too obtrusive—holding an elderly gentleman, a large black woman and an older woman, wearing a dress unsuited to the weather and her age, at gunpoint.

Naturally they had tackled the security guard, thinking him some demented English terrorist.

After considerable argument as to just what had happened they arrested everyone and fanned out in an all-out search for Vera Dillingham.

"Something," on the part of the Clive Royals, had turned out to be to take the fugitive's pulse and, having determined she was alive, to drag her to their apartment and pour vodka stingers down her throat until she snapped out of it. Vera had become quite tipsy, as she had missed dinner, and had been the hit of the Annual Spay and Neuter Society Ball.

She and Louden became fast friends and drinking buddies and Clive took them to official functions, giving Louden something to do and greatly improving their marriage.

Jo Ann Henson had become Jo Ann Henson Hoffman after a brief courtship following her incarceration with Albert. They sold the deli and one of the condominiums and traveled the world extensively, coming home only for the Christmas/Chanukah season and to gloat over long lunches at Faye's Kosher Deli.

Ella Jenkins got a job as a parole officer and left the employ of the much relieved Boyds, who hired a housekeeper as diminutive and obsequious as they were themselves.

Betty Ann and Joseph Johnson conceived their third child that evening.

She had returned home in an excited state and found her children asleep and her husband inebriated. In their mutually unbalanced state they neglected to include birth control in the evening's festivities.

She left her post as senior English instructor the following fall, prompting the headmaster to hire a man to replace her.

They named the child Blue, after the wine, which he remembered, and they never discussed the incident in the laundry room, which she forgot.

Owing to his valor and the fact that all parties involved wanted the charges dropped, Mert Hager was made head of security by the homeowners' association.

And the crystal chandelier was replaced with an art deco glass monstrosity, which Michael liked much better.

◠ ◠ ◠

"So it's agreed then," Bill Stockbridge was saying into the phone in Michael's dining room.

"There was a shooting in this building last night," Michael said, looking up from his newspaper at the breakfast table.

"Who?" Gray asked, coming in from the kitchen. "More coffee?"

"Please," Michael said. "As best as I can make out the only casualty was that Reign of Terror baroque chandelier."

"Okay, Harvey. See you in court," Bill said, and hung up. "I'm a little worried about this."

"Why on earth?" Michael said, folding up the paper. "I think everything has worked out surprisingly well."

"They gave in too easily," Bill said, tamping tobacco into his pipe as he sat with Michael at the table.

"Lookit," Michael said, lowering his voice after Gray had left the room, "after the way things went yesterday, they were probably afraid Gray would only substantiate the innocence of all their cloak-and-dagger innuendos."

"Harvey is still too happy or something," Bill said through the cloud from his pipe.

"Well, he's just relieved not to have to go through it again today. Anyway, I don't care. Gray has done everything but sing and dance he's so happy."

"Why didn't you want Gray—"

"I don't want to talk about it," Michael said with a wave of his hand.

"I'm your lawyer. Remember?" Bill said.

"If I thought it would make any difference, I'd tell you," Michael said quietly.

"Michael," Bill began, then paused, looked as if he might be passing a kidney stone and asked, "You all are not . . ." He wiggled his fingers in the air as if that completed the question.

"We're not?" Michael asked, imitating the gesture.

"You know," Bill said, staring intently at the cream pitcher.

"Having a taffy pull?" Michael suggested, laughing.

"Michael!" Bill said, blushing.

"Eating melted candy bars? Out of toilet paper?" Michael continued, enjoying the game.

"If it weren't so good to hear you laughing, I'd hit you." Bill snorted.

"No," Michael said kindly. "We're not having a taffy pull."

"What's the joke?" Gray asked, coming in with a plate of muffins.

"Isn't Scott joining us for breakfast?" Michael sidestepped the question.

"He threw strained persimmons on your sweater yesterday morning," Gray said with an air of finality. "He can eat in the kitchen until he's twenty-one."

"Sounds like a stiff sentence to me." Bill chortled.

"Strained persimmons?" Michael asked. "I'd have thrown them, too."

"It's all set," Harvey said, returning to the sitting room of Senator Miller's suite.

"Great," Robert said without conviction.

"I know yesterday didn't go very well," Harvey said, sitting at the rolling room service table. "But today will be all ours. Cheer up."

Robert grunted and made patterns in his grits with his fork.

"Are you gonna eat that or hang it on the wall?" Harvey asked, trying at humor.

Robert smiled weakly.

"How's Sylvia?" Harvey asked quietly.

Robert shrugged. "I don't know. Haven't heard."

"She'll get over it," Harvey placated.

"I don't know if I will," Robert said.

"Do you want me to go to the drive-through and get you something?" Mindy asked.

"What?" Allen said, suddenly aware he was sitting across from her.

"Well, you're not eating," Mindy said. "I just thought maybe . . . I know I'm no cook."

"You're fine," Allen said, smiling at her. "I'm just nervous."

"Don't be," Mindy said, buttering toast, burned beyond recognition. "All we have to do today is sit there. Yesterday was just horrible. Did you hear what Bill said about my housekeeping?"

"I'm not marrying you for your housekeeping," Allen said, grinning.

"When are we going to set the date?" Mindy asked, oblivious of his leer.

"As soon as this mess is over with, I promise," Allen said.

"Today should take care of that," Mindy said, gesturing with the square of blackened, butter-covered floor tile—formerly a slice of bread.

"A toast," he said, raising his slice to meet hers. "To us."

"To victory."

The two pieces of carbonized bread shattered on contact.

They laughed.

"What are you thinking about?" Ann asked.

"Allen," Ashton said simply without looking up from the crossword he hadn't touched. "Do you think he really hates his brother so much?"

"I don't think he hates him," she said, warming her hands on the mug of coffee she supported just beneath her chin. The steam that rose around her face gave her an ethereal, dreamy quality.

"Resents him then," Ashton said, a little less dispirited.

"I'd like to believe it was all that girl," Ann said, blowing wisps of steam across the top of the cup, "but—" She sighed, shrugging. She took a sip of coffee.

"You heard him in court yesterday," Ashton said, looking up. "He called Michael a pervert."

"He said Michael's lifestyle was perverted," she cut in quickly.

"Whatever." He looked back at the puzzle.

She took another sip.

"Maybe he'd be less resentful if you'd talk to him," Ann said tentatively, testing the waters.

"Ann . . ."

"Hear me out now," she said, setting down the mug and putting her hand on his shoulder. "You're accepting Michael for doing what Allen feels is the wrong thing. And rejecting Allen for doing what he thinks is right."

"But Allen is wrong," Ashton said.

"He doesn't think so," she said quickly. "And neither does Michael. And neither do you."

"Neither does anybody," Ashton said with a little snorting laugh.

They sat for a while in the comfortable silence of people whose love makes it pleasurable just to be with each other, no longer desperate for something to say.

"I'll talk with him," he said at last.

She only nodded.

"What's a seven-letter word for conflict?"

"Children."

"That has eight letters."

"See."

Everyone was startled. There had been quite an uproar in the courtroom.

Judge Dukes pounded her gavel and called for order, but the request had made her pleas impotent of threat.

"Your Honor," Harvey Turnbul explained above the din, "it is important that the room be cleared of all but the immediate family prior to the announcement of the name of the next witness."

"Your Honor," Bill Stockbridge demanded, standing as he had been since Harvey had asked that the courtroom be cleared, "we object to this grandstanding and to clearing the courtroom without knowing why."

"All right, all right," Judge Dukes said, tossing aside her gavel and standing. "Everyone sit down and shut up or I'm going to start having people arrested at random on contempt charges."

The new teeth in the threat brought a modicum of quiet.

"Now," Dukes said, sitting down again. "Will counsel approach the bench?"

They did.

"All right, Harvey," she snarled, switching off her microphone. "Who is it? And this had better be good."

"Hugh Golden," Harvey said quietly.

"That's pretty good," Judge Dukes said, sitting back. "Bill?"

"A moment, Your Honor?"

She nodded.

Hugh Golden was a former local television personality who had risen to national prominence. His job as host of the highly rated morning talk show *SunUp* had made his blond good looks, six-foot-four-inch frame and sincere blue-green eyes as familiar as national treasures.

"Who is it?" Michael asked as Bill came within range of a whisper.

The room was absolutely silent. Everyone craned to hear.

Bill, who was facing the crowd, took a pad of paper, wrote the name, folded the page and handed it to Michael.

A rustle of annoyance blew through the room.

"Clear the room," Michael said after a quick, covert look.

"What is it?" Bill asked, offering the pad and pen.

"Taffy pull," Michael said.

"Are you acquainted with Mr. Reily?" Harvey asked, surveying not his effect on the witness but the effect on the few shocked faces dotting the empty room.

"Yes," Hugh said in his well-modulated, though somewhat hollow, voice.

"How were you acquainted?" Harvey probed, looking at Michael.

"We met through mutual friends," Hugh said indolently, making it difficult for Harvey as much from the habit of lying as for spite.

Michael smiled at Harvey.

"Were you . . . intimately acquainted?" Harvey said, snapping his head to look at Hugh. A flash of anger flickered in his eyes and went out.

"Yes," Hugh said simply, the announcer's voice gone.

"How so?" Harvey said, and stopped. He stared hard at Hugh.

Hugh stared back at him. He hated Harvey for doing this to him. He hated himself for doing it. "We were lovers," he said evenly, measuring out each syllable. "Briefly," he added, looking away.

"How would you describe your relationship with Mr. Reily?" Harvey asked, arms folded, looking from one to the other.

"Your Honor," Bill said disgustedly, leaving it at that.

"Mr. Turnbul," she said like a prim schoolteacher calling down an errant pupil, "this does seem a bit afield. This is a probate hearing, not a fishing expedition."

"Judge Dukes," Harvey said, sidling in her direction, "we are seeking to create an accurate picture of life with Mr. Reily. The home environment is of crucial interest in considering the welfare of the child."

Hugh's cheeks burned. His heart raced. He felt oddly afraid and exhilarated by his public admission of something so long held private.

He looked at Michael. He was a little pale, he looked a little older, he wasn't smiling, but that was Michael's only real concession to time and to the horror surrounding him. Michael sat doodling on a pad in front of him, mussing his hair on one side with the hand he leaned his head against. He looked good in a suit, Hugh thought; it must have taken some argument from the lawyer to get him into one. Michael had hated even going places where a suit was required.

"It's so hypocritical," he had said to Hugh. "I mean, you know no one else there wants to wear one. So why go?"

Michael smiled to himself as though he could hear Hugh's thoughts. Hugh smiled, exhilarated by the same freedom he had always felt around Michael.

"All right, all right, Mr. Turnbul," the judge was saying. "But when the court feels the portrait is complete or that you are gilding the frame, we will stop this."

"Certainly, Your Honor," Harvey said, turning on Hugh, who was smiling absently, lost in memories. "Mr. Golden," Harvey said, startling Hugh a bit, "how would you describe your—"

"I remember the question," Hugh said, cutting him off.

Michael looked up.

"I've just been thinking about that," Hugh continued. "I think the best description would be tumultuous."

"Tumultuous?" Harvey repeated it as a question.

"Yes. Michael's life was always so frenetic. This sort of high drama," he said, gesturing to indicate the courtroom. "It doesn't really seem out of the ordinary for Michael."

Michael smiled.

"There was a kind of honesty about him that seemed almost confrontational, like a child saying or asking what everyone was avoiding. It either made people furious or made them love him, but no one ignored him."

"How did you feel?" Harvey asked.

"What is this, analysis?" Hugh snapped.

"Just answer the question."

"Well, it attracted me. And it made me furious. It was like being on a runaway bus in rush-hour traffic. Everything that happened was somehow larger than life—out of control."

"How long were you together?"

"Oh, maybe six months, but we saw each other around for some time afterward."

"Was Mr. Reily unable to make a commitment?" Harvey asked, bored with the sentimental ramblings.

"I don't know," Hugh said honestly. "I think I never really gave him the chance. I was afraid of him."

"Afraid of him? How?"

"It's hard to say," Hugh said, shrugging, searching for the words. "It was like there was a choice—Michael or the rest of the world—and I was afraid to make that choice."

"Were you physically afraid?" Harvey asked, needled.

"No." Hugh laughed. "No one would be physically afraid of Michael. No, it was more like . . . life burned more brightly in Michael and I didn't want to be burned up. I know that's a little poetical, but well, you know Michael. Isn't he sort of intimidating?"

"It would be inappropriate for me to say," Harvey said, blushing and looking away, certain of the feeling and equally unable to describe it. "What was the cause of the split between you?" he asked, changing the subject.

"I was," Hugh said curtly.

"Was there an incident that brought the—" pause, two—"situation to an end?" Harvey pried.

"You mean, what was the dirt?" Hugh asked, sneering.

Michael was looking down at the pad, obviously repressing a laugh.

"Was there—"

"Yes," Hugh said. "We had a major ripsnorting, domestic disturbance, four-alarm fight, during which Michael climbed onto the kitchen cabinet and threw dishes at me. How's that?"

"And that brought an end—" Harvey began, beaming at having finally gotten to the testimony he was after.

"No, it didn't," Hugh said, cutting Harvey's glee short. "That was the dirt. Michael's behavior was my fault. He found me on the sofa with someone else. More dirt. We split up several days later, following a long, rational, and thoroughly embarrassing conversation. But that's hardly worth mentioning when there's dirt."

"Had Michael been drinking?" Harvey asked, jaws stony with anger.

"When?" Hugh asked blankly.

"When he threw the—"

"Yes."

"Did he drink a lot?"

"Well, not—"

"Did he—"

"Yes."

"Did he tend toward violent or wild behavior when he drank?"

"So did every—"

"Did he tend—"

"—college student—"

"—toward violent or wild behavior—"

"—I've ever known."

"—when he was drinking?"

Both men were shouting and breathless.

"Yes or no?"

"Yes," Hugh shouted. "And no."

"Either he did or he didn't," Harvey shouted back.

"Nothing is that absolute," Hugh said, matching Harvey's tone. Then quietly: "Certainly not Michael."

"He was unpredictable?"

"You're putting words in my—"

"Is that why you were afraid of him?" Harvey demanded.

"Is that why you're afraid of him?" Hugh shouted back.

"No further questions," Harvey said, turning away.

"How about you, Senator," Hugh shouted. "Is that what frightens you?"

"We'll take five minutes to calm down," Judge Dukes said with a perfunctory tap.

"He's better looking in person," Mindy said under her breath. "What did he see in Michael?"

The statement made Allen feel defensive. He thought of a whole list of reasons but suppressed his urge to respond to the offense.

"Allen?"

He turned to see his father standing at the end of the aisle where he and Mindy sat. He stared. His father hadn't spoken to him since throwing Mindy and him out of the house.

"Allen, your mother and I would like to have lunch with the two of you," Ashton said, looking intently at the empty seat next to his son. "If you're free."

"No," Allen said stupidly. "That would be fine."

"Great. We'll, um, see you at lunch recess," Ashton said, backing away like some shy, awkward schoolboy after asking for a date.

"Yeah. See you," Allen said.

Mindy punched him. He turned and shrugged in response to her comically overdone, cross-eyed, inquisitive look.

Hugh had sat in the witness box, sipping water brought him by the bailiff. He stole occasional glances at Michael, who was talking quietly with Bill Stockbridge. Michael's laughter rang out in the quiet. He was nodding vigorously and smiling when Hugh looked. He must be confirming the dishes, Hugh thought smiling. He looked over and saw Harvey chattering away to Senator Miller, who didn't seem to be paying any attention.

Judge Dukes rustled back into the courtroom. "Keep your seats," she said, preempting the bailiff, who sat down in a slighted huff. "Mr. Stockbridge?" she said, wrestling her enormous chair into place.

"Thank you," Bill said, rising and crossing up to Hugh.

Hugh set his half-finished glass of water on the flat wooden rail in front of him.

"Mr. Golden," Bill said, nodding deferentially.

Hugh smiled, amused by the formality.

"Do you remember your tumultuous times with Mr. Reily fondly?" he asked abruptly.

"Yes," Hugh answered, smiling. "Very."

"In spite of the tumult?"

"Yes."

"In spite of the fact he threw dishes at you?"

"Yes," he said, laughing a little.

"He must be a terrible shot," Bill said.

"Michael?" Hugh asked, surprised. "You should see him play boccie ball."

"I have," Bill said. "But he missed hitting you with all those dishes? Maybe it was the drinking."

"I don't think I've ever seen Michael play boccie sober," Hugh said.

"Yet he missed you with every single plate?" Bill asked.

"Well, he wasn't throwing them at me," Hugh said.

"Oh, I'm sorry," Bill said. "The attorney for the plaintiff had given me that impression."

"No," Hugh said, relieved to have a chance to defend Michael. "Michael breaks things when he's angry. But he's never hit anyone that I know of."

"Then you were not ever afraid of Michael attempting to injure you, even when he was drinking?" Bill asked, rubbing his chin.

"No. Never."

"And this drinking, was Michael drunk frequently at work or in class?"

"Never. Michael likes to drink, but even in college," Hugh said, looking at Harvey, "Michael showed good judgment about when."

"Do you think anyone need fear physical harm from Michael?"

"No."

"Even when he's drinking?"

"No."

"One last question, Mr. Golden," Bill said, walking halfway back to the desk and then turning. "Do you think Michael would make a good parent?"

"The best," Hugh said, catching Michael's eye and smiling. "I've never known Michael to do anything halfway."

"Thank you," Bill said, turning and walking back to his desk.

"The plaintiff rests," Harvey said without conviction, half standing.

"Court is adjourned until two o'clock."

They sat in uncomfortable silence, trying to eat lunch. Everyone had taken turns at breaking the chill.

"Ann, isn't Hugh Golden even better-looking in person?" Mindy asked with that conspiratorial "us girls" tone that Ann hated.

"I've known Hugh since . . . for some time," Ann said. She had not picked up the thread, and "How long?" was too uncomfortable a question, so it died.

"This is certainly a nice restaurant," Allen said.

"Yes." Ash smiled. "You know Michael handles—handled their advertising. Before."

All roads led back to the problem.

So everyone sat in embarrassed silence for some time.

"I know you're doing what you think is right," Ashton mumbled.

Everyone looked up and eyed one another sweatily.

"I understand," Ash said, focusing intently on the greasy leaves of his spinach salad. He cleared his throat. "I don't agree, but I understand." He waited for a response.

Allen stared at the top of his father's head.

"We all do what we think is right," Ashton said, looking up and startling himself as he found himself looking into Allen's eyes.

They both looked away.

"Thanks, Dad," Allen said, looking back.

"We're still a family," Ashton said, meeting his son's gaze. "Even after this mess."

"That means a lot," Allen said quietly.

"You're just as important to me as Michael is," Ashton said, reaching to put his hand on his son's. Instead he spilled his son's iced tea.

Ann laughed. Then Ashton. Then Allen. Then Mindy.

While the waiter didn't find it nearly as amusing, he did find the table easier to wait and the tips Ann and Allen left to compensate for Ashton's quite satisfactory.

"Are you prepared to present your case, Mr. Stockbridge?" Judge Dukes asked after bringing the once again noisy courtroom to order.

"We are, Your Honor," Bill said, standing.

After the morning's quiet the crowd was clamoring for information. The fact that Harvey had rested his case in secret had whetted their appetites for some hint as to the nature of the morning's secrecy. The best place to look was in the defense. It was understandable, then, that the crowd sat starved with anticipation as the defense began.

"Proceed," the judge pronounced.

"We call Ashton Reily," Bill said.

Ashton rose and crossed to the stand.

If Harvey's presentation had been characterized by tension and formality, Bill's program was its antithesis.

"Ashton," Bill began, dispensing with preliminaries, "you are Michael's father?"

"Yes," Ashton said, at once at ease with an old friend.

"Are you homosexual?" Bill asked with the same casual ease.

The feast was served. The room erupted like a banquet following the invocation.

"Quiet," Dukes said. Even she was surprised. "Mr. Stockbridge, I hardly see—"

"Our meaning will become clear, Your Honor," Bill said, still smiling and pleasant. "With your permission?"

The judge shrugged her bewildered assent.

"Are you homosexual?" Bill repeated.

"No," Ashton said simply, a little stunned as well.

"To the best of your knowledge, is your son Michael a homosexual?"

Dessert was served—flambé.

"Last warning," Dukes called, pounding.

Ashton looked at Michael. Michael smiled and nodded. Ashton looked back at Bill, sighed and said, "Yes."

"Do you think your heterosexuality had anything to do with your son's homosexuality?" Bill asked, rising above the clatter.

"No." Ashton laughed nervously.

"Was your daughter a homosexual?"

"No."

The crowd was becoming numb to the word as the questions continued.

"Was she aware of your son's homosexuality?"

"Yes."

"Was her husband?"

"Yes."

"Do you think Michael would make a good parent?" Bill asked abruptly.

Ashton looked startled. "Yes, of course," he said.

"No further questions," Bill said. "Thank you, Mr. Reily."

"Mr. Turnbul?" the judge asked.

Harvey and the senator sat in stunned silence as they had throughout the questioning. Stockbridge was proving beyond a shadow of a doubt what they had spent two days trying to imply.

"Mr. Turnbul?" the judge prompted.

Harvey sat considering what he should do.

"Aren't you going to ask him anything?" Robert said, punching Harvey in the arm.

"What would you ask?" Harvey hissed over his shoulder.

"What is Bill up to?" Robert asked, sitting back.

"Mr. Turnbul?" the judge demanded.

"Uh, Your Honor," Harvey said, half standing, "we think the defense is making our points for us very nicely."

"Very well," Judge Dukes said. "You're excused, Mr. Reily."

"We call Ann Reily," Bill said.

Ann and Ash exchanged a look and a shrug as they passed.

The room was strangely quiet. Everyone wondered what Bill was up to.

"Ann," Bill began in the same easy tone, "you are Michael's mother?"

"Yes."

"Are you homosexual?"

"No," she answered, more prepared for the question.

"To the best of your knowledge, is your son Michael a homosexual?"

"Yes."

"Do you think your heterosexuality had anything to do with your son's homosexuality?"

"No."

The questions continued as before.

"Do you think Michael will make a good parent?" he concluded.

Ann glowed. "Yes," she said, beaming at Michael. "Tops."

"No further questions," he said. "Thanks, Ann."

She smiled and nodded.

"Mr. Turnbul?"

Harvey shook his head.

"We call Allen Reily."

Allen was shocked.

"Your Honor," Harvey said, rising, "Mr. Stockbridge has already had his chance with Mr. Reily."

"Your Honor, this is a hearing, not a trial, and Mr. Reily has always been a part of our plan for defense. It would not have been effective to question Mr. Reily at that time—"

"Mr. Reily?" Judge Dukes said, cutting Bill off. "Allen," she clarified. "Would you mind testifying for the defense? I think you have a pretty good idea what you will be asked."

Allen looked from the judge to Harvey, who was shaking his head, then to his parents. His father only smiled. "No, Your Honor," he said, looking at her.

There was some minor rumbling in the courtroom. Harvey turned around and folded his hands smugly in his lap.

"I would not mind testifying," Allen concluded, rising.

"Allen," Mindy grabbed his arm.

Allen looked at her. She released his arm. He took his seat in the witness stand.

"Thank you, sir," Bill said.

Allen nodded coldly.

"You are Michael's brother?"

"Yes."

"Are you a homosexual?"

"No."

"To the best of your knowledge, is Michael a homosexual?"

"Yes." Allen's answers were quick and expressionless. He knew what to expect.

"Do you think your parents' heterosexuality had anything to do with Michael's homosexuality?"

"No."

"Do you think your parents' heterosexuality had anything to do with your heterosexuality?"

"No," Allen said, then realizing: "Well, I mean yes."

"Well, which is it? Yes or no?"

"Yes," he said, flushed with vehemence.

"But you don't think it had any effect on Michael?" Bill asked.

"Well, no."

Harvey shook his head in disgust.

"How is that possible?" Bill asked. "Did they treat you differently?"

"I don't know," Allen said, looking at his parents. They sat quietly, solemnly looking at him. He smiled as he thought of how much he loved them. "No, they didn't treat us differently."

"How do you account for this inconsistency?" Bill asked calmly.

"Your Honor," Harvey shouted, jumping to his feet, "the witness is not qualified to speak on the causes of homosexuality. Even medical experts cannot agree on the cause."

Bill stood silent.

"Mr. Stockbridge?" the judge prompted.

"The plaintiff is making our point for us very nicely. No further questions," he said.

Harvey trembled into his seat; hot beads of anger stood as sweat on his upper lip.

"Aren't you going to ask me what kind of parent I think Michael will be?" Allen asked suddenly.

Everyone looked up.

"I think we all know how you feel about that," Bill said pleasantly.

"Because I think he'd make a terrific parent," Allen continued. "Don't get me wrong, I don't think Michael should raise Scott but not because I think he'd make a bad parent."

Everyone sat stunned, silent, staring at Allen.

Michael smiled. Allen was making his first scene.

"I mean, look at the evidence so far," Allen continued.

"Your Honor," Harvey said, finding his voice and his feet.

"He's been dragged through the mud; he's lost his home, his job, everything. Shut up, Harvey. If being a parent is being willing to sacrifice for the good of the child, no one here has been as willing as Michael."

Allen paused.

There was an unfriendly silence that no one wanted to disturb.

Ashton gave Ann's hand a squeeze in response to her sniffle.

"I'm sorry, Michael," Allen said at last, as surprised by his outburst as everyone else was.

"Do you have any questions of this witness?" Judge Dukes asked a still-standing Harvey Turnbul, in an effort to get back on track.

"Uh. No," Harvey said hoarsely.

"Mr. Reily, you may return to your seat if you're through," she said gently to Allen.

He nodded and rose. He crossed back through the silence to his seat. Mindy stared straight ahead, hands tucked under her arms, as Allen joined her.

"We call Michael Reily."

Michael rose. He found his way to the stand in the mist of whispers that filled the courtroom.

"Michael," Bill began, "are you a homosexual?"

"Yes," Michael said into the vacuum of silence that followed the question.

"Were your sister and brother-in-law aware of that fact?"

"Yes."

"Yet they chose to leave the care of their child to you?"

"Yes."

"In your opinion, were Bob and Kathryn competent to make decisions regarding the welfare of the child?"

"No one tried to take the child away from them while they were alive." Michael smiled.

"Do you want to raise the child?"

"More than anything."

"No further questions."

"Mr. Turnbul?" Judge Dukes said, tensing, anticipating the blow for Michael.

Harvey rose slowly. He walked to the stand deliberately, as if choosing each step carefully. "Michael," he began with the same deliberate air, "do you have a lover?"

"No."

"Have you ever had a lover?"

"Not really."

"No emotional commitments?"

"Well, I have friends and family . . . and Scott."

"But none beyond that?"

"Well . . . no."

"Do you plan to"—pause, two—"take a lover?"

"No more or less than anyone else plans to."

"But the possibility does exist."

"It hasn't happened yet."

"But it could."

"I suppose."

"So Scott could find himself raised by a homosexual couple?"

"It's possible."

"And you don't see any problem with that?"

"No."

"No?" Harvey said, his voice tinted with irony. "What about casual affairs?"

"What about them?" Michael asked, unsuccessfully battling the irritation in his voice.

"Will you subject the child to them?"

"No."

"So you'll stay away from home?"

"No. I won't subject myself to them either. There won't be any."

"A healthy adult male with no"—pause, two, three—"lover? How will you take care of those urges?"

"I'm not an animal in rut, Harvey," Michael said contemptuously.

"But surely you have the same needs as the rest of us?"

"Yes. Including parenting."

"And sexually?" Harvey asked.

"Yes," Michael said tensely.

"Well, what about those needs?"

"My parents had a healthy sex life while I was a child."

"They were married."

"They had that option."

"Your Honor," Bill said, rising, "Mr. Reily has admitted to being homosexual. What is counsel's point in this line of questioning?"

"Your Honor, our point is that the child will be raised in the home of a practicing homosexual. We don't feel that's a suitable environment for a child. Irrespective of the wishes of the child's parents."

"Point taken," Judge Dukes said tersely. "Move on."

A strange quiet had settled through the room. The matter-of-fact tone of the defense had infected the hearing. There was no sensational testimony, no reluctant admissions sweated out under intense cross-examination. It was dull by comparison to the previous few days.

Mindy and Allen sat rigidly, merely occupants of adjacent seats. Senator Miller had become sober, silent, detached from the proceedings. Ann and Ashton held hands, their grip tight with tension.

"Do you think that you can provide a suitable environment for raising the child in spite of your sexuality?"

"No one knows that going into it," Michael said, smirking. "Ask me in thirty years."

"But you have no plans to change your lifestyle during that period."

"No."

"Then you cannot assure this court that the child will not be exposed to homosexual behavior?"

"I can assure this court that the child will not be exposed to sexual behavior of any sort—at home, anyway."

"You think so?" Harvey asked mockingly.

Michael only looked at him.

"No further questions," Harvey said with a derisive snort, and turned away.

He was as annoyed with his cross-examination as he was with Michael. The brevity and openness of the defense had diffused him. Rather than answer his charges, they had admitted everything. His charges seemed petty even to him. He looked at his client. Robert sat leaning on folded arms, looking at his reflection in the shiny surface of the desk.

All the juice had been squeezed out of the case and all that remained was the ugly, distorted rind.

"If I could, Your Honor, I'd like to say something," Michael said quietly, almost confidentially to the judge.

Harvey stopped short.

Everyone woke up, looked up. The boredom was broken. An electrical charge of tension buzzed in the room.

"Certainly you may," Judge Dukes said. "This is a hearing, not a formal trial."

Michael looked back at the capacity crowd. Ever since the funeral it had seemed that all of his personal life had been in the windows at Bloomingdale's.

He looked at Bill, who smiled and nodded. He smiled at his mother, took a deep breath and began.

"It's sort of hard to remember now, but all this is about a little baby and his life. We all want him to grow up to be happy and healthy. The question at hand is: Can I insure that. My answer is no. No one can insure that. Not me. Not the senator, no one. All I can do, all any of us can do is try. And that much I can promise.

"We don't know so much about what makes one man a murderer and another a saint. About what determines who a child will be. And love. And that's what this has really come to be about. Can a single homosexual man be a good parent?

"I didn't even think so at first. My sister and brother-in-law did. And part of the reason that they did is that they didn't know a single homosexual man; they knew me. A person. A person who was a man and who was a homosexual but who was a lot more than that. Hardworking, settled, funny, pretty bright, who was a lot like them, except in one small way.

"Being gay is not the main thing to know about me. It's comparatively minor next to other parts of me. It isn't something that I think about all the time. It isn't a set of standards by which I make decisions. My lifestyle is a lot like yours. Ordinary. Middle-class. Quiet.

"Just as it's now deemed unfair, even offensive, to perceive blacks as ignorant or promiscuous or *Amos and Andy*, it is unfair and offensive to judge me as a stereotype.

"The image that most people have of gay men is one of child-molesting, orgiastic, hedonist interior decorators involved continuously in lewd sexual activities in bars, baths and bushes. And the threat of AIDS hasn't helped. It's an offensive and repellent picture. But you must know I think it's offensive and repellent, too.

"There is a substantial segment of the heterosexual population who are child-molesting, orgiastic, hedonists. Even interior decorators. It outnumbers the same segment in gay men and women. But that is not the picture we have of heterosexuals.

"If ten percent of the population is gay, a sizable number of those people must just be leading ordinary lives. You don't know about them because they are afraid of your persecution and because they are—save the one small difference—just like you. So they're invisible.

"I don't hang out in bars, attend orgies, molest children or want to wear women's clothes. I want the same things you want. I want a home, work that makes me feel useful, love and companionship. And I want this child. It's my chance to do something that ordinary circumstances would have denied me.

"I love him so much that I won't lie to you to protect myself. I won't participate in the bigotry.

"And I want to be judged here. Me. Not the picture bigotry paints. I wouldn't give that person a child to raise either. But I'm not that picture.

"So in a way, this is a trial about something bigger than a baby. It is a trial about prejudice. There is no indication that being raised by heterosexual parents is a guarantee. Most homosexuals had heterosexual parents, I guess. I did.

"So am I a fit parent? I don't know yet. I won't know for some time. But I do know this: I will share my strong belief that people are unique and should be taken that way, not by some arbitrary standard. And that you should stand up for what you believe. It's obvious Scott's parents felt that way. Maybe that's why they chose me."

Michael met the senator's stare.

"We're all doing what we think is right. But right isn't absolute.

It's what we think. And it's what we've learned. We used to think separate but equal was right. We learned we were wasting people. And that isn't right anymore.

"What I think is right now, Scott will have trouble with in thirty years. Because he will have learned things I didn't. That's the wonder of children."

The senator's eyes stung with tears he shared with Michael.

"I ask to be considered and granted or denied custody as a parent, not as a single gay man.

"And please bear in mind, your honor, that Scott has already learned to say uncle."

BOOK

II

SCOTT

My first memories of my uncle are of his nose.

When I was young, I'm not sure how young, he owned and operated a small theatre during the summer season at the beach. As part of his marketing program, he acquired one of those bicycle-powered hot dog carts that vendors pedal up and down the beach, selling their wares to the greasy tourists caking the shoreline. From his cart Uncle Michael sold tickets to the theatre.

Each day, during prime suntanning hours, he piled me into the modified relish tray of the cart and we went in search of theatre patrons.

From my vantage under the green and white canvas umbrella affixed to the cart, my gaze fell not where we were headed but back into the face of the cart's power source—Uncle Michael. It was quite a face. Hat emblazoned with the name of the theatre, dark glasses and about a quart of zinc oxide protecting his nose.

The white contrast against tanned skin and ebony glasses made his nose float, disembodied before my eyes. Six hours a day, five days a week. I probably never spent so much time since looking into his face, and I suppose, like a baby duck, I imprinted that face—that nose—on my young mind and carried it forward into life.

Like Uncle Michael's nose, my memories of those years of dawning recognition float disembodied in my mind. Vague images and feelings, like faces and unicorns in the clouds, materialize and dissolve in my memory without design or order.

It was a time of fantasy, as are most childhoods, but I tend to feel that it was more fantastic than for other children. Maybe everyone feels that way. I guess the world seems magic to the uninitiated. But the hard edges of reality were only a small part of our lives then and growing up was more a matter of finding those edges than simply coming to accept them.

Though I was not aware of the necessity for some years, I eventually discovered that I had had parents but that they were killed when I was quite young. Even then, I felt the loss only insofar as I understood that the other children possessed something that I did not.

To be fair, I truly never wanted for family.

I grew up in a world of adults, all of whom were my aunt or uncle somebody—in that casual sense that the title is granted to imply closeness without establishing a specific relationship with a child who has no need, or understanding, of such things.

There was always Uncle Michael, Gray, Uncle Allen, but because of the theatre, there were always great quantities of uncles and aunts who came and went as the bill changed. And because the requirements of one play and the next were different, I found that my family included every hue, shade, and gradation of humanity. They were none of these labels to me, just aunts and uncles.

And they could do the most wondrous things: dance, sing, play the piano, laugh and cry without meaning it.

Gray and I sat with Uncle Michael through rehearsals and openings, hits and bombs. I saw my aunts and uncles undergo miraculous changes in the way that they behaved and looked and treated one another and then returned to themselves at the appointed time.

And I grew up with no illusions about the theatre—only life.

The first play that I remember, as such, was a production of *Cat on a Hot Tin Roof*. I actually appeared as one of the "no-neck monsters" and, I think, remember the play only because it marked my stage debut.

The experience sticks with me not because of the terror it struck in my young soul—indeed, I had spent so much time in theatres that nothing seemed more natural to me than standing before a crowd of people to speak my part—but because it was the first time I realized what a play was: that there was a plot, a point to be made and that the performers were trying to simulate real life, to behave as "real people" would.

It was not enough for Uncle Michael that I merely be pushed onto the stage to sing *"Skin-A-Mirink"* or that I run across the stage with a sparkler at the appointed time. He was determined that I understand the play and my part in it.

"Scott," I heard Uncle Michael call, "it's time."

"Now pay attention," Gray said, brushing my hair. "This is *très important* to your uncle."

"*Oui, oui,* Gray," I said, struggling to get away from his preening grasp. "*Donne-le moi—*"

"Hold still," Gray said gently. "No French. He doesn't understand and it makes him crazy."

"*Oui,* I mean yes," I said.

"Scott?" Uncle Michael screamed. "Gray? For crissakes. Where the hell is everyone?"

"In here," Gray shouted. "*Allons.* Run along, Scott."

I rose and ran to the door. Then, with a more solemn gait, I walked down the hall.

I loved my uncle, but he could be a forbidding man. At home he was easy and fun. But when there was business to be handled or the topic was *très important,* he became another person—the way the actors at the theatre did when the curtain went up.

I had seen him become this other person at the theatre with the actors when things were going badly. And with Uncle Bill Stockbridge on occasion when he arrived with "papers" for Uncle Michael. And with me on such occasions as the time I brought the hose into the living room to water the potted plants.

So as I approached the door to his den, I was not entirely sure if the curtain was up or down.

"There you are," he said, catching sight of me through the open door. "Come on in and sit down."

I obeyed, sitting stiffly beside him on the small sofa.

"How's it going, pal?" he asked.

I shrugged.

"You look lousy," he said. "Underwear on backward?"

I laughed.

"That's better," he said. "Let's talk about the play."

"Okay."

"Now, the most important part first," he said, putting his hands on my shoulders and looking into my face. "Do you really want to do this? Either way's okay with me."

"I'm sure," I said, trying to sound serious and grown-up.

"Scott," he said, letting go of me and reaching for a cigarette, "acting is work. Hard work. It doesn't seem that way to you and me because we've been there and we take things for granted when they're around all the time.

"Like me being your uncle," he said, lighting the cigarette. "I'm around all the time, and we have fun together, but I'm still responsible to see you have food and a home and that you go to the doctor when you're sick. Do you see?"

"I guess," I said, not really seeing.

"With acting you are responsible to the play and the other actors. See, a play is really just a story in a book, like the ones that Gray and I read to you. But with a play, you and the other actors pretend to be the people in the story and you act the story out.

"Now, how good you are depends on how real you make your part of the story. You have to make people think you really are that person, not Scott anymore. And the other actors do the same thing. And if you all do a very good job, then to the audience the play looks real. And it's a success.

"So, let's talk about this story and the little boy you're pretending to be. Okay?"

"Okay."

"Now this is a story about selfishness. Selfishness is when you are thinking only about yourself and not about anyone else. Remember your birthday and how you got upset because you didn't want anyone else to have any of your cake or the candy or favors?"

I nodded, solemnly remembering the ghastly thing and running to my room and crying myself to sleep, feeling oddly betrayed because neither Gray nor Uncle came to comfort me.

"Well, the feeling you had at the party was selfishness. And this play is about a whole family who felt that way. They were all very rich because the grandfather had worked hard and made a lot of money. But now the grandfather is going to die and all the aunts and uncles want the money.

"What the people in the story don't realize is that what they really want is love. Not the money. And to get that love, they all pretend to love the other people in the family. But the only way to get real love is to give it. And since it isn't real love they're giving, it's not real love they get back.

"Uncle Bob and Aunt Susan will play your mother and father.

And in the story they try to get the grandfather to love them because of you.

"And the little boy you play tries to get his mother and father to love him by doing what they want him to do. Kind of like you doing this play because a little part of you thinks I'll love you more if you do," he said, looking straight at me.

I felt my ears grow hot and red in my embarrassment. It felt as if Uncle Michael could read my mind and I felt hot waves of guilt welling up into tears in my eyes. I looked away.

He left me to squirm in the silence for an eternity. He rose and crossed to his desk, sat behind it, lit a cigarette and then blew a shaft of smoke into the autumn sun, cut out of the sky by the window behind him.

"Two things," he said at last. "First and most important, don't feel bad if a little part of you is doing this play to please me. We always do things to please the people we love. But I will love you just as much if you don't do the play. I want you to do what you want to do. I love you for who you are. That's real love. Okay?"

"Yes, Uncle," I said. "I really do want to."

"Good man," he said. "Come give me a hug."

I ran to the safety of his lap, and he held me there caught with him and the smoke in the warm shaft of light, the rest of the world hazy and dark around us.

"All right," he said, perching me on his knee. "The second part is harder to understand but *très important*."

I smiled in response.

"You must try very hard to remember the feeling you just had when I told you your secret. Those feelings were real. And that's the way the people in this story feel. Your job is to convince the audience that you feel that way during the play. And to do it, you must know how it really feels and pretend you really feel that way. That is acting, and it is the work of art—to capture real human feelings. Can you do that?"

"I'll try," I said, not wanting him to catch me again.

"Good," he said, lifting me down. "Now go and play. Gray will help you with your part tomorrow. It's up to you to make it real."

And so I came to be in my first play. Of it I have blurred

remembrances of the tension and triumph that are always back-stage and of the tears in Uncle Michael's eyes as he embraced me after the opening night.

But mostly I have the memory of my first acting lesson. It comes to me often, oddly enough, as my first brush with reality. For as Uncle Michael would say, "Good acting is just like real life."

Cat, as I came to call it, since everyone did, was fairly successful and ran most of the fall at the off-season theatre we had in town for income during the fall and winter months.

The fall and winter brought serious plays, the spring romantic comedies and the summer brought the beach and musicals. The summer theatre was what Uncle called "cabaret," which meant there were tiny tables and chairs and cool drinks and nibbles were served before, during and after the show in the chilly dark refuge from the thick heat of muggy, southern, coastal summer nights.

The theatre in town was called a "dessert theatre"—more mar-keting. What it boiled down to was that there was a restaurant and a theatre and you could have dinner and then a show with your dessert. Or just dinner if you'd seen the show. Or just dessert and a show if you'd already had dinner. All in all, the place was as popular as a restaurant as it was a theatre and it came to be open year-round as both.

Holidays were the best. We threw huge parties, and hundreds of people paid one price for dinner and a show and sometimes dancing and even champagne breakfast on New Year's.

There was a costume party for Halloween, a Thanksgiving buf-fet, a Christmas wassail, Fourth of July fireworks at the beach, green beer on St. Patrick's and, when I was still small, Gray dressed me in banner and diaper as the New Year and carried me in at midnight.

And there was always a family table reserved for us: Gray and Uncle, of course, but also Uncle Allen and Grammy Ann and Paw-paw Ash and the senator.

Those were the best times. I guess all former children feel that way.

And there was always fabulous food pouring out of the

kitchen, drawing crowds and making my family bigger and bigger.

Now that I think of it, it was that kitchen that changed our lives, that brought an end to my childhood fantasy and that brought real life to me—or brought me to real life.

It was my sixth Christmas. Because my birthday was in the spring, it was still only my fifth year.

"Wondrous school," a topic on which Gray and Uncle waxed poetic, was coming. *Cat* was over a year behind me and I was an old hand at theatre, having appeared in two other plays since.

The only private party we gave was on Christmas Eve, a tradition of Uncle's, and it was approaching.

Every year all the aunts and uncles conspired in secret to put together a play for Uncle and me. The theatre and the restaurant were dark—theatre talk for closed—for the holiday and the party was held there. There was an eight o'clock curtain and then a party till midnight and then Uncle gave out the presents. The shows were parodies of the shows from the previous season with lots of rewritten songs and playful pokes at Uncle, mainly, but also everyone else.

While the aunts and uncles conspired to put on the show, Uncle and Gray conspired to put on the party.

In spite of the fact that he owned and operated a very successful restaurant, Uncle Michael was no cook. So he helped plan, but Gray ran the kitchen.

And that's really how it happened at breakfast one morning. I use the term "breakfast" pretty loosely. Since our life in the theatre kept us up nights, breakfast was late and rare.

"Scott," Gray said, tapping on my door as he opened it, "breakfast, if you want."

"Maybe cocoa," I said, stirring.

"Well, you know where it is," Gray said, starting to withdraw. "Oh," he said, turning back, "Uncle's hung over, so hold it down."

And he left.

I groaned and began climbing out of bed.

By the time I got to the kitchen, Gray was frying bacon as quietly as possible and Uncle sat staring ambivalently at the glass of tomato juice, and God knows what else, sitting before him. The only sign of life coming from him at all was the occasional glowing of the ember on the cigarette stuck haphazardly into his mouth and the subsequent gusts of smoke as he exhaled.

"Cocoa, s'il vous plaît," I said, dropping heavily into my chair.

"No French," Uncle said, and then began to cough violently.

"You know, Uncle," I said as the fit died down, "you shouldn't smoke. It's so bad for your health."

"You know, Scott," he said, "you shouldn't nag me about my smoking. It could be so bad for your health."

"Don't be a smart-ass," I said. "What would you do if I smoked?"

"The same thing I'm going to do if you don't piss off about the smoking." He snorted, hiding the smile I could still see in his eyes. "Kill you."

"So it's do as I say, not as I do?" I asked as Gray set my cocoa in front of me.

"You see, Gray," he said. "I told you we should have taken that baby we saw at Bloomies. The one labeled kind of stupid but very respectful. You," he said, turning and pointing at me, "are the last baby I'm ordering out of the back of the *New Yorker*, yes the *New Yorker*."

"I'm serious," I said.

"Piss up a rope," he said, lighting a fresh cigarette off the end of the last one.

"Okay, boys, no fighting at table," Gray said, sitting down as he put a platter of food in front of us.

"No food," Uncle groaned.

"If you didn't drink and smoke . . ." I began.

"I'd have to take up a hobby," he cut in. "Like child abuse."

"Michael," Gray said, shifting the conversation, "speaking of food."

"We were not speaking of food," Uncle said, turning green as he watched me shoveling breakfast onto my plate. "Smelling it is bad enough."

"Well, we have to," Gray said. "Talk about food, I mean. For the party."

"Not now," Uncle said, waving him away. "Let's talk about coffee."

"Well, when?" Gray asked, rising to get the coffeepot.

"Later," Uncle said. "I'll work it out."

"Hunh," Gray snorted, putting the coffee in front of him. "What you'll do is come up with lots of impossible *merde* for me to work out at the last minute."

I laughed and choked slightly, spitting cocoa back into my cup.

"No French at breakfast," Michael said, sipping at his coffee. "And what do you mean 'for you to work out'? We do the food together."

"Don't be ridiculous," Gray said, sitting down. "You couldn't slice a cake with the recipe, set aside bake one."

"I could so."

"Mendacity," I said, sniffing the air. "I smell mendacity."

"You know a lot of men get respect at their own breakfast table," Uncle said, slouching in his chair.

"A lot of men can cook, too," Gray said. "You're just not one of them."

"*Merde*," Uncle muttered, slouching further.

"Uncle Michael," I said, giggling, "French? At breakfast?"

"And you," he said to me. "I can't believe you'd take sides with this Canadian mukluk against your own flesh and blood. You know," he said, leaning toward me and whispering dramatically, "I understand he's in the country illegally."

"Okay," Gray said. "I challenge you."

"To what?" Uncle asked. "The Constitution at twenty paces? All spies know that stuff. Who turned down the Academy Award for best actor in 1973?"

"I challenge you to a bake-off," Gray said, undaunted.

"A bake-off?" Uncle said incredulously.

"Yes. We'll let the guests at the party decide."

"And if you lose, you have to quit smoking," I jumped in, clapping my hands.

"That's it," Gray shrieked, leaping to his feet.

We burst into an impromptu version of the *"Marseillaise,"* and we sang and danced all over Uncle's hangover.

"That does it," he said, wincing and leaning into his hands. "I'm never coming to breakfast here again."

And the bet was on.

When there was not a play in production, Uncle Michael actually had quite a bit of free time, and he began spending it in the kitchen at the restaurant.

After more than a few fires and one small explosion that occurred when he left a can of spray shortening in the oven, we agreed that cheesecake, which required "limited pyrotechnics," as Uncle put it, was an acceptable gauntlet.

Uncle Michael had always loved cheesecake and plunged with renewed vigor into the project. Aside from making such an extravagant mess that the kitchen staff symbolically threw him into the Dumpster out back, the project proceeded without incident.

When I was a baby, Gray had read me the story of the tortoise and the hare. Often. And at Uncle Michael's insistence. He liked it because it taught hard work as a virtue. And though he dismissed the "ass-aching moralizing" of most other fables as "simpering tommyrot," this one was okay. At the time though, we didn't remember and sat idly by, a pair of napping hares laughing at Uncle Michael's plodding culinary project.

Confidently, Gray assembled his own cheesecake on Christmas Eve morning.

By the time the evening began everyone at the party knew about the bet. There was even a song about it in the show, sung to the tune of *"You're Just in Love"* from Irving Berlin's *Call Me Madam* and performed by Gray and yours truly:

> [Me] *I smell burning in the evening air,*
> *I hear explosions from the kitchen there.*
> *Someone's been baking in the Tupperware*
> *I don't know why.*
> *I wonder why?*
>
> *Our kitchen's ready for the last rites,*
> *The busboys look ready for another fight.*
> *The guy who used to live with me and Gray*

Is now always away.
I wonder why?

[Gray] *You can't bake under the broiler,*
You still need water in a double boiler.
We don't know how you got so far in life.

We challenged you to bake a cake, but
You misunderstood and baked a quake. Now
You're measuring in Richter, not Fahrenheit.

We think you're still a great director,
But as a cook you ain't worth heck, dear.
And let us say this once, our turtledove.

There is nothing you can bake
That's won't make our stomach ache.
You can't cook, but you're still our love.

Then both verses are sung in counterpoint. The effect was wonderful and quite the hit of the show.

Of course, we had underestimated Uncle Michael there, too.

He had hired trumpeters and arranged for a tabbed-curtain opening that might have heralded the Second Coming more appropriately than a cheesecake. But this was no ordinary cheesecake. This was Uncle Michael's nougat, caramel, hazelnut cheesecake with cream cheese crust and glacé du Napoléon—French yet. It was premiered after the play and entered "humbly" against Gray's Lindy Chocolate Cheesecake Supreme. Needless to say, we overconfident hares were found wanting, having underestimated our opponent. Uncle Michael's "Gambler's Cheesecake," as it came to be called, was, and is, the best cheesecake I have ever tasted. It was also no contest and Uncle passed out golden souvenir packages of cigarettes to celebrate.

He was not, however, so generous with the recipe. That he wisely guarded.

Gambler's Cheesecake was added to our menu, but our customers were soon no longer content to buy it a slice at a time, and before long we were selling whole cakes by the order.

And then it happened that a top dog from Macy's New York, who was visiting the local branch operation, came by to see *Anything Goes* and ordered a piece of Gambler's. He loved it; everyone did.

And after a period of intense negotiation between Macy's and Uncle Michael and Uncle Bill Stockbridge, it became possible to buy Gambler's Cheesecake at Macy's.

And then there was a specialty shop in Macy's called Gambler's.

And then there were specialty shops everywhere called Gambler's.

And then we were rich.

And then everything changed.

But I'm getting ahead of myself.

～ ～ ～

Until we can more fully understand the birth trauma and its effect on the human psyche, it is my firm assertion that the first day of school is the greatest trauma affecting the modern human experience.

Try as they might, neither Gray nor Uncle could adequately have prepared me for the sense of desolate abandonment that was school.

Aside from the ordinary pangs of nest separation, I had little experience of other children and absolutely none of "real people"—more theatre talk meaning nontheatre people. I was a stranger in a strange land and I wanted an exit visa from the first.

Of course, the boys had done their part.

Gray and I had spoken of the joys of being with other children my own age. And Uncle Michael and I had had "a talk."

"Sit down, Scott."

I climbed into one of the armless stuffed chairs facing his desk—the ones I was always afraid of falling out of—and held on for dear life.

"Scott," he began so seriously I thought I was in trouble. "Scott, you're about to begin the most important experience of your life. School. You will gain the skills you need for the rest of your life. Your first year will introduce you to math and science, but that'll be a lot of crap like 'If I have two apples and I eat one, how many will I have left?' And science will be gathering leaves and petting cows in barnyards, which might actually be fun; I don't know how you feel about agriculture. But they will also begin intense instruction in the language. And that is the key to everything."

He paused—for effect, I knew. I sat smiling weakly, thinking of running away from home.

"I know that you feel that you already speak the language and French besides. And Gray has helped you with your reading. But what you don't know is that reading and writing will allow you to do anything you want for the rest of your life. Those two skills will unlock the greatest thoughts of the greatest minds that have been and will be."

Heady stuff for a six-year-old.

"Now, when I was young, and dinosaurs ruled the earth, they began the process with the alphabet and a lot of 'A is for apple' horseshit that will drive you out of your mind. And I have no reason to believe that's changed. But be patient with them because what they don't tell you is that the alphabet is a tool that has taken thousands of years to develop. You can't toss that off. It is the basis for all human knowledge. Pay attention. Eventually they'll start letting you read. And the books will be dreadful. Miserable story line, one-dimensional characters and a lot of sneaky moralizing. But those stupid books are like the scales Gray is teaching you on the piano. They are a test of skill, warm-ups for the good stuff. Once you've learned the notes, you can play anything you want.

"Now I expect you to do well; you're bright. Do what they ask of you in math and science. Pursue the visual arts if they appeal to you. But do more than you have to in language. Okay?"

I nodded solemnly, trying not to cry.

"And now the other important thing," he said, rising and coming from behind the desk to sit in the other impossible armless chair. "I'm sure you've heard that there are going to be other children there."

I smiled a little.

"They will be the hardest part of school."

My smile died.

"They will all seem to know one another. They will seem united in the purpose of hurting your feelings and humiliating you. You will feel like you're in a play and you don't know your lines. At least that's how I always felt."

His eyes got a little misty and he started blinking a lot, the way he did when he cried, and I suddenly felt as if I should comfort him.

"They'll do this," he said, rising, his voice breaking a little, "because you're not just like them. Because you'll know things they don't know. And because they'll know things you don't know.

"You see, school is also a place where we learn to be a part of the world. And while you're there, they'll try to make you fit easily into the world by making you the same as everyone else. Hold out. You're special. Don't let them change you."

Suicide, I thought. It's been fun and now I'll just kill myself and avoid all this.

"You do what you want. And you know that Gray and I love you and support you, and that's enough. If you have friends, great, but if you're lonely, that's okay, too. We're your friends. And the kids will come around. And they'll respect you for holding out.

"You see, what I didn't know was that all the kids felt just like me. But they gave in and became like everyone else. They were sorry they made that choice. And I reminded them they had made that choice. So they weren't really mean to me; they were trying to destroy the memory of what they had felt. Like Brick's drinking in *Cat*.

"So," he said, flopping down in the chair next to me, "learn to read and write and deal with assholes and you'll have a great life. Okay?"

I nodded.

"Pretty scary?"

I nodded and the tears shook loose.

"I know," he said, taking me in his arms. "But it would have been worse if I lied. And worse yet, you might have given in to them."

He held me, more or less, for the rest of the night. I got the feeling he was as frightened as I was. Once he even broke down and cried, squeezing me so tightly that it hurt.

But whatever his feelings then, they were obviously gone by the first day of school.

I was quite angry with him.

He got up early, a painful experience for all of us, and we had begun rehearsing a week or two in advance, Uncle Michael cursing whatever "son of a bitch had decided school should start at dawn" and getting into a heated argument with Gray about how "sleep deprivation was used in brainwashing."

In any case, the morning I was to depart for my date with

destiny he was quiet, morose, rushed through breakfast and left before we did. "Things to do at the theatre to get the Macy's order ready," he said.

I was furious. How could he just casually pitch me to the lions and rush off to make cheesecake?

So chip placed securely on my shoulder, I went with Gray to school.

Well, to say the least, it was far more hideous than I had imagined.

Gray and I arrived at the appointed time for "orientation," which meant a sort of grahams and juice mixer for parent types, students and teachers.

The building itself was a Victorian fright which might comfortably have housed Dr. Frankenstein and company. We were greeted out front by the headmaster, a dried-up old horror who might easily have been any of the aforementioned.

The school was what was locally called a church school, which meant small and private. While there were more notable private institutions locally, Uncle Michael refused to "countenance those bastions of bigotry" by supporting them. In truth many had come into existence as a result of the desegregation of the local public schools, but those reasons were largely forgotten and those campuses were largely integrated as well.

Still and all, Uncle was having none of them or of the public schools that he hated for imprisoning his spirit for so long.

So I was sent to an Episcopalian Church-run academy where chapel and religion were a part of the curriculum. Ironic really, considering I had been to church only at Christmas and Easter— Uncle Michael declaring his relationship with the Almighty "none of anybody's goddamn business."

In response to the seeming contradiction, Uncle had said simply that I was to be "exposed to all sorts of questionable influences" all my life and that I'd have to make up my own mind.

And so I stood on the steps of St. Francis Hall, shaking hands with a man of indeterminate age who wore what, for all intents and purposes, appeared to be a skirt and a Nehru—strictly passé—collar. He smelled of apples ripening and spoke like some demented idiot.

"Master Miller," he said.

I looked over my shoulder to see whom he was talking to.

"How are we today?" he asked.

"How would I know?" I asked, bewildered.

Gray discreetly pulled my hair in the back.

"Excited?" he asked.

"Get back to me after lunch," I said, trying to be jovial with this obviously deranged man with bad taste in clothes.

Another tug at my hair.

I turned on Gray.

"I'm Gray Rambeaux," he said, covering.

"The governess," I put in.

Nervous laughter and a glare from Gray.

"Headmaster Wilbury," said the crackpot, shaking Gray's hand.

"Pleased to meet you," Gray said.

"Best of luck to you, young man," the headmaster said, messing up my hair.

"You, too," I said, wondering what it was with my hair.

"You come see me if you need anything." The old man chortled.

Little did I realize that the senator had donated a fortune to the school, once Uncle had picked it out, in order to "grease the wheels," as he put it to the headmaster. So there was a good reason for the Wildebeest—as I came to call him—to know my name and meet us outside.

We had not walked twenty feet into the lobby before Gray yanked me into an alcove with a statue of St. Francis. "You have got to be nice to these people," he hissed at me.

"*Pourquoi?*" I snorted. "Uncle Michael said—"

"I might have known," Gray snapped. "Well, I'll handle Uncle. You must be nice. Promise."

"I was nice," I said with a shrug. "I didn't say a word about that absurd outfit. What is this? A remake of *The Bells of St. Mary's?*"

"Being nice doesn't just mean not insulting them to their faces, although I'll bet Uncle didn't mention that."

I shook my head no.

"Well, lookit," he said. "Try to be polite and respectful like—

well, you must have seen it on TV somewhere. Remember Heidi?"

"What a simp," I snorted.

"Oh, God," he moaned. "Just try to be nice. We'll talk about it when you get home."

Well, the day was downhill from there. The food at the mixer was ghastly. All the adults talked like the Wildebeest.

"How are we?"

"What's our name?"

Gray explained that that was because they expected him to answer, as most children were shy.

"Why ask me then?" I snorted.

The hair again.

Looking around me, I could see his point, though.

The choice seemed to be either rampaging little shit or thumb-sucking ninny.

When the time came for the great divide, I preferred to sit with the adults and said so.

More moronic laughter and hair pulling.

I relented.

We were seated at laughably small tables. The adults got coffee and doughnuts while they "observed" us "interacting." We got watery grapelike drink and stale graham crackers. I ordered cocoa. It never came.

I tried to make conversation. "Eating together is really a very symbolic act," I observed to the young man on my right.

He threw his juice on my sweater.

So much for chat at table.

But nothing, absolutely nothing could compare to the disturbance when the adults left us alone with Miss Tidwell. I thought the wailing and bellowing would never die.

Eventually, though, the hullabaloo was quelled and we got down to business. And what a business it was. The morning included a fascinating discussion of our daily schedule, the making of name cards for our desks and vague references to the alphabet suspended above the chalkboard with the promise that one day we would know all the letters and be able to make our own name cards.

What a thrill.

It was along about then, my attention wandering, that I first noticed him. He was an elderly gardener mutilating the shrubbery outside the window. I watched him for a while and eventually caught his eye. He smiled, his weather-beaten face wrinkling like some tropical Santa Claus, and he winked at me.

It was, thus distracted, that I missed the call to line up and go outside for a little "constructive play."

"Mr. Miller," I heard, realizing suddenly that Miss Tidwell was speaking to me.

"Oh, I'm sorry," I said. "Call me Scott. Everyone does."

I was trying to be nice.

"Mr. Miller," she repeated sharply.

"Well, if you prefer," I said blankly.

"Will you be joining us for a little trip to the playground?" she trilled, birdlike.

"Um, no," I said after a moment's thought. "You go ahead. I think I'll just stay and enjoy the quiet. Is there any of that tasty punch left?"

I was still trying to be nice.

"Mr. Miller, get up and get in line."

So this is it, I thought. The confrontation starts right away. I heard Uncle's words: "They'll try to make you fit easily into their world."

"No, thank you," I said, matching her tone, but mindful to be nice.

"Mr. Miller!"

"Piss . . . off."

The cloakroom was quiet.

Dinner wasn't quiet at all.

"Hello," Uncle called. "Scott? Gray?"

"We are in here," Gray called testily from the kitchen.

"Are we eating here or the restaurant?" Uncle said, coming in.

"I hope you're satisfied," Gray said, arms folded.

"Well, whichever is fine with me," Uncle said, shrugging. "I just thought it might be pleasant to go out and celebrate the first day and all."

"There is nothing to celebrate," Gray said, hands on hips. "Thanks to you, this one told Miss Tidwell to 'piss off' before lunch."

"Oh," Michael said seriously, taking the chair beside mine at the table. "Scott, you should always wait until after lunch to tell people to piss off."

"Michael," Gray fairly shrieked.

"They're much more reasonable on a full stomach." He giggled.

I smiled for the first time since the incident.

"Michael," Gray demanded.

"Oh, all right," he said. "Lookit, that was pretty stupid, Scott. What happened?"

"She locked me in the cloakroom," I said indignantly.

"Umm," he intoned. "Pretty big stuff. What provoked this tumult?"

"She was trying to make me go out for recess."

"I always hated recess," he muttered.

"Michael!"

"But I always went right out when they asked me," he said quickly and for Gray's benefit. "You really have to do what they want. No matter how dizzyingly stupid it seems."

"Michael!"

"Why didn't you want to go?" he asked, searching for a cigarette.

"Oh, Uncle, you should have been there," I said, still more than a little angry that he hadn't been. "It was awful and the children were idiots and I just wanted a break."

"That's what recess is," he said, lighting a cigarette.

"I wanted a break from them," I persisted.

"Well, you have to look for your options," Michael said. "Find ways to do what you ought and still do what you want. Go out and sit under a tree and read a book or draw. Escape inside your mind. Let your imagination protect you. You know," he said off-handedly as he took off his jacket, cigarette still in his mouth, "you might try meeting some of the children. They can't all be awful."

"Uncle Michael," I said disgustedly, "you don't know. You weren't there."

"All right. Do as you like," he said with a wave of his hands. "I take it from Nanook's tone we're eating in."

The next day was more of the same. Uncle was up and out, all consumed with his stupid cheesecake. Gray dropped me off and I went into class.

It was "*A* is for Apple," as Uncle had predicted. Followed by having to write an entire page of the blasted things. I counted the characters on the frieze above the blackboard and realized what the next twenty-five mornings of my life held in store.

I dashed off a quick page and got up to look for a book to take to recess.

While I was at the bookcase, I caught the gardener looking in at me. I smiled and he turned quickly away.

"Mr. Miller." I heard the familiar birdsong.

"Yes . . . ma'am," I said, remembering the morning's tirade from Gray.

"What are you doing?" she asked, looking over her spectacles.

"Getting a book . . . ma'am," I said, indicating the bookcase and pointing to the book in my hand. What an idiot this woman was.

"I mean," she said through tightly pursed lips. "What are you doing up?"

"Oh," I said, nodding as if this were a revelation to me. "I'm getting a book, ma'am," I said again, repeating the gestures and speaking clearly.

"Mr. Miller," she said loftily, "what do you suppose would happen if everyone just got up?"

All eyes on me.

"Gee," I said, shrugging, "I don't know. Probably nothing."

"That's right," she said—to my total amazement. "And we are here to do something." She gave the word something special emphasis. "At the moment that something is writing our *A*'s."

"Oh. I did that," I said.

"Then you should sit quietly at your desk until the others have finished," she said primly. "Or practice your writing."

"Let me get this straight," I said to her shocked face. "I can't get up until you say so. And then I have to get up?"

"Mr. Miller. Sit down."

"What about a call from nature?"

"Mr. Miller, if you had been paying attention, you would know that we covered that yesterday."

The class laughed.

"You are to wait until recess," she said as I slunk back to my desk. "If it's an emergency, you raise your hand, and I will come to you, and you may ask."

"I am not believing this place," I muttered, slouching into my chair.

At recess things went from bad to worse. Miss Tidwell steadfastly refused to let me take a book or crayons and paper to the playground.

"What if everyone did that?" she demanded.

"What if they did? . . . ma'am," I answered tensely.

"Why, there would be books and crayons all over the playground."

"I give up," I said resignedly.

Because I had been branded a troublemaker, the other children were a washout. I'd just get them in trouble, they said.

So I found a pleasant bench under a tree and sat. From my vantage I noticed the gardener talking to some of the other children. Well, I thought, there's a friendly face. And I got up to ask if I could watch him work.

Before I could get to him, though, I was besieged by a couple of other boys. "Hey, you want to get some Coke and candy?" asked Thom Berford, a chubby little boy who had minutes before told me to take a hike.

"Sure," I said, delighted with the prospect of a break from the dreary fare we had been offered thus far. "Where?"

"There's a canteen just inside the front door," said another boy.

"Great," I said, a glimmer of hope for school flickering in the distance. "I wonder why no one mentioned it sooner."

"Come on."

"Yeah."

"Wait, I don't have any money," I said. "I didn't realize there was a canteen."

"Oh, that's okay," Thom said. "We've got plenty. The gardener gave it to us if we'd—"

"Hey, Scott." Greg Andionegi—the other boy—cut him off. "What's a canteen?"

"A place to get a snack." I shrugged.

"Let's go."

And we were off.

We had just settled down to M&M's and cherry Coke at a nice table by the window when Miss Tidwell walked by on the path outside. I waved genially. She stopped dead for a moment and then she was on the move with a purpose.

"Cripes," Thom said, "here comes Miss Tidwell and she looks mad."

"Let's get out of here," Greg shouted and they were gone.

No sooner had the door closed than it reopened and there stood Miss Tidwell, face blazing red from running and anger.

"What are you doing in here?" she demanded breathlessly.

Clearly this was the stupidest woman on God's earth. How was I supposed to unlock the secrets of the great minds with anything she might offer? Still and all, I had to be nice.

"Having a bit of a snack," I said, smiling. "M&M?"

"All right, that does it," she snapped, grabbing me by the arm and dragging me across the room.

"Okay, okay," I said. "Take the whole bag. I'm not that hungry."

"I'm taking you to see Reverend Wilbury," she huffed, dragging me along.

"Wait," I said. "My drink."

"Really," she snapped, and off we went.

"Now, Master Miller," Headmaster Wilbury said after listening to Miss Tidwell's rather hysterical and exaggerated report, "what were you doing in the teachers' lounge?"

These people were the limit.

"I was having a snack, sir," I said patiently.

"In the teachers' lounge?" Miss Tidwell shrieked.

"I didn't know I was in the teachers' lounge," I said. "It isn't labeled."

"Didn't it seem unusual that there were no other children there?" the Wildebeest asked.

"Well, now you mention it, yes. Of course, I wasn't really alone. I came in with some other guys."

"Oh?" said Wilbury.

"Yes, Thom and Greg, from my class," I said. "In fact, I wouldn't even have known it was there but for them."

"Oh, really," he said, eyebrows raised, nodding sagely.

"Yes," I went on. "Thom, I believe, suggested it out on the playground. In fact, it was his treat."

"Oh. And where are they now?" he asked.

"I don't know really," I said. "They ran off when they saw Miss Tidwell coming. I'm sure it was nothing personal, but you did look a fright."

Reverend Wilbury smiled, but she didn't take that very well.

Anyway, after some stern talk about not returning to the teachers' lounge and an absolute no to retrieving my drink, I returned to the cloakroom.

During the afternoon session of "If I had two apples," Thom and Greg were absent. I didn't see them again until I was waiting for Gray when I saw their parents, presumably, dragging them across the parking lot to their cars.

Such a fuss.

Right up there with the one Gray pitched after Miss Tidwell, who was waiting with me at the curb, filled him in on the day's events.

Uncle came straight to the kitchen when he got home.

"Déjà vu," he said, finding us in a pose not unlike the previous day's.

"This time it really is your fault," Gray snapped. "He got in trouble for getting a book and for trying to take it to the playground."

"Oh, well, live and learn," he said, flopping into a chair.

"Is that all you have to say?" Gray demanded.

"Well," Uncle stammered, "who knew that was against the rules?"

We exchanged a mutual shrug of disbelief.

"That's not the worst of it," Gray went on. "He and some other boys were caught having a snack in the teachers' lounge."

"Teachers' lounge," Uncle Michael repeated. He looked genuinely shocked.

Then his cheeks began to tremble and he looked for all the world as if he might cry.

"At least he met some other boys," he said at last, rising to leave. "Look, I've got to run down to the theatre for a while."

The swinging kitchen door was the only indication he had been there.

Then from down the hall it erupted. It had not been tears but laughter he was suppressing. And it was uproarious.

It was also more than Gray could stand and he stormed after him, the kitchen door was swinging again. What followed was what Uncle Michael liked to call "a really good fight," and I had ringsides. Gray was furious and screaming and Uncle couldn't stop laughing.

"I cannot believe you think this is funny," Gray screamed. "You are being very irresponsible. What will he think?"

"I can't help it." Uncle choked out the words through waves of hysterical laughter.

"You've got to do something," Gray persisted. "This is the second bad report he's taken. And he's only been there two days."

This sent Uncle into new waves of laughter.

I went to the dining room door to spy.

"Michael. Stop it," Gray demanded. "I'll call your mother."

That was it. Uncle was rolling around on the floor in convulsions.

Gray's face was beginning to twitch. "Michael," he said, stamping his foot. And that was the end of it. He was laughing, too. "Goddamnit, Michael," he yelled through his own laughter. "This isn't funny. It's serious."

"I know, I know," Uncle said, still laughing.

Gray got a throw pillow off the sofa and began pounding Uncle Michael with it. "Stop laughing, you son of a bitch," he screamed.

Uncle began crawling across the room, to get away, it seemed. Gray followed, pounding away. I thought they were heading out onto the balcony, but as they neared the door, Uncle Michael made a quick move and grabbed the old-fashioned CO_2 canister.

The blast of water caught Gray in the face.

Gray cried out in surprise and indignation and the chase was on. Out the door, down the hall, through the kitchen, back in through the dining room. I had to step out of the way. Gray was pounding Uncle on the back, and Uncle in turn would stop and blast him with another shot of seltzer.

Finally, out of breath and, worse yet, out of seltzer, they collapsed, gasping, onto the living room sofa.

I walked quietly into the room and stood facing them.

Uncle Michael looked up, caught my eye, waved a limp finger at me and said, "Let this be a lesson to you, young man."

The blow from the pillow took him straight across the face and muffled a new wave of laughter.

The following day was a date with destiny, although there was no indication that it held special portent when we arose.

Things went pretty much as usual. Up early—I was getting used to it—grunts at one another across an otherwise silent breakfast table, Uncle off early to another hard day of cheesecake. Then a silent ride to school accompanied by the golden tones of *Morning Edition*, into the Victorian mausoleum and the shining countenance of the charming Miss Tidwell.

The morning was abuzz with *B*'s. Another quick page, a covert wave to the gardener out the window and I spent the extra time secreting paper and crayons in my jacket.

No faux pas for me. I was silent, smiling, obedient, seated and on line when I ought.

As we strolled out for another delightful day's recess, I began scouting the grounds for a spot conducive to serious coloring.

"Hey," Thom called, interrupting my survey of the grounds. "Hey, Scott."

"Good morning, Thom," I said, glad of the company as he and Greg approached. "Greg," I said, nodding in greeting.

"Listen, Scott," Thom said, "you got to see this, man. It's real neat."

"No more trips to the teachers' lounge," I said.

"No way," Greg said. "Come on."

"Boy, I got a lickin' for that," Thom said, whistling for emphasis, as we started across the grounds.

"A lickin'?" I asked.

"You know," Thom said. "A whipping from my parents."

"Me, too," Greg put in.

"Oh," I said, a little shocked that such things weren't relegated to melodrama, ABC movies of the week and remakes of *Tom Sawyer*.

"Didn't you?" Greg asked.

"Didn't I what?" I asked.

"Didn't your parents give you a whipping?" Thom asked.

"I don't have any parents," I said distractedly, thinking it was just as well if that was the price one paid. "Where are we going?"

"It's right over here," Greg said, running ahead to a break in the hedge nearly overgrown.

We squeezed through into a small garden with benches, a dried-up fountain and the obligatory statue of St. Francis. The garden, obviously forgotten, was wedged between the hedge and a jog in the wall of the library.

"Pretty neat, guys," I said a little surprised, not taking them for admirers of the aesthetics of such places. "Look what I've got," I said, pulling out crayons and wrinkled paper from my jacket.

"This isn't what we want to show you," Thom said with a new tone in his voice as he knocked the crayons out of my hand.

"We want to show you what we do to rat finks," Greg said, grabbing me from behind.

The rest is sort of a blur. There was the pain of the first punch in my stomach and then the taste of blood from either the split lip or the bloody nose. And then there was the blast of cold water that caused Greg to let go and the old gardener, with agility surprising for a man of his age, sprang forward, tackled the other two and called to me, "Run!"

I did, as best as I might under the circumstances. The disturbance was beginning to draw attention and as I ran to the more crowded areas of the schoolyard, I realized that everyone was stopped and looking past me. I turned and saw the gardener and Thom and Greg emerge, struggling, from the hedge. The gardener had a firm hold on Thom, but Greg had a firm hold on the hose and was dousing the old man pretty well in defense of his friend.

From where I stood it looked as if Thom actually pulled out part of the old man's beard, which really set him off and he turned Thom upside down, holding him by the heels and using him as a shield from the hose.

A couple of the men teachers, one of them the PE coach, broke ranks and began running across the grounds. Old Wildebeest, bringing up the rear, made up in animation what he lacked in speed.

The gardener suddenly dropped Thom and turned and ran away from the boys and the approaching men. And stranger still, the men ran right past Thom and Greg and after the gardener. The PE coach actually felled the old man, clip tackling him from behind.

That poor old man, I thought, righteous outrage rising in me.

It was at that point that a firm adult hand grasped me by the shoulder and spun me around. "I might have known you'd be at the bottom of all this," said pink and snarling Miss Tidwell. "Look at you. We're going to the nurse's office, and then we'll see what Headmaster has to say about all this."

It was pointless to argue, and she was more than twice my size.

I looked over my shoulder as she dragged me across the playground. Mr. Wilbury had Thom and Greg firmly in hand, and the two men teachers were more or less carrying the struggling old gardener.

By the time I was through in the sickroom and led to Headmaster's, a strange quiet had settled in the office. The secretary stared silently at me over her still-humming typewriter, half-finished letter still protruding from the bale.

"Go in," the secretary said at last. The nurse relinquished her hold on me.

As I walked through the room of silent, unblinking stares, I couldn't help wondering what I had done. I was, after all, the one with the rapidly developing black eye. It must have been the crayons, I thought, shaking my head as I turned the knob on the great door to the office I was becoming much too familiar with.

Headmaster sat at his desk facing me, expressionlessly, black eyes bright and piercing under bushy Irish eyebrows. He looked like Ponsious O'Pilot.

"Close the door, Master Miller," his voice rumbled strongly and evenly.

"Headmaster . . ." I began after closing the door.

"Not another word," he said, snapping a hand up beside his face like a traffic cop. "I have only one question for you, Master Miller," he said, teeth clenched. "Do you know this man?" The hand changed from stop signal to a finger of accusation aimed to my left.

Slowly I turned to look behind me. There, his beard in his lap, most of his wrinkles washed away by the garden hose, shoulders hunched in shame and dripping on Headmaster's leather sofa sat the old gardener.

I nodded.

"How do you know him?" Headmaster demanded.

"He's my uncle Michael," I croaked.

Uncle smiled sheepishly and wiggled his fingers in a pale wave.

"Cut that out," Headmaster snapped. "Sit down, Master Miller."

I did.

The Wildebeest rose from his chair and slowly, ominously crossed toward Uncle. "Never," he said so loudly and suddenly that we jumped, "never in my reputed one hundred and forty-two years as an educator have I ever had to contend with such people as you two.

"You," he said, turning on me, "are without doubt the most troublesome first-year student I have ever seen. You come steaming in here like the crowned prince arriving at a grand hotel, willful and demanding, speaking to the teachers like maidservants, sending food back to the kitchen in the cafeteria, on report three times in as many days. God help us, what will the next six years be like for us all?

"I'll tell you frankly, Master Miller, Miss Tidwell stunned me when she broke with a long-standing tradition and asked that you be transferred from her class. She said it was you or her. And after yesterday, transfer to Devil's Island was becoming a consideration.

"But I can hardly hold you up to too sharp a reproach when I discover that your young mind is being shaped by this man," he shouted, wheeling on Uncle. "Because," he said, closing the distance slowly between them, "you, sir, are insane. You come in here got up like Halloween, spying on the children, trespassing, encouraging them to break school rules, assaulting them, giving them money. Not to mention the irreparable damage you've done to the shrubbery outside Miss Tidwell's classroom—and don't you dare laugh.

"The most terrible part of it all is that I punished those children out there for lying to me, as did their parents, because they insisted the gardener had given them the money and told them about the lounge. We have no gardener.

"So," he said, folding his hands behind his back and pacing away from us, "what shall we do?

"I'll tell you frankly," he said, turning back before we could answer. "I'm more than a little inclined to refund the tuition and the money the child's grandfather donated and wash my hands of the lot."

Uncle Michael and I exchanged a look, more than a little surprised about the senator's secret donation.

"But I can't do that. Do you know why?"

We shook our heads silently.

"Well, I'll tell you. I can't do that because I feel it is my duty, now that I understand the situation, to try to be a sane and responsible influence on a child in the care of such a loon.

"What's more, I could not in good conscience turn the two of you loose on another unsuspecting institution of learning and a full report might well preclude the child's ability to gain access to any further educational opportunities. Ever.

"Therefore, it is my decision that Master Miller is to remain, but—and I do mean but—only so long as you, Mr. Reily, promise that you will never set foot on this campus without first notifying me. And then only in the company of no fewer than two employees of St. Francis at all times. And all this until the day you die. Clear?"

Uncle nodded.

"Any violation and you're all out and I'm keeping all the money."

And so it came to pass, as Uncle Michael liked to tell it, as the issue of his age became harder to nail down, he became a millionaire the same year he was thrown out of elementary school.

All told, the incident did me a world of good. The other children, being what they are, held me in a new awe and esteem as much for my crazy uncle as for my shiner.

Greg Andionegi and I became fast friends, enduring to this day.

But most of all, I found a new love for my uncle.

Gray wouldn't speak to him at all when he found out and we ate at the restaurant for the better part of a month. But I thought he was the tops.

Gone were my feelings of betrayal because Uncle hadn't accompanied me that horrible first day at school. He had been rising early and going to the theatre where the makeup artist did him up as a gardener so that he might be there to watch over me always, not just for a cursory observation of my "interacting" over grape juice.

There was something so thrilling then about his outrageous behavior, a thrill I soon lost, but growing up, for most of us, is necessarily coming to behave as a part of the real world.

My reprieve as disciplinary scourge came about a week after the gardening incident. In typical school fashion, after we had settled in and I had buckled down with renewed vigor to the arduous task of acting like the other children, the school began administering diagnostic intelligence examinations. One by one we were taken out of the classroom and into the cloakroom for a few hours' brief stint at showing the stuff we were made of.

My big break came the morning of the letter *I*.

With much ceremony and exhortations to practice that most singular letter in the alphabet and bring in a page the next day, I was ushered into the cloakroom, very much relieved at not having to make the writing assignments take up the allotted time and call no particular attention to myself.

Our school counselor, Mr. Frotham, a tall, willowy man with the longest, most wrinkled fingers I have ever seen, was administering the tests. As the process began, he spoke in that strange plural way, thick with "we" 's and "our" 's, that everyone used at St. Francis when talking to the first years.

"And how are we today, Master"—he paused, looking at the folder—"oh, Miller." His face colored slightly as he read the notations. "You're the one," he breathed.

"We're fine . . . sir," I said with my best Freddie Bartholomew smile. Gray had started me on a program of movies on videotape in which nice and polite children were depicted.

"Do you know what we're going to do today?" he asked, leaning down to face me across the small oak table.

"I've got a pretty good idea," I said casually.

"Oh, ho," he said, smiling and chuckling. "And just what is that?"

"Some sort of IQ test," I said. "Gray said it might be the Sanford Benet."

"Stanford," he said without thinking and then looked slightly surprised.

"Who is Gray?" he asked. "A school chum?"

"No, he's my—" I stopped. I'd really never thought about it as having an official name. "What's the masculine form of governess?"

"I, well." He stumbled. "I don't know," he said at last, staring at me with a new intensity.

"Well, I hope that's not on the test," I said, trying to lighten the mood.

I laughed alone.

Eventually we got the bloody thing off the ground.

It was a pretty skimpy test really, full of arranging colored blocks and spotting what was wrong with pictures and linking such trying concepts as cup and saucer. I was quite surprised at how quickly we got through it as it had taken the previous kids simply hours and they had emerged visibly worse for wear.

Oh, well, I thought. The other children are amazingly fragile.

Mr. Frotham stared at me for some time after he had said the test was over.

"Did you attend any preschool?" he asked, having—thank God—dispensed with the "we" shit.

"No," I said frankly. "My uncle believes we rush children too much as it is."

"I see," he said sagely. "Do you . . . read?" he asked as though he were prying loose state secrets.

"Only English," I said apologetically. "My French she is not so good"—another attempt at humor wasted on Mr. Frotham. ·

"Would you mind reading to me a bit?" he asked coyly, as if it might be an embarrassment to me.

"Sure," I said kindly. Another nitwit, I thought privately.

He got a book, one that we had been promised as our reward for learning "the whole alphabet."

All I had to say was Uncle Michael had been right again.

"What tripe," I said after reading to a rapt Mr. Frotham about the dullest children I had ever heard of.

"What?" he said, startled from his educational epiphany.

"This story," I said. "What idiot wrote this stuff? Not you, I hope," I said, flushing.

"No," he said, no longer blinking at all. He did not look well.

"Good," I said, smiling with relief. "But I mean really, the stilted language aside, the subject is just the pits. Lookit, the whole point of this story seems to be about a ball being blue. I just don't see the point. What difference does it make, I ask you? If it's supposed to be symbolic, it's wasted on me. Got any Mark Twain?"

The test stretched on for days. Reading, writing, French, the theatre, I was middling at math and said so in advance, but it made no difference to them.

I was pronounced a genius and my "precocious nature"—as it came to be known after the tests—was put down to extreme intelligence.

Uncle Michael was escorted to Headmaster's office.

He told me at dinner that I could be in a higher grade, special classes or go away to a special school. "It's up to you," he said.

The decision was easy. The older children scared me, I was not leaving Gray and Uncle and there was no love lost between Miss Tidwell and me.

Special classes were tutorial sessions with the teachers from the higher grades in those periods when they didn't have classes.

I met my class and Miss Tidwell only for official functions like school pictures and school assemblies. And I kept pretty much the same schedule as before. So there was lunch and recess with my classmates, but no more pretending to take forty-five minutes to write a page of I's.

"I" is for independence.

So I had school under control.

Gray was beside himself with joy and prouder than I was. Or Uncle.

The new classes cost a great deal more, but that was increasingly not a problem. For as I was making my way through grade school, Uncle Michael was becoming a Captain of Industry, although I didn't really notice.

The changes were slight enough in our slapdash life to be barely recognizable.

We got a houseboy, Bert, to do the cleaning and help Gray in the kitchen, and we got a driver named Smitty—a name I thought was too cool—to haul Uncle and me around in what Uncle called "our rrridiculous new car."

Mostly, though, I was concerned with the things I guess most boys are concerned with.

Greg and I spent most of our time together. Thom and his family had moved to the coast and it was some years before our paths crossed again.

Greg's family was great. Mr. Andionegi, originally of New Jersey, was a quiet, older man, aloof and scary.

Greg said that his grandpa made his money bootlegging before the family went legit, but Mr. Andionegi looked and acted like a refugee from an Edward G. Robinson film—not on Gray's list of preferred role model videos, but Uncle Michael slipped me more piquant fare when Gray wasn't looking.

Mrs. Belle Andionegi, by contrast, was at least twenty years the junior of her husband and possessed of all the grace and charm of a stripper. She was lots of fun and called me "sweethot" in her stolid Brooklynese.

I spent many weekends at their large baroque rococo home in The Grove which Uncle branded "Very late Reign of Terror."

"*Quel* snob you are," I said at breakfast the morning following his first sighting of Andionegi Acres.

"Yeah, well, you ought to be more choosy," he said. "Gray, I swear to God when I met the man I didn't know whether to shake his hand or kiss his ring."

"Well, I think they're good people," I said, staunchly defending the family of the boy who had become my blood brother in the same private garden at school where he had drawn my blood more forcefully several years earlier.

"Well, they may be good people, but I bet they're better shots," he said, slopping marmalade onto his toast. "Never sit with your back to the door."

"I like them, and besides, they have a pool and tennis courts," I said.

"So do you," he snorted.

"Theirs are private," I snorted back. "We have to share ours."

"Well, that's sure the end of civilization as we know it." He laughed.

"Just the same," I said, smiling, "I like going over even if there is a cherub spitting water into the pool and the tennis net is held up by gilded dolphins."

We laughed.

"Lookit," he said, "I've got to go to California, we're opening another Gambler's. You want to come?"

"Don't you have a play in rehearsal?" I answered with a question.

"It doesn't open for a couple of weeks," he said, munching on his toast.

"Oh," I whined. "Can't I stay at Greg's?"

"Sure, pal," he said strangely. "If it's okay with Belle. I'm sure that'll be a lot more fun. You better run. Smitty'll be up in a minute to drive you to school."

"Thanks, Uncle," I said, running out of the room.

And so we went on about our lives.

Aside from the Andionegis I also spent time with Grammy and Pawpaw Reily and the senator—Miller.

All in all, I thought my family was Looney Tunes, and I often longed for the "real lives" of my classmates.

The senator was about two hundred years old but still shuffling around. Every so often Smitty would drive me up to visit. And while it was not the sort of weekend an elementary school age boy might dream of, days with the senator did have their appeal. It was like a weekend in Stalingrad—with Stalin. I watched in awe and not just a little fear as this ancient despot roamed through his fiefdom.

Evenings at home with the senator were stranger still. The stately country residence reeked of old money and older upholstery. Among its many rooms was a tremendous library. Two storeys of books lined the walls of the great room. We sat dwarfed on leather club chairs before a marble fireplace large enough for me to walk into without stooping. There was always a fire, even in the summer, when the air conditioner was turned down to "light frost" to make the fire bearable.

As the servants wandered shivering through the great house, we sat before the fire, I with cocoa, the senator with brandy, each of us with a stack of books and a black Magic Marker. The books were all classics and first editions and too valuable or venerable to burn. So instead, as we read, we censored disturbing ideas and passages with the Magic Markers. As we finished with the books, we put them on a small mahogany cart to be returned to the shelves.

The senator eradicated rather more than I did, but to keep him happy, I struck out parts that I thought badly written. He, on the other hand, struck out points he disagreed with like the line from the Declaration of Independence about all men being created equal, a good deal of Sinclair Lewis and *The Tropic of Cancer* in its entirety.

I found the process disturbing, but he was reading them first, I reasoned, and he fell asleep too quickly to do too much damage to the books.

His wife's portrait hung above the fireplace, the only aspect of her presence in the house. She was rarely mentioned and if she was, it was as "that bitch."

When the senator was sound asleep and I was bored with my book, I went and hung out in the kitchen with Burke, a marvelous old black woman who had apparently always been there. She alone was unafraid of and undaunted by the senator's irascible nature, saying simply, "I knew you before." And his storms would end.

She ordered the old man around, forced him to eat his vegetables, cut off his brandy when he'd had enough and disciplined him when he was too hard on people. I guess she ran the place, as I never really saw her do anything except bake me chocolate chip cookies, as big as my head, which we sat munching as we watched the demon HBO—strictly verboten by Herr Senator—on the kitchen TV.

Eventually the bizarre weekends would end and I'd be returned home by the senator's driver, always someone new as he ran them off as fast as Burke could hire them. The leaving was as dry and formal as my arrival. I can't ever remember actually touching the senator.

By contrast Grammy Ann and Pawpaw Ash couldn't keep their hands off me. They picked me up themselves, treasuring every moment, every word, every observation of mine. It was pretty sickening, but they were old and I made allowances.

Their driving was harder to forgive. Ash drove in a series of lurches. Stopping, starting, speeding up, slowing down, everything was another jolt. I didn't care for seat belts, but I wore mine without question when riding with Pawpaw to insure that I remained in the car even if my stomach didn't.

On the other hand, I could have walked to their house faster than I got there with Grammy. She said I was valuable cargo, when asked, but she could have kept the Waterford on the hood of the car and arrived with it intact.

Their differences were much the same in all things: Pawpaw abrupt, startling, and Grammy even and gentle, but deliberate. Their bipolar styles made visits with them pretty interesting.

Pawpaw was always "up to something," as Grammy called it, and she had to keep an eye on him to make sure he didn't injure himself or do irreparable damage to the house or cars.

One spring they decided to put up a fence around the pool they had installed for me. Despite the fact that a crew of men was hired to put up the fence, Pawpaw had to help. After knocking the fence down a time or two, nudging one of the workmen into the pool with the wheelbarrow and sawing Grammy's Samsonite card table in half, cutting pickets, he was assigned to mortar stirring.

"It'll harden if you don't keep stirring," one of the men told him.

Grammy and I watched from the breakfast room with pangs of amusement and pity as the poor man stirred mortar all afternoon for a wooden fence.

Uncle Allen was really my only ordinary relative. That is, he was pretty dull and preferred not having me around. He did occasionally drag me to sporting events, movies, fairs and on one abortive trip to Disney World; it wasn't a total loss as he seemed to enjoy the rides. But by and large, I saw him only at mandatory family events.

In fact, it was at one such gathering that he began the rites of admission to the family fold and came ultimately to attain honorary "*Looney Toon*ness" by marrying weird.

It was the year Uncle Michael bought the first hotel.

We had continued our annual summer treks to the cabaret theatre, but Gambler's was doing so well that Uncle decided to expand the operation. To do this, he bought an old rambling hotel,

The Sandpiper, that had seen its glory concurrently with Elizabeth
I. Uncle saved the old place, slated for destruction, snapping up
at the same time an isolated peninsula of private beach.

The Sandpiper Gambler's swallowed suitcases full of tax-
exempt dollars—some deal of Uncle's about historic some-such.
He spent a year renovating and creating "a grand hotel in the old
style," but with new-style plumbing, air-conditioning and massive
ballroom-cum-theater.

We kept the "cabaret" and the hot dog carts, but the new centerpiece would be The Sandpiper. "And," as Uncle pointed out
with absurd irony, "we can stay there rent-free."

The annual summer migration of the strange birds that were
my family was a much-heralded event. The family table at the
Summer Party was the coup for nonfamily, and a place setting for
an outsider was the peak of many small-time Carolina social
climbers' careers. I thought the view of the stage was bad.

But there we sat, luggage already en route to The Sandpiper.

Our company included, of course, the senator—and Burke at
my insistence—Grammy and Pawpaw, Uncle, Gray and me, the
Andionegis and Greg—who was coming with us that year—
Kevin and Shanah Perdue, old friends of Uncle Michael's and minor film producers, Frankie and Anna Gilliam, our advertising
agent and his wife and several other people far more thrilled to
be there than we were to have them.

Uncle Allen had been a bit of a problem. For years he had
arrived squiring a series of ghastly women, never the same twice,
whom Uncle and Grammy took delight in torturing for the evening. But the year of The Sandpiper Allen had refused to bring
anyone.

"I'm not really seeing anyone," Allen had said to Uncle. "And
anyone I ask will just be coming to meet you, Michael," a remark
Uncle had laughed about for quite some time.

To solve the social crisis, Uncle appointed Liz Pastur to "look
after Allen." Liz had been Uncle's business partner for some years,
but he had long since bought her out and put her in charge of
promotions. I dearly loved Aunt Liz, but she was defiantly not
Allen's type.

Uncle described her as "a whippet in a dress."

Her boundless energy manifested itself in behavior almost as outrageous as Uncle's. Her dress tended more toward Coco the Clown than Coco Chanel. She drank heavily and her frequent laugh sounded like the scream of the brightly plumed tropical birds she resembled.

"Allen will be miserable," Grammy said to Uncle when the plan was hatched. "But we won't for a change." They laughed conspiratorially.

We were seated for dinner, everyone was pretty tight and Allen, seated to my right, looked miserable, fidgeting and pulling at his collar. Liz, who was seated across from Allen, was faced and enjoying it. She insisted on arm wrestling with Greg, who was sitting on her left.

Greg, who was already bigger than Aunt Liz's four-foot nothing, was having a pretty easy time of it. They were going for best two out of three, while Uncle Allen died a quiet death, as much from Liz as from the bank president's wife to his left, who was telling in no uncertain terms how "the nigras were ruining public education"—this in spite of the fact that there was a black state senator at the table.

Things were reaching a peak with the wrestling and the racism when Liz lost her balance and the match, bringing her hand down at full force onto the chocolate-filled tart in front of her.

The delicious liquor-spiked filling made Mrs. Bigot look like those denizens of the hallowed halls she had been denouncing so vehemently only moments before. "You stupid bitch," Mrs. Bigot screamed, wiping at her face.

"Now, honey, I'm sure it was—" Mr. Bigot began.

"Shut up, you ass," she wailed. "Just look at me."

The table and surrounding area fell silent. The string quartet stopped playing one at a time—cello last—as all eyes came to rest on the Kalúa-chocolate-cream-horror.

There was a moment of gut-wrenching, "meet me under the table, I dropped my napkin," uncomfortable silence.

Liz stared blankly at Mrs. Bigot for a moment. "No, no," Liz said, waving her hand limply in Mrs. B.'s direction. "I insist. Dessert's on me." And with that she hit herself in the face with Greg's chocolate tart and let out that screaming laugh.

The din was deafening. Even Mrs. Bigot laughed.

"Liz," Allen said sharply, "you were wrong to do that."

Oh, God, we thought, move over, Reverend Falwell, here it comes.

"Dessert," he snapped, pointing at her, "is definitely . . . on me."

And with that his rites of initiation began as he smashed his tart onto his face and laughed as I had never heard him before.

Gray grabbed my hand in time, and Belle took care of Greg, but Grammy was slowing down as she got older and Uncle Michael beat her to the tart.

"It's my party," Uncle screamed. "And dessert's on me."

Splash.

Within minutes the room was filled with the tastiest faces assembled since the Three Stooges discovered pies.

It was the highlight of the party, upstaging even Liz and Uncle's biannual rendition of their song *"Bosom Buddies."*

Liz and Allen danced until they were alone on the dance floor, laughing and screaming and cutting up long after the other guests had crawled home.

Uncle and Grammy were beside themselves. Unfortunately they were on different besides.

Needless to say, our arrival at The Sandpiper grand opening fell just short of the Second Coming on the Sunday magazine scale of social significance.

Months of advance work had assured that opening week was not just a full house but a royal flush. Every suite, room, nook, cranny and broom closet was filled with the stars from every quadrant of the heavens.

The preseason quiet of the resort community had been shattered.

The first-magnitude luminaries of business, government, entertainment and just plain rich people were flown in on private jets and whisked to The Sandpiper in limousines and helicopters, all carefully timed for simultaneous night arrival. The hotel and the grounds burned with light from torches and twinkled with Tivoli lights wound into the trees on the hillside leading up to the hotel's perch astride the ridge. The sky was rent by searchlights, the landing lights of helicopters, awaiting clearance on the available pads, and fireworks.

The photographs in the papers and magazines would have put Mad King Ludwig to shame. Their perspective from a distance in the dark gave the place an Olympus-like quality as the hotel balanced on a mountain of light.

The next day and the rest of the season were in sharp contrast with the debauched opening night. The Sandpiper became a bastion of quiet pleasures. The only real disturbance came in the form of the six shows in rolling repertory in the hotel theatre, and that was over by eleven each night.

Late night the only noise came from the jazz bar, which stayed open till sunrise, and it was pretty subdued.

Greg and I enjoyed ourselves tremendously.

Gray and Uncle were occupied with the continuing series of disasters that always accompany the opening of a new hotel. Bad food, bad service, bad plumbing and bad feelings; nothing serious, but steady enough to keep them off our backs.

We had the run of the hotel. We spent days on the beach and in the pool, gorged on the desserts and from the restaurant menus—available to us for free—and saw all the shows until we knew them by heart. Our sins, which we considered black as ink on our souls, were in truth easily erased by time and a greater knowledge of what we might have done. But we were young and unaware of how much fun we could have been having.

Allen was there often. And under Aunt Liz's jaded tutelage, this man who looked like Uncle Allen did things my uncle would never have done.

His sensible BMW gave way to a bright yellow convertible, which roared up the winding drive every Friday like some Technicolor lion. Oxford cloth and khaki gave way to Hawaiian prints and Jams, a brandy after dinner became Dom Pérignon in the afternoon and romance became scandal when some rather staid guests from White Plains came upon Liz and Allen, naked in the public Jacuzzi, just before dawn, although the White Plainsians never said what they were doing there at dawn.

The greatest shock of all came at a relatively quiet family dinner in the roof garden.

It was on the occasion of Grammy and Pawpaw's "two hundredth wedding anniversary"—or so Uncle Michael called it. Aside from Grammy and Uncle's bickering about seemingly everything, it had been going along fairly smoothly.

The arguing had soared to new heights on Saturday afternoon, but Uncle had won out and Liz was to come to the dinner.

As the weather was nice, it had been decided that we would dine al fresco. Everyone congregated in the pavilion off our living room for before-dinner drinks.

"Well," Grammy sniffed as an opening gambit. "I see we're all here." She gave Liz a sidelong glance.

Liz and Allen were, of course, oblivious.

"Batten down the hatches, Gray," Uncle said, raising his glass and the bid. "Looks like we're in for a hell of a squall."

"It's clear as a bell," the senator grunted, pouring himself another brandy.

"It certainly is," Grammy enunciated acidly.

"I'd say you've had just about enough brandy," Burke said, snatching the bottle from the senator.

"And a high-pressure zone," Uncle said, giggling.

"What would you boys like?" Gray asked Greg and me, trying desperately to change the subject.

"Chocolate fudge soda," I answered, taking advantage of the situation.

"Me, too," Greg said, delighted to know at last what somebody was talking about.

"Drinks all around," Uncle Michael said, wobbling to his feet. He had begun drinking almost before Grammy's luggage was all in from the car. "A toast," he cried once everyone was served. "To the happy couple," he said, deliberately facing Allen and Liz and then turning at the last second to Grammy and Pawpaw. The moment was electric. "May your second two hundred years be as . . . exciting? . . . as the first."

"I wish you'd stop saying that," Grammy said testily. "If for no other reason than it makes you one hundred ninety-five years old."

"One hundred ninety-six. Next March." He grinned, more or less falling back into his chair. "And I've still got all my teeth," he said in an old man's voice as he careened into Greg and me.

We laughed with him alone.

"So, Michael," Allen tried, "what have you got planned for the theatre in town this fall?"

"*I Remember Mama* and *The Bride of Frankenstein*," he said, going off into gales of laughter.

Grammy ground her teeth.

"I've always thought you should do *The Odd Couple*," Pawpaw said, missing the point but continuing the joke inadvertently.

Uncle Michael choked on his drink and doubled over, laughing.

"Don't encourage him, Ash," Grammy said acerbically.

"Well, I just think folks'd like to see some good old Neil Simon," Pawpaw huffed.

"You ought to do something with some moral fiber to it," the senator said, wrestling with Burke for the brandy.

"How about the *Passion Play*?" Liz said, feeling no pain.

"We could serve Mogen David and sacramental wafers— they're very high in moral fiber, I understand," Uncle shrieked.

Liz and he were both laughing.

Grammy slammed down her glass, but before she could speak, Dewars waddled out of the house. "It's the oldest dog in the world," Uncle yelled, throwing his arms wide in greeting.

Dewars, gray-haired and almost totally bald, stopped, snorted, looked rather embarrassed by Uncle's behavior and sat with a thud. Much to her dismay Neveu, our Irish setter, bounded out, crashing into her.

We had gotten the dog to ease my transition when Dewars finally croaked. Or at least that's what Gray and I told Uncle Michael.

The three of us hated the thing.

Four if you count Dewars.

We'd have gotten rid of the dog, but Bert had grown attached to the animal. Since Bert was live-in, he kept the beast away from us, even taking him on vacation. So there we were.

Dewars hated Neveu more than the rest of us and growled threateningly as the monster nipped playfully at her.

Greg, who liked the dog well enough and was desperate to get away from the rigors of the adults' conversation, seized the opportunity to escape. "Where's the ball?" Greg asked the dog, inciting one of the lummox's more annoying tricks.

Neveu darted through the door, almost toppling Gray, who was coming out with a tray of hors d'oeuvres in the vain hope that a little food would sober Uncle up—or at least shut him up.

Then, as quickly as our appetites disappeared, Neveu was back, depositing a spittle-covered rubber ball at Greg's feet.

The game was on. Greg and Neveu and—just to be polite—I played fetch the ball until dinner was served.

By the time we got to table Grammy and Uncle were plenty mad. As best as I could make out it was some crack about theatre being the second oldest profession and some thinly veiled riposte about marriage being the first.

Whatever, they were seething, the senator was besotted, Pawpaw was gaining fast and Gray was miserable and snappish as Burke kept adjusting and recommending.

To top it off, Liz and Allen were chattering like magpies, which seemed to chafe everyone's wounds.

"Well," Pawpaw said, "this is excellent, Gray. Thank you. And, Michael, thanks for a lovely bicentennial. Don't you think, Grammy?"

"I'm so overwhelmed I can't think," she said with frozen mannequin smile firmly affixed.

"How long have you two been married?" Burke asked.

"Long enough to have a serpent's tooth necklace," Uncle sniped.

Grammy sighed. Of course.

"I gave that bitch a shark's tooth necklace when we were in Australia," the senator snorted, obviously sorry of the gift.

"Not at dinner," Burke snarled.

"Get that dog away from the table," Gray said to me.

Neveu was a persistent animal, and he was making the rounds at the table looking for another game of fetch, the previous having been cut short by dinner.

"More salmon?" Gray asked.

"Just a touch more dill," Burke said, winking at Gray. "Don't you think?"

"What's brown and full of holes?" Greg asked.

"What?" Pawpaw asked.

"It's a riddle," Greg explained. "What's brown and full of holes?"

"I don't think—" Liz said, startled back to reality.

"I give up," Pawpaw said.

"Swiss shit!" he proclaimed triumphantly.

Uncle howled, as did Pawpaw, but that was about it.

"Where did you hear a thing like that?" the senator demanded.

"Aunt Liz," Greg said in a small voice.

"How . . . colorful," Grammy said.

Uncle laughed harder.

"Greg, that's not a dinner riddle," Liz chastised him mildly.

"Liz—" Grammy began.

Allen, Uncle and Pawpaw stiffened.

"I know it must be easy to feel like one of the gang," Grammy said imperiously, "but we really must be careful what we say around the young people."

"Yes, Liz," Uncle said gravely. "You should never say 'cock-sucker' in front of the children."

We hung our heads to hide our laughter.

"Michael," Grammy snapped, "you are incorrigible."

"It's genetic." He smiled.

"Dessert?" Gray asked to break the silence. "Neveu, get away from the table."

Bert brought dessert.

Greg and I covertly played slobber ball with the dog as Gray fussed the dishes into place.

"Would anyone like brandy?" Gray asked, hovering nervously around the table.

"Not you," Burke said, reeling on the senator.

"Or coffee?" Gray said through gritted teeth. "Scott, stop encouraging that goddamned dog." Gray froze.

"Well," Allen said, taking advantage of the dead spot, "as long as we're here together . . ."

"Get away from me," Grammy snapped at the dog, who had chosen her as his new victim/playmate.

"I just wanted to tell you all at once," Allen went on, "that Liz and I are going to be married."

"Shit," Grammy screamed as Neveu deposited the spit-covered ball into her white silk lap.

She leaped to her feet, upset her chair and instinctively grabbed the rubber ball before it fell. Of course, it was even more repulsive to touch than it was to have in your lap, so she threw it away in disgust and frustration. It was a good strong overhand toss. It was also the object of Neveu's game.

The ball took a bad bounce on a grass mat, reversed directions, ricocheted off a large terra-cotta planter and sailed over the low garden balustrade formed by the hotel's rooftop facade.

And, of course, so did Neveu.

There was what seemed an unduly long pause as the members of the dinner party stared expectantly at Neveu's point of departure.

Everyone except the senator, who seized the opportunity to refill his brandy snifter.

At last came the crash and subsequent screams as Neveu came suddenly to rest in the crowded terrace dining room eight stories below, which Uncle renamed "Neveu's" some months later.

As we sat in speechless horror listening to the clamor below, the senator rose from his chair, raised his brimming full snifter and said to Allen and Liz, "Congratulations."

Aunt Liz was from a small southern town, rich in poverty and horse manure—owing to the seasonally imported elite's penchant for the animals. Liz was from the privileged class ultimately, but her family had risen to that position, and they had never been truly admitted to the holier-than-thou order of the leisure class.

Because the bride's family decides these things, the wedding was to be in "Turdsville," as Uncle called it. He had been unable to bribe her family out of it as the Pasturs wanted to showcase the "good marriage" their daughter was making, for the benefit of their tiresome, inbred neighbors.

Under the guise of a wedding present, Uncle more or less paid for everything, so he could call the shots. "The show," as Uncle persisted in calling it, was to be a post-Easter spring affair to coincide with the Turdsville Dogwood Festival, which opened the horse racing season, and with the spring break, which closed the theatre for two weeks.

Planning for the event began almost before Neveu hit the Campari umbrella.

The fighting which had preceded his descent persisted and turned the wedding plans into a family free-for-all worthy of the Borgias.

Though I was not immediately involved, the strategizing was difficult to ignore.

The wedding pervaded everything.

Even the Christmas show became a satirical Wagnerian operatic salute to the battles between Uncle, Grammy and the Pasturs, complete with tap-dancing horses and cows singing "Watch Your Step" as they avoided conflicts and horse turds.

But the mock drama was no contest when compared with the reality of the situation.

Uncle took a suite for the duration at one of Turdsville's finest from which to coordinate overall planning. But he soon moved due to yet another of his practical solutions.

The problem was that the annual Turdsville Dogwood Festival and racing season conflicted with the wedding. The pinnacle of the social events was the annual Vanderhorst Hunt, held each year at Vanderhorst Inn. The inn was formerly a private residence that had been bought by a very exclusive resort hotel chain, but the traditional hunt remained even though the Vanderhorsts themselves did not.

Unfortunately the Vanderhorst was the only location deemed large enough and of suitable quality to accommodate the wedding party.

Actually the whole conflict was a ploy of Grammy's to delay the ceremony by insisting on a location they could not get at the appointed time. To defeat Uncle, Liz's mother, Andrea Pastur, joined on Grammy's side.

Uncle, however, outflanked Grammy, Andrea and the Turdsville Equestrian Society Dogwood Festival Planning Committee by purchasing the chain that owned the Vanderhorst and canceling the eighty-ninth running of the Vanderhorst Hunt. There was a huge public and private outcry from both groups, but owing to the town's long tradition of being bought and sold by outside interests, the public complaint died quickly enough. The private dispute, however, lasted right up to *D* day.

I was relieved to have had school to keep me in town during the long series of embarrassing public brawls over music, flowers, ushers, menus and every other trivialty and minutiae the three terrors of Turdsville could dredge up. The fighting over the invitations had been so bitter that three different versions were mailed at random to every third entry on the guest list.

By the time Gray and I arrived at the Vanderhorst, almost no one was speaking to anyone else in private, only at official functions.

Greg and I beat everyone down to dinner and were generally annoying Dewars by the fire when the rest of the party started to drift in. Grammy and Pawpaw came down first with Liz's parents, Andrea and Jimbo Pastur.

Everyone messed up our hair in greeting and then headed for the bar. Drinks were all round when Greg's parents, Belle and Sam Andionegi, came in. They had outdone themselves. Sam was passable in black tie—albeit black crushed velvet—but Belle had on a blue-green sequined satin sheath that made her look like a pudgy mermaid.

Andrea choked slightly as they came into the room.

"Idn't this some place?" Belle intoned as she swept in. "That Michael's really goin' places, hunh?"

"Belle, Sam," Pawpaw said, delighted to see nonaligned faces. "Good to see you. Drink?"

"Don't mind if I do," Belle said, hustling it over to the bar.

"Yeah," Sam grunted, following.

"All right, what's the meaning of this?" Uncle Michael blasted into the room.

"Meaning of what?" Grammy asked, exchanging a quick look with Andrea.

"These menu cards," he said, waving a few around for emphasis.

"What's wrong with the menu cards?" Andrea asked, batting her eyes. "Aren't they the ones you ordered?"

"You know good and well they are not," he snapped.

"What are you implying?" Grammy demanded haughtily.

"Why, that the printer made an error, of course," Uncle said, voice suddenly coy. "We're having bouillabaisse, not vichyssoise; these are useless." With a grand gesture he tossed them into the fire.

"Bouillabaisse?" Grammy said, slamming down her drink.

"Didn't I tell you?" Uncle asked. "We couldn't get fresh chives this time of year, so we went with bouillabaisse."

"This is the last straw," Grammy yelled.

"I hate bouillabaisse," said the senator, waddling in.

"You do not." Burke waddled after him.

"I do, I tell you," he said, heading for the brandy decanter. "It's all that vile sherry."

"You hate she-crab soup, is what you hate," Burke said, trying to head him off. "One brandy before dinner."

"When was the decision made about the bouillabaisse?" Andrea insisted.

"The first time I ever tried it," the senator said, tossing off his brandy and pouring another.

"We decided days ago," Uncle said. "I was sure I told you."

"You didn't," Andrea shrieked.

"You don't," Burke said, taking the decanter. "You've always enjoyed bouillabaisse."

"What will we do?" Grammy said, sinking onto the sofa.

"I'm having Frankie send some new cards up tomorrow afternoon, late," Uncle said, pouring some gin in a glass.

"Now we'll have two fish courses." Grammy sighed dramatically, of course.

"And besides, Liz just hates bouillabaisse," Andrea wailed.

"Hi, all," Liz said as she and Allen came in.

"Don't you?" Andrea implored.

"Don't I what?" Liz asked, looking puzzled.

"Just hate bouillabaisse," she moaned.

"I do," said the senator. "I just hate it."

"You don't," Burke snarled.

"What is bouillabaisse?" Jimbo, Liz's father, asked.

"Fish stew," Belle said.

"With gallons of dry sherry," the senator added.

"That's she-crab soup," Burke yelled.

"I like she-crab soup," Aunt Liz said, trying to be helpful.

"I'd like another drink," Sam said, being uncharacteristically verbose.

"We're not having she-crab soup," Grammy said impatiently to Aunt Liz. "We're having bouillabaisse."

"I just hate bouillabaisse," the senator confided to Belle, who was seated next to him.

"So does Liz," Andrea announced.

"And the menu will have to be changed," Grammy said with an air of finality.

"Thank God," the senator said. "I just hate—"

"You do not. You do not hate bouillabaisse," Burke said in an unbridled rage. "So stop saying that you do."

"Do what?" Gray asked, coming in.

"Hate bouillabaisse," the senator said.

"You don't," Burke said, actually striking him on the shoulder.

"We're not having bouillabaisse," Gray said, blinking in surprise at the intensity that the topic of soup was receiving. "We're having vichyssoise."

"Thank God," the senator said.

"I knew it," Grammy said, rising in triumph.

"We can use those cards after all," Andrea said.

"My mistake," Uncle said. "I'm always getting those two confused."

"Well, we're having vichyssoise," Gray said.

"Great," the senator said. "I love that."

"No, you don't," Burke said, shaking her head in disgust.

"And we can use those cards," Grammy said.

"No, we can't," Michael said, shaking his head.

"Why not?" Andrea said insistently.

"I burned them," Uncle said, pouring more gin.

"You did that on purpose," Grammy said, crossing in close to his face.

"It would be difficult to burn five hundred menu cards by accident, wouldn't you say?" Uncle said, not moving an inch.

"Actually," Liz said to no one in particular, "I really like bouillabaisse."

Dinner was no better.

And it got worse. The volume rose in direct proportion to the pettiness of the offense.

The brunch for the wedding party the next day was rocked by a huge fight over the tiger lilies Uncle Michael had ordered by "mistake" instead of lilies of the valley.

Uncle Michael was mysteriously locked in his room for the duration of the bridal luncheon he had insisted on attending when a chair accidentally fell and wedged itself under his doorknobs.

And the luncheon came down around everyone's ears when Belle Andionegi coldcocked Andrea Pastur after a remark of Andrea's about "Blood will tell." To which Andrea had replied, "Let's see."

Greg and I had a pretty good time messing around the grounds and stables, where we met Andy, the son of the stable master. In exchange for a ride on my new horse—a gift from Uncle in honor of the occasion—Andy showed us his private menagerie. He raised foxes, which he sold to locals for hunts. It seemed rather barbaric to me, especially after we took one of the little guys out on the lawn. He followed us around like a dog and ate out of our hands. He would even curl around your shoulders like a live stole.

But business is business, Randy explained.

We were still out enjoying the great outdoors when Pawpaw came out on the back terrace and called for me.

"All right," Pawpaw said. "We're all here. Scott, shut the door."

I complied and sat with the others in the small second-floor sitting room where we were all gathered. All except Allen and Liz.

"I want everyone to try to shut up and listen up. Now Jimbo and I have talked and we are in full agreement that you people are behaving like a pack of jackals. Now we realize that's nothing out of the ordinary for this lot, but it simply has got to stop.

"We don't have anything to threaten you with, so we can't say 'or else.' But you people are ruining Liz and Allen's wedding. And if you care about them, that should be threat enough. This is the most important day of their lives and the people they care about most had a fistfight today at the bridal luncheon."

"Wadden much of a fight," Burke snorted.

"And you screamed the place down at brunch," Pawpaw went on, "over some flowers.

"I'm shocked and appalled, but how I feel doesn't matter. It's how you're making them feel that matters. Everything is set now. Right, wrong or indifferent, the match is made, the troth is plighted, the candles and the flowers and the napkins and what-ever else the three of you can think of to fight over are done. Now I want you to stop arguing, stop picking on the guests and stop making such a spectacle of yourselves.

"Oh," he said. "One other thing. Jimbo and I have decided that if you ignore this little chat and decide to start making fools of yourselves, we're going to finish the job and personally carry you out in front of God and everybody and throw you into the lily pond."

"That's all," Jimbo said.

And so it came to pass that at the appointed hour, in the appointed manner, the three terrors of Turdsville arrived at the Turdsville United Methodist Church.

The only nod to the previous unpleasantness were the sunglasses Andrea wore to conceal the shiner from Belle.

As usual, I felt weird being in a church with my irreverent family. Our family's casual brush with religion seemed to make it important that we get it right the first time as our contact was so limited.

Rehearsal was a breeze. A tense breeze, but a breeze.

Really, though, the only uncomfortable moment had come when Uncle yelled, "Cut," because the wrong music was being played. But it was merely unusual, not unpardonable.

After we rehearsed the ceremony, the orchestra arrived for its rehearsal. Only the wedding director and the three terrors stayed for that. The rest of the party went back to the inn for the rehearsal festivities.

It was obviously a mistake to leave them unsupervised, but it seemed like a good idea at the time.

The three arrived at the dinner dance and behaved as though they had never exchanged cross words. Grammy and Andrea raved about the menu cards and Uncle danced with them both.

Clearly something was up.

The day of the wedding arrived without incident.

Turdsville's dogwoods and azaleas outdid themselves to oblige the occasion. The day had that clean, clear, early-spring quality where, because of winter's long gray, sensory deprivation, everything suddenly looks dazzling and new.

The day at the Vanderhorst started early. There was the church to be gotten ready and the reception to be prepared for.

Owing to the stunning weather, the reception was to be a largely outdoor affair. The dozens of glass doors across the back terrace were to be thrown open and the lawn dotted with white silk tents and white linened tables. The band was set up on the terrace so that guests could enjoy the music in the large public rooms across the back of the inn as well as on the lawn.

By the time I awoke and stumbled down for breakfast, the

preparations were well under way. The house was overrun by people with ladders and tent poles and chafing dishes.

Better still, the three scourges were already at the church, tormenting the florists who were there to do the decorating.

Greg and I ate breakfast in the kitchen with Gray, who was up and down a lot, so we were left pretty much to ourselves. After breakfast we got ready and went down to the stables to escape the crush and to go for a ride.

"Nope," Big Andy told us. "Your Uncle said, 'Absolutely no more turds at the party than were on the guest list.' "

"Where's Little Andy?" I asked, hoping at least to get a chance to play with the foxes.

"He's gone," Big Andy said, resuming his buffing on an old saddle. "He's handling foxes this morning. For the hunt."

"I thought that was canceled," I said.

"Nah. They're having it at the old Wiley Place," he said. "Even your uncle can't stop a thing like that."

"Let's go down to the pond," Greg said, having had enough and looking for fun, not conversation.

We complimented Andy on how splendid the stables looked and went down to the pond.

We'd hardly skipped a stone before we heard Gray screaming for us. "Where have you been?" Gray asked breathlessly when we rejoined him. "You have to start getting ready. Do you want lunch?"

"At the pond. We're going. No," I said trying to cover everything. "And try to calm down. It's Liz and Allen who are getting married."

"Smart kid," he said, smiling. "You sound like Michael."

"Right this minute, I hope not," I said, turning to leave. "What time are we going over?"

"One-thirty," he called after us.

Unlike at the rehearsal, at the wedding I had to sit farther down front. We sat on Uncle's row, which was third back on the groom's side. And as none of us was in the wedding, we had to be in place long before the procession began.

Uncle had come back to the inn in a state of total panic. He came in the front door, screaming, and stopped only once the car arrived at the church. "Gray," he screamed as the huge front doors slammed behind him, "what the hell is going on around here? Where are the azalea garlands that are supposed to be wrapped around the columns out front? And what in the hell is this ice sculpture doing in the lobby?"

"Relax," Gray said, taking him by the elbow and steering him toward the stairs. "The garlands are in the refrigerators so they'll be fresh and the ice sculpture is only there until they get the table set up for it in the ballroom."

"Have they got the tents up? Has the band arrived? Who's setting up the bandstand? Oh, my God," Uncle shrieked. "Why on earth do they have only one rehearsal for these things?" And then the door of Uncle's room at the end of the hall closed and all we could hear was muffled screaming for a while.

Bert was just pinning on our boutonnieres when the doors to Uncle's room burst open as though unable to contain the fury any longer. "Scott, Greg," he screamed. "Oh my God, who's been getting the children ready? We're going to be late."

"Bert is getting them—" Gray began.

"Where is everyone?" he went on. "Belle, Sam, Andrea, Mother!"

The doors along the hall began to spring open and Grammy and Andrea joined the general alarm.

"Michael, where are the garlands for the front columns?"

"Did the orange blossoms arrive for the table settings?"

"Where is Ash? If he's late, I'm putting myself up for adoption," Uncle chattered. "Oh, Scott, there you are. Don't you look wonderful. Daddy! Gray, Scott should wear light gray more often."

"Oh, God," Andrea screamed. "Where's Liz?"

"Liz," Uncle screamed.

"She's your daughter," Grammy snapped.

"She's already gone to the church," Gray tried to shout over the mass hysteria.

Pawpaw emerged from his room and, like whirling dervishes, we made our way to the car.

Greg and his parents rode with Gray and Uncle and me as both Andrea and Grammy were afraid of Belle.

The chorus of panic became a monologue as we rode to the

church: "Oh, God, did Allen look all right? Has he gone over to the church? If those idiot florists aren't finished before the guests arrive, I will just drop dead at the communion rail. Can you imagine, there were no ladders at the church. They don't even have any sort of crew on staff to set up for these kinds of events. And naturally the florists didn't have anything but flowers, so it was practically ten o'clock before we even got under way. Did Allen have his boutonniere? Oh, my God, the ring!"

We were all privately thrilled that the church was only five minutes away.

As Smitty opened the door, the tirade shut down, and Uncle emerged from the car with the air of smug calmness cultivated for the public on opening nights. He strode into the church as if down the gangway after an extended and restful cruise. And with the same casual ease he led the party to our place on the third row. Uncle sat closest to the aisle; next to him was Gray, then me, then Greg and his parents.

The senator and Burke were seated behind us and the row in front of us was reserved for Grammy and Pawpaw. The first row was left blank.

The orchestra began shortly after we were seated.

I sat swinging my legs and praying for my family's salvation, feeling God could see us better on the third row.

As some Bach fugue or other blasted away, the mothers-in-law were squired to their seats. Grammy and Pawpaw took their place in front of us.

The fugue concluded and there was a moment of silence filled only by the rustle of the orchestra in the balcony turning dozens of pages and the choir at the altar rising.

Then everything was drowned out as the orchestra began the choral movement of Beethoven's Ninth. Everyone was so rapt in the fervor and idealism of its sentiment that no one in a position to know noticed as an attractive older woman with iron-gray hair tinged with blond whispered into the usher's ear. "Groom's side," she said. "I'm Mrs. Robert Miller."

The usher nodded solemnly and took it upon himself to lead her to row four, right where he had seated Senator Robert Miller only a moment before.

The choir and the orchestra reached the crescendo, drowning

out almost every petty thought—and the first parts of the skirmish just behind us—wringing out every dram of emotional intensity of the movement's conclusion. The room was aquiver with the storm of silent applause, stilled only by the place and the moment.

"You bitch," the senator's voice cut through the moment of personal reverence. "How dare you come here."

"Perhaps I'd better sit somewhere else," said the woman I recognized from her portrait in the senator's library as my grandmother.

"You're goddamned right you better sit somewhere else," screamed the senator, standing, cane flailing as Burke struggled to pull him back by his coattails. "You can sit in hell."

"Sit down," Burke growled.

"Robert, please," she gasped, stepping back to avoid the ebony wood cane.

"I thought you took care of this," Pawpaw said to Grammy.

"Get out of here, you harlot," he shouted, struggling to break free of Burke's iron grasp.

"Well, we had," Grammy whispered to Pawpaw. "We told her it was at a different church. But after your little talk we thought we were interfering. So, after the rehearsal the other night, we called her and told her it had been moved here. And you were right, darling, we felt so much better."

"You can walk down that aisle like you walked out on me," the senator was bellowing. With that he grasped a hymnal out of the rack on the back of the pew in front of him and threw it at her.

She dodged and the weighty tome struck the usher on the shoulder and knocked the unsuspecting and semicatatonic man into the laps of the people on row five, bride's side.

"You crazy old son of a bitch," Sylvia shrieked, "I may go to hell, but I'll see you there." And she turned and stalked up the aisle.

As the entire congregation turned to watch her exit, we found ourselves looking into the horrified faces of the wedding party, queued up just outside the doors, their entrance originally planned to coincide with the conclusion of music.

Burke unfortunately misjudged the moment and let go of the senator's morning coat as she said, "Now sit down and shut up."

Free at last, the senator bolted and ran down the aisle after his ex-wife. "You got your way, you flint-hearted fishwife." His words echoed through the otherwise silent chamber bathed in the colors of the sun pouring through the stained glass windows.

Sylvia turned to speak, saw him bearing down on her, cane in hand, thought better of it and fled up the aisle with a desperate scream.

The escort who had brought her in and taken the blow from the prayer book for her had righted himself with the help of the worshipers on whom he had landed. The usher was a friend of Allen's, one Carl Bledsoe, a lawyer at Allen's brokerage house. Prior to taking his law degree, he had been a very successful member of his college track team. Though he didn't compete any longer, he still kept up with his running and as such was able to overtake the senator before he bludgeoned my grandmother.

In a rather spectacular flying leap, Carl took out the senator. The force of the assault, however, sent the two of them flying and together they took out Grandmother Miller and the front ranks of the wedding party, toppling several bridesmaids and knocking the breath out of the flower girl.

The senator was old, but he recovered nicely and came up swinging, whereupon the groomsmen, who remained standing, covered him with their bodies as they piled on in a second tackle.

The wedding director silently pushed the chapel doors closed.

Everyone continued to stare at the doors.

There was the sound of breaking glass, and Sylvia was screaming, "Get off my husband."

More crashing around and then silence.

Uncle turned around into the respectively furious and desperate stares of Pawpaw and Grammy. Uncle shrugged slightly and said, "She was supposed to sit on the bride's side."

With that the doors banged open again, the orchestra struck up *"The Prince of Denmark's March,"* and the wedding party, disheveled and limping, began its somewhat anticlimactic procession.

"I cannot believe you did that," Gray said fiercely as the car door closed.

"I didn't do anything," Uncle said evasively as he looked out the window, smiled and waved at someone. "Isn't it a lovely day for—"

"Don't be coy," Gray snapped.

"Look, it was the senator who had the grand mal," he said, beginning to laugh.

"Don't you dare laugh," Gray said. "It was a catastrophe."

"I can't help it," Uncle said, laughing anyway. "If you put that onstage, no one would believe it. The looks on the wedding party's faces as Sylvia and Robert came flying straight for them. I thought I would die laughing."

I had just thought I might die. Clearly, I thought, there had been some cruel joke of fate, and I had been inadvertently given over to some family of crackpots. Worse still, some appropriately maniacal little boy had been foisted off on some unsuspecting and otherwise normal family.

The car pulled up and I bounded out the door, not waiting for Smitty.

To judge from the expressions on Pawpaw's and Jimbo's faces, similar topics had arisen in their car. Uncle, Grammy and Andrea met on the front porch and scurried off in a cloud of whispering and laughter.

Gray joined Pawpaw and Jimbo down the drive a bit and they stood talking seriously for some time.

"That was some wedding," Sam said with a low whistle.

"No shit," Belle said as they climbed the front stairs.

"Come on," I said to Greg. "Let's go get some drinks before Gray gets there."

"I don't know," Greg said, shaking his head.

"We'll be outside," I said, striking out. "We can throw up in the bushes."

"Okay, great," Greg said, following.

We went straight out back to a still relatively quiet bar. I waited for my chance. Just as Allen and Liz made their entrance, and the band struck up a rousing and terribly big band rendition of Lohengrin's "Wedding March," I made my move.

"Excuse me," I said in my very best wide-eyed little boy's voice, as I came up on the barman's blind side.

"Hello, sir," he said. "What's your poison?"

"Two gin and tonics with a twist of lime," I said into his startled face and then added innocently, "for my uncle. And we'd like cherry Cokes with lots of ice."

"Certainly, sir," he said, looking relieved and turning briskly to oblige my uncle.

As he turned, I snitched a fifth of rum and handed it to Greg, who hid it under his coat and headed for the stables.

"Here you are," he said, handing me the gins. "Where's your friend?"

"Oh," I said, looking around foolishly. "I don't know."

"Well, you're going to need two more hands for these Cokes," he said genially.

"I'll be right back for them," I said, smiling sweetly. And I, too, was off to the barn.

Greg and I were just finishing our gin and tonics when we heard a familiar voice.

"Hey, you-all," little Andy said. "Whatcha got?"

"A whole fifth of rum," Greg said, pulling the bottle of Myers's best out of the hay.

"Got any Coke?" I asked.

"Shicheah," he said. "There's a Frigidaire full in the tack room."

We poured out most of the contents of three bottles of Coke and mixed the rum in the bottles.

"I thought you were gone to the hunt," I gasped, trying to sound unaffected by the sip of the highly flammable mixture I had just swallowed.

"The last heat just started about a half hour ago," Andy gasped back. "The Wiley place is so small they had to have three runs."

"Um," Greg said, unable even to gasp.

"Which one did you take out?" I asked, getting a little more acclimated to drinking gasoline.

"Reddy," he said. "The one we had out yesterday."

"Gee, man," Greg said, "aren't you a little sad?"

"Nah," Andy said. "That's the way it goes."

Then he laughed and, eyes twinkling, said, " 'Sides, I've never lost one yet."

"What do you mean?" I asked.

"All right," he said. "I'll tell you, but you got to swear you'll keep a secret."

"Swear," I said.

"I swear," Greg said, recovering from another sip.

"Shit," he said. "These assholes go to the hunts and get so tanked up they wouldn't know a fox from sweat socks. Hell, half the time they shoot their own dogs in duck season. Anyway, I train the foxes to come home. So them hot shits go out and follow the dogs around for a while and then give up. And the houndsman pulls out a bloody rabbit skin we get for next to nothing, and those drunks cheer and blow their horns and tip the houndsman like anything, and we split the money for that and the fox."

"That's great," Greg said, starting to look glazed already. Greg just couldn't hold his liquor.

"Let's freshen these drinks and go get some food," I suggested.

By the time we arrived the party was in full swing. And for that matter, so were we.

Sylvia and the senator were sitting on opposite ends of the lawn, she nearest the house, he nearest the farthest bar.

Peaceful enough, I thought and, with half a pint of Myers in me, I was starting to feel that the whole thing was pretty funny.

We had just hit the oyster bar when Gray apprehended me. I figured we were done for, but he hardly seemed to notice me. "Have you seen your uncle?" he asked distractedly, looking past me as he surveyed the crowd.

"No, thank God," I said. "What's he done now?"

"Nothing," he said distantly, and wandered off.

"That was close," Andy said.

"What's the matter with him?" Greg asked.

"Who cares?" I said. "Let's go steal a tray of something and get out of sight."

We filled our pockets with sausage balls, snagged a platter of stuffed mushrooms and hid in a grove of oleanders on the far side of the lily pond. The view of the party was great and we finished off the last of the rum in private.

We were all coughing our way through some cigarettes Andy

had found on an empty table by the dance floor when we heard screaming.

It was some moments later when we made out the distant shapes of three, no, six people coming down one of a pair of staircases that led down to the lawn from the terrace. Actually only three of them were coming down the stairs. The other three were over the shoulders of the first three, and they were doing all the screaming.

It was, of course, my family. And they were headed our way.

As they drew nearer, we made out that Allen and Carl Bledsoe were standing in for Pawpaw and Jimbo, but Gray had Uncle Michael. Pawpaw and Jimbo calmly brought up the rear.

It seems they had actually chopped down the doors of an upstairs sitting room to get at the co-conspirators. And now, as promised, they were going for an afternoon swim.

We hid behind a stand of bamboo that surrounded a moldy statue of Mars and Venus directly opposite the house on the far side of the rectangular pond. The pond was the width of the lawn which was in turn the width of the inn. The entire corridor was defined on both sides by thickets of laurel, oleander and azalea at the base of several carefully planted rows of old, fat live oaks.

In our hiding place the only people with a better view of the proceedings than the three of us were Mars and Venus.

In total silence and with an air of casual nonchalance the three carried their kicking, screaming charges to the edge of the pond.

"Don't you dare throw me in this pond," Uncle Michael shouted indignantly.

"Can you give me one good reason—" Gray began.

"Shhhh," Uncle hissed. "What is that?"

"What is what?" Gray asked.

"That sound. Listen," he said.

"It's not going to work, Michael," Allen said to Uncle's wrong end, turning Andrea to face the left hedge as he did so.

She screamed suddenly as a fox shot past them and made for the party, presumably to lose himself in the crowd.

"Oh, jeez," Andy said, rising and breaking through the screen of bamboo.

"Andy, get down," I said, but he paid no attention.

"Jump," he called to the already startled party on the opposite bank.

At that moment a pack of dogs broke through the hedge, heading straight for them. With no further question they all jumped into the cold, waist-high, mucky water.

And then it really hit the fan.

All down the left-hand side of the vista, surprised horses and drunken riders began to burst through and leap over the hedge only to find themselves face-to-face with the still more surprised and drunken wedding guests. A couple of horses even landed in the pond.

It was pretty much a rout as the guests ran screaming for the house. The bucking and terrified animals trampled tables and chairs, threw their riders and made a real mess in the serving tents.

The fox, hounds in hot pursuit, made straight for the nearest protection he could find. This, unfortunately, was the senator, and he scampered up the old man's body and wrapped himself around his neck as he'd done only a day earlier for me. The hounds were not fooled, and they pretty well flattened the senator.

Sylvia alone made her way through the debris and destruction to come to his rescue.

"Jesus Christ," Uncle said, beginning to laugh, "it looks like a Japanese horror movie."

The other bathers began to laugh.

Suffice it to say, it was a memorable occasion. But Uncle Michael always says, "You throw a really good party like you're trying to hit someone."

The wedding was pretty eventful all round.

The Vanderhorst Hunt was moved permanently back to the inn, and a good deal of local regulation was enacted regarding the running of hunts and the preparation of hunt animals.

Andy was more or less out of business. He retired from the sport with an almost unblemished record. He had finally lost one.

And so had we.

The shock or, very possibly, just the indignity of being set upon by the dogs was more than the senator's sense of propriety, and his heart, could stand. He was gone before the sun set on Allen and Liz's wedding day.

"I, Senator Robert Augustus Miller, Jr., being of sound mind and body, do hereby decree and direct that my worldly goods be dispersed as follows," Harvey Turnbul intoned.

The strange party of mourners sat in varying states of reverence around the dusty and unkempt office. Sylvia was there, face as hard and cold as basaltic rock. Uncle Michael was there, as were Burke and I.

Burke was the only member of the party who seemed truly grieved, though. Sylvia was frosty and quiet. Uncle and the senator had only ever really just tolerated each other and it had surprised me when Uncle had wept on receiving the news of the old man's death. And though I had known him well enough, I had never really felt close to him or even that he liked me very much.

"To my dearly departed wife, Sylvia," Harvey droned on, "I leave all of the dogs in my kennels of the female persuasion so that she might keep the company of those to whom I have always felt she was of a kindred spirit."

Sylvia smiled and snorted.

"To my whatever-the-hell-in-law Michael Reily, the only man I've ever known to keep his word, I leave my profoundest respect and the executorship of the foundation I have established to begin the Robert Augustus Miller Memorial Library and as such grant access to him and him alone to all of my notes and personal effects, for whatever our differences, I know that I can trust him to be fair in establishing an accurate picture of me for history."

Uncle Michael smiled.

"To my gadfly and conscience Burke Halloran, I direct that whatever funds necessary be put in trust that her outrageous salary might be paid her all the days of her nagging life. I further direct that she be allowed to live out her life in residence in the house that has been her home, certainly longer than I could stand, because I am sure that no one would take in such old and ornery baggage."

Burke began to cry.

"Finally, to my grandson, Scott Reily Miller, the only person on earth whom I truly love and am sorry to leave behind, I leave the bulk of my estate to be held in trust until he is of age to receive it, such trust to be administered by Harvey Turnbul and his uncle Michael and to pay Scott the sum of one hundred thousand dollars annually free and clear so that he might enjoy his youth, something that too few of us are allowed."

I was dumbfounded. Not because of the bequest, for I was his only blood kin and I'd rather expected it but because of his rather emotional codicil regarding his affections for me.

I was dazed and silent through the remainder of the legal procedure. The funeral had seemed merely curious and macabre, and I had again been more concerned about being in church with my unholy family than with the corpse in the box in the front of the room.

In addition, the death of so prominent a citizen had brought us into a strange glare of public scrutiny.

All in all, I had been occupied in the same way as during the wedding, with the details and not with the meaning. And it was not until this, the least personal and emotional of de rigueur—the will reading—that I felt the loss.

I did not speak at all until we had been hustled into a car and were speeding home. "Uncle," I said.

"Mmm?"

"Why do people wait so long to tell you how they feel about you?" I asked, feeling the first tears in my eyes for the senator.

"Because," Uncle said, smiling gently and putting his arm around me, "because they're afraid."

"Of what?"

"Of being hurt, rejected."

"But the senator wasn't afraid of anything that I ever saw."

"What do you want? An argument?" he asked brightly, trying to cheer me up.

"No," I said, crying in spite of his efforts. "I just don't understand why he never said he loved me, because—" I broke off, crying too hard to finish.

"Because you never told him you loved him?" he said, hugging me and rocking me gently.

I only nodded.

"You see," he said, holding me at arm's length, "that's how love is. You didn't tell him because he didn't tell you. It's the same for everybody."

He hugged me tight again.

"Love is very hard," he said in a strangely detached voice. "Especially for people like—like the senator. When everything else is easy for you, when you're not afraid of anything, love is the hardest.

"You feel love when you don't expect it. And you can't control it. When you feel in control of everything else around you, that's very frightening. You can't wave your cane and demand love. And yet you feel you need it very badly. So love defeats you, even though nothing else can. And that can make you very afraid. When you're someone like the senator. So you must try very hard to be brave and tell people that you love them even if you feel afraid."

"I love you," I said, sniffling.

"I love you, too," Uncle said, squeezing me.

And so minus one of the flock we went on with our lives.

Of course, nothing was the same, but nothing ever is.

Uncle became more involved in his ever-expanding business. The flighty purchase of the hotel chain to gain control of the Vanderhorst proved a tremendous new responsibility.

Gambler's Gourmet Package Goods was booming as well. There were TV dinners and frozen foods, a line of chocolate, a line of soft drinks and then wine and liquor, and Uncle was more and more caught up in business.

The theatres remained as a trademark of Gambler's hotel operations, but they, too, were being mass-produced, and scores of directors and designers were put on staff to do what Uncle could no longer manage single-handedly.

Even Christmas Eve and the summer migration celebrations were handled by committees that did nothing else all year.

I went my own way more as well.

Greg and Gray and I spent most weekends during the school year at the senator's house, now mine. I became more taken over by the demands of schoolwork and the joys of school activities. Greg and I both made the lower school soccer team in our last year at St. Francis.

Uncle never missed a game no matter how extreme the measures to be there. Once he actually landed on the soccer field in a helicopter minutes before game time.

"Why did you do that?" I demanded, almost as angry as I was embarrassed.

"I'm afraid to sky-dive," he said.

We didn't speak for days.

Increasingly, as Uncle became more and more successful, he became more and more outrageous. Or so I thought.

He bought me a ludicrous antique limousine. I hid in the back and made Mel, my driver, leave me outside the school grounds, preferring to walk.

Uncle's visits to school only heightened the legend of the gardener story. He got control of the PTA by donating the senator's library. He bought hundreds of tickets to school fairs and dinners and then actually brought hundreds of his overdressed friends.

He endowed the theatre.

I switched to soccer.

He endowed the soccer team.

I stopped telling him the dates and times of games or school events.

He endowed the school paper and found out anyway.

When at last sixth-year graduation was at hand, so, too, was the question of secondary school. Through Harvey and Mr. Frotham I made discreet inquiries into schools where Greg and I might both be accommodated and accepted, settling at last on The Academy.

It was a local private school with an open curriculum of classes and seminars that would allow me to progress at my own pace without leaving Greg behind. It was also one of what Uncle called those Halls of Hatred, meaning it had come into existence following the fall of separate but equal. Despite the fact that it had a fully integrated staff and student body by the time of my proposed enrollment, I knew Uncle would hate it. And eventually I could proceed no further with admission without his assent.

But I was my Uncle's nephew, and I had a plan.

"I've decided to go to Pietre," I announced one morning when Uncle was in attendance at breakfast.

"What?" he asked blearily.

"I'm going to Pietre," I repeated irritably.

"To go shopping?" he said. "Don't you have school?"

"Not Carson Pirie Scott. Pietre is a boarding school in Virginia," I said.

"Boarding school?" Gray asked, abandoning the stove.

"Never heard of it," Uncle said, slurping coffee. "Gray, I think something's on fire over there."

"Boarding school?" Gray repeated, not moving.

"Jesus," Uncle said, rising and crossing to the stove, "when did you start thinking about boarding school?"

As he spoke, he poured his coffee into the smoldering skillet of bacon. The hissing and steam attracted Gray's attention.

"*Mon Dieu*, Michael," Gray said, charging over, "what are you doing?"

"Warming up my coffee," Uncle said, pouring another cup. "Why boarding school?"

"Mr. Frotham feels that I've exhausted the possibilities at St. Francis," I said, taking a muffin.

"The soccer stadium isn't even finished," he said in disbelief.

"The bacon is ruined," Gray moaned.

"The bacon was ruined when I got there," Uncle said, picking grapes off the centerpiece. "Do I need to go down and talk to Mr. Frotham?"

"No, it's all arranged," I said.

"So when do we go up for a visit?" he asked, crossing his feet and leaning forward in excitement.

"A visit?" I asked.

"Well, sure," he said. "We can make a vacation of it. You know, tour boarding schools all over."

"Why?" I asked, terrified by the prospect.

"To decide which one you like," he said, taking a muffin, looking it over and then tossing it back. "Gray, have we got any doughnuts?"

"We have bran muffins," Gray said primly from the sink, where he stood scouring the charred remains of the bacon.

"But I'm going to Pietre," I insisted.

"Here I sit, one of the largest manufacturers of doughnuts in the free world and all I can get is a bran muffin," Uncle wailed, hand on his hip.

"You make bran muffins, too," Gray said, drying the pan and putting it back on the stove.

"I do?" Uncle said, blinking in surprise.

"Yes, you do," Gray said, peeling bacon off the slab and lining it up on the griddle. "And your TV commercials say that the bran fiber in your muffins helps reduce the risk of cancer."

"They do?" Uncle said, lighting a cigarette. "For crissake, I smoke three packs of cigarettes a day. What do I care about cancer? Besides, I hate bran muffins."

"So does everyone else, but they're good for you. You used to eat them all the time," Gray said, poking at the bacon with a pair of tongs.

"Well, I didn't like it," he muttered, chewing on one. "Where shall we go first? There are boarding schools in Switzerland. We could go skiing—"

"I said I was going to Pietre," I snapped.

"But you never even mentioned it," Uncle sputtered. "How did you find out about it? Is it a good school?"

"Uncle Harvey recommended it," I said flatly.

"Uncle Harvey?" Uncle shrieked. "That flaming asshole. Well, that's the first mark against Pietre. We'll go up and have a look at it, but I can tell you right now—"

"I'm already enrolled," I said with an air of finality.

"Well, don't you think I ought to have some say in the matter?" he said indignantly.

"I'm the one who has to go to school there," I said nastily. "Besides, I am nearly thirteen years old."

"Oh," Uncle said, waving a hand dramatically, "I forgot. How silly of me."

"The tuition is already paid," I said to end the matter. "Try to be happy for me."

"The tuition?" Uncle shouted. "When the hell—"

"Uncle Harvey and I arranged it," I said. "You were out of town."

"In darkest Africa, where there are no telephones, right?"

"I'm sorry," I said sarcastically. "I had no idea you'd be so upset."

"Well," Uncle said after a longish pause. "Where is this school? I do hope you don't feel I'm prying."

"It's in the mountains in Virginia," I said. "And don't be so dramatic."

"Humnh," he snorted, brightening. "Maybe we could get a mountain lodge nearby so we could visit on weekends—"

"I wouldn't bother," I said. "It's a very strict school and parental access is limited to officially designated days."

Gray was back at the table.

"I'm going to kill Harvey Turnbul," Uncle said, leaping up from the table. "And you are definitely not going to Pietre."

He stormed out of the room.

"What a fuss," I said. "Gray, stop staring at me like that."

"You have hurt his feelings very badly," Gray said expressionlessly.

"How can you tell?" I snorted. "He's always overacting."

"Because he has never said no to you before," he said, not moving.

We stared at each other for a moment.

"The bacon is on fire," I said, looking away.

Of course, by the time I relented, Uncle was thrilled with the "progressive curriculum" at The Academy, and Gray was just happy I was staying at home. I was just happy.

My graduation from St. Francis came and went with only mild humiliation. The continuing obligations of the business kept Uncle out of my hair and precluded his having time to do anything really embarrassing.

He did, of course, show up at the ceremony with what seemed to be hundreds of his wild and glittering friends, easily outnumbering the audience, the class and the faculty combined. And as I was graduating with highest honors and had to make a valedictory speech, he had pretty well manipulated audience reaction.

The speech itself had been quite a bone of contention between us.

I tried to keep my graduating status a secret, but his contacts at the school paper kept him well informed. Uncle began an unabated campaign to get his hands on or in the speech. He began leaving favored quotes on Post-It notes in my room and other places he thought I might be. He cut out magazine articles and put them on the refrigerator. He marked passages in books and left them on my pillow. He even put a list of suggested topics in place of my homework one morning, an unpleasant surprise, but the instructor who had assigned it had also met Uncle, so he understood.

"Leave me alone about the goddamned speech," I said, storming into breakfast the next day.

"A lot of thirteen-year-olds just leave it at 'Good morning, sir,' " he rumbled, voice still craggy from sleep.

"A lot of parents just leave it at 'Let me know if you need a hand,' " I shot back.

"I was only trying to help," he complained.

"Replacing my geometry homework with your ideas for speech topics is not helping," I said.

"Michael," Gray said disapprovingly.

"I was just trying to get your attention," he muttered.

"I appreciate the offer, but no, thanks, all right?" I said harshly.

"Michael," Gray said, "you took his homework?"

No answer.

"Where is it?" he asked.

"We could do with a deal less democracy around here," he pouted.

"Where is it?" he asked again.

"It's on my desk," he said.

Gray left to get it.

"Uncle," I said, "I'll do fine. I earned this speech. I'll make it."

"I just want to be involved in your life," Uncle said quietly.

"I'm growing up," I said. "I still need you. But I need to do some things myself. All right?"

"All right."

At last exams were done, grades posted, annuals signed and graduation day was at hand.

I was introduced to give the first-form valedictory. Uncle stood to applaud, so did his entourage, and so did the few remaining people in the school auditorium not wanting to feel left out. I was embarrassed but not surprised.

Silence.

"Hello," I said to the quiet. "And good-bye. That's what this afternoon is about. Spending one last time together to mark our achievement and, more important, to pay tribute to those who got us here.

"Someone I care about and whose opinion I greatly respect said to me a week or two before I started school that I was starting on something very hard but very important. He told me that I would be receiving the keys that would unlock the secrets of the greatest minds of all time. And that if I applied myself and learned my lessons, I could do anything that I wanted to for the rest of my life.

"In six years at St. Francis I have only begun to discover just what on earth it was he was talking about"—

Laughter—

"Let alone unlock the secrets of the ages. But his advice is still true. What I have learned, what I am learning is preparing me and all of us who will be graduated today to think for ourselves and, if we are wise, we will, like Socrates, realize just how little we know.

"And we're only starting to find out. Every new idea raises a hundred new questions. What we are here to find out is not the answers but how to find the answers for ourselves so that we can keep looking and keep learning all our lives. It seems to me at this moment that that is education.

"And so I say good-bye to my friends who have shared St.

Francis with me for six years. To you I say, 'Keep looking.' It's better to ask good questions than to have all the answers.

"To my teachers I say, 'Thank you for helping me to find the answers for myself.'

"But most important, I say thank you to my adviser from six years ago and today, for teaching me to ask. Thank you, Uncle Michael."

My favorite part of the speech was that I started the applause and precluded Uncle Michael's standing up since it was for him. I got a standing ovation anyway, but it was mine.

None of us can imagine our parents' having sex—or wants to. Clearly mine did at some point.

Uncle Michael?

To be honest, I'm really not sure.

Still, there comes a day when the topic of sex does come up naturally.

Naturally, for us it fairly exploded in a firestorm of high drama.

After first-form graduation we summered at The Sandpiper, Greg and I reveling in those halcyon days of youth, Uncle Michael coming and going as the bill and the business demanded, Gray there solid and unchanging as the sphinx. Family came and went, as did the gilt-edged hours of the summer, and in time we migrated inland for the fall and Greg's and my first year at The Academy.

As we settled into the rhythms of a new season and the demands of a new school, we fell easily into a new habit of being.

The Academy's seminar-styled lecture program and unstructured promotion put me in classes as I was ready for them, not simply when I was old enough. So school became more of a challenge and took more of my time in preparation.

Thus preoccupied, like Emily's family in Thornton Wilder's *Our Town*, we met for meals when we were all in town, shared our lives and generally ignored one another. But the trouble with sleepwalking is that when you wake up, your surroundings are unfamiliar and the alarm that should have awakened you is in another room. So as we phoned in another dinner together, we missed the bell.

"Michael, you're not eating your squash," Gray said, monitoring Uncle Michael's atrocious eating habits.

"I've got a mother, sprout breath."

"You won't get dessert."

"We should eat out more."

"We're at a restaurant," I pointed out, almost looking up from my book.

"Well, at other people's restaurants then," Uncle said, turning a page in his evening paper.

"Eat your squash."

"Don't you want something to read?"

"Michael."

"Why don't you yell at Scott?"

"Uncle Michael, eat your squash."

"Tag team dining," Uncle said, pitching his paper and shoveling down the squash.

"That reminds me," Gray said, picking up the paper and beginning to leaf through. "Kevin Perdue called the house today."

"Do I need to call him?"

"Don't talk with your mouth full," Gray said, not looking at him. "No, he's flying in from L.A. and wants to come to dinner. I said Friday was okay."

"Shanah?"

"He didn't say. So dinner at home on Friday. Okay?"

"Okay."

"Sure," I said, highlighting a salient passage.

"What's for dessert?"

"Eat your green beans."

"Check!"

And so without paying any particular attention we stumbled through the week and found our way to the table. Actually Uncle Michael went to the restaurant and Smitty had to be dispatched to retrieve him.

Uncle Kevin and I talked about the movies and who we thought would be in the running for Oscar among the fall releases.

"Kevin," Uncle called from the front door, "there you are. I've been looking everywhere for you. How's Shanah?"

"Oh, fine," Kevin answered affably, rising for a hug and air kisses.

"So, to what do we owe the honor?" Uncle asked, taking a seat across from our guest.

"We might ask you the same thing," Gray said, coming into

the living room drying his hands on a dish towel tucked into his waistband.

"Why, yes, Gray, I'd love a drink. And don't the hors d'oeuvres look tasty."

"You can have wine at table, dinner's ready."

"Oh, good, I hope we're having lots of squash. I'm starved."

"Smitty told me you already had chocolate terrine."

"I live with the food police."

Dinner proceeded without undue incident. Uncle had a little too much wine—no surprise—and wolfed down all his vegetables—a little surprising, but he was trying to get back on Gray's good side before dessert.

We talked of those things that friends do at dinner—work, books, movies, current events—passing the evening in the comfort of one another's familiar company.

"Dessert?" Gray asked eventually.

"Just a soupçon," Uncle Michael said, flinging his arms wide apart dramatically, redefining the word.

"More zucchini?" Gray asked him.

We all accepted the invitation to dessert, and Gray and Bert cleared up to make ready.

"So," Uncle said over the clatter of dishes, jump-starting the conversation, "Kevin, just what brings you back to the bosom of the people who brought you beige?"

And the bell tolled.

Kevin burst into tears and sobbed uncontrollably. As he put his head in his hands, we looked on silently.

Gray came back into the room, carrying a tray of sweets. "Dessert is served," he said, his announcement growing slower and softer with each word, falling silent and still as he took in the scene.

"Justly," Uncle Michael said. "Kevin? Are you okay?"

No answer.

"What's the matter?"

No answer.

"So, how about those Lakers?"

"Michael."

"Well?"

"I'm in love with Richard," Uncle Kevin wailed. "Since college. We've been . . . having an affair."

"Who's Richard?" I asked.

"Time for bed, Scott," Gray said, more or less dropping the platter on the table and heading for me with a purpose.

"Get a life, Gray," I answered, gripping the chair preparing to defend my ringsides.

Uncle sat staring at Kevin as he began to sob with renewed vigor.

Gray struggled with me briefly and then picked up the chair with me in it. I slipped out of the chair as it rose from the floor and then turned and grasped it to keep it between Gray and me. It was thus that, distracted momentarily, we missed Uncle Michael's sidearm pitch of his wineglass.

The smash punctuated the melee with a large red stain on the wall that looked rather like the island of Honshu.

We dived for cover under the table as Uncle screamed, "You son of a bitch."

The isle of Honshu was followed in rapid succession by the cheesecake archipelago and the sea of tea pitcher, as Uncle punctuated his continuing remarks. "You have sat by for thirty years and let me twist in the wind and the entire time . . . you and Richard? Or should I say Dick?"

Uncle Kevin leaped to his feet and joined the cartographic frenzy with a few condiments and comments of his own. "So this is about you?" Kevin screamed. "Fuck you, Michael. It's always about you, isn't it?"

"What's going on?" I asked Gray as we peered over the end of the table, ducking at appropriate moments.

"I tried to get you to leave," Gray said between the centerpiece and the remains of the dessert platter. "But no, you couldn't just leave."

"How could it not be about me, you self-involved sack of shit?"

"On three we go for the kitchen door."

"Right," Gray said.

"This is about me. For once this is all about me."

"One."

"Oh, right. Even though it's me you've been lying to since high fucking school."

"No, Michael. Just this once this has nothing to do with you. It's all about me."

"So why tell me about it?"

"Three."

The kitchen door was one of those spring-hinged things that swings both ways—an ironic choice under the circumstances but not a bad escape route. Unfortunately we were not alone in the house, and Smitty and Bert, with the coffee things still in hand, were glued to the other side of the door. The impact sent them flying back into the kitchen and flung us back into the dining room just as Uncle snatched the tablecloth off the table, dislodging everything but the still-lighted candelabra like the old magician's trick—sort of.

We all stared at the candelabra.

"That's amazing," Uncle Kevin said at last.

"I need a drink," Uncle said, dropping the cloth and walking across it toward the living room.

"Make mine a double," Kevin said, following.

"We should eat out more," I said to Gray, who only nodded.

And so, naturally, the subject of sex came up. Or out.

The conversation between Uncle Michael and Kevin continued in quieter tones long into the night and involved glassware only insofar as it accommodated their highballs.

We found them asleep and tear-stained amid heaps of Kleenex on the living room floor. We left them there—aphorisms about sleeping dogs flickering through our minds—and went out for the day. Uncle Kevin was gone when I returned that evening, but the topic of his tumultuous visit remained like the stains on the dining room wall, unmentioned and unavoidable.

We painted over the stains. Honshu took three coats, but Uncle Michael's distance at our already detached family forums grew.

Shortly before the third coat was applied to Honshu, Gray and I were having an innocuous enough meal with Uncle. "Michael?" Gray asked. "Have you tried this fried eggplant?" It was a new ploy, Grammy had suggested, that Gray had been trying since the world atlas food toss. It wasn't working any better, but the airplane and hangar method had failed miserably.

"That red wine stain is still there," Uncle said, staring at it.

"Don't change the subject," Gray said, sighing.

"I think we should talk about Uncle Kevin's visit, Scott."

I choked slightly and looked at Gray, who looked at Michael.

"Well, I'll get us all some dessert," Gray said, leaving so abruptly that he struck his shoulder on the doorjamb.

"So that's how to get dessert around here," Uncle said, lighting a cigarette. "I should have tried it sooner."

I realized I still had food in my mouth and resumed chewing, looking away from Uncle.

"This isn't exactly how I'd planned this," he began. "I guess I really hadn't planned anything at all. Would you consider just not growing up?"

"Um, hmm." I nodded, mouth full. If I just kept shoveling it in, I reasoned, I wouldn't have to say anything.

"Well, that's sporting of you," he said, patting my hand. "But it isn't very practical. And anyway, this is all about growing up, right? And we have to deal with these things as they just naturally come up, right?"

"What are you talking about?" I asked, unable to think of anything else to say.

"What am I talking about?" he said, lighting another cigarette, the last still smoldering in the ashtray. "It's just that—" He broke off and started again. "There's something we need to talk about."

"What?"

"Well, I'd rather hoped that you'd ask when you were ready. You know how I feel about rushing kids to grow up."

"Some nice fruit and cream," Gray said, coming back in.

"Gray and I have discussed it, though, and we feel I need to bring it up now because it's important that you know how I feel."

Good God, I thought. What now?

"It's about sex," he said.

"Oh," I said, much relieved.

"Coffee," Gray said, hurtling out of the room.

"Now I know you've had biology and all that," he said, waving me off. "So I'm not going to embarrass us both by getting into mechanics, unless you have specific questions. Do you?"

I shook my head.

"Well, Gray and I are always around if you do," he said. "And God knows there is loads of how-to literature if you have questions of technique you'd rather not ask us. Either way feel free, okay?"

"Okay," I said, focusing on the dessert.

"Okay," he said. "Now the part I think needs discussing. You're getting to what is euphemistically called that awkward age," he said. "What that means is that for a while your body is going to start doing things you're not prepared to deal with. It's like going to your first formal dinner party. You don't know what fork to use or what's expected, so you feel and act awkwardly. After a while you figure out what to do and you're not awkward anymore. It's not just like that, but that's the general idea," he said, laughing.

I tried to look at him but couldn't.

"So, your body is going to start maturing sexually," he said, trying to sound serious but actually only getting louder. "Outwardly that'll mean you'll start getting hairier and taller and your voice will get deeper. Don't be alarmed. I'm sure you know that's natural.

"The reason, I'm sure you also know, that all these changes in your body start taking place is that glands in you start dumping hormones into the works. That's okay, too. It's already made your baby teeth fall out and gotten you this far.

"Now these hormones mean well, but sometimes they go a little haywire. Your face will start to break out. Let us know when that starts to happen and we'll get you a dermatologist. There's no point in suffering any more than necessary. And while we're at it, please don't start shaving without talking to us. It's okay. I just don't want you messing up your face, okay?"

"All right," I said, starting to relax a bit.

"In addition to lousing up your face and making your voice crack, these hormones have other side effects," he said, lighting yet another cigarette. "That has to do with the way you feel. You're going to feel . . . weird. You'll be depressed for no good reason. You'll get restless and nervous, and well, I felt like a caged tiger pacing the boundaries of his cell. Go kick the soccer ball or take a walk or run around the block. That'll release other more friendly hormones. You'll have to try different things to find out what works best for you. But mainly, try to remember you're okay; it's just your body going crazy.

"Worst of all, this will all start to happen at a time when the people around you want you to act grown-up. Which means sitting still and worrying, both of which will make the restlessness and the depression far worse.

"There's nothing I can do about all that," he said with a shrug. "That's just the stupid way the world works. You have to deal with being pulled in two different directions."

"Who wants coffee?" Gray asked, coming in with the carafe and putting out cups.

"Let me know if I can help. Talk to Gray. Do what you have to do. Just try not to do anything rash. Everybody's been through it, everybody hates it and grown-ups act like asses about it because they don't want to be reminded. Okay?"

"Sure," I said, calm and confident, my appetite for dessert slowly returning.

"Now, what all this mess is leading up to is you're getting ready to have sex."

So much for dessert.

"Some cake," Gray announced, bound for the door. "I'll just bake one."

"Gray," Uncle said, exasperated.

Gray returned and hovered near the door.

"Anyway," Uncle Michael continued, "there's a term you've probably heard or you'll soon hear from the other boys—horny."

Gray was gone, and I heard the back door close.

I put my fork down and began pouring coffee.

"There's not a thing in the world dirty about the word," he said, lighting another cigarette. "It's actually a very apt description."

I tried not to die.

"It refers to young buck deer and other bovine creatures. Instead of getting acne, they get antlers. As their bodies begin to mature sexually, little velvety horns start to appear on their foreheads. And that's horny. Now, people use it to describe a rather more personal experience where—"

"I know what it means," I said, feeling the heat in my face and ears.

"All right," he said. "So on top of everything else, you're going to start feeling horny."

"Could you stop saying that?" I said, shoveling sugar into my coffee cup.

"Don't be embarrassed," he said. "It's all right. That's really what I want to say anyway. You're going to start feeling . . . we'll call it *funny*, okay?"

"Fine," I said, looking away.

"You're going to start feeling *funny* just in general and for no particular reason. And then you'll start feeling *funny* about all sorts of people in all sorts of situations and all of it is okay. Don't be embarrassed. Just go ahead and feel that way.

"I'd like to recommend that in spite of feeling this inclination toward other people, you wait at least until college before trying to do anything about it. There's nothing wrong with feeling *funny*, but you need to be surer of yourself before you start having sex. I think. Now masturbation is another story—"

"Uncle Michael, please," I said, slamming my cup noisily back into the saucer, hands shaking wildly.

"Okay, all right," he said placatingly. "I won't say that word either. I do want to say that not only is *it* all right, but *it's* a way of venting the fantasies that make you feel *funny* without getting involved with emotional reactions you're not ready to deal with. I just want you to know that I feel very strongly that you shouldn't have sex with—"

"Really, Uncle Michael," I said, getting up from the table.

"Oh, come on," he said. "Can't I say that either?"

"I wish you wouldn't," I said, folding my arms and looking out the window.

"It's going to be pretty limiting, but I'll try," he said, leaning back in his chair. "Let's see. I feel that you're better off not . . . getting involved with another person in *that way* until you love them and that you have more in common with them than just . . . sex—sorry.

"Now that's only the way I feel," he said calmly. "Everyone feels differently. You'll have to decide for yourself when the time comes. Whatever you decide to do and whoever you decide to do it with is okay with me. If you need help or you feel bad, please try to talk with me about it.

"And then there's the risk of AIDS. Do you know about condoms?"

"Yes."

"Do you want some?"

"Uncle Michael."

"I can tell you're a little embarrassed right now," he said. "And I don't mind telling you this hasn't been an easy talk for me. For some reason this topic embarrasses parents and children. But I want you to promise me that you'll try to get round that and speak with me if you're troubled. Promise."

"I promise," I said, tremendously relieved that the talk was over.

"And now, about Kevin's little tirade the other night," he said, pouring himself some coffee.

"Oh, my God," I said, having completely forgotten that that was what all this was about in the first place.

"Feeling, what's it, *funny* is a tricky thing," Uncle went on heedlessly. "You just can't say who you're going to feel *funny* about. You just feel *funny*. Most boys feel *funny* about girls, and most girls feel likewise about the boys."

I was catatonic, transfixed on Honshu.

"And it would seem Uncle Kevin feels *funny* about boys and girls though maybe he feels *funniest* about boys," Uncle said, an edge creeping into his voice. "Now that's called—"

"Gay," I said. "Or bisexual. Okay? Can we please talk about something, anything else?"

"Not yet," Uncle said quietly.

"Jesus," I said, putting my head on the table.

"You see, Scott, I feel *funny* . . . oh, for God's sake," he said, lighting yet another cigarette. "I'm gay. So is Gray. And the reason I got so mad at Kevin is that I was . . . am . . . was, I don't know, in love with him."

I kept my head on the table and listened to Uncle Michael smoke for a while. I guess I knew that, I thought. I mean, he never dated. But he never dated anyone. And Gray was, well, Gray was Gray. I looked over my arm. Uncle Michael wiggled his fingers at me in a little wave and grinned.

"So what does this mean?" I asked, rising slightly.

"Nothing." Uncle shrugged. "It just is."

"Are Bert and Smitty gay?"

"Heavens, I don't know. Ask them."

And then, of course, it hit me.

"Are you and Gray having sex?"

"Well, so much for feeling *funny*," he snorted.

"Well?"

"You know, my sex life really isn't any of your business."

"Why not?"

"Most parents don't discuss their sex lives with their children."

"It isn't the same."

"Because I'm gay or because I'm not really your parent?"

That shut me up.

"But no," he said at last.

"And Uncle Kevin?"

"No, and that is the end of this line of questioning."

"The important thing," he said after a pause that lasted for a-whole-nother cigarette, "is that none of this has anything to do with you. You'll feel *funny* about whoever you feel *funny* about when the time comes. And whoever that is, is okay. Okay?"

I suppose I could adopt the popular pursuit of blaming everything that happened in my life on the strange revelations of Honshu. But despite Mr. Tolstoy's views to the contrary, happy families are indeed happy in their own way.

The only real change in our lives was that Uncle Michael's mediaphobia abated somewhat. And while he didn't pursue the attention of the press, he was far less shy of it, I realized, because he was no longer protecting me. So, as the business and our fortunes grew so, too, did Uncle's notoriety.

Like most teenagers, I was supremely indifferent, focusing instead on the really important issues: soccer, the horrors of the school dance, school politics, popularity. You know, the earth-shattering stuff. Our sophomore year saw the return of Thom Burford—of the grade school gardener and the bloody nose incident. He shared classes with Greg and fell in with us initially.

Thom was no longer the lard butt he had been in first grade. His time out of Columbia had seen him spread that weight over a longer, leaner, much more flattering frame. It had also witnessed his growth into a longer, leaner, better-looking jerk than he had been previously.

He and I began competing for everything. A place on the soccer team. We both got one. Greg didn't. That all-important sophomore class presidency. I won.

Then it happened. Amy-something-Greek-and-unpronounce-able-with-silent-T's-for-God-sake transferred into our homeroom midyear. Suddenly, the topic of girls overtook school politics and got pretty close to soccer in its world-shaking importance. And Thom and I turned a new corner in competitiveness.

Thom's professed prowess with girls—actual or apocryphal—exceeded mine easily since I neither had nor professed anything of the sort. Still in all, something in me rose to the challenge that marvelous first day when "Miz" Davis first presented Amy to homeroom.

The tiny waist and hands, the play of the late-winter sun on her long dark hair and her braces, I felt *funny* all over the place. And that marvelous silent *T* in her name put her alphabetically appointed seat only four away from mine. My joy rose and crashed as homeroom passed and again and again as each new class arrived, ripe with the possibility that she might be there.

By lunchtime she had not reappeared in my miserable existence, and I felt so *funny* I couldn't eat. And when I saw that precious metal smile in world history later that afternoon, I lost all feeling in my legs and complete knowledge of the Napoleonic epoch.

Such was my state of mind in soccer practice that afternoon when I headed the ball to a member of the other scrimmage team. And it persisted on to the dinner table that night at the restaurant. I spoke perfunctory greetings and then sat rereading page 237 of my biology text, hoping that the next time through some of the words would form themselves into comprehensible thoughts. I was so conspicuous by my absence that I occasioned comment even at that dinner of the living dead.

"Scott?" Gray asked to rouse my attention. "You haven't touched your chop. Is something wrong with your food?"

"Music to my ears," Uncle said, snapping his paper for emphasis. "No one ever asks me if anything's wrong with my food."

"Scott, do you feel all right?" Gray asked me, reaching for my forehead.

"I'm fine," I managed to say, shrugging him off.

"That must be some book," Uncle said archly. "Why, you've been reading that page alone for about twenty-five minutes."

"Eat your broccoli," I dodged.

"Michael," Gray warned.

"It was a short but memorable melody."

I hazed on through the evening as Gray forced holistic home remedies on me. Uncle seemed to find the whole thing amusing and teased us both. They finally wore themselves out and I got some peace after they were asleep, eventually finding some fitful facsimile for myself as I drifted off, clutching my pillow and savoring my life with Amy.

Sleep-worn and worse for wear, I made my way to homeroom. I rounded the corner and froze as the hideous scene assaulted my view. There was Thom, leaning—if you please—on the wall beside the homeroom door and the mother of my unborn children and they were—dare I say it?—talking. It was a shocking spectacle, and I murmured the tersest of greetings as I pushed past them into the classroom.

Talking.

My mind reeled. How could she betray me like that? And Thom? That snake.

My response at roll call was cold and sardonic. "Present," I said.

They knew.

With an unmistakable air of tragic nobility that would have brought tears of admiration from Sydney Carton I went to class.

Everyone knew. I was humiliated, but I wasn't giving them the satisfaction. I met my classes, answered questions, calling on my inner strength to rise above this personal tragedy. Everyone knew and hated them for what they'd done to me.

Talking? Ha!

I stormed into the house, announced I would not be attending piano lessons and went to my room to pretend to study. Gray stood in the foyer, as always, eternally wiping his hands on a dish towel tucked into his waistband.

"Scott?" Gray said, gently tapping on my door a little later. "What's the matter?"

"*Nothing!*" I said reasonably.

"I called Greg—"

"You called Greg?"

"—and he said you had been OTR all day."

"You called Greg?"

"What is OTR?"

"Will you just leave me alone. I have a big test tomorrow."

"You want me to help you study?"

"I want you to leave me alone."

Gray withdrew silently.

Of course, I didn't want to be left alone. I wanted wide-screen, Technicolor, Dolby sound, self-indulgent, CinemaScope, emotional wallowing with an SRO crowd.

I went to the kitchen. Studying always makes me hungry.

Gray said nothing in greeting as he and Bert went about the business of preparing dinner. I got some juice and muffins and malingered at the kitchen table until Gray finally couldn't stand it any longer.

"Don't you have to study?"

"For what?"

"Eh, *mon Dieu*," he said, wiping those hands and sitting across the table to snap beans Uncle Michael would not eat later at dinner. "Scott, I am very worried. What is wrong?"

The cameras rolled; the music swelled.

"I told you I don't want to talk about it," I announced, storming out of the room and out to the balcony. Exteriors are so good for dramatic confrontation, and I could easily be seen through the glass when Gray followed.

"Scott," Gray said, following me out on cue, "should we get someone for you to talk to?"

"You mean, like a therapist?" I asked, considering the dramatic potential: Driven mad by love, hmm?

"If you can't talk to me . . ." He left it at that, concluding with a shrug.

"There's this girl," I said abruptly.

Gray sat heavily on a wrought-iron chair. "Is she . . . embarrassed?" he asked at last.

"What?"

"You know, in trouble?"

"In trouble?"

"Pregnant," he whispered.

"Jesus, Gray, she just started at our school yesterday. How would I know?"

"So you haven't been . . . Oh, thank God."

"I . . . kind of . . . like her." I was clearly going to have to get the scene back on track.

"Oh, but this is wonderful." He was up and crying and headed straight for me. "What's she like? What does her family do? What does she look like? How did you meet her?" he babbled, alternately embracing me and wiping his face and his hands on the dish towel. "You're growing up," he sobbed. The scene stealer.

I finally got him calmed down enough to get him back in the kitchen to annoy Bert with his blubbering.

"Don't tell Uncle," I said, stationing him at the snap beans, getting him a fresh dish towel and secretly hoping he would tell; Uncle would know whose scene it was.

"But why?"

"I don't know," I sputtered. "Because he'll dress up like Cupid and shoot her with a real bow and arrow and there'll be an ugly trial."

"True," Gray said pensively.

I went to my room and waited for Gray to tell. Of course, he took me at my word and didn't tell—no sense of drama whatsoever, unless it was his scene, which dinner definitely was.

We had been at table about five minutes and Gray was so distracted that Uncle was openly hiding his snaps in the centerpiece.

"Well," he announced startling us both back to consciousness, his plate uncharacteristically clean, "what's for dessert?"

Gray looked at him blankly, then at me and burst into tears.

"Oh, all right," Uncle said, pulling the epergne to his place and beginning to fork snap beans into his mouth. "Jesus, what a fuss."

Gray took his histrionics and his dishrag into the kitchen.

"I'm eating, I'm eating," Uncle called after him.

"Uncle Michael," I said, becoming aware that he was eating the centerpiece, "stop that. That's disgusting."

"Well, I'm glad someone sees my side," he said, throwing his napkin on the floor. "No dessert again. If you'll excuse me, I have to stick my finger in the dike. No pun . . . oh, never mind."

Gray was not only stealing my scene but taking my audience.

Well, at least he would tell Uncle now. I finished dinner and went to my room to await my close-ups. Uncle never came. Finally I broke down and went to Uncle's study, where I found him smoking and drinking and eating a box of Godivas he had concealed in his stationery drawer.

"Scott, come in," he said, slamming the drawer and wiping his mouth inconspicuously on his sleeve.

"Well," I said, flinging myself onto one of the odious armless chairs, "I guess Gray told you."

"Told me what? Jeez, he was ridiculous this evening. I mean, more than usual. Do you think it's . . . the change?" he asked confidentially.

"He didn't tell you anything?"

"After about forty-five minutes I managed to sweat out of him that you were in a mood. And he asked me what OTR means. Do you suppose I should tell him?"

"Is that all?"

"Well, you know how queasy he is, and 'on the rag' is not strictly PC. And I don't want to get Greg in trouble. Why was he talking to Greg anyway?"

"To find out what's wrong with me," I ventured, valiantly trying to shift the focus of the scene back to me.

"You?" He snorted derisively. "You're just in love."

I was speechless.

"You knew?" I demanded once I relocated my voice. "Gray didn't tell you?"

"Oh, my God," he said. "You didn't tell Gray? You know how weepy he gets about that sort of thing, Scott. I think it's something to do with being French. Do you remember the time—"

"You knew?"

"Well, of course. You've been mooning around like Andy and Judy."

"Why didn't you say anything?"

"You're the one in love. I figured you'd talk about it if you wanted to, but to Gray? Scott, what were you thinking?"

"Will you shut up about Gray?"

"Boy, Greg was right."

"Well, I'm talking about it now."

"And I'm sure the people downstairs are fascinated, so speak up, would you?"

"Would you be serious?" I asked more quietly.

"No. Do I have to?"

"Then shut up and listen."

"OTR."

"Uncle Michael."

He held up his hands in surrender and smoked quietly as I described the whole affair with particular attention to the sickening spectacle of that very morning.

"So what do you think?" I asked when he didn't volunteer anything at the conclusion of my grand revelation.

"About what?"

"Uncle Michael."

"Okay, okay, let me get this straight. You're in love with this girl who's been in your class for two whole days and you've seen her four times, five if you count the leaning-in-the-hall incident."

I sighed and nodded.

"Well, I'm going to go out on a limb here, Scott, but, have you considered talking to her?"

I could only stare.

"I mean maybe she's a jerk or a Republican. Or both. That's been my experience."

"Uncle Michael," I wailed.

"I'm sorry. Are you a Republican? Maybe she's a Democrat. Or worse yet, a Libertarian."

"No, I mean, what about Thom?"

"Let him get his own girl."

"That's it? That's all you've got to say?" I asked, incredulous.

"Who do I look like? The Dalai Lama?"

"So that's your last word?"

"Rosebud," he said, shrugging.

I went to bed—very dramatically. Talk to her? I thought. And yet it was so simple. It just might work. I lay awake, rehearsing what I would say. Snappy riposte, charming phrases fraught with meaning. She would be dazzled. I got up a little early—around 4:00 A.M.—so I would be ready and at school when she arrived. I changed clothes several times and was practicing my laugh in front of the mirror when Uncle burst in.

"What the fuck are you doing? It's four in the morning," he whined. "Nice shirt."

I sprained my neck, grabbing for the hairbrush and trying to look as if I were working on my hair. "Oh, just, um, up a little early. Studying to do."

"Christ," he sighed, turning to go. "Well, study quietly, hmm? Oh," he said, turning back at the door. "I like the sort of wise, knowing laugh. You know, heh-heh," he imitated. "It's so, how you say . . . artificial."

The hairbrush narrowly missed his head as he ran laughing from the room.

And so, clad in the fourth or fifth outfit of the day, I arrived an hour early for school and took up my post outside the homeroom door, casually leafing through the *Wall Street Journal* I had forced Smitty to go to three 7-Elevens to find.

"Where the hell were you this morning?" Greg said in greeting.

"Oh, sorry," I said, reddening. "I came in early this morning. I guess I forgot to pick you up."

"No shit," Greg said, pushing past. "Nice blazer. Who died?"

I turned back and looked directly into Amy's face.

Hours of practice, a dashing outfit, dozens of clever bon mots at the ready, I looked directly into her braces and said, voice cracking across two octaves, "Hi."

"Hi," she said with a small smile. "Nice blazer."

"Thanks," I whispered into the empty hallway, no moisture remaining in my mouth.

"Will you be joining us for roll call this morning?" Miz Davis asked. "Or have you dressed up to be the doorman?"

I slunk through the laughter back to my desk, ditched the jacket in my locker and hid out for the rest of the day.

Gray and I were already at the table when Uncle came home. "Glad you could join us," Gray said tartly.

"Pass the centerpiece and give me a break," Uncle said. "Is it your turn to be OTR, Gray?"

"What does that mean?"

"You're not old enough to know."

"I spoke to her today," I cut into their bickering.

"Scott, please not in front of Gray," Uncle said, flipping out his napkin.

"And why not?"

"If you cry, I'm having you deported. I can do it, I swear to God. I have connections at INS," he said, waving cutlery at Gray, then turning to me. "So, that wasn't so bad, was it?"

"It was horrible," I moaned.

"Uh-oh," he said, serving his plate. "What could be so horrible?"

"It just was," I said, picking bread crumbs off my squash casserole.

"Oh, I see," he said, defending his plate from Gray and the casserole with the salad tongs. "What? Did you fart? Pick your nose? What did you say? What did she say? And what did you say back?"

"I said, 'Hi,' she said, 'Hi,' she said, 'Nice blazer,' I said, 'Thanks.' "

"That doesn't sound too incriminating. You wore a blazer? Who died?"

"It was the way I said it," I whined.

"Michael, just try a little squash casserole," Gray said.

"Oh, for God sake," Uncle said, abandoning the salad tongs, "just give me the bowl and I'll eat the whole thing."

"There's broccoli, too."

"How many vegetables are we having?" he demanded, pounding the table.

"Stop talking about those vegetables," I screamed. "We're talking about me."

"Yeah, Gray," Uncle said. "We're talking about Scott and what's her name. What is her name?"

"You don't know?"

"I missed the paper today."

I told him.

"How's that?"

I spelled it.

"Tah-blah-blah-blah." He nodded. "Amy Tah-blah-blah-blah. A fine old Greek name."

And that was it. I have never since been able to remember her name.

"The *T* is silent." I snickered.

"Thank God," Uncle said, laughing with me. "Okay, lookit. I

think it's all this face-to-face stuff—vis-à-vis, as you and the out-back spy would say. You should call her on the phone, introduce yourself. Tell her you're the one in the blazer."

"Uncle Michael."

"Sorry, leave out the blazer. Ask her to lunch, you have tons of money. You even have a car and a driver. How many other sixteen-year-olds can say that?"

"I'm fifteen."

"See, even fewer fifteen-year-olds have a car and driver. It's a known fact."

"I don't know her number."

"How many Tah-blah-blah-blahs can there be in the book?"

"Right," I said, leaping up from the table. "This is a great idea."

"Scott . . ." Gray started.

"You're excused, Scott," Uncle cut him off with his and-that's-the-end-of-that-voice.

I headed for the hall phone.

"Michael," Gray said quietly.

"I'm not eating the squash casserole," Uncle said. "It looks like someone already did."

"That's not what I was going to say," Gray said patiently.

"Well, sometimes I get to say, 'You're excused.' "

"I was going to ask if you were ready for dessert."

"I was born ready for dessert." Uncle grinned, pushing his plate away.

Go have parents.

I closed the hall door.

I will spare you the details of a romantic three-course luncheon at Chez McDonald's shared by a gangly pair of adolescents. Suffice it to say, it was heaven. Amy and I were soon going steady— "As opposed to dating all those other people?" as Uncle put it.

Thom was not a gracious loser, eventually raising the ire of Mr. Tah-blah-blah-blah for calling too often to pester Amy.

Soccer was in a nip-and-tuck race for first place with Amy, and the horrors of the Spring Dance subsided into terrified anticipation.

Dancing lessons with Uncle Michael were memorable mainly for complaints from the neighbors about the music and the stomping and the subsequent arrival of the police owing to Uncle's redressing the complaint by turning up the stereo and jumping up and down on the floor with his tap shoes on. He taught one of the arresting officers a time step.

It was one of the final few fleeting moments of childhood worship that I felt for Uncle and I began to slide slowly down the backseat of our ride through life together, hiding in my embarrassment from the guilt by association everyone comes to feel for parental units.

Life's seat covers started getting noticeably slippery around the time of the much-dreaded and anticipated Spring Dance.

Uncle, unable to leave well enough alone or take no for an answer or take a hint or mind his own goddamned business, once let in on the Amy romance was as hard to be rid of as an eyelash on your finger.

The Spring Dance was a school building fund-raiser, and Uncle wrested control out of the hands of the unsuspecting parents' association by underwriting the entire affair. He began at once to create an evening so opulent it would have made Louis Quatorze blush. The headmaster of The Academy had ignored the advice of the Wildebeest from St. Francis to limit Uncle's access to campus. Dr. Huggins, ever mindful of a potential big donor, gave

Uncle free reign, which of course, became a reign of terror. Dr. H. was thrilled with the addition of the local Philharmonic to play waltzes. We were not. He was leery of the topiary rosebushes and downright nervous about the silk canopy suspended from the gym ceiling. But when Uncle replaced the light fixtures, had the basketball lines sanded off the floor and repainted the gymnasium walls a dusty rose, Dr. H. saved me the trouble and denied Uncle any further access to the school and—best of all—the dance.

Undaunted, Uncle put together an after-the-ball-breakfast for Amy and me and a few intimates, I think, as an excuse to wait up for me. Gray was allowed to be a chaperon at the *dans macabre* and was with me when I returned home.

"Happy spring," Uncle called from the living room when he heard us come in. "Where is everyone? Oh, my God. You look like shit. Are you all right? What the hell happened?" He was picking up speed.

"Calm down," I said through cracked and bleeding lips.

"Gray?" Uncle fairly screamed.

"Enh," Gray exhaled, throwing up his hands. "I'm going to get a steak."

"A steak?" Uncle called after him. "How can you eat after looking at that?" he concluded, pointing at my face.

"Thanks," I said, going into the living room.

"It's for his eye," Gray called from the kitchen.

"Will someone tell me what the hell is going on?" Uncle was screaming in earnest.

"Calm down," Gray and I shouted back in unison, if not harmony, from our respective parts of the house.

Uncle came into the living room, lit a cigarette and stared.

Bert arrived, unbidden, with a martini for Uncle.

"Tell Gray I said thanks," Uncle said snidely.

"You can tell me in person," Gray said, steaming in with a steak and an ice pack.

"I take it breakfast is off?" Uncle asked.

"*Mon Dieu,*" Gray muttered, putting the steak on my eye, "look at you, such a spectacle."

"Owww," I moaned, trying to get away.

"It will help take down the swelling."

"Not if you keep beating me over the head with it."

"You deserve to be beaten over the head—"

"Shut up, shut up, shut up," Uncle screamed. "Gray, out. Scott, talk. And not about the breakfast steaks."

"Idonwannatalkaboutit," I said, fleeing out onto the balcony, slamming the doors behind me. I could hear him and Gray screaming for a bit and then all was quiet. I sat for a while, staring off into space.

"You know," Uncle said, suddenly there, startling me, "it takes the light of the stars years to reach the earth. Sometimes millions. So when you look into the sky at night, you can see the light of creation. Pretty cool, hunh?"

"I guess."

"I like to think it puts me in perspective. I mean compared with all that, what's a little black eye between friends?"

"Gray told you."

"No, oddly enough, that I believe is the one thing Gray didn't tell me. I did rather feel that it was my fault somehow, but he said I should ask you for the dirt. So give."

"I had a fight with Thom."

"What, again?"

"Uncle."

"Was it over Amy?"

"Sort of."

"He's jealous?"

"I guess."

"Were you there tonight? Or did he send that face parcel post?"

"It was something he said."

"About Amy?"

"About you," I admitted after a long pause.

"Well, the Wildebeest is wrong. I can now cause fights and wreak havoc without even showing up," Uncle sighed, putting out his cigarette and crossing to take me in his arms. "No one can see," he said, overcoming my halfhearted attempts to squirm away. "You can tell me now."

"He asked Amy how she liked dating a fag. He said I must be a fag because you are."

"So you hit him," Uncle said, squeezing me tighter.

"I asked him to stop saying that word first."

He rocked me back and forth in his arms for quite some time. "I've got to be a parent here for a minute, okay?"

I nodded.

"First, I love you very much. And I know you're hurting and I'm here to love you and support you unconditionally for every day of our lives here on earth together. And afterward, if I can work it. Now, the hard stuff," he said, letting me go. "You must never hit people. Never."

"But he called you a fag."

"You've called me worse."

"You're mine, not his."

"I didn't hit you, though. Fag is just a word. It used to be your mother's pet name for me."

"Besides, he ruined my date with Amy."

"You did that, dear heart. And you lost the fight as soon as you swung. Bigotry and violence are nothing but fear brought on by ignorance. You let Thom win when you showed your ignorance."

"He called me a fag."

"Are you?"

"No."

"Would it be so horrible if you were?"

"Well, no, I guess not."

"Well, what's the difference?"

"I don't know, but there is," I spluttered, getting mad.

"Is it fear and ignorance? Is that the difference?"

We stared at each other a moment.

"You're good," I said at last.

"You think?" he said, nodding. "It was pretty good, wasn't it?"

"How do you do that? What? Did you go to uncle school?"

"This is uncle school," he said, pointing down with both index fingers. "I think it's a genetic thing I inherited from Grammy. I'm making this shit up as I go along."

I shook my head and made a low, whistling sound.

"I may get the hang of this parenting stuff yet." He shrugged. "Gives me an appetite. Feel like helping me eat breakfast for eight?"

"Beats wearing it," I said, pitching my steak aside and following him inside. "What about Amy?"

"Send flowers, then call and apologize."

"Good, good." I nodded. "You just make this up, hunh? What about the gardener thing?"

"Okay, so there's a learning curve," he conceded.

I apologized to Amy and did Uncle two better by apologizing to Thom and Dr. H. Amy was gracious, Dr. H. blamed Uncle anyway. And Thom? Well, two out of three. School continued to lurch along with those limited successes and failures so crucial at the time, so insignificant in retrospect. My ardor for Amy faded along with my memory of her last name, and we dated on and off on into college, comfortable with but not committed to each other. We never really stopped going steady. I think we just forgot. All in all, I was closer to Greg. We elected to attend the large state university there in town primarily because of that friendship.

Uncle, deprived of his access to The Academy and, as a result, to me for eight or more hours a day, began devoting himself to expanding the business and to meddling in the lives of other innocent and unsuspecting victims.

Pawpaw and Grammy took an early retirement. Not because either wanted or planned to, I think, but because Uncle forced them into it. "You can enjoy yourselves," he said.

"We're not unhappy," Grammy snapped back.

But in the end she relented. Uncle bought out their mortgage and sent them away for six months in Europe. While they were gone, he completely redecorated and remodeled Grammy's house. He had a huge ribbon and bow stretched across it when they returned exhausted from being dragged around the Continent.

She hated it and she and Uncle spent the better part of my junior year not speaking.

I really only saw everyone at official family functions. The Christmas party, New Year's, the spring closing, the summer opening—all continued as sacred family/company traditions, or so I felt. I was away mostly, and so was Uncle.

His business interests continued to expand and he was forever away, opening a store or a hotel or buying something new.

Gray stayed at home for a while, but as I wasn't there and Uncle was away most of the time, he tendered his resignation.

So Uncle started taking him on all his trips to "see to everything." He even had business cards printed for Gray proclaiming him "Senior Executive Vice-President in Charge of Nagging." More to the point, though, Gray was happy, and the resignation was forgotten.

As the family residence increasingly became an airport, I spent more time at the senator's with Burke, eventually becoming a voting resident there.

Allen and Liz stayed to run things at the main offices of Gambler's. Allen handled business investments, and Liz promotions.

But all this is surface detail that even a stranger might have known about us. Such was my relationship with my family.

I was consumed with myself and spent not nearly enough time on anything of real importance. The curse of youth is the innocent belief in your own immortality. And for me reality has always come harder than illusion.

My decision to attend a state university was met with mixed reviews at home. It was my first public schooling, and Uncle, who had actually graduated from the same college, was still reluctant for me to have "my spirit flattened under the roller of peer pressure and eviscerated by the cookie cutter of conformity."

"Stop being so dramatic," I said, staring out the window in the back of Uncle's car, where he and Gray and I were trapped one Sunday·on the way home from the senator's old house.

"You just don't know those people like I do," he wailed.

"*Quel* snob you are."

"Scott's right," Gray said, looking up from the needlepoint he had taken up to kill time during his and Uncle's endless business traveling.

"I am not," Uncle whined.

"Well, you're being a big baby," I said, folding my arms.

"Scott's right."

"Okay, I am being a big baby, but I am not a snob. And needlepoint is faggoty."

"Michael."

"Such talk in front of the children," I said.

"Well, if I'm being a big baby, I'm going to enjoy it." Uncle simpered. "And besides, I get to say 'faggoty.' "

"Michael," Gray said, putting the hoop in his lap and taking off the little magnifiers he had started wearing for "close work," which included just about everything within twenty feet, "if Scott goes to State, then he can stay at home with us."

"Well, actually," I said, dragging out the words to avoid the rest, "I've decided to get my own place."

"No," Gray said, almost raising his voice. "I will not permit it."

"Who are you? The pope?" I snorted.

"Ha, ha-ha, ha, ha, HA, ha," Uncle sang. "Welcome to the playpen."

"Fag."

"Bitch."

"Stop it."

And so it went.

I graduated with highest honors from The Academy but was edged out of the valedictory by a Philippine girl with more science AP grade points than I, but "no stage presence," as Uncle stated rather too loudly at one of his rare and officially sanctioned visits to The Academy—my graduation.

There' was the Summer Party and yet another season at The Sandpiper.

To my great surprise and Uncle Michael's furor, my life began to be of interest to minor media figures, who I felt, then and now, were covering me only as a highlight to their overall coverage of Uncle, since I hadn't ever done anything more newsworthy than having been born into one of the weirder and, ultimately, wealthier families in the South. And given the level of poverty and the average level of weird among southern families, that in itself is something, I suppose.

Uncle screamed at Liz, who handled PR with Frankie Gilliam, they screamed at assignment editors, I got my first picture in the tabloids and Uncle screamed some more.

It's ironical how the demand for privacy occasions so much comment.

At the time I thought the attention was sort of a kick, but I lived to regret it upon my arrival that fall at State.

It was hard at first. The news was still fresh and there were stares and whispers. New acquaintances always came back around to one version or another of "I don't want to pry but . . ." or "Do you mind if I ask you a personal question?"

But the fall was rife with politics and the flurry of real news that follows the summer season and, soon enough, news of the Millers and the Reilys was pushed farther back in the pages of the paper until we were overgrown by the leaves of fresh scandals.

I helped my cause by dating heavily and conspicuously. I tried out for and made the soccer team. And I wrote personally to the president of the fraternity to which my father and the senator had belonged, requesting membership.

Before the fall was out, a trained reporter couldn't have picked me out of the crowd at Alpha K. My studies were easy and I wasted little time on classwork. Life was a haze of beer busts and football games.

My off-campus apartment was a haven for parties that ran late, long and loud. So much so that Harvey Turnbul—still the executor of the senator's bequests—and I discreetly bought the building to control the flood of complaints.

I parked the limousine Uncle had given me and left it and Mel with Burke at the senator's, preferring instead a little red sports car. It was better for my new image.

Of course, family command performances continued to intrude on my education and my coverage continued sporadically, usually accompanying a photo of some young lady and speculative captions about my intentions and her lineage. And, in that it put to rest questions about my sexuality despite my ambiguous upbringing, I smiled for the cameras.

By my first spring semester, my studies continued to present no real challenge, and while my lack of attention had not distinguished me in the outcome of the first semester, I still got by and was getting by. My contemporaries, however, were more occupied than ever, resolved to buckle down in the new year.

So while I sought their company constantly, I found it mainly at parties.

My fraternity's annual Valentine's Sweetheart Ball was a feast of companionship, and I was starving. I had gotten myself on the planning committee and managed to stretch the social sustenance into a month of meetings and donations drives. All the profits from the evening went to the Heart Fund.

I was tremendously successful in my efforts, or so my fraternity brothers thought. Actually the owner of a local hotel, Chaz Montreau, had called me at home and offered to underwrite the entire affair.

That donation really started the ball rolling, and door prizes, a band and the rest seemed to fall into place. It was going to be a great party, and I got credit from my fellow Alphas.

I took Amy. Her long, dark hair and golden skin played counterpoint to her pale blue eyes. She was an overwhelming beauty, though I was no longer overwhelmed. She made me conspicuous by her presence, but given the choice, I would have kept the red coupe over Amy.

As I did not have to choose, the three of us arrived at the twenty-third annual Alpha Kappa Lambda Valentine's Sweetheart Ball fashionably late and after a complimentary dinner at Amy's family's restaurant.

We got applause as we strode into the packed ballroom.

Our reserved table was in front of the dance floor and we made good use of the easy access: dancing and drinking and enjoying a procession of tributes from couples as they came and went from the polished parquet rectangle beside us.

"Great party, Scott."

"Helluvah good job."

"The best ever."

The only dark spot on the glowing evening was our tablemate. We shared our place of honor with Greg and his date, Sims Simson. Greg was no problem, but Sims made up for his social ease by being absolutely impossible. She was from one of those ancient, coastal families and never missed an opportunity to remind us all. The food, the band, the hotel, everything paled by comparison to the coast.

The blackest moment of all, though, came when Sims refused to join Greg on the dance floor. "Really, they are just too amateurish," she sniffed at the band.

"Amy." Greg sighed. "How about you? This is one of my favorites."

"Sure, Greg," she said, squeezing my hand under the table. "We'll be right back, Scott."

So as I mouthed silent protests like a goldfish gasping for air, they swept off to the dance floor, leaving me alone with Sims, the impossible.

We sat in sweaty silence owing to the fact that my modesty precluded bon mots like "Great party, eh?" That and the fact that Sims was already on record on the topic.

"Why on earth did they have the party in this dump?" she moaned.

I shrugged and looked around nervously, trying to locate Greg and Amy on the dance floor.

"Well, after all," she said grandly, "there is the new Gambler's down by the river. It's not The Sandpiper," she went on, ever mindful of the superiority of the coast, "but it is a Gambler's after all."

"I can't imagine," I said, looking at her only because I couldn't see Greg or Amy anywhere.

She wasn't bad-looking but the sneer spoiled a delicate, fine-boned face. Glossy blond hair was overshadowed by a knitted brow. Clear gray eyes were crushed under the weight of a critical glare.

"It's all so bourgeois," she sighed, listlessly tossing a heart-shaped doily that had adorned her hors d'oeuvres plate—pinkie extended as she did so.

"Umm," I said pensively, wishing the earth would open up and swallow her.

"Amy seems to be enjoying it, though," she said in a forced contralto trill, accompanied by a smile that turned the corners of her mouth down.

"Sims," I said sweetly, "I'm so awfully sorry I met you."

She started.

"You are an irreconcilable bitch," I went on. "And I wouldn't wish an ass-aching snob like you on my worst enemy, let alone my dear friend Greg."

She stared.

"I don't know where you get off, but I could buy and sell you and your coastal clan twice before breakfast," I snarled. "And I only hope you will be returning to your trumped up, seaside society shitheads in time for hurricane season."

As if on cue the band broke into a protracted drumroll and the assemblage applauded. Actually they were applauding the president of our fraternity as he took the mike from the band's singer.

"How dare you speak to me like that?" Sims hissed.

"I know that I'm not only speaking for myself," I hissed back. "Consider it a sort of tacit plebiscite from everyone here tonight who has had the misfortune to meet you."

"Is everyone having a great time?" the president shouted into the microphone.

There was feedback and applause in answer.

"You rude little man," she went on. "If I weren't a lady, I'd slap your face for speaking to me that way."

"Look, lady," I snapped, "you've done everything but this evening. Perhaps the estimation of a lady is different at the coast."

"Well, I'd like to take credit for this soiree," the president went on. "Particularly since the fifteen thousand dollars we've raised is the largest kitty ever."

More applause. More feedback.

"You just wait till Greg gets back to this table," she said like a schoolchild. "He'll teach you some manners."

"Is that how the upper crust at the coast settles things?" I asked calmly. "Like white trash in back of the bowling alley?"

"And so I'd like to ask you to join me in giving a warm round of applause," the president went on, "to the man who made this all the success it is . . ."

"You bastard," she said, leaping to her feet.

"You bitch," I said, joining her.

"And the man I'll be supporting as my successor next year," the president continued.

Sims drew back to slap my churlish face. I caught her hand in mid-flight.

"I give you the next president of Alpha Kappa Lambda, Scott Miller," the president shouted.

During the applause we realized that we were suddenly the focus of attention.

I continued to hold Sims' hand but forced it down by my side and dragged her forward in a stumbling bow.

"Let go of my hand," she snarled through the clenched teeth of her forced smile.

"Shut up and smile," I hissed back.

"And now will the two of you lead off in the traditional Sweetheart's Waltz?" the president urged.

We stood stunned as the dance floor cleared and the band began "Moonlight Serenade."

"Come on, you two," the president coaxed as we stood transfixed, blinded by the spotlight.

"Come on," I said, half dragging her to the floor.

"I'd rather die," she snapped.

"I'm prepared to deal with that," I said, slamming her into position like a game of two-man crack-the-whip. The maneuver partially knocked the breath out of her and I got the upper hand as I pushed her around the dance floor, the spotlight tracing our every move.

"There they are," the president said, "tonight's Sweetheart Couple."

There was applause and the other couples joined us on the floor.

Sims put her head on my shoulder. Her body began to tremble against mine.

"Don't you dare cry," I snarled into her ear as I danced us momentarily out of earshot.

With that Sims threw back her head and laughed a loud, coarse, unladylike laugh. "Cry?" she gasped. "Why should I? We're the goddamned Sweetheart Couple."

We spent more or less the rest of the dance and the evening laughing.

Life with Sims was life as I had only imagined it. She brought a dimension of propriety and effortless elegance to everything.

It wasn't that she made any changes in my life. She was more an editor, blue-penciling certain details and giving other elements more emphasis by their omission.

She became my hostess, striking kegs of beer in favor of wine and then increasing my appreciation of the wine; jugs gave way to dated vintages. The omission of dips and chips meant actually eating the cheese and crackers and whetted my appetite for Bries and blues. Triscuits gave way to table waters. Sporting events gave over to ballet. The mall to the museum.

I was not a stranger to these things, but I felt that with Sims I gained more than a passing acquaintance. She gave me an appreciation that I had not had before. With Sims it wasn't just the thing to do but the best thing to do. She could always answer why.

Love had a good deal to do with my receptiveness, I'm sure, but the plebeian fare of my first semester in college had given me a point of contrast.

With Uncle it was always the best and the finest. But if you have caviar and cream cheese every day, it has no more significance than peanut butter and jelly. And eventually the latter becomes the delicacy.

My taste and my school standing improved.

Sims planned the parties or was, in their absence, the companionship I had ached for in lieu of the accustomed weight of familial obligation. And I could again focus on my studies.

Sex, too, was a matter of gourmet appreciation with Sims. What had been an embarrassing and belated detail, like waiting all day to eat breakfast and then gorging indiscriminately and with no regard for manners or convention, became an individual and important experience.

There was no longer a need for the protracted prologue of the date to introduce the obligatory scuffling at its conclusion. An evening could be devoted to nothing else. Sex, I discovered, was an end unto itself.

She said no at first. Not as a denial, but as though it were the wrong wine. I assumed that Sims' sense of propriety precluded the possibility.

One evening I returned to my apartment and found it filled with fresh flowers, lighted candles and incense. Samuel Barber's *Adagio for Strings* trailed through the air with the scent of tea olive.

Sims came into the room. She wore the vaguest of peignoirs, but she held me off, declining even a kiss. Gently she took my hand. She led me to the bedroom, where she removed my clothes, savoring each button and flap. She laid me down on the bed and massaged my body with oils and cologne until I thought I might pass out if I restrained myself any longer.

Still, she resisted.

She took me instead to the tub. The feel of the cold porcelain was like an electrical shock as she sat me down and the steaming water she filled the tub with came as a tremendous relief.

Again she drove me mad, removing her slight robe and joining me in the water she had flavored with scented oils and bubbles. The maddening massage continued as she washed me from hair to toenails with soaps and sensations. She encouraged me to explore her body in the same tactile cleansing way, then pulled the plug and left us clothed in the bubbles.

My last bits of restraint went down the drain with the sweet warm water. But she slipped easily through my fingers and blew my brains out with a shower of icy cold needles of water rinsing away the soap and the passion. As she carefully dried my body with mountains of soft, sweet towels, every nerve synapse in my body rattled and I shivered though I wasn't cold.

At last she took me to bed to explore and appreciate all of me, and I her.

The soft tickle of her eyelash, the mole on the inside of her right knee, the textures of her skin as it roamed over her body, all of her was there for me to experience with all of me.

When at last she spoke the first words since I had returned home, "Yes" was all she said.

Sims became more and more the focus of my life. Like a favorite cologne, she was always with me. Every decision I made hinged on Sims. She was always all around me.

She redecorated the apartment and then the entire building and grounds. She planned my time and filled my days and my life.

Along with Brie and sex and art, she taught me the taste of love.

As the spring semester drew to a close, a dark mood—mine— began to cover us like the thunderheads of summer. Sims and I had never discussed my family. Of course, she knew what everyone could have known, but I avoided the topic. What was unspoken began more and more to drown out our conversation.

"So, how the hell are you?" Uncle's recorded voice blared out of the answering machine. "Where the hell are you? Gray and I are—where are we, Gray? What? Oh, for God sake. Well, we're on some plane anyway. We're not there, but we will be. Isn't it about spring break? Call Alice and tell her when you're free. Maybe we can get together for lunch or something. I miss you.

And who is this Sims person I keep seeing you with in the papers? Three pictures? It must be serious. Anyway, we'll be home—Gray, when will we be home? Oh, for God sake, Gray." And then there was extended dial tone.

Several messages later Uncle's voice blurted out the single word "Tuesday."

I phoned Alice, Uncle's administrative assistant/keeper and made arrangements to meet Uncle Michael for lunch at his office in the new steel and glass Gambler's monolith downtown. The company had gotten to be large enough to justify building one of those "Van der Rohe houses," as Uncle called it, to accommodate all the aspects of the business.

To this day it amazes me that Uncle was a successful businessman.

I can remember as a child being struck by the two different Uncle Michaels. There was the one I knew, warm, fun-loving, almost another child. And there was the Uncle Michael who could reduce an actor to tears or run off teamsters trying to force a contract on his restaurant deliveries.

In the beginning "the office" had been wherever Uncle Michael was, but as Gambler's started and grew, the second Uncle Michael had become more and more estranged from me. "The business" was something that didn't concern me. Consequently I knew very little about it.

I had been to the building only once for the opening, about a year before, and I found it as overproduced as I did my arrival for lunch that day. Uniformed guards took my car and escorted me into a private elevator with credit card keyholes instead of buttons. The doors opened onto the executive floor.

The combination of black marble and stainless steel made the hall before us seem more a sanctuary or a vault housing some national treasure than the headquarters of a cheesecake company.

Ambient light bounced off the mirror-bright surfaces illuminating the G inlaid in the floor in front of us. The G was echoed in the etching on the frosted glass doors, flanked by guards at the end of the hall opposite us. Aside from the two walls of other elevators they were the only doors in the hall.

"Golly," I said, realizing that this was what Uncle Michael saw every morning as he came to "the office."

Solemnly we walked toward the doors, the two guards snatching them open as we approached.

Inside was no less intimidating. More black marble in an arched colonnade stretching to the right and left and topped with a glass arcade roof. Our steps echoed as we walked through an archway into an enormous luxe sitting room dominated by a pair of still more enormous glossy ebony doors.

"Mr. Miller," one of the two people seated on either side of the doors said as she got up and crossed to us, "I'm Alice, your uncle's assistant. We talked yesterday. Thank you, Joseph."

Joseph, my escort, touched the brim of his hat and left.

"This is Jonathan," she said, referring to the young man who sat opposite her.

"Mr. Miller," he said, nodding.

"Can we get you anything?" she asked as she led me toward the doors.

"No, thanks," I said, staring around like a tourist.

The monastic silence was broken as she tugged open one of the doors.

Sunlight flooded over us as we entered the almost entirely glass room. The ceiling and three walls of the basketball court–size room were glass, so that you felt even more vulnerable than the rest of the tomb might have made you feel.

But more overwhelming than the room, the gallery of objets d'art, museum-quality furniture, rugs, trees or even the Olympian desk that he stood behind, was Uncle Michael. The room was built to his scale.

He was on the phone facing the other way as we entered, and he dominated his out-of-scale surroundings: The master of all he purveyed.

"Goddamnit, Harold," he yelled into the receiver. "You contracted at that fucking price, and you'll goddamn well deliver at that price. I've got too much tied up in the thing now to change my pricing structure this season because you can't run your own operation."

Alice left me and scurried across the great room to Uncle.

"Then get out of the business, Harold. Your lack of planning"—he broke off as Alice whispered to him—"doesn't constitute my emergency."

He slammed down the receiver and turned into a different person as easily as he turned to face me. "Scott," he said warmly. Then the metamorphosis again as he said crisply, "Al, have Allen find out how much it would cost us to buy out Harold's company and fire Harold. Thanks. That's all for now."

"Sure, Mic," she said as she bustled past me.

The door clicked shut.

"Give us a hug," he asked, childlike Uncle Michael once again. I hugged him.

"This is a hell of a place," I said, breaking the hug and the silence.

"Do you like it?" he asked like a little boy showing off a school project. "You've been here before, haven't you?"

"Sort of. For the party. It's incredible," I said. "If God had an office, it would look like this."

"We wouldn't even have to change the monograms," he said, giggling.

"We must be really rich," I said, laughing. "Where do you want to go for lunch?"

"Go? For lunch?" he asked.

"Yeah, you know, like a restaurant?" I said sarcastically.

"How about over there?" he said, pointing to a smaller set of doors to the right of the entrance.

"What?"

"Come here," he said, leading the way.

We walked over and into a restaurant. There was no one there, but it was a restaurant.

"Mr. Reily," an attendant said in greeting, "would you like to have lunch now?"

"Scott?" Uncle said, turning to me.

"What the hell," I said.

"What the hell," Uncle said to the attendant.

"Would you like a table by the window?" the attendant asked.

"What the hell," Uncle said, laughing.

"Jesus," I said as the waiter handed us menus, "I can't believe this place."

"We really haven't talked enough," Uncle sighed. "Scott, Gambler's is a really big company."

"No shit," I snorted.

"There's the theatres, the resorts and hotel properties; there's, uh, a movie production company, construction, television and radio stations, newspapers, publishing, an amusement park, food processing, vineyards; we're getting ready to get into fast food. But the largest part of the business is food brokerage."

"Well, I've got a rich uncle," I said, leafing through the menu.

"Scott," he said so seriously that I looked up, "I've got a rich nephew."

"The senator's money is peanuts compared to this," I said, taking in the room with a wave of my hand.

"This all belongs to you," he said flatly.

"You're going to be around for a while yet," I said nervously.

"No, no," he said. "In two years when you're twenty-one. All of this, except for the apartment here and The Sandpiper, will belong to you. Outright."

I only stared.

"Gambler's and all its divisions and subsidiaries belong to a company called Scotty, Inc., which your uncle Bill Stockbridge and I set up for you when your parents died. It's your trust. I'm only your guardian. Even Gray works for you."

I stared.

"You see the seed money for everything came from what your parents left you," he said. "I've just been managing the money for you."

"You did great," I said numbly. "You invented the cheesecake."

"You dared me," he said lightly.

"No, seriously," I said.

"Seriously, yes, I invented the cheesecake, and Gambler's pays me an obscene royalty for it and the Gambler's name. And the apartment here and The Sandpiper belong to me. I'm fine. But the facilities and the money to go into production came from the restaurant and the theatres, which you owned."

"But you founded those businesses," I insisted.

"What? Are you trying to get out of it?" he said, smiling. "I opened the theatres and the restaurant because I didn't have a lot of options at the time. I was in public relations at the time of the fight with the senator over your custody. What with all the publicity, that was pretty much shot to hell and the theatre was all I knew how to do. Gray could cook, so we did food, too. It was real Andy Hardy, 'let's do a show' time then. Who knew it would turn out like this? It was a fluke."

"A fluke?" I said.

"Yeah." He nodded. "You invested in the properties, or rather your trust fund did, so I could work to support you. I didn't just want to live off your money. And accidentally your trust fund became all of this. You see?"

I snorted and shook my head.

"What do you want for lunch?" he asked.

"A drink."

"You're too young to drink," he said, looking at his menu.

"Get me a drink or you're fired," I said, laughing.

"Oh, way-tah," he shouted, "da boss wants champagne."

We laughed conspiratorially.

"So I own all this," I said, giddy from the news.

"Worst luck," he said.

"What am I supposed to do?" I asked.

"Well, that's sort of why I wanted to talk to you," he began. "You have to make decisions about school and I don't want to pressure you, but I thought you should factor this in. You have to figure all this out and it's a lot to figure out."

"Can't you just run things like always?" I asked, more intimidated by each new development.

"I'm not going anywhere," he said, patting my hand. "And there are thousands of employees to help. You don't have to do it all. But I've been on a nineteen-year leave of absence from my life and I'd really like to get on with it."

"So, tell me about this fight with the senator," I said after pausing long enough to process the information overload and for the waiter to pour.

"Well, that's not what I expected," he said, sipping. "But then you never are."

"Well, everyone's always referred to it obliquely around me, but no one's really explained."

"Don't you want to hear about being the scion of one of the great fortunes of the late twentieth century?"

"That's definitely a follow-up."

"Okay." He shrugged. "Well, there's not a lot to tell. When

your parents died, they named me as your guardian in their will, and the senator—you remember how conservative he was—opposed it because he didn't approve of my *lifestyle*," he concluded, affecting Long Island liberal lockjaw with a knowing wink and a nudge. "It was a family fight really, but since the senator was so infamous, the press was on it like vultures on road kill. It was a sort of prehistoric outing."

He stared out the window for a bit.

"Why did you . . . go through with it?"

"Because my sister wanted me to," he said without a pause. "I loved her very much, almost as much as I love you."

"Thanks," I said simply. "I'm glad you won."

"Don't mention it." He smiled, lightening. "Anyway, I didn't win, really. The senator dropped the case."

"He did? Why?"

"There's the sixty-four-million-dollar question," he said with a sort of drunken laugh. "I really don't know."

"You don't know?" I said incredulously.

"Not really," he said, playing with his napkin. "The fight just went out of him. His wife—you remember her from the wedding and all—she left him during the trial. I don't know. He was just never the same. I think it broke his heart or at least his spirit. And he didn't know what to think."

"He didn't say when you settled?" I asked, prodding him along.

"No," Uncle said, shaking his head. "And yes, I asked."

"What was the settlement?" I asked as we slipped into an easier, more conversational tone.

"That is none of your business," he said firmly.

"What is that supposed to mean?" I asked in surprise.

"It didn't have anything to do with you," he said, leaning back in his chair and folding his arms.

"Oh, come on, you have to tell me what the terms of the settlement were," I said, amazed by his reticence.

"I never will," he said to me.

"Well, I'll just get Harvey to get me the documents," I said hotly.

"There are no documents," he said, finishing the last of his drink. "We shook on it."

"Shook on it?" I howled. "Do you mean to tell me my whole life and this giant company are based on a secret agreement that you two shook on?"

"I never thought of it like that," he said. "I guess you're right. It's really kind of funny."

"Only if you know what 'it' is," I snapped.

"You're right." He nodded. "Don't let's talk about it. It isn't fair and I'm not telling."

"Have you decided what you'd like for lunch?" the waiter ventured.

"Yes, I have," Uncle said. "But I've eaten here before."

I stared at him.

"Perhaps my companion needs more time?" Uncle chirped glibly, belying his cloak-and-dagger pronouncement. "Do you need more time?"

"No. Thank you," I said, venting my irritation in my words.

"Fine," Uncle said, matching my tone. "What'll you have?"

"I'll have the goddamn veal and pasta," I said angrily. "And a tossed salad."

"Dressing?" the waiter asked timidly.

"Blue cheese," I shouted.

"Mr. Reily," the waiter said.

"I'll have the motherfucking crab salad," Uncle said politely. "And some damnable French bread."

I slapped the menus into the waiter's trembling hands and he fled.

"I don't think the waiter likes us," Uncle said confidentially.

"I don't see how you can say it doesn't affect me," I said.

"It does affect you," Uncle said coyly. "We'll get terrible service."

"Will you shut up about the goddamned waiter?" I exploded.

"I thought it was the goddamn veal and pasta," he said.

"Shut up!"

We looked out the window and drank champagne in silence.

The waiter brought my salad and Uncle ordered more "shit-headed champagne."

"Look," Uncle said once my mouth was too full to answer, "you have a decision to make. Win, lose or draw, in two years the company is yours. Hear me out. You can either take it over or hand it over. It's your choice. But if you want it, you need to find out more about it. Come to work here some. After school."

I snorted. "A part-time job as CEO?" I asked, laughing at the absurdity. "Minimum wage? Extra hours at Christmas?"

"Something like that." He smiled.

"I don't know what to say about all this," I said, blotting dressing off my face.

"Well, I don't expect you to decide now," Uncle said, lighting a cigarette. "It's a lot to take in in one afternoon. Think about it. Let me know. And, uh, you don't necessarily have to work with me," he went on. "Allen handles investments and Liz is in marketing. They can work with you if you'd rather. Okay?"

"I'll think about it," I said begrudgingly.

"Good," he said. "One more thing and then I'll drop it. There is no CEO per se. We don't have that kind of structure. We're a private company. No stockholders to answer to. You can have complete autonomy."

"Great," I said without feeling.

"That makes a big difference," he said, knitting his brow sternly. "To me, anyway. And it's an important part of what—of what I wanted to give you. Of what I've worked to give you. Independence. Whatever you decide."

"Thanks," I said tersely.

"So let's talk about really important stuff," he said in his spy voice. "Who is Sims?"

The joy of Sims washed over me, and my irritation was quickly forgotten. We howled over the details of the meeting at the Sweetheart Ball and glowed together as I savored each detail I shared.

"She seems very important to you," he ventured at last as I fell into a quiet reverie.

"She is," I said, grinning stupidly in the afternoon sun.

"Well, then we must meet her," he said with finality.

That woke me up.

"The Summer Party is coming up," he said, slamming the conversation into foregone-conclusion planning gear. "You'll certainly want to bring her to that so she can meet everyone, but it's so public. Maybe we should plan something more private."

"Well, I'll have to check with Sims, and finals are coming up,"

I said, trying to grab the wheel of fortune and steer us to a safer stretch.

"Just a quiet dinner then," he said, heedless of the curves I could see. "First anyway. I'll talk to Gray. Let him know what day is good for you two. And the Summer Party, of course. I'll have Alice handle it. What about her family? Do you know them?"

Oh, God, I thought, queasy from the downhill speed. "And of course, the Marine Color Guard," I put in nastily.

"What?" Uncle said, almost stopping to listen. "Should they come to the dinner or the Summer Party?"

"I um, well . . ."

"The Summer Party," he said, starting to write stuff on a cloth napkin. "That'll be less formal. I mean it's not like you're engaged yet. Are you?"

"Engaged?" I asked, reeling. It was out of control. "Uh, no."

"So do you have their address?"

"Wait a minute," I said weakly, a paper ribbon to stop a freight train.

"You have Sims tell Gray, so he can tell Alice. I'll tell Gray and Alice," he said, writing furiously. "Listen, I have got to get back. Alice has those credit card key thingamies for the doors here, so you can come and go. Let me know what you decide about things. I can't wait to meet Sims."

Hugs and air kisses, and he was vestibuling me out to the elevator before I could say anything constructive.

"Sims," I said with such gravity that she rose from the table at the library where I had found her studying.

"What's the matter?" she asked, coming to me.

"We have to go to dinner," I said flatly.

"It's three in the afternoon," she pointed out, snapping her pen shut.

"What?" I asked, distracted.

"You said we had to go to dinner," she said, the little canals between her eyebrows belying her patient tone.

"We do," I said, nodding.

She sighed and began gathering her books. "Okay," she said. "Where do you want to go?"

"Go?"

"Dinner," she said, raising her voice a little. "Where do you want to have dinner?"

"I don't know," I said stupidly. "You're supposed to call Gray."

"Who?"

"Or is it Alice?"

"What?"

"Shhhhhh," a fellow patron hissed.

"Do you want to go to dinner or not?" she whispered violently.

"I don't really know," I said, sitting down. "I suppose we have to."

"Well, I'm not really hungry," she said, trying to be reasonable and reasonably quiet against almost insurmountable odds. "And who the hell are Gray and Alice?"

"They work for—" I broke off, laughing. "They work for me."

"*Shhhhh.*"

"Have you been drinking?" Sims asked, sitting back down.

"I had some champagne at lunch," I answered automatically, still puzzling over the revelations of the meal with Uncle.

"Lunch?" she asked. "When did you have lunch?"

"I just came from there," I said, shrugging.

"Then why do you want to have dinner?" she was yelling.

"What?"

"How can you say what when you know what what is?"

"What?"

"I'm going to have to ask you two to leave," the guard said, guiding us toward the nearest exit.

Eventually Sims was able to pry the details of our proposed encounter, the identities of Gray and Alice and the specifics of my lunch with Uncle out of me. Much to my consternation she was delighted by the prospect of bringing the two families together and made plans, heedless of my predictions of disaster, to consummate our date with destiny.

The die was cast, and the dinner was set to follow exams.

And so summer approached like an August storm, banding the landscape with ragged stripes of light and dark. By the final week of exams I had become morose and brooding.

We sat, one of those last nights, in a local café.

Sarah Vaughan, dim light, muted conversations, bread and cheese and fruit and wine and Sims' insistent chattering surrounded me.

"So what do you think, Scott?" I heard her asking.

"About what?" I answered blankly.

"Where have you been?" she said, taking my hand. "Would you like to go to Mom and Dad's beach house at Pawley's after The Sandpiper?"

"Maybe we should wait to see if we're still on speaking terms to decide," I snorted, pouring myself more wine.

"Okay, that's it," she said, withdrawing her hand. "What the hell is up with you?"

"Sorry, I just have a lot on my mind," I sighed.

"Like what?" she asked. "You can tell me, can't you?"

"You just don't know my family," I said obliquely.

"But I'm going to meet them."

"That's what worries me."

There was a long silence between us in the noise of the café.

"You think I'm not good enough," she said flatly.

"What?" I asked with a nervous laugh.

"I embarrass you, don't I?" She was yelling.

"Keep your voice down," I said, reaching for her.

"Admit it," she demanded, pulling away. "You're embarrassed to be seen with me."

"Right this minute, yes," I answered hotly.

"And you're embarrassed for your family to meet me," she went on, unabated.

"Who the hell do you think my family is?" I demanded, matching her volume.

"I don't know. You've managed to keep me hidden from them," she said, overpowering the muted jazz and the neighboring conversations. "Why is that?"

"Do you want to know why? Hunh? Do you?" I demanded, forgetting the surroundings and leaping to my feet.

"Yeah," said a man at an adjacent table.

"Me, too," Sims said, pointing at herself with her thumb.

I realized that the room had gone quiet, save for Miss Vaughan, and that most everyone was waiting for my answer.

"Because," I said quietly, nervously, slowly sitting down again, "I—I'm in love with you and I, well, I want to marry you. And," I continued, picking up speed to cut her off, "I'm afraid that you won't want to if you meet them or that they'll screw it up somehow."

I looked at her.

Everyone looked at her. Bar service paused.

"Is this a proposal?" she asked.

Sarah Vaughan stopped singing.

"Maybe," I said furtively, looking away from her and playing with the cheese knife.

"Then yes," she said simply. "No matter who you're related to."

The room erupted into applause.

"You're so romantic," she said, taking and squeezing my hand.

"Let's go for a walk," I said, smiling sheepishly. "We need to talk."

"Is there anything left you feel you can't say in front of these people?" She laughed.

We paid the check and left to wander through the hot breeze and crowded streets.

"That's Uncle Randy's restaurant," I said, stopping in front of the Urban Greenery. "Gray and I used to eat lunch here a lot. Gray was—is our majordomo, governess, tutor. You talked to him about dinner. He's kind of my mom. Sometimes he used to leave me here to spend the afternoon while he went shopping.

"Uncle first met Gray there," I said, walking on, bringing Sims by the hand. "Randy and Uncle were friends before, and Gray was working part-time in the kitchen here and part-time at Randy's sort-of-wife's Montessori school. I guess that's complicated. Anyway, Uncle hired Gray to take care of me after my parents died.

"That's partly why the senator, my grandfather, sued Uncle for custody of me because Gray was sort of a hippie—he's still a vegetarian—and he's . . . gay. Uncle is, too. They weren't, uh, lovers or anything. That's where we lived when it all started," I said, pausing again in front of the old duplex Uncle had pointed out to me a hundred times. We had wandered up the hill into the oak shadows of the streetlamps in the residential area adjoining the ever more chic little cluster of shops and restaurants where we had been.

And so, like a tour guide, I conducted Sims through the broken phrases of my life. I told her what I had never said before. I shared parts of my life that I hadn't known until then and discovered only in the telling.

ᔐ ᔐ ᔐ

Dinner was a loaded proposition.

There was the question of the company, the introduction of
Sims and the simultaneous announcement of our engagement.
Sims and Gray had made arrangements for dinner at Uncle's
condo the night before the Summer Party. We had decided to
include Sims' parents for obvious reasons and so both groups
could meet "quietly" before the public theatre party. We were all
to travel to The Sandpiper for the opening and then to Sims' parents' place at the beach to "relax" after running the social gauntlet.

So, by the time we left for dinner, we were both fairly green
and largely uninterested in food.

"Have you decided what you're going to say about the company?" she asked in the car on the way over.

"Not really," I said tartly. "But thanks so much for reminding
me. I had actually managed to stop worrying about that. Looking
forward to seeing your parents?" I added nastily.

"Thanks," she said sarcastically.

"Don't mention it." I grinned.

"Too late," she snapped.

"Say," I said glibly, "I have an idea. Let's drive down to the
river and jump."

"No. I know," she said, adopting my wry tone. "I'll take a
sleeping draft and you sharpen your dagger."

"It's been done to death," I said, laughing. "Well, Juliet, here's
Montague Manor. Ready for the masquerade?"

"Yes, but not the unmasking." She scowled.

I parked the car, and we walked into the lobby in silence. I
nodded to the security guard, who recognized me as we walked
past toward the elevators. I fumbled with the key that signaled
the elevator to stop at our floor.

"The Capulets are everywhere," I said dramatically as I turned
the key. "Can't be too careful."

"It does seem a bit much," she said, smiling.

"Uncle has always been that way." I shrugged as we began to climb. "You should see the office. Oh, God, I did it again."

"What if we just don't say anything else?" she said, laughing.

The door opened into the little reception hall just outside the doors to the apartment.

"What? No gun turrets?" she asked, laughing.

"Look," I said, pointing at the cameras in the corners. "And the doors are solid steel."

"Maybe your uncle is a mobster," she suggested wildly.

"Gay gangsters?" I said. We were laughing. "I like it. The brotherhood of the ruby slippers."

"If you're late with your payments, they break into your house and rearrange the furniture," she added, continuing the joke.

"When they say it's curtains for you, it's really curtains."

We howled.

Gray threw the door open. "Are you going to come in or are you going to stand out there in the hall?" he demanded hotly.

"Can we have a few minutes to think about it?" I asked.

"Get out of the way, Sasquatch," Uncle said, pushing Gray aside. "Pay no attention to him. Come inside. He's been a perfect beast all day. He's made dinner three times because he can't decide what we should have. And he just dressed me down because we don't have the right wine for any of it."

Gray stomped off into the living room.

"Uncle, this is Sims," I said by way of introduction. "Sims Simson."

"How monochromatic." He giggled. "I'm Michael Reily, but you can call me Ri. Good to meet you. You-all come in and have a drink. Don't ask for rum, though. We're out and Gray might seriously injure someone."

We followed him into the living room. I felt more at ease already. Sims gave me a conspiratorial wink of approval.

"Gray," Uncle said as we walked into the room, "we'll have three rum and sodas on the deck."

"But the hors d'oeuvres are set up in here," Gray said tensely.

"So they are," Uncle said, shooting us a look. "See you outside."

We went. Uncle giggled as he closed the door.

"You shouldn't provoke him," I said without much conviction.

"Oh, he's been spiteful all day," Uncle said, taking a seat. "The only reason the food's in there is that I wanted it out here. Sims, come and sit by me."

We took seats near him.

"Mr. Reily . . ." Sims began.

"Ri or Michael," he corrected.

"Michael, I'm so pleased to meet you at last," Sims said cordially. "Scott has told me so many nice things about you."

"He has?" Uncle said. "Well, that's a shock. I bet that's not all he's told you."

"Uncle," I warned.

"Excuse me," Gray said icily as he opened the French doors. "We seem to be out of rum."

"How careless," Uncle said, lighting a cigarette. "I suppose I'll have a nice dry martini. Kids?"

"A glass of white wine?" Sims said.

"A beer," I said.

Gray shot Uncle a glance and slammed the door.

"Now he's mad," I said.

"Oh, no," Uncle said, waving it off. "He was mad before now. Sims, tell me about you. How do you know Scott?"

"We met by accident," she began.

"Doesn't everyone?" Uncle smiled.

"Yes," I said, giving him a "shut up and be nice" look over Sims' shoulder. "But this was a serious accident."

"Casualties?" he asked.

"Just us." Sims smiled. "We were at Scott's fraternity ball—with other people."

"Wouldn't have been much of a ball if you'd been there by yourselves." Uncle smiled.

I frowned.

"No," Sims persevered. "We were with other dates."

"Sounds like more casualties," Uncle put in.

I sank back into my chair and calmed down a bit as the two swept each other into waves of giggling over the stormy first meeting.

He could be as charming as a real estate salesman.

"Ah, drinks," Uncle said.

Gray snarled and began passing them out.

"Gray, you're missing all the fun," Uncle said. "Sims was just telling us how she and Scott met at—" He broke off in a coughing fit after sipping at his drink.

"You bitch," he screamed at Gray as he recovered.

"Uncle," I warned.

"You're trying to poison me," he went on, yelling at Gray. "This is a glass of lukewarm vermouth."

"Oh, dear," Gray said calmly. "I must have gotten the recipe backward. Let me fix you another."

"I've got a better idea," Uncle snarled. "Why don't I get myself a drink and you bring the canapés out? I mean, as long as we're out here."

"What a great idea," Gray said, holding the door for him and slamming it behind them.

We heard the sounds of screaming muffled by the glass.

"Volatile," Sims said with a little laugh.

"Not really," I said, pouring my beer into the glass Gray had brought. "They just bicker all the time. Like an old married couple. Do you suppose they'd notice if we just sneaked out?"

"Yes." She nodded. "Who would introduce my parents?"

"Just a thought," I sighed.

"Bing, bing," Uncle shouted as he and Gray reentered. "Round two."

"Michael," Gray said quietly, "move the stuff off the table."

Gray got the food situated at last and the four of us sat down with drinks.

Conversation was light and abrupt as we struggled to conceal the specters of what was unspoken with the transparent divisiveness of what was.

The phone rang and Gray went to answer it. We fell silent, knowing it was the guard announcing the Simsons' arrival.

"They're on their way up," Gray said, returning.

Sims rose and straightened herself as she headed in to greet them.

"Uncle," I said, grabbing his elbow to keep him behind a moment, "try to behave."

"Like what?" He chuckled maniacally.

"Oh, God."

"Don't worry so much." He nudged me with the elbow I'd

been holding. "Everyone's parental units are humiliating to be around. Just think how nervous they are."

"I guess," I admitted, releasing him.

"Trust me on this one," he said, heading for the door. "The fact that I behave so badly puts everyone at ease because they know they couldn't possibly act worse.

"Hellooooo," he shrieked, flinging the glass door open. "You must be the SimSimsons. I've heard absolutely nothing about you. Come in. Tell me everything."

"Snag. Snag Simson." A beefy red-nosed man who I assumed was Sims' father was bellowing as he appeared to be attempting simultaneously to wrench Uncle's one arm out of the socket and to break the other pounding on it. Then in one deft move that looked like a square dance step, he snatched Uncle to his side with their shaking hands and tried to break Uncle's collarbone with his free arm around Uncle's shoulder as he presented Sims' mom. "Janine. Neen Simson."

"Snag Snag, Janine Neen," Uncle gushed, dropping straight down to escape Snag's grasp and scurrying across the hall to push Gray in Snag's direction. "This is Graham Gray Rambeaux. Hit him."

"Ha-*ha*," Snag guffawed, pumping Gray's hand and pounding his sturdier shoulder. "How the hell are you?"

"Language, Snag," Neen chirped. "Mr. Reily," she said sweetly. "So pleased to meet you."

"Michael, please," Uncle corrected, taking her hand in both of his.

"Mom, Dad," Sims said, "this is Scott Miller."

"Scott." Snag sounded the attack and bore down on me. I braced for the assault. Snag took me by surprise and flung his arms around me, pounding my back with his open palms and almost lifting me off the floor.

"Scott, we've heard so much about you," Neen said, taking one of my hands dangling behind Snag.

"Well-heh-hell," Uncle cackled, rubbing his shoulder. "Now that we're all black and blue, let's go out on the deck for some painkiller."

Snag let fly with this water-buffalo-in-heat laugh and took a swipe at Uncle, who dodged it.

"And you thought I was embarrassing," Uncle said to me under his breath as we ushered them out.

I pinched him on his sore shoulder.

Much to my surprise everyone seemed to hit it off. Neen raved about Gray's hors d'oeuvres and they talked about cooking and children and house stuff. Uncle and Snag got started on the martinis and seemed to be competing with each other to see who could be the loudest, most obnoxious drunk at the party. They regaled each other with tales from the battlefields of business and got into a heated discussion about taking your business public for the investment capital—as Snag had done with his family's chain of furniture stores—or keeping the family business private—as Uncle had done. It was boring as all hell, but they had a ball drawing fever charts of profit and loss with anchovy filets on the coffee table like two old war heroes reenacting a battle.

"Michael, that's disgusting," Gray said, sneering at the greasy graph.

"Snag," Neen chided her husband, chiming in.

"Aw, hell, Neen."

"Aw, hell, Gray.

"Language."

"Everyone," I called over them, caught up in the warm glow of familial parsimony, "before we eat, there's something Sims and I want to say to you."

Gray and Uncle struggled briefly over the anchovy chart, and then the group fell silent.

"Well, I, um," I began adroitly, and ground to a halt.

"Oh," Uncle said, nodding sagely, "I see."

I gave him a look and he made the hand signal for tick-a-lock. Everyone sat down.

"Seeing you all together tonight has made this a lot easier for us," I said, taking Sims' hand. "It reminds me how important family is. And how family is made more by commitment to one another than by social convention—by love, not by law.

"This past year I've come to understand what it means to care more for someone else than for yourself." The room swam around me. "I met Sims, and through her eyes, I see your love, Uncle, Gray. Through my love for her I saw your love for me. And I ask you now to love Sims as you love me, for I can offer her no greater gift than that. What I have offered her is my life and she has accepted it and offered me a place in your family, Neen, Snag. We are engaged to be married."

Everyone cried. Everyone. We hugged and welcomed each other to one another's families and hugged and cried and hung on each other like farewells at the *Titanic*'s lifeboats.

Eventually we toddled off to dinner, where we had roast chicken, swordfish steaks and beef Wellington owing to Gray's indecisiveness.

"Too simple, too trendy and Scott's favorite," Uncle said as he introduced each dish. "Take your pick. We're airlifting the balance to Ethiopia."

Dinner conversation was ablaze with plans—the Summer Party, The Sandpiper, the Simsons—and crackling with questions about setting the date—we hadn't beyond sometime after graduation—and Gambler's—I was switching my major to business administration and coming to work at the company with Liz in marketing. And so as we broke up for the evening with hugs, congrats and promises of days to come, Neen and Uncle banked their burning coals of anticipation for wedding plans.

"Well, that didn't suck," I said, belting myself into the car, alone with Sims at last.

"Didn't hate it," Sims concurred, nodding.

"Who knew your father was a bigger lunatic than Uncle Michael?" I grinned, backing out. "And I was worried."

"Oh, I don't know," Sims said with a knowing suck on her teeth. "You've got yourself one pretty weird litter of pups there."

"No doubt, but your folks fit right in."

"Yours were the strangest."

"Oh, you're just saying that."

"No, no, no. I mean it. I mean, I really, really mean it."

"I don't know, it was nip and tuck there when Snag Snag put the spoon on his nose."

"Too true." She started to break up. "But I really think your folks took the day when Gray played airplane and hangar to get Michael to eat his baby carrots before we could get dessert."

"That trick never works."

We lost it, dissolving into rounds of laughter and "Your family's the weirdest," "No, your family's the weirdest," "No . . ."

We wore out the laugh and rode in silence for a bit.

"Oh, my God," Sims said eventually.

"What?"

"They're all our family."

"We should start saving for the children's therapy."

"Do you think, knowing what we know about both sides of the gene pool, that it would be responsible for us to have children?"

"I'm not telling those people they're not getting any grandchildren," I snorted.

"Umm, good point. Could be ugly."

"Speaking of ugly," I began ominously.

"And we were."

"We've got extended family tomorrow. That should be heartstopping."

"Definite defib."

Once again the family surprised us. They still behaved badly, but they behaved badly with each other, not toward each other. Like children at a social gathering, they incited one another to greater and greater offenses.

The announcement of our engagement, which began privately at the family table, grew into waves and waves of toasts, flooding the room with champagne and good cheer.

Grammy kissed us about a thousand times. Pawpaw was more reluctantly sentimental, allowing in his terse affectation of crusty curmudgeon that would never have played past the third row, that he "could only wish for us as much happiness as he'd known the last two hundred years with Grammy."

Burke buttonholed Sims to confide Miller family stories, the secrets to a happy marriage—though she herself had never been so much as engaged—and her secret recipe for my favorite chocolate chip cookies.

We danced with Liz and Allen and made merry with the usual suspects, indulging our moment of celebration to extremes.

Thus distracted, those cooler family heads left Uncle and Snag unchecked to take stage and steal the show. They chased the champagne with a bourbon drinking contest and among other things sang *"Oh Promise Me,"* set off a jumbo pack of Black Cats and cleared the dance floor with a jitterbug exhibition to the band's obliging and extended rendition of *"Sing, Sing, Sing (with a Swing),"* concluding with Uncle Michael's flying leap into Snag's waiting arms that took out not only the two of them but two or three dinner tables and an hors d'oeuvres station. It brought the house down, and while they did finish the dance, they were more or less willingly confined to their chairs for the remainder of the evening.

The Sandpiper opening was considerably more sedate, owing to the diminished capacity of the potential agitators. We took a rest cure at the hotel for a week and then moved on to more mayhem at the Simsons' beach house at Pawley's Island. Grandma Simson joined Neen, Snag, Gray, Uncle, Sims and me for a weekend of terrorizing the tourists. She showed surprising resilience and a remarkable tolerance for alcohol in a woman of her years.

All too soon the world beckoned us back, and blinded by the glow of happiness, we returned to the sunrises and sunsets of our day to days.

That summer I went to work at the company and began to participate in the bizarre rituals that Uncle had created and in the more rote lessons of business school. The Simsons joined the family table at the Winter Party, and I followed in the footsteps of the Uncle worshipers at Gambler's. But the more I followed, the more at odds I grew to be, with Uncle and the things he stood for.

The way he ran the company was outrageous and flew in the face of everything I was learning in business school. Gambler's, I found, was as eccentric as Uncle himself. But, as it was a private company, he had no stockholders or boards of directors to answer to.

My lessons in insanity began with Aunt Liz. I started my apprenticeship with her in the marketing wing of the company.

Things went smoothly at first as I fell in with the handling of programs already in place. But a month or so into my practical application of my newly acquired knowledge from marketing class at school, I began to see the problem.

Uncle came into the office after a trip to Asia to kick off the expansion of our fast food operations in that market. "Liz," he shouted from the door, "Liz, where are you?"

"Michael," she shouted back from the table where we sat in conference with lawyers over the wording of some frozen food product labeling.

Shockingly informal, I thought.

"Darling," he said, hugging her in the hallway outside.

"How was your trip?" she asked as they came into the room together.

"Hideous." He giggled. "But not a total loss. Try one of these," he said, producing a bag of crisps.

She did.

"Ummm," she said, munching. "Shrimp?"

"That's right," he screamed. "Shrimp crisps."

"They're delicious," she said, taking another.

"Aren't they?" he said. "Here, have some," he said, offering the bag to the lawyers and to me. "The Japanese have been making them for years. These were the best I found, so we hired the guy who makes them."

"What do you want to call them?" she asked earnestly.

"Sea Biscuits," he shrieked with delight. "We can shape them like little sea horses."

"Wonderful," she said, joining in the gleeful rout.

The lawyers concurred and they began talking uproariously about TV commercials with singing mermaids styled after the Andrews Sisters.

"Sounds like a good start," I said, trying to get in on the enthusiasm. "When can we start product research?"

"Didn't you try one?" Uncle asked.

"Yes," I said.

"Did you like it?" he continued.

"Well, yes," I said.

"Me, too," he said "Let's go talk to Allen about aquaculture investments," he said jovially. "Who knows? We may already own a shrimp ranch."

He and Liz howled with laughter, and they headed for the door. "If you'll excuse us, gentlemen," Uncle said, nodding to the lawyers.

"Certainly," the senior partner said.

"Scott?" Uncle asked. "Are you coming?"

"What about the label?" I said numbly.

"What label?" Uncle asked.

"We were meeting about package labeling for the frozen fruits line," Liz explained, rolling her eyes.

"Bleh," Uncle said, grimacing. "What a stupid—"

"Scott thought we should make sure that the labels were legal and appetizing," Liz cut in.

"Oh," Uncle said blankly. "And these gentlemen know about product labeling?"

"Yes," I said. "They're from our legal department on product—"

"So they know what the labels ought to say?" Uncle cut me off.

"Yes, sir," one of them said.

"Swell," Uncle said. "We'll just let you gentlemen get on with your work. Come along, Scott."

"But what about the label?" I persisted.

"They're going to write it," Uncle said matter-of-factly.

"But don't you think we should be involved?" I asked, getting more flustered.

"Why?" Uncle asked. "I don't know anything about product labeling, do you?"

"Well, no," I admitted.

"Great," he said. "So let's go find out about shrimp."

And he was off.

As it turned out, we had extensive aquaculture holdings that Uncle knew nothing about either. "Well," he said in explanation, "Allen bought it as an investment. If it'd been a bad investment, he wouldn't have bought it. I don't know anything about investments. Everybody does what they do best."

We went on from there. And try as I might, I could not get Uncle interested in the first thing I was learning about business. "I never went to business school," he would say by means of explanation.

I tried talking with Aunt Liz about it, but she was no better than Uncle. "That's the way he does things," she told me after my impassioned plea to test the shrimp crisps. "It's kind of exciting, isn't it?"

"I guess," I said, bewildered.

"And one day you can be just like that," she said wistfully.

I didn't answer.

I did predict extensive failure of Sea Biscuits, which were, of course, a smash hit. I attributed the success to luck and brooded on.

And I found that new product development was only the beginning.

I transferred to work with Uncle Allen in the investments and financial planning division and became more horrified every day. Uncle would waltz in with the same nonchalance as with marketing, back from some trip or dinner or with some magazine article and say, "Let's buy the food distribution rights on the moon."

And we'd buy them, over my perfectly reasonable protests. And then in the face of sound business practices the investment would turn gold.

"Look," Allen carped at me when I was in a rage over some idiosyncratic purchase, "your Uncle only accounts for about one percent of the investment decisions around here. The rest are made on sound, tried-and-true businesslike methods."

"Thank God," I sighed.

"Yeah, well, I went to business school, too," Allen said, patting me on the arm comfortingly. "And it took me awhile to get used to it. But your uncle's one percent of new investments accounts for about eighty-five percent of all investment profits."

"But he's a flake," I wailed.

"Maybe so." Allen shrugged. "But he's a flake of gold."

My discoveries only continued to heighten my anxiety. I found out that company policy—that is, Uncle's policy—mandated that all our labor force wages and benefits exceed comparable union or industry standards by 5 percent. "They're our customers," he said. "We want them to have disposable incomes."

Another rule was that no new plant or substantial new work force development project be located in a successful or accessible area. Our site-planning department actually had to locate depressed and inaccessible areas to develop for new projects. Uncle for his part explained these rules by saying, "Well, we want to help people out, don't we?" And though it cut into profits sharply, he was beloved by everyone associated with the company.

My recommendations that we could either pay workers in depressed areas less or save money by locating in more well-developed markets were met with the childlike horror one receives in breaking the news about Santa Claus.

Snag and even Sims were equally stunned when I shared my frustrations over development and other practices. "You mean to tell me," Snag bellowed at one such revelation, "that when you can streamline production with a new technology, you buy the machinery and keep the displaced workers?"

"At the same salary," I said, nodding. "And we pay to retrain and relocate them in the field of their choice."

"Even though they become inexperienced workers?" Snag sighed in disgust. "Well, all I can say is I hope the company survives till your twenty-first birthday and you can take control."

I was amazed but undaunted.

So it began, innocently enough. Uncle's strange song in dissonant counterpoint with the strains of business I was practicing at the keyboards of my laptop. It's always easier to hear the chorus than the soloist.

And like patient parents, the Simsons, increasingly Harvey Turnbul, and I tolerated Uncle's off-key performance and orchestrated my taking the baton to conduct business as usual.

Uncle, for his part, had spent my entire senior year planning the circumstances of the official transfer of power. Uncle's planning got as far as the family dinner following graduation.

We were all of us gathered at Uncle's, following the ceremony: Simsons, Reilys, Millers, et al.

Uncle and I had adopted a sort of formal détente from which we had been able to deal with one another during my "career development" phase. It was frosty but workable.

So was the dinner party.

Everyone was correct and pleasant. We all pretended not to notice the underlying themes of tension that had become a part of any family gathering, like a tune you can't get out of your head.

Uncle was explaining my ascension rather loudly so that Pawpaw, who had grown quite deaf, could hear. Neen and Grammy were working out wedding plans, setting up my new household with Burke. Snag and Harvey Turnbul were talking quietly. Gray was overseeing dessert. Allen and Liz were talking with Sims about her soon-to-be social obligations for the Summer and Winter parties, The Sandpiper opening and God knows what else.

Everyone in short was busy planning and conducting my life.

"I think there is something you should all know," I said, topping their collective volume, "before this charade goes any further."

"What?" Pawpaw said, raising his glass. "A toast?"

"A toast," Uncle beamed, raising his glass.

"Yes," I said. "A toast. To destiny."

Everyone drank.

"You see," I went on, "I thought you-all should know that things are changing."

"What?" Pawpaw shouted.

"Things are changing," I shouted again. "I've thought about it for a long time now. And I thought that before you went any further with your plans, you should know mine."

"What?" Pawpaw said.

"Plans," Grammy screamed. "Scott's plans."

"Yes, my plans," I went on. "I'm going to start reorganizing Gambler's."

"You're going to do what?" Uncle asked, lowering his glass.

"Reorganize Gambler's," Pawpaw screamed at him.

"I'm going to streamline the operation and get the company in shape for sale. I'm taking Gambler's public."

Uncle only glared at me.

"What does that mean?" Allen asked in the hush that followed.

"It means I'm going to clear out the deadwood," I said. "Like the movie production units and the nurseries—the nonmoney-makers. We're unloading the cumbersome policies, and we're turning Gambler's into a business."

"No," Uncle said calmly. "No, you're not. Now sit down and we'll talk about this later."

"No?" I laughed. "What do you mean, no? You can't tell me no."

"Oh, yes, I can," Uncle said rising. "I just never have. But this is my limit, Scott."

"There is nothing you can do," I snapped. "Gambler's is mine. And I'll do as I please. And we're going to stop running my company like a charitable institution and start acting like any other business."

"You will never learn," Uncle said, hurling his napkin onto the table.

"Oh, I've learned all right," I said, rising to meet him face-to-face. "You are the one who carries on as though the rest of the world is wrong. You are fired."

"What?" Pawpaw asked.

"Fired," everyone at the table whispered at once.

"Oh, I am, am I?" Uncle said with a sardonic catch in his voice. He pushed his chair away from the table with the backs of his knees.

"No," he said icily. "I'm not fired. I've just failed. I'm a failure because you are my fault. And you are the most hideously spoiled and selfish human being I have ever seen. But you're mine. And it's time I listened to everyone who has ever met you. It's too bad you're too big to spank now."

He glared at me for a moment.

I met him with the calm assurance of victory.

He looked away at Harvey, Snag, and the Simsons. "You should choose your friends more wisely . . . Scott," he said.

Then he sat down at the table and ordered dessert. It was a pretty gloomy cherries jubilee.

Just as calmly as he had resumed his seat at the table, Uncle canceled the processes of the transference of ownership to me.

And so the battle began.

I went to Uncle Bill Stockbridge's law firm to demand my inheritance. Bill, who was about a hundred and fifty years old by then, was not around, but I was referred to Billie Stockbridge.

"Mr. Stockbridge?" I said, barging into his office.

"Miss," Billie said, looking up from her desk.

"Oh, I . . . sorry," I said. "I thought Billie was—"

"It's me," she said, rising politely.

"Yes, well, I'm Scott Miller," I said, thrusting out a hand.

"Oh, yes, I know," she said, taking it. "What can I do for you?"

"Well, I'll come right to the point," I said, shaking her hand brusquely and then taking a seat.

"Please do," she said, sitting also.

"Yes, I want my uncle removed as executor of my estate and I want to begin whatever procedures to receive my full inheritance."

"Oh," she said, coloring. "This is awkward. Then you haven't been served?"

"Served?" I asked.

"Yes. I thought that's what this was all about," she said. "You see, just for openers, we're, rather I'm, the executor of your estate. I took over for my grandfather, Bill Stockbridge. Just this year."

"Congratulations," I glowered. "Then give me my money."

"It's not quite that simple," she said. "You see your uncle is your guardian and he advises us."

"I'm twenty-one years old," I said irritably. "I don't need a guardian."

"No, indeed," she said. "And we will, of course, make whatever monies available to you that you need. But your uncle feels that you're not ready to direct the company at this time."

"Who cares?" I said. "It's mine. He said so."

"I am sorry you haven't received the brief in this matter," she said. "You see, based on the basis of your behavior, we don't feel you are ready to receive ownership at this time either."

"I'm sorry you feel that way," I said caustically. "But frankly I don't care how you feel."

"Well, it isn't just me," she said patiently. "You see there are hundreds, thousands of other people involved now. I'm afraid that the situation of your trust isn't typical."

"Tell me about it," I snapped.

"And we can't deal with it in a typical fashion. The assets and profits of the company are yours."

"You're damn right, and I want them," I was shouting.

"You can have them. All you want within your means," she said, still calm. "What we'd like to do is work out an arrangement with you. What we are proposing—what we proposed in the brief—is that you accept certain financial latitude in lieu of assuming holdership of Gambler's outright."

"Well, to hell with that," I screamed, leaping to my feet.

"We wish that you would try to be reasonable," she said tensely. "Think it through before you decide."

"I'll have my lawyer think it through," I said through clenched teeth.

"Well, that's certainly your prerogative," she said, no longer hiding her irritation. "We don't want a fight, Mr. Miller. But we're not afraid of one either."

"You don't have a leg to stand on," I said wildly.

"Well, be that as it may, Mr. Miller, we are prepared to stand fast," she said, rising and crossing to the door. "I'm sorry that we had to meet under such . . . strained circumstances. We'll talk again soon. Good day."

She held the door and stared evenly.

"Have a nice day, Miss Stockbridge," I fumed, storming out of her office.

I was much more comfortable in the sympathetic atmosphere of Harvey Turnbul's office.

Harvey shared my outrage at the developments, and like children in their parents' absence, we ranted and raged at Uncle Michael, plotting and scheming our revenge.

The brief that Billie Stockbridge had referred to had been delivered to the apartment and Sims brought it over to Harvey's office. We had calmed down some by the time she arrived and we began poring over the document and planning in earnest. Harvey was surprisingly avid, canceling all other appointments and even sending a junior partner to court to request a continuance in another matter.

"Harvey," I said apologetically as he sent the young lawyer to the courthouse, "you don't have to do that. We can talk about this tomorrow."

"Oh, no," he said fervently. "This will go between me and the attorney general's office. This is personal."

Prior to making the action official, we scheduled a meeting with Uncle and Billie Stockbridge.

We met at Harvey's offices on a sweltering June afternoon. Everyone was sticky and irritable and the chill of the air-conditioned air, rancorous with stale cigar smoke, struck a chilly note at the outset.

"Well," Harvey began, "here we go again, eh, Michael? I'm only sorry your grandfather couldn't be with us, Miss Stockbridge. I'd like to have the chance—"

"Get on with it, Harvey," Uncle said in the same threatening tone he'd used with me a few days before. I felt sweat trickle down my back in spite of the chill on the air.

"I'm sorry, Mr. Reily," Harvey needled. "I just thought it was ironic that we should return to the same point of law after twenty years. And on reversed sides of the same question."

"What is this?" Uncle asked, tamping a cigarette on the surface of the mahogany table that separated us. "Are you writing a novella or a legal brief?"

"All right, all right," Harvey said. "I just thought old friends could exchange a few pleasantries before we got down to business."

Uncle snorted as he lit the cigarette he'd been packing.

"It seems that you-all feel"—Harvey began pacing the length of the table, dragging a finger over its sticky haze of fifty years of polishing—"that my client isn't capable of being in receivership of his rightful inheritance."

"We're not trying to say anything of the kind," Billie cut in crisply. "We simply contend that ownership is a separate issue from the management of Gambler's, which was not actually a part of the original bequest."

"Yes, ma'am," Harvey said with an obsequious little bow. "That is true. And you feel that Mr. Reily is better qualified to manage the affairs of the property of my client."

"In a manner of speaking, yes," Billie said. "Though we wouldn't put it quite that way."

"I'm sure not, Miss Stockbridge," Harvey said, adding a circle to the smears he was making on the table.

Uncle didn't seem to be paying attention and sat idly blowing smoke at the ceiling. "What's your point, Harvey?" he asked without looking.

"Just this, Mr. Reily," Harvey said, wiping his hands on his suit. "We feel, conversely, that you aren't the best qualified to run the Gambler's companies."

"Which I founded," Uncle snorted.

"With my client's money," Harvey shot back.

"With money I earned for . . . your client," Uncle said, looking at me.

I looked away.

"And to which, by your own agreement, my client is entitled as his rightful inheritance," Harvey said as if to conclude it.

"He can have the money, Harvey," Uncle growled. "He just can't have the company."

"Because you don't think he's qualified to run it?" Harvey queried.

"Déjà vu," Uncle Michael said, his voice sweet with sarcasm.

"I guess we are covering the same old ground," Harvey said with a short coughing laugh. "Our point here, Mr. Reily, is that we don't feel an ugly trial is in the interests of the company or anyone."

"I'm sure not," Uncle said, catching my eye again.

I looked at Billie to avoid him. She was writing something and was startled when she looked up into my eyes. I smiled nervously. She smiled and looked away.

"Not to put too fine a point on it," Harvey said, making a cat's cradle of his fingertips. "We are in possession of certain evidence that would indicate your management of the company has been somewhat . . . eccentric, shall we say?"

"You're right, Harvey," Billie said. "That doesn't put a very fine point on it."

I laughed in spite of myself. Sims shot me a withering look.

"We are prepared to introduce court records, which we feel prove Mr. Reily had a highly questionable relationship with a man who is now director of the movie production unit of Gambler's, which has not lost less than a million dollars in any of the fifteen years since Mr. Reily purchased it," Harvey said, building to a crescendo. "And we are prepared to present case after case of Mr. Reily's misuse of my client's money and resources to support and further elements of his personal life, which he himself admitted to in court under oath twenty years ago."

"It always comes back to this, doesn't it, Harvey?" Uncle said with an oddly bemused lilt in his voice. "You got yourself some pretty classy friends there, Scott."

I looked away again. Unfortunately I looked into the disapproving gaze of Billie Stockbridge, a gaze I couldn't meet. I looked into my blurry reflection on the greasy surface of the old table.

"Now we don't want to dig up old bones," Harvey continued. "We'd rather not have to fight about this at all. We propose a suitable period of transition be established during which time my client can be made more fully aware of the duties involved in the management of the Gambler's companies. We think this is a reasonable way to mend up this problem and avoid any unnecessary unpleasantness."

"Well, you know, Harvey," Uncle said, stubbing out his cigarette, "it's like I always say. Fuck you."

The complaints were filed. The court date was set. The flood began anew.

Harvey's sense of irony over the combatants' returning to take up an unresolved twenty-year-old case was shared by the press. The scandalous nature of the original case, the intermittent publicity over the years and the fact that an enormous and secretive private company had been added to raise the stakes of victory all combined to produce a storm of historical reporting and a rain of new personal questions.

Harvey astutely put us in the position of fighting for my rightful inheritance.

Uncle, for his part, didn't say much, which meant even more was said about him. The business press speculated about the Gambler's future, and the press at large speculated about Uncle's past.

The entire process put the family under a strain in general and made times difficult for Sims and me in particular. The Simsons were angry that I hadn't waited until my position was secured to announce my reorganization plans. Their irritation became the theme of all our legal meetings and most of the personal ones.

One particularly unpleasant encounter occurred about a week before the court date. We were at Harvey's—the Simsons and I. Things had started out okay but had begun to degenerate into a new chorus of "if you had only waited."

Snag had sung the opening aria.

"Okay," Harvey was summarizing. "When they get here then, our offer is that Michael stays on as director of the company after we take it public but that Scott becomes majority stockholder and votes the controlling interest with Michael as his adviser."

"He's not going to go for that either," Snag said, slamming his fist on the table.

"We have to try to suggest something," I sighed.

"We did suggest something," Snag said, stressing "we" to the extent of its tensile strength. "We suggested that we lull your cotton-headed uncle into a false sense of security, and then, after he was out of the picture—"

"We," I said, matching his stress on the syllable, "have been over this bridge before. And I am sick to death of your crossing it."

"There's no need to snap at my father," Sims said petulantly, drumming her fingers on the table.

"He has been pretty snappy himself," I raged. "Nobody told me that there was any reason why I should wait. Who knew he'd have any grounds for blocking my inheritance?"

"Well, he really doesn't," Harvey said, playing peacemaker. "The burden of proof rests with them."

"So why are we building a case?" I demanded.

"Because we have to refute their claims that you are a rash, unskilled hothead," Snag shouted. "But I'll be goddamned if I couldn't testify for their side."

"Snag," Neen warned. "Language."

"Sorry, Neen," Snag said sheepishly.

"Well, excuse the hell out of me," I said, grinding my teeth.

"You're doing that intentionally," Sims growled. "And stop grinding your teeth."

"Doing what?" I whined. "And I am not grinding my teeth."

"You are," she said with a superior tone.

"I am what?" I wailed.

"Everyone," Harvey said, trying to restore order.

"Don't you talk to my daughter like that," Neen threatened.

"You're using foul language," Sims said, folding her arms.

"You want to hear foul language, you-all just keep this up," I said hotly.

"This isn't getting us anywhere," Harvey tried vainly again.

"Are you threatening us?" Snag demanded indignantly.

"Do you see anyone else in the room?" I shot back.

"Well, we'll just leave if that's what you'd like," Sims said, rather too dramatically.

"What I'd like is for all of you to get off my back," I was shouting.

"We are only trying to help." Neen simpered.

"Do we make the offer or don't we?" Harvey said, shouting over us all.

"Really, Harvey," Neen said, "there is no need to raise your voice."

"I want an answer," Harvey went on, not backing off his initial volume.

"Honestly," Neen said primly.

"Well?" Harvey screamed.

"What's the goddamned question?" I screamed back.

"Language," Neen clucked.

"Scott," Sims chided me.

"The question is 'Is the offer of directorship a suitable compromise?' " Harvey bellowed.

"No," I shouted.

"Yes," Snag said at the same moment.

"No," I reemphasized.

"Yes," Snag said again at the same moment.

"I'll do whatever I want to," I shrieked.

"That's what put us here in the first place," Snag said.

"Daddy's right," Sims said irritatingly.

"In the first place," I said, "Uncle is never going to accept figurehead status as a solution to the problem. He opposes going public."

"Yes, but we're going public with more than the stock," Snag reasoned. "He can avoid the scandal—"

"Do you think that is going to stop him now?" I asked, almost laughing in amazement. "What can we possibly say at this point that hasn't already been on the evening news five times in the last twenty years?"

"Scott's right," Sims said.

"So what do you propose?" Snag asked, calming down a bit.

"I'm no lawyer—" I began.

"You're right about that, too," Sims put in sarcastically.

"Stay off my side," I said, cutting my eyes at her. "Anyway, it seems to me, in my vast ignorance, that it's my inheritance and that the will has stood before—"

"That case was never decided," Harvey said. "There's no precedent."

"So subpoena the judge and ask her," I said in disgust.

"Scott, that's stupid," Sims said flatly.

"Thanks for the vote of confidence, sweetheart," I said sourly.

"Anytime," she snarled back.

"No, wait," Snag said. "I like it. Why can't we?"

"Even if we could," Harvey said plaintively, "we don't know what she was going to decide."

"So we ask her," I said.

"Look," Harvey said, his exasperation mounting, "supposing she is willing to do something so outrageous and unethical, if she was going to give custody to the senator, then the whole will is invalid and everyone has a claim to present against the estate. And if she was going to let the will stand, then your uncle is back in the driver's seat."

"I see," Snag intoned with a dry, toneless whistle as he became lost in thought.

"I told you it was a stupid idea," Sims said to me.

"Don't you talk to your father like that," Neen said.

"I am not talking to Daddy," she said, wrapping her knuckles on the table.

"And why not?" Snag demanded, snapping out of his momentary reverie.

"Jesus," Sims said, putting her face in her hands.

"Language," Neen said.

"Scott, don't grind your teeth," Sims said, looking up.

"I am not," I said.

"You are," she insisted.

"It's your father," I said.

"Snag," Neen threatened him.

"It isn't," Snag said on the defensive. "It's Scott."

"You see," Sims said with an air of finality.

"What are we talking about?" I screamed as I leaped up.

"There is no need to adopt that tone—" Neen began.

"Shut up. Shut up. Shut up. All of you shut up," I wailed hysterically.

"Well, I never," Sims said, flouncing around in her chair indignantly.

"Look," I said, trying to regain my sanity, "they called this meeting, so I say let them talk. Like it or not, this is my decision and I'm not making any deal. I don't think we have to," I concluded, sitting down.

"Fine," Sims said angrily.

"It's your funeral," Snag yelled.

"Don't raise—" Neen began.

"Shut up," I screamed.

There was a knock and Billie Stockbridge stuck her head in.

"If you're through screaming," she said with sarcastic charm, "your secretary said I'd find you in here."

"Barge right in." Sims scowled.

"Thanks ever so," Billie said, coming into the room and closing the door.

"Where's Uncle?" I asked, surprised she was alone.

"Belgium," she said after looking at her watch.

"Belgium?" I asked. "But I thought you wanted to meet with us?"

"I do," Billie said pleasantly.

"What is he doing in Belgium?" Sims asked.

"Buying a chocolate manufacturing company," she said, laying some papers on the table and closing her case.

"We already own a chocolate manufacturer," I said, irritated that Uncle hadn't come.

"Not in Belgium," she said brightly.

"Well, I can hardly see the point of meeting then," Harvey said. "If Mr. Reily doesn't even feel he—"

"You seem to forget, Harvey," Billie cut him off. "I am the executor of the estate. Mr. Reily is Scott's guardian. We appointed him director at Gambler's. And we are the ones opposed to Scott's appointment."

"If you think you can get around me," Harvey said, "by confusing the issue of whose job it is to manage the company—"

"Actually that's not how I plan on getting around you," she said calmly. "I have met with Mr. Reily and I'm afraid he's gotten around all of us."

"And what the hell does that mean?" Snag demanded.

"Language," Neen and I said in unison.

Sims stomped my foot under the table.

"Really I'd rather discuss this with Scott," Billie said. "Alone," she clarified when no one responded.

"No," Harvey said.

"Yes," I said at the same time.

"Scott," he implored, "you should be represented by legal counsel in any negotiations."

"May I remind you, Harvey," Billie said unfolding her glasses to put them on, "that I am Scott's legal counsel as the executor of his estate."

"We are not leaving," Sims said defiantly.

"Oh, yes, you are," I said nastily.

"Scott," Sims said, shocked.

"I really can't allow it," Harvey said pompously.

"I am afraid you will have to," I said.

"How could you?" Sims wailed.

"Like this," I said, rising, crossing to the door and opening it. "Good-bye."

They stormed out in a cloud of harrumphs and protestations. I slammed the door.

"My, what a big crowd you have," Billie said, peering at me over the tops of her glasses.

"Is this going to take long?" I asked.

"Well, no," she said, clearly rather put off by the question. "A few minutes—thirty maybe."

"That won't do," I said.

"Well, I'll talk as fast as I can," she stammered, still a little surprised.

"You'll have to take a good deal longer than that," I said, opening a side door of the conference room, which opened into Harvey's office.

"What are? . . . What?" Billie asked, puzzled.

"In fact," I said, wiggling my eyebrows, "I think it's going to take so long that we're going to have to get some late lunch. Yes." I nodded, gathering up her things. "And the news will be so bad that we'll have to have quite a number of drinks."

"We will?" she asked with a smirk.

"Yes," I said solemnly. Then I dropped my voice to a whisper. "Come on. The coast is clear and there's a private exit in here so we can escape the Mr. and Miz Godzillas."

"You know," Billie said after we were safely seated at a private booth in a very dark nearby restaurant, "that was just the sort of thing your uncle would have done."

"You see what a bad influence he is," I said, waving a playful finger. "If I'm irresponsible, it's his fault."

"Very possibly," she said, smiling mildly. "Now to the business at hand," she went on, putting on her glasses and reopening her attaché case.

"You're not drinking your wine," I said.

"Mr. Miller—" she began.

"If you're not at least as drunk as I am, I'll agree to everything and then accuse you of taking unfair advantage of me," I said, raising my glass.

"Mr. Miller . . ."

"Scott."

"Scott . . ."

"A toast."

"A toast?" she asked. "To what?"

"Absent friends?" I suggested slyly.

She laughed.

"Aha," I said. "And if you take off your glasses, I'll bet we can be friends."

"What has taking off my glasses got to do with it?" she asked.

"Well, you might not recognize me as the same man who's been so rude to you the last couple of times we've met," I said.

"To absent friends," she said, raising her glasses and ringing them against the side of my glass.

"Good," I said, taking a sip. "Now let's try to discuss this pleasantly. All right? I haven't had a pleasant discussion recently."

"Okay," she said. "Good."

"What's the story, counselor?" I asked, pouring more wine in our glasses.

"This is the situation," she said, tapping the folder in front of her. "As the executors of the estate which now includes all the Gambler's holdings, we have appointed your uncle director."

"Right," I acknowledged, taking a sip.

"Well, if you assume your estate," she said, "you also assume responsibility for appointing the director of Gambler's."

"I'm still with you," I nodded, taking a handful of the nuts on the table between us.

"Obviously you can appoint anyone or take responsibility yourself," she went on. "Are there cashews in that?"

"Uh, yes," I said, examining a handful.

"Good," she said, and began sorting through the bowl to find them. "Anyway. What neither you nor I have any control over is the name Gambler's."

"The name?" I asked.

"Mmm, yes," she said, munching on her cashew harvest. "We license it and all the recipes from your uncle."

"So?" I asked. "Don't take all the cashews."

"But I only like the cashews," she said. "So, if I give you control and you appoint yourself director, your uncle will revoke the license and we won't have a name or any products to sell."

I stopped eating nuts and got back to drinking. "Hmm," I said at last. "Uncle Michael only looks like a flake."

"He's smart enough to have made Gambler's in the first place," she said, pausing from the cashew carnage to have some of her wine.

"So if I take him to court and take control, he'll destroy the company?" I asked, pouring more wine.

"That's about the size of it," she said, running a finger around the rim of her glass.

"Well, then," I said loudly, the wine hitting my empty stomach, "as I see it, I can either give in to Uncle Michael or I can get drunk," and I downed my glass.

"You want some free legal advice?" she said giddily.

"Sure," I bellowed, pouring us more.

"You can do both," she said.

We laughed and had another toast.

And another.

In fact, we had quite a few toasts. And a really good time— something I hadn't had in quite a while. She talked about her grandfather, and I talked about Uncle.

We agreed that working with family was a terrible idea. We also agreed to meet again before the trial and after I'd had a chance to work something out.

By the time I got home I was quite drunk.

Sims was coiled and ready to strike. "Where the hell have you been?" she said, opening the floor for discussion as I walked in.

"Language," I taunted.

"I'm going to kill you," she screamed.

"That's the mature and adult thing to do," I snorted with drunken laughter.

"We waited hours for you to come out," she went on.

"I didn't ask you to," I said, beginning to undress in the living room.

"And you come home in the middle of the night drunk and ridiculous," she wailed.

"It's eight-thirty," I said calmly, trying to focus on my watch.

"What the hell has that got to do with it?" she demanded.

"Language," I said, giggling.

"If you say that again, I'll castrate you with the kitchen shears."

"You said it was the middle of the night," I said, unbuttoning my shirt and casting it aside. "But it's only eight-thirty."

"There is just no talking to you," she said in disgust.

"Then don't," I said, kicking off my shoes and fumbling with my fly.

"What are you doing?" she asked, looking at me in disbelief.

"I'm undressing," I said confidentially.

"I know that," she said. "Why are you undressing?"

"Because my clothes will get all wet in the shower," I answered simply as I shucked my trousers down around my ankles.

"You can't," she said tersely as she leaned down to pick up my shirt. She made as if to hand it to me.

"It is a little difficult," I said. "But I assure you I can."

I lifted a foot and leaned down to wrestle myself free from the pants leg.

"No, I mean you can't because any minute—" she began.

"We're here," Snag bellowed, bursting in with Neen and Harvey.

I lost my balance during the process and fell over backward, upsetting the coffee table and a straight chair in my wake.

"What the hell?" Snag injected, surveying the disaster.

"Language," I guffawed.

"Get up from there," Sims whispered.

"Never," I shouted, still laughing.

"What is going on?" Harvey asked Sims.

"Perhaps we'd better leave," Neen suggested.

"He's drunk," Sims said by way of explanation.

"I am," I said, waving a finger up at them.

"Well, we'll just be going," Neen persisted on her theme, trying not to look at me.

"No, Mother," Sims said, "please stay."

"Now you listen to your mother," I said to Sims. "I think she's really on to something there."

"It's bad enough you're stinking," Sims hissed at me. "Don't be rude, too."

"What the hell," I gurgled drunkenly. "I didn't invite all these goddamn people to my house. Language," I added, and began laughing again.

"Scott," Sims said sharply, "you just try to get a grip on yourself. We're here to help you. The least you can do—"

"I'm sick of your help," I slurred. "And stop looking down

at me like that all of you. I feel like I'm on an operating table."

"Scott," Sims said angrily as she grabbed my hand and began to try to drag me up.

"Leave me alone," I yelled, snatching my hand away. "All of you just leave me alone."

There was a moment's silence.

Sims glared at me hotly. "You want us to leave you alone?" she asked tersely.

"Is this a rhetorical question?" I tried to pronounce.

"Fine, we'll leave you alone," she snapped. "All alone. Come on everyone."

"But, Sims—" Snag began.

"Just come on," she said tensely.

And that was the end of it. They left.

I woke up the following morning with a shattering headache, my pants around my ankles and an unobstructed view of the living room ceiling. I would never have awakened at all except there was someone pounding on the door.

"Scott?" It was Grammy. "Are you in there?"

"Oh, God," I muttered.

"Scott, are you all right?" She tried the door. Naturally it was open.

"Scotty," she wailed. "What happened? Are you okay?"

"Yes," I said, rolling my eyes. "This is how I receive guests now."

"What happened?" she said, trying to kneel beside me.

"I was drunk, I passed out, I'm hung over, talk quietly," I said, starting to get up. I had to help Grammy back up.

"Get a shower," she said. "I'll make coffee. You want something to eat?"

"I not only do not want anything," I said, pulling up my pants. "I don't want you to mention food in my presence ever again as long as we live."

"Okay," she said, smiling.

"Say 'I swear,'" I said, buttoning my fly.

"I swear." She chuckled. "Coffee?"

"Coffee," I said, heading for the bathroom.

I felt better after my shower.

The kitchen smelled like coffee and Grammy's powder. "Here you go," she said, handing me a mug. "Nice bathrobe."

"Sims gave it to me," I said, taking a swipe at my hair with the towel around my neck. "Jesus. Sims," I said, remembering.

"What about Sims?" Grammy asked. "Where is she?"

"At her apartment," I said, trying to sound offhand.

"Come off it," she said, sitting at the kitchen table beside me. "I may be old, but I'm not stupid."

"No?" I said, raising my eyebrows and sipping at my coffee.

She slapped my shoulder playfully. "No," she said. "I know perfectly well that Sims has been living here for the last couple of years. It must be nice to be rich enough at your age to maintain the pretense of two apartments."

"It's swell," I said lamely.

"So where is she?" Grammy asked.

"We had a little fight," I began, and then interrupted myself. "No, we had a big fight. And so she probably is at her apartment."

"Maybe Ash and I should try that," she said. "What about?"

"I'm sorry?" I said, knitting my brow.

"What did you fight about?" she asked.

"I was drunk," I said with a shrug.

"And pretty disorderly," she said, pointing at the clothes she had stacked neatly on a chair.

"Yes, fairly," I said, smiling.

"And you fought." She prodded.

"Yes," I said, and took another slurp.

"Don't slurp," she corrected. "Fought about what? Being drunk?"

"Sort of," I admitted vaguely.

"Did you go to a party without her?" she persisted.

"Sort of," I said.

"Are you 'sort of' going to tell me what happened or not?" she asked wryly.

"Or not," I answered.

She sighed, of course.

"All right," I said. "No sighing. We met with the lawyers yesterday. And she and her parents are driving me crazy. So I told them to butt out. Okay? Let's don't talk about it."

She nodded and slurped her coffee.

"No slurping," I said with a wink. "Now, what brings you here this morning?"

"It's afternoon," she said evasively.

"Okay," I said. "I stand corrected. What brings you here this afternoon?"

"Well," she said, not looking at me, "I did stop by your office first."

"Yes. And?" I nudged.

"And you weren't there," she said.

"Are you 'sort of' going to tell me or not?" I asked, squeezing her hand.

"Or not," she said. "You said you didn't want to talk about it."

"Oh, not you, too," I moaned, taking my hand away.

"Yes, me, too," she said. "Lawyers and court and the evening news. I had planned such a quiet family."

"You blew it," I said, smiling.

"I know," she said, rolling her eyes up. "Tell me about it."

"So go ahead," I sighed. "Take your shot. Everyone else has."

She looked at me a moment. "Don't give in," she said at last.

"What?" I coughed, choking slightly on my last sip of coffee.

"Don't give in to Michael," she repeated in the same simple tone.

"Well, I have to say," I said in amazement, "if I was writing this script, that's not the role I would have cast you in."

"Poor Michael," she said, rising. "He's always looking for a fight. I think it's all he understands. It's all he's ever had in his life. I don't know why. He's such a wonderful person. But he was born with a chip on his shoulder. I think he started out too ide-alistic. It made him bitter." She sighed and poured herself more coffee. "More for you?" she asked, waving the pot.

"Please," I said pensively. "And so you want me to fight with him?"

"Yes," she said, pouring. "Because he'll understand that. I made him fight, you know?" she said, putting the pot back. "He just wanted to give up. Hide. And I couldn't let him do that."

She sat down again. "It's my fault he's so high-minded any-way," she went on, folding her hands primly. "Too many fairy tales. Not enough reality. So I made him fight. And then I criticized him for fighting. And so he fought me, too. Now all he has is fighting. And you. And he doesn't even realize it. And now he's fighting you. Fight back," she implored.

"Okay," I said quietly. "Okay."

"I'm going to fight," I said, walking through the door of Billie's office.

She laughed mildly.

"What's so funny?" I asked.

"Your uncle said you would," she said, smiling.

"The wily old son of a bitch," I said, grinning.

"Umm, hmm." She nodded. "You know it could ruin the company."

"Maybe," I said. "But I don't care anymore."

She smiled again.

"Did he say I'd say that, too?" I asked.

"Umm, hmm," she said, smiling more broadly.

"Go have parents," I said, shaking my head.

We laughed.

"You know," she said. "That's the first time I've ever heard you call him anything but Uncle."

"I haven't felt like it in a long time," I said.

"Why the change?" she asked, looking over her glasses at me.

"Oh, I don't know." I shrugged. "A lot of things. Seeing Sims and her parents together. Grammy stopped by. Some things she said. Seeing her and Uncle together in my mind. I don't know. All of it, I guess."

"Definitive," she said glibly.

"Feelings never are," I said, looking her straight in the eye.

She smiled nervously and looked away.

"So what does Harvey say?" she said, changing the subject.

"I haven't told him," I said. "Or the Godzillas."

"Then why tell me?" she asked.

"Wanted to see you again?" I suggested.

"I hope you won't feel we have to sue each other every time we get together," she said.

"I guess that would make for a fairly strained . . . friendship," I said, still looking.

She blushed slightly.

"So," she said, taking a deep breath, "do you want to negotiate or do you want to talk with Harvey first?"

"I'm going to talk to Harvey," I said. "And I'm going to tell him the same thing I'm going to tell you. The only difference is I'm going to tell you over dinner. Eight o'clock?"

"Actual food?" she said with a smirk.

"Done," I said.

"Sit down, Harvey," I said, bursting into his office.

"I am sitting down," Harvey said, blinking.

"Good," I said. "Then shut up and listen. This is it. We're going to fight. Or rather we're not. We're going to ask for my inheritance, all of it. No deals. No negotiations. Period. If they want to fight, that's fine. But they're going to do all the swinging. You should know that if we win, Uncle says he's going to take back the name and all the recipes and wreck the company. But that's fine with us. I don't care what you think, I don't care what the Simsons think and I don't care who Uncle has or has not been sleeping with—which is probably no one. I have a plan. If you want to know what it is, see you in court. Or not."

"And so what did Harvey say?" Billie asked me over dinner after I recounted the story.

"I don't know," I said with a shrug. "I left right after that."

"You just walked out?" she asked incredulously.

"That's it," I said. "And yes, I know that's just what Uncle would have done."

She smiled. "So you're just going to let him ruin the company?" she asked.

"He won't," I said calmly.

"How can you be so sure?" she asked, toying with her pasta salad.

"Because I wouldn't," I said cockily. "Besides, you haven't heard my plan."

"Pretty sure of yourself," she said archly.

"I guess I am," I said.

I was in a pretty good mood when I got home, in spite of everything. I was whistling as I entered the darkened apartment.

"Harvey told us." Sims' voice came out of the darkness, startling me back to earth.

"Jesus," I said, switching on the light. "You scared me."

"Sorry," she said.

"Why are you sitting around in the dark?" I asked, unloading my pockets onto a table.

"Just thinking," she said.

"Uh," I said, examining the change in my hand. "A dollar and fifteen, sixteen, seventeen cents for your thoughts."

"Free," she said tonelessly. "Special introductory offer."

"I do care what you think," I sighed, tossing the change onto the table with everything else.

"Then why didn't you discuss it with me?" she asked plaintively.

"We haven't been doing much discussing lately," I said, heaving off my jacket. "You probably haven't noticed because you've been doing all the talking."

"Oh, ho, ho," she said, rising along with her tone of voice. "So it's my fault, is it?"

"No, it isn't," I said. "It's still Uncle Michael's, but you and your family and Harvey have been driving me off the edge."

"I thought you'd be glad of the support," she said angrily.

"Support?" I crowed. "The only thing I've been glad of lately is that you're an only child."

"Oh," she said, tears suddenly in her eyes.

"Shit," I inhaled. "I'm sorry. I didn't mean to hurt you."

"Too late," she sobbed.

"We've been hurting each other a lot lately," I said quietly. "Too much. I think we need some time. Apart."

"Just hold me," she said.

"No," I said quietly.

She looked at me, all her pain focused on me, in that one stare.

"I'm sorry," I said. "I can't. We'll just start all over. Maybe after all this is over . . ." I trailed off.

"Maybe," she said. "Maybe."

There was a knock at the door.

"Not now," I muttered, looking at the ceiling.

"Scott? It's Aunt Liz."

"And Allen."

"What do they want?" I said.

"Scott," she called, "are you in there?"

"Just a minute," I called. "Look, Sims—"

"Maybe later," she said, grasping for her bag.

She let Liz and Allen in as she shoved past.

"Are we interrupting?" Liz asked in the confusion.

"Yes," I said in exasperation.

"We can come back," she said, pointing at the way out.

"Well, there's nothing to interrupt now," I said rather unpleasantly. "Come in. Join me for a drink?"

"No, thanks," Liz said.

"No," Allen said.

"What can I do for you?" I asked, heading off to fix one for myself.

"I don't suppose you'd believe we were just in the neighborhood?" Liz said, grinning as she followed me into the kitchen.

"Uh, no," I said tersely.

"How about, just wanted to see what you've done with the apartment?" Allen said, leaning in the doorway.

"Looks better in the daylight," I said, starting my drink. "So what do you want?"

"To . . . talk," Liz said haltingly. "Maybe I will have a drink."

"Talk, talk, talk," I said nastily. "I'm going to put in a revolving door. I don't think anyone I know in all of Christendom hasn't been here in the last two days. Maybe a receptionist in the living room."

"Scott, we don't want to interfere," Allen said from the doorway where he'd anchored himself.

"No one does," I said, kicking out a chair and sitting.

"No, really," Liz said, sitting across from me. "We've been debating about this since everything started."

"Which everything?" I asked pointedly. "This has been going on for twenty years."

"The you and Michael and Gambler's everything," Liz said with a snort of nervous laughter.

"There are just some things you should know," Allen said.

"There's more?" I said incredulously.

"Well, yes, kind of," Liz said. "There are things you don't understand about Michael."

"Oh, I understand Uncle Michael as well as or better than any-one else," I said nastily.

"And the company," Allen put in. "It's a very eccentric operation."

"No shit," I said.

"Like the movie company business," Allen said, hanging spread-eagled by his fingertips on the door facing like a spider's web.

"That seems clear enough," I said.

"Did you know that Gambler's Films does all of our commer-cial production for free?" she asked.

"Which saves the company millions," Allen went on, taking up the story. "And that all the creative work, movies, TV produc-tions, that kind of thing is sold at a loss to other divisions of the company for distribution?"

"Why at a loss?" I asked.

"So Gambler's Films will lose money," Allen said, leaning his body into the room from his bizarre stance in the doorway.

"Lose money?" I parroted.

"And the distribution profits are all reinvested in Gambler's Films," Allen said. "So we don't make any money. On paper. But it's actually a huge profit center for the company. And a tax loss."

"Pretty slick," I said with low whistle.

"And very eccentric," Liz said knowingly. "Your uncle is a brilliant man."

"What about Kevin Perdue?" I asked. "That's still pretty questionable."

"Not really," Liz said. "He's very good at what he does. We've won lots of awards for the work."

"And there would be no profits to reinvest if his film work wasn't good," Allen said, still swinging on the door facing, the web blowing in a breeze.

"Well, this is all well and good," I said. "But it's a moot point. I've told Harvey we're not pursuing this kind of thing in court. There's been enough public discussion of our private affairs."

"But it still matters," Liz said. "If you take the company public, that kind of unusual business arrangement won't be possible."

"Why not?" I said. "Is it illegal?"

"No," Allen said. "But it doesn't pay dividends."

"There's just a lot about the business you don't understand," Liz said earnestly. "You need to give Michael another chance."

"I'll tell you what I don't understand," I said, rising to get another drink. "Is why are you two sticking up for him?"

"What?" Allen said, letting go of the door.

"Your uncle has been wonderful to us," Liz said emphatically.

"Wonderful?" I said in amazement. "Not only does he run you around on a leash, but he meddles in your lives like some demented Greek god."

"What are you talking about?" Liz asked, rising and joining me at the liquor cabinet. "Got any bourbon?"

"Yes," I said, handing her the bottle. "I'm talking about, well, what about your wedding? He turned that into a three-ring circus."

"He bought a chain of hotels so I could have the reception where I wanted it," Liz said.

"I guess," I said, slicing a lime.

"Don't you see? Michael saw the conflicts with Mom and your grandma, and he ran interference. We had a great time. We did what we wanted. Your uncle is always trying to make people happy. He does really stupid things to do it. Like dressing up like the gardener. But he is really trying all the time. He can't ask you to like him 'cause he's too proud, so he tries to make people like him—by force. Do you see that?"

"I guess," I said, tasting my drink.

"Look, who do you think paid for the Sweetheart Ball?" Liz said, screwing the lid back on the ginger ale.

"Liz," Allen warned.

"What do you mean?" I asked, pausing as I put the ice back in the freezer.

"It's time, Allen," Liz said. "I mean Chaz Montreau is one of your uncle's oldest friends. Michael knew you wouldn't take anything from him, so he underwrote the whole thing through Chaz. To make you happy."

"I see," I said quietly. "But I don't see how it changes anything."

"It doesn't really," Liz said, stirring her drink with her index finger. "We just thought it might change the way you look at Michael. A little."

"I'm sure that Uncle has had the best intentions," I said patiently. "But he has the worst judgment. He's pushy, meddlesome and, very possibly, stark raving mad. This whole business is typical," I said, shaking my head. "If you can call Uncle typical."

"Look—" Allen began.

"No, you look," I cut him off, beginning to get worked up. "Even if Uncle is a saint, he is always interfering in my life like —like—"

"Someone's mother?" Liz suggested coolly.

"Yes," I said, and then stopped.

There was a long pause, punctuated only by the rattling of ice cubes in my glass as I finished my drink.

"Look, Scott," Allen said, coming into the room, "I understand how you feel. Better than you know. When this all started, when Michael was fighting for custody of you. Jesus, was that really twenty years ago? Was it really you?

"Anyhow," he went on, "I was just about your age. And I was so sure he was wrong. He was always wrong. He had never fit in. He was a real oddball. And we were all convinced, all of us —the senator, me, everyone—convinced that he couldn't possibly raise a child.

"All we could see was that he wasn't like us. Or anyone else. So he had to be wrong. But then Michael said something in court that changed my mind. It changed the way I was looking at everything. I think it even changed the senator's mind.

"Let me ask you something," Allen said, putting his hand on my shoulder. "You don't have to answer me even. Just think about the question. When was the last time you thought of Michael as just a person? Just like you. Wanting and needing the same things you do. He's such a rare bird it's hard to think of him as one of the flock," Allen said, patting me. "Isn't it? We need to go now. Come on, Liz."

"Okay, sure," Liz said, rising and pecking me on the cheek. "See you, Scott."

Our day in court arrived.

I hadn't been able to stop thinking about what Allen had said. I also hadn't changed my mind. I arrived, a man with a plan.

The Godzillas had gone back to the coast, so court was pretty much a family affair. Aside from a couple of hundred spectators and fifty or so reporters it was positively intimate.

We had had to fight our way in from the cars and everyone was in a pretty foul humor. There were terse greetings. Uncle and I spoke. I shook Billie's hand and sneaked a squeeze. We shared a smile.

Grammy and Pawpaw had a spat about who to sit behind and Grammy asked Harvey if we could all sit at the same table.

Harvey was explaining as the judge entered, so Grammy sat behind us and Pawpaw sat down in exasperation next to Gray behind Uncle and then had to get up again in response to the bailiff's call.

"All rise."

"Judge Henry Arnold presiding."

"Siddown," Judge Arnold said. "All right, look, I've heard about you people. I've read about you; I've seen you on the evening news. I've read the transcripts of the previous trial, and it was like leafing through the scripts from *Dynasty*. Judge Dukes was never quite the same after you people. So let me just start things out on the right foot. I'm having none of it," he said, wagging his jowls. "You may all be insane, but this is my court, and we're going to behave here. Is that clear?" he asked.

We only looked stunned.

"Is that clear?" he demanded, pounding his gavel for emphasis.

"Yes, Your Honor," Harvey and Billie said.

"And ladies and gentlemen of the press," he said, gesturing to include the room, "and you folks in the gallery, if you came for a soap opera, go home and watch *The Young and the Restless,* 'cause this ain't it. Report what you want," he said, waving them away. "There's no gag orders on this mess, it's too late, it didn't work last time and these people don't deserve it."

Uncle Michael made a snorting sound.

"Shut up," the judge said, pointing at him. "And counsel, don't bother to ask me for a gag order 'cause you ain't gettin' one. Now the plaintiff is going to present some material and then the defendant and then I'm going to rule on it. No theatrics. Legal facts that have a real bearing in this matter, and that's it. I've got a pad of contempt writs already filled out except for the names, so let's begin, Miss Stockbridge."

"That's quite an act to follow," Uncle Michael said.

"How's that?" the judge demanded, leaning forward.

"Just conferring with counsel, Your Holiness," Uncle said.

"Watch it," the judge said, leaning back. "Pro-ceed."

There was a lot of legal blathering, most of which Judge Arnold wasn't having any of, and then Uncle Michael took the stand. I waited for my chance.

"State your name and occupation," Billie said.

"Michael Reily," Uncle said. "Chief executive of Gambler's."

"How long have you been with Gambler's?" she asked.

"I founded the company," he answered with a nod.

"Roughly what are the present assets and holdings of the Gambler's company?" she asked.

"It has been my experience that people who know what they are worth aren't worth much," Uncle said calmly.

There was a small stir which the judge leaped on.

"Would it be safe to say that Gambler's current value would probably be about two and half billion dollars?" Billie said.

"Roughly," Uncle said. He seemed a little embarrassed.

Another rumble.

"So you have supervised the growth of Gambler's from nothing to its present worth?" she asked.

"Yes," he said smugly.

"And the company began with your recipe for cheesecake and grew on your business savvy, is that correct?" she asked, looking at me.

"Well, it would be immodest for me to say it quite like that," Uncle began affably.

"Just answer the questions," Judge Arnold snapped.

"Yes," Uncle said through clenched teeth, nostrils flaring.

"Do you own the Gambler's company, Mr. Reily?" she asked.

"No," Uncle said more calmly.

"Who does?" she asked.

"Scott," he said. "Scott Miller."

"Why is that?" she asked.

"He was my ward," Uncle said. "The money that started the company came from his trust and I set up the company as part of that trust so that it would be a part of his inheritance."

"And he is of age to receive that inheritance now?" she asked.

"Yes," he said, nodding.

"Have you made any effort to deny Mr. Miller his inheritance?" she asked.

I sat forward.

"No," Uncle said calmly.

"No?" I shouted. "What do you mean no?"

"Mr. Miller," the judge warned.

"I mean no," Uncle shouted at me. "No means no."

"Mr. Reily," the judge yelled, pounding his gavel.

"How can you say that?" I asked, leaping to my feet and toppling my chair.

"Scott, please," Harvey said, grabbing my arm.

"Mr. Miller," the judge said, turning from Uncle to me like a tennis linesman, "I'm warning you—"

"Like this," Uncle said, jumping up to demonstrate. "Nnnnoooo," he pronounced. "No, no, no, no . . ."

"Mr. Reily," Billie said, putting her hand on his as he leaned on the front of the witness box.

"Mr. Reily," the judge wailed, pounding indiscriminately on the desk, "sit down or I'll hold you in contempt."

"That's not what I mean, and you know it," I yelled.

"Scott," Harvey admonished as he struggled to right my chair.

"Bailiff," the judge wailed, pounding furiously.

"You can have all the money you want," Uncle screamed. "You just can't run this company into the ground."

"Mr. Reily."

"Scott."

"And why is that?" I demanded, striding toward the witness box.

"Because you don't deserve it," Uncle hissed, climbing down and crossing to meet me.

"Bailiff," the judge bellowed.

"Mr. Reily," Billie said, taking Uncle's arm.

"Don't deserve it?" I said, topping his volume and slapping the back of my hand into my palm.

"That's right," he yelled into my face. "You just take the money and go play with your tiresome, snotty little bourgeois friends."

"I don't believe you people," the judge trumpeted.

The bailiff was just about on us when Smitty vaulted the railing and headed him off. They struggled.

"Who's the snob here?" I asked, giving Uncle's shoulder a little push.

"If the nose fits . . ." Uncle said pushing back.

"Order in the court," the judge shouted vainly as the bailiff's gun went off, blowing out a ceiling tile and raining sparks and debris on the packed courtroom.

Chaos reigned. The crowd was pandemonium.

"Do you know who you are acting like?" I said, punctuating my words with my index finger on Uncle's chest. "The senator."

"Oh. Oh," Uncle puffed, momentarily speechless with indignation. "The senator. That old fart. Most of this is his fault anyway."

The gun went off again, winging the judge's desk. Judge Arnold took a header underneath, screaming, "You're in contempt. Every goddamned one of you is in contempt of this court."

"It's true," I yelled into Uncle's face. "You're just convinced I can't do it, just like he thought you couldn't raise me."

"Well, he was apparently right," Uncle screamed. "Oh, my God. I can't believe I am agreeing with that old buzzard."

"You see, you see," I said, hopping up and down.

"All right, all right," he said. "Look, I just don't think you understand what taking the company public would mean."

Smitty had knocked the gun free, and Grammy picked it up and held them both at bay. Most of the occupants of the court had fled, and those who remained made a break for it as the threat of more random gunfire was temporarily eliminated.

"Look," I said more reasonably, "you can't control every-thing—or me—forever. You're going to have to let go."

"I can't," he wailed. "I blew it. You turned out all wrong. You got these ludicrous values."

"You are the one with ludicrous values," I snapped. "I turned out to be a normal kid, which is amazing in itself."

"Well, if I'd said bourgeois, it would just have pissed you off," he said petulantly.

"Lookit," I said. "I have learned one thing and that's that peo-ple's values are different, but they all basically want the same things."

The last of the spectators was gone, and court fell strangely quiet save for me.

"It's not fair to judge people as stereotypes. You have to judge the person," I continued. "Judge me, not what you think of what I believe."

"What's going on now?" the judge asked, peeking over the top of his desk.

"You shut up," Grammy said, pointing the gun at him.

"That's pretty smart, Scott," Uncle said hoarsely. "Where'd you learn that?"

"From you, Dad."

BOOK

III

MICHAEL

~ ~ ~

What to say?

Whoever said beginnings were the hardest never had children.

It certainly wasn't something I planned or prepared for. Scott just sort of showed up. I guess some people get the nine months' notice thing, but they really only get to make sure their insurance is in order and read a few how-to books. Beyond that, every day is a surprise party.

I think the biggest mistake most parents make is in believing that they will be guiding and shaping a young mind, that this new life is theirs to make.

Oh, sure, you do the basic stuff, walking, talking, and the potty-training thing—Jesus. And along the way you offer up your views and values—your take on the world and life and death and sex and politics and religion. But that's a take-it-or-leave-it proposition. You're a director; the performance is still up to the actor.

Now the Act III denouement is that the biggest mistake children make is believing their parents are responsible for their lives.

It's like people on those interview shows. The interviewer asks, "Who were the influences in your life?" And the dissectee has a list of people. What amazes me is that the respondent's name is never on the list.

I am the biggest influence in my life.

And it seems to me that's the story with being someone's kid.

Black, white, gay, straight, Catholic, abusive, alcoholic, workaholic, bad taste in shoes—the big impact isn't who your parents are but how you choose to cope with it.

As I look back on it, Scott had a much bigger impact on my life than I had on his. But I made the choice to make Scott a part of my life.

The best role model I can offer to other parent types is Glenda, the good witch, in *The Wizard of Oz*. Dorothy could have gotten what she wanted all along, but she had to find that out on her own.

But what a lot of unasked-for advice, huh?

What you want to know is how everything works out. And the answer is: I don't know.

That answer is as long as the history of mankind. Asking how it ends is like asking where it started. Family is really only the way we share our love and shape destiny a little at a time. What I got from Ann and Ash, what I gave to Scott, what Scott will give to his family—it's as gradual and as continuous as evolution, but it's more remarkable because it's spiritual, not physical.

What I can tell you is where we are now—at an ending and a beginning.

Scott is getting married tomorrow. He's marrying Billie Stockbridge, but you knew that, right? Surprised the hell out of me. I thought sure he was going to marry that twit Sims and I was going to spend Christmases for the rest of my life with that buffoon Snag—can you believe that name?—Simson.

No, I didn't like them, but Scott loved her. And I think all too often when people we care about tell us they're in love, we come up with reasons why it won't work. "Be careful," we tell them. Hell, life is for the living of it—all the way. Sure, be careful not to walk in front of a speeding truck, but be careful, deny yourself love? Love is too precious a gift for that.

Anyway, Scott learned what he needed from that one and moved on for whatever reason. Maybe I had a greater influence on him than I think.

Scott has gone into politics. He was always getting elected to things, so we'll see. He's in the House of Representatives now, and former actors have been faring pretty well in the field of late. Maybe it's just a phase he's in. Anyway, I voted for him.

Greg works on his campaigns still.

Billie is running Gambler's now. She's doing fine, and since we didn't go public, she has her work cut out for her, I can tell you. Of course, I still stick my big fat nose into it, but she's patient with me. That old fossil of a grandfather of hers, Bill, will be taken out of the cryogenics unit to attend the ceremony. He must be two hundred and fifty by now.

And Burke Halloran, who is even older, has a new career. Scott and Billie have put the senator's mausoleum on public tour. Burke takes a surprisingly active role. She doesn't conduct tour groups, but she yells at the gardeners and such.

Sylvia, the senator's widow, married a real estate mogul from Charlotte. They're retired to a place on the Outer Banks and have turned into a pair of those lizard-skinned golf addicts.

Allen and Liz—another of those relationships I kept my mouth shut about—have proved me wrong. They're still together dividing their time between Gambler's and Columbia and Turdsville and her parents. For their part, Jimbo and Andrea have scaled the social heights and chaired the Vanderhorst Hunt for time immemorial and managed the inn for about as long. Allen and Liz never had any children. I guess it's ironic that I'm the one in the family who raised a kid. But Allen and I are it for the Reilys.

Ann and Ash are in love with each other and long distance and have become quite the globe-trotters sharing their love and the world with each other. They're never home, so Scott and Billie are taking over their house—Ann never liked what I did with it anyway—and Ann and Ash have taken our old condo, which Ann has taken perverse delight in redecorating.

Gray went back to Canada and to school, where he got a degree and a professor. He's running a Montessori school in Toronto, and Jean teaches at a university there. Who would ever have thought that impossible old mukluk would find a boyfriend? Maybe there's hope for me.

Nah.

I'm living at The Sandpiper and directing and acting. I'm thinking of trying my hand at the movies. Kevin and Richard are always after me to go to Hollywood. We'll see. Who would look after Bert and Smitty?

And my custody deal with the senator? See? I said it wouldn't make any difference.

So, that's where we all are today. Tomorrow we'll all be at the wedding—the ending and the beginning of my family. After that who knows, but that's the fun part.

Scott's leaving home.

And I'm supposed to speak at the ceremony. After that, who knows?

So, what to say?

That's where I began this ending.

I wish them joy and happiness.

And the secret to happiness? Well . . . I learned that from Scott.